Kingdom of Tricksters and Fools

Kissed By Thorns, Volume 1

R.A. Vincent

Published by R.A. Vincent, 2024.

Chapter One

"Jaclan? Jaclan!"

The eight-year-old stopped spinning wildly on the browning grass and frowned at me. Seemed I interrupted vital business.

"What?"

"The clouds grow heavy. Bring in the sheets, please. Get Gisela to help you."

"I don't need help. I can do it myself." Jaclan ran headfirst through the quilt, swinging and swiping his arms at the fabric, and ended up blinking and confused on the other side.

I hid a smile as I bounced the baby. Jac had been on this independent streak since he started school. No doubt his instructors were filling his head with stern words of how he would soon be the man of the household—tasked with using his magic to protect his mother and sisters, then one day his wife and daughters.

Jac tried again to tackle the quilt and ended up flat on the grass.

His instructors clearly hadn't known him long enough. It'd be a while yet before this dreamy, clumsy boy untied from the apron strings, and what was wrong with that? A child should be a child. Not a protector. Not a provider.

My eyes drifted over his head to the sign once again plastered on our door. They narrowed.

And not a pawn.

"Ahh," Savia cooed.

Shaking myself, I settled my squirmy sister in the sling and knelt down in the vegetable patch. It was doing well despite the sorry state of the rest of our small scratch of land. Meliora and I had been forced to ration our water through the dry season, sharing it with the patch. It paid off in enough green beans, radishes, carrots, and squash to make a vegetable soup that would actually fill our bellies that night.

I worked in a steady rhythm of weeding, digging, cleaning, and singing to the baby. My croons carried on the wind, covering the sounds coming through the window overhead.

Fat, stinging pellets of rain struck my back, signaling its final warning to go inside. I rose on aching knees with my basket of goods. Turning around, I found the sheets exactly where I put them and no Jac in sight.

Sighing, I dropped the basket and quickly took them down myself—running inside as the heavens opened. I paused only to rip that cursed sign from my front door. It'd be back again in a few days' time, then that parchment would meet the same fate.

Jaclan sat at the table with my second-youngest sister and his twin, Gisela.

"—is the rune for water." He stuck his tongue out, concentrating hard as he drew directly on our worn, splintered table. "See?"

Nodding, Gisela scrunched up her sweet, cherubic face, swiping her unruly golden curls out of the way as she copied him. A wave of such sadness hit me, I would've sworn it summoned the crack of thunder that struck that moment.

"Haeowen, look!" Gisela waved at me, bouncing in her seat. *Haeowen* as in honored sister. The young weren't allowed to address those older than them by their given names. Not even within families. I didn't care in the slightest and told her so, but even as a babe there was a seriousness about Gisela—the perfect balance to her wild twin.

She followed the rules. Did things in the right order. Asked permission before taking a step. She sought law, order, and structure in our world of chaos, as if following the rules would one day bring rewards.

Eight years old was too young to shatter her dreams.

"Did I do it right? Is it good?"

A smile tugged on my lips. "That is the best water rune I've ever seen. You're a natural, Gisela."

My sweet sister beamed so wide, I saw all of her missing teeth. The smile was a dagger through my heart.

"I can't wait until I go to school with Jac. He says they're learning mind riding next week. I've gotten better. Look!" Gisela spun around, hand up and face scrunched. Not a second passed before a lump of fur and whiskers crawled out from under our threadbare couch.

I laughed as it bounded up to me. "So that was the mewling noise I heard last night. You and Jac said it was Savia."

The kitten looked at me through too-intelligent eyes. Behind them, was Gisela. Or at least her mind and thoughts pushed into a smaller, weaker being. It was said her namesake, Gisela Raekin of legend, could meld her mind with her familiar and companion, a dragon.

I suspected that was why our Gisela was so taken with mind riding magic. She'd been practicing with the mice and other critters that have long shared our home, since she was practically in swaddling. Successfully melding her mind with an animal the size of a kitten was a grand accomplishment for a child her age. An accomplishment that would name her a prodigy to be praised in the same name as Gisela Raekin.

But the legend she admired was from a time when dragons still existed.

And freedom.

"Haeowen," Meliora called. "The water's boiled."

I patted Gisela's head on the way to the kitchen. "You keep practicing, faywen." *Sweet one.* "You're going to leave your instructors speechless."

Meliora looked up from the pot when I rounded the corner. She didn't let her voice carry. "You shouldn't tell her those things," she said, taking the basket from me. "It'll just make her hate you when she learns the truth."

"Did my lies make you hate me?"

She didn't answer.

She didn't have to. My sixteen-year-old sister was called stoic, and other unkind things, for the blank, unsmiling expression she carried through our village, but her thoughts always shone like fireflies in the night to me.

She did not hate me for letting her believe in a fantasy... most days.

Today was not that day.

"She keeps asking to go to school with Jac." Meliora gave her back as she set about washing and chopping the vegetables. "We don't have two years' worth of lies to keep her from realizing there's a bigger reason to why she can't go. It'll only take one word from one of Jac's new friends to shatter her illusions. They've started following him home."

"Because Jac tells them all sorts of fanciful tales of the pet dragon we keep in the barn, and that one of the faeriken visits him at night and tells him the secrets of the wild kingdom."

"Yes," she said flatly. "He's almost as experienced a liar as you. His study of you rivals any accomplishment he could achieve at school."

I winced. Yes, Meliora wasn't too pleased with me that evening.

"I sense I'm not all that's set your teeth on edge." The line of her shoulders hardened. "After all, you're quite used to the stories I tell the children. What's added to your ire today?"

She didn't speak for so long, I assumed she wouldn't answer. I turned to put Savia down for her nap.

"The royal wedding approaches."

The whisper tickled my ear, stopping me in my tracks. "Yes. So?"

"A procession from the wild kingdom arrives in a week's time. They say the king of Wind and Wild is bringing a hundred men with him. Wonder what it says that despite his upcoming marriage to Princess Emiana, he won't set foot on our soil without a small army."

"Why are we speaking of this, Meliora? The likes of us aren't invited to the wedding. We won't even be among the crowd of people lined along the main road, watching the procession arrive."

Her shoulders hunched. The *chop-chop-chop* slowed as her blade settled on the wood, and stayed.

"They've been having trouble finding war wives willing to service King Alisdair's people. Kirwan offered me."

Clang! Clang!

I spun, knocking over our drying tin cups and bowls. Savia jerked awake—screaming.

"No! He can't— You won't!"

Meliora hunched over, resuming her chopping. Her refusal to look at me proved one thing at that moment.

She was crying.

It was no wonder she was furious with me that day. When she was small, I encouraged her every wish and dream. I filled her head with stories of all the wonderful things she could be.

I certainly never told her that she'd be denied education, work, status, and opportunity. That we'd struggle for food, medicine, and money... until one day a loathsome man offered her up against her will in service of the one thing our kingdom still valued of women—our bodies.

"He can't do this. Once you take official work, it's branded your profession for life. A nobleman could take you from us. You could be called to war. And none of that comes close to what the faeriken men would do to you. They're little more than beasts."

"I offered s-such arguments," she rasped. "They fell on deaf ears. The palace has raised the reward to one hundred and fifty kiruna. Kirwan means to have a cut."

"No." I spoke with a finality that silenced Savia's wails. "This will not happen. I lied about many things, Meli, I know. But I did not lie about this. I promised you'd never be forced into that life. Your body will always be your own."

"He's coming for me tonight," she cried. "No doubt he thinks I'll run and ruin his plans. He told me to be ready by the break of moon's light."

"You will leave this to me." I touched her shoulder. "You're not going anywhere."

"Haeowen—"

"Look at me." I tipped her chin. Mossy pools rimmed with starlight drowned in a salty, spilling sea. Only sixteen years old, and the lovelier of the two of us by far. Meliora claimed everything from our beautiful mother. The lush, flowing dark locks; shining two-colored eyes; full, dusky lips, and a glow in her cheeks that gave the appearance of health, happiness, and radiance even when nothing could be further from the truth.

It was because her frustration so clashed with the perfect little petal people wanted her to be that they mocked the dull reflection in her eyes.

But my sister was not cold and emotionless. Her feelings—her fear—dangled from her sleeves for all to see. I was just the only one who bothered to look. "I will take care of this, faywen. I promise."

She searched my face, and I knew she found no lies. "Okay," she croaked.

I kissed her cheek. "Start the soup. Mama hasn't eaten all day. I bought some shaela bread from the market this morning to tempt her appetite. It's her favorite."

"That must've cost half our purse." My serious sister returned quickly. "How many times, Haeowen? Stories, gifts, and sweets cannot change our reality. Cease wasting our hard-earned coin on them."

"The bread was half price today in celebration of the royal marriage. Even if it wasn't, I would still spend the coin. It's not about changing our reality. It's about the fact that a life without stories, gifts, and the occasional sweet that brings a smile to Mama's lips, isn't a life worth living.

"Once I've stopped caring enough to lie to you, then you'll know I've given up on you. That day will never come."

She sniffed. "I will not make a liar into a hero by praising that speech."

I laughed. "I'm going to put Savia down and check in on Mama. The shaela bread is in my bag. There's enough for all of us."

Baby Savia did not go down easily. I rudely woke her the first time, and she fussed and flailed her anger at me until the sun retreated and the rain stopped. Finally, her lids fell heavy and she drifted off—holding tight to my finger.

I smiled gently while that finger stroked her soft cheek. "I will tell you the same pretty lies too, sweet one," I whispered. "Because in this reality, we can only be happy in a fantasy."

I left Savia to her rest and went out into the main room. Meliora came in from outside carrying a sign.

"Why do you have that?"

"They hung another one up." She glanced behind her. "And they're waiting to do it again."

Frowning, I looked past her shoulder outside. Three young men stood on the wrong side of our fence—bold in their intrusion and their glares. In their hands were the signs and glue they were taking through the Gutter Galley—a fond name for the poorest part of town that we lived in. They were most aggressive about their recruiting in this neighborhood.

"Yes," I called, "we have a young boy in the household, and tonight he curses this door so that misfortune befalls any who touches it without permission!"

I slammed the door, so angry that I took the sign and ripped it to pieces. Meliora didn't comment on my outburst and instead went to prepare the table for dinner. I moved to the curtain, watching them through the window.

They were low-powered fae. Only two had a crystal on their lapel and they were small ones at that. I watched them debate if they planned to test me.

"It's because of the wedding," Meliora said. "King Alisdair agreed to marry the princess and sign a treaty to end the war. But he did not, and would not, agree to end the curse. We are no closer to attaining what we began this war to achieve.

"While we are sticking to the terms of the treaty, Alisdair's people will grow stronger until he and Emiana give birth to the rightful heir of both thrones, and they return to conquer our kingdom once and for all. Everyone capable of looking beyond the immediate future sees this marriage for what it is. They believe the war to end us is coming, and we don't have enough men to stop it."

"We might if women were allowed to join the army, and not as bedwarmers," I returned. "The war to end us has always been coming. We fight because we have to, but I don't believe anyone—not even the king—thinks we can win. One day Jac will have to decide if he wants to fight this unwinnable battle, but that is not today. It is not when he's eight years old. I will protect his childhood the same as I protected yours and Gisela's."

Meliora did not answer me. I looked back and landed on her back as she went into the kitchen. I knew she agreed with me on this—in theory. In practice, one nineteen-year-old girl from Gutter Galley was an unimpressive match against the Royal Army.

King Alisdair will soon arrive with a hundred soldiers, and the response to save us is to conscript my young brother into the army.

I watched Jac roll across the floor, making faces at the kitten.

We're doomed. I laughed at my private joke—a short, sharp one that ended quickly.

Only boys were allowed to attend magic school, but at eight years old, they were given another choice as well. They could join the academy and begin the ten-year training that would end with a sword, a coudarian crystal, and the name of the regiment they'd go to war with. The end result was non-negotiable. Even if Jac became an advisor to the king himself, if his regiment was called up, he'd have to go—no exceptions. No excuses.

The only men who could not be conscripted were those who did not attend the academy. Naturally, they did not have ten years of fighting experience and would be a liability on the field. But most young men were signed up. That is what happens when the crown pays the families five hundred kiruna for each name on their roster, and then one hundred every year that they complete training.

Surprisingly, the choice to sign our sons up for training was not left solely to their fathers. Both parents had to agreed, and though Jac's father argued loudly and constantly that Jaclan must do his duty, my mother continued to refuse.

That didn't stop recruiters from haunting Gutter Galley—home to many a struggling single mother.

One of the recruiters broke the pack, and marched on our door with a recruitment sign—the payment for doing so was written larger than anything else on the parchment.

"Gisela," I said. "Hurry."

My sister ran into the next room and got what I needed. I threw open the door just as he touched the wood.

"You were warned." I tossed the basket of Savia's soiled wrappings in his face.

He bellowed like he was being murdered. "Filthy little kakka!"

I slammed the door before he could lunge at me. He settled for pounding on it instead.

"Don't think yourself better than us! I was born on these streets too. There's no future for the likes of you other than whoring for my regiment. You'll wish you were nicer to me then."

Walking off, I left the fool to his squawking. He'd do no more to that door other than yell on the other side of it. Magic would allow him to blow it off the hinges and deliver on his many threats, but that was a tiny crystal on his lapel. He didn't have much magic to waste, and it wasn't worth wasting it on me.

His noise, and the twins' giggling at his crude language, muffled as I closed myself in Mama's room. The lump on the threadbare mattress didn't stir.

I was gentle withdrawing the sheets, and taking Mama's hand. She curled around me instinctively—though she did not wake. My chest squeezed gazing at her.

A gaunt cheek rested on the pillow, appearing as though even its gentle touch could break her. Bony fingers wrapped around mine, each tipped with brittle cracked nails. A crown of hair once so shining and full of life, draped limped and oily across the sheets.

Drained.

That is what my mother was. She was drained of life, health, vitality—and there wasn't a single thing I could do to stop it.

"Mama?" I gently shook her. "It's time for supper. I bought you shaela bread. Why don't you try a little?"

A watery eye cracked open. "Fay... wen..." Mama's voice was thin and brittle like the crust on shaela bread. Wind blowing in from the open window tried to steal her soft words away before they reached my ears. "How are you... my precious girl?"

Tears stung my eyes.

This last bout of sickness was worse than ever. For the past two months, Mama's stomach rebelled at the notion of food. She had not been able to keep anything down and had taken to eating one meager meal a day—if that. And even that single bare meal wound up in the bucket beside her bed most days.

For twelve years, she's battled bouts of the sickness that's gotten worse and worse, longer and longer each time, but every day all she wanted to know was if I was okay. She would be such a great mother.

If she could get out of bed.

"I'm well, Mama. It's you I'm worried about. I stopped by the apothecary this morning. He said we could work out a deal on your medicine if I look after the shop in the evenings."

She shook her head. Doing so caused her great effort. "Costas Lightfellow will work you more than the medicines are worth at full price. He has used the young women of the Galley for free labor since the shop opened. The man has no concept of fair business, nor of keeping his hands to himself."

I slumped, dropping my forehead on the mattress. "What choice do I have? You're getting worse and this is the only way I can afford your medicine."

"We both know that medicine does little for me, my darling, and less and less every time." She smiled in spite of everything. "We cannot continue to waste the coin. It does not help me. Nothing can. Nothing will."

"While it does little for you, it still does something. We will waste the coin until that changes. I will not see you suffer any more than you must."

"My girl." Mama stroked my hair as Meli came in with her supper. "So strong. So stubborn. Never lose that, faywen. Your obedience is taken, but your fire is surrendered."

Mama has told me this since I was old enough to remember. I was certain she said it when I was a babe as well, but I did not know what it meant. If my choices were gone and obedience was taken from me on the knife's edge of everything I held dear, what did fire matter? I already surrendered. I already lost.

"Here you are, Mama." Meliora spoke to her with a softness no one else received. "Do you need help?"

"No, celesi." She squeezed her fingers. "I will manage."

Celesi. Treasure. We were all Mama's faywens, but only Meliora was her treasure.

This did not fill me with jealousy—only sadness. Mama did her best to love Meliora twice as much to make up for what my sister did not receive from *him.*

A fist pounded on the door, snapping both our heads up. Meliora and I exchanged a look.

"What?" A mother's eagle eyes missed nothing. "What is it?"

"Nothing, Mama." I got to my feet and tucked the sheets tight around her. "You eat. I'll see who's at the door, and get them acquainted with Savia's wrappings if they dare shove another recruitment letter in my face."

A chuckle sounded from beneath the blankets. "There's that fire."

I mouthed *stay here* to Meli and left, softly closing the door behind me. Our small little hut claimed only two bedrooms. One for Mama and one for the young children. I picked up Jac's and Gisela's bowls and sent them all to their room. I crossed to open the—

The door banged into the opposite wall, rattling half off the hinges. A man in a silken tailored coat stepped over the threshold, wiping his hands on his coat as if the mere act of his magic touching our home sullied him.

His coldly handsome face swept our living space, his mouth curling up at the edges.

I wished I could stop describing him at cold, but there was no denying that Kirwan Dawnbreaker was the handsomest of men. Streaks of silver wove through his raven locks, giving him distinction instead of age. Lily pads floating in a clear stream did not come close to the crisp green of his eyes, and when he smiled at those he deemed worthy of his attention, the wonder of his full lips and teasing amusement knocked you on your back.

Yes, Kirwan earned the turned heads he collected everywhere he went, and it wasn't just because the hem of his coat was lined with coudarian crystals bigger than my fists.

He was handsome. But to me, I'd never seen a more hideous creature in all my days.

"Where's the girl?" he asked by way of greeting. Kirwan pushed me aside and came in. "I told her to be ready."

"Which girl are you referring to?" I got in front of him, halting Kirwan with his mere refusal to be touched by me. "There's no girl here who answers to you."

Kirwan looked me up and down, then dismissed me. "You will be silent, kakka. You were not given permission to address me. Meliora? Meliora! Get out here now."

The hairs on my neck stood on end, giving rise to choking rage. It was one thing to be called kakka by a squawking man-boy covered in baby waste, but for the likes of Kirwan to call me such?

Kakka was the worst of insults. Scrapings from a horse's hooves. Flies that feast on rotted dung. Old chamber pots left in the sun. All of these had more value than you.

"There is only one kakka in this room, and for all his money and station, he's little more than a soulless broker." I sniffed. "What am I saying? Even brokers have more honor than you. They don't barter with their own blood!"

Meliora's father stiffened. "How dare you. The girl is stepping up in service for the king himself. It is her honor and her duty to aid in the union that will bring our kingdoms together."

"Strange how her honor and duty fattens *your* coin purse. You wouldn't deign to remember her name otherwise."

Kirwan brushed a thumb over the crystal on his chest, and I went flying.

Screaming, I was blasted off my feet and thrown onto the table—tipping us both over with a resounding crash.

"Haeowen!"

"What's going on!"

Meliora raced out of the room amid Mama's shout. She ran to me and Kirwan snatched her off her feet, hauling her back by the wrist.

"Let's go. The carriage is waiting."

"No, please!" Meliora strained against his hold. "I don't want to do this. Please, don't make me, Kirwan. Please!" She cried in earnest. "They'll kill me!"

My head lolled, wetness running down my forehead. "N-no..." I tried to get up and pitched forward on my face. "Stop..."

"Meliora?" Mama screamed. A loud thud sounded from her bedroom. "Children, what's wrong?"

"Enough!" Kirwan dragged her to the door. "You will be silent or I'll spell your mouth shut."

Meliora was not silent. She sobbed and wailed, fighting her father harder than she ever had. His mere presence, and the swirling cloud of disdain he brought with him, used to strike her quiet. Not that day. "I won't go! I won't!"

I crawled over the splintered wood, vision spinning. "Meli!"

"Leave Haeowen alone!" Jaclan burst from his room, wielding his wooden spoon like a club. He struck Kirwan between the legs, doubling him over.

"Argh!" Snarling, Kirwan raised a backhand to Jaclan.

"Don't—!"

"I'll go!"

My scream stopped everything.

Kirwan spun on me, hand still raised. "What?" he barked.

"Take m-me." I rose on shaky knees. "I'll do it."

"No one wants you, girl."

"No, *you* don't want to offer up Meli." My gaze burned him where he stood. "Advisor to the king. Lord of the House of Dawnbreaker. One of the highest-powered fae in Lyrica... and his daughter can be had for three coppers. You'll never hear the end of it," I rasped. "Your comrades will laugh and taunt you of the taste of her, and don't pretend they won't."

Frowning, Kirwan looked from me to her. No denial came.

Kirwan knew well what would happen if Meliora wound up in the grip of men as vile as him. Not for her sake, but for his reputation. His only love in this life and the next.

"I'll do it," I repeated. "I'll become a war wife, you won't be known for selling your own daughter, and you'll still get your one hundred and fifty kiruna. Surely you have no objection? You'll get everything you want."

His lips peeled back from his teeth. It was the hard, unfeeling monster in him that wanted to say no just because I asked this of him. But—

"Fine. You'll do just as well."

"No!" Meliora broke from his loosened grip and ran to me. I gently dried her tears. "Haeowen, you can't do this. We promised we would never."

"I promised that you would never be forced into this life," I whispered. "I promised we would choose, and I choose to protect you. That's what I'll always choose, faywen."

"But not faeriken. They'll k-kill you. We'll never see you again."

"Let's go," Kirwan ordered.

Ignoring him, I forced a smile on my lips. "Of course you will. Nothing's going to happen to me. I'll be back after the wedding, and when I do, I'll tell you all about the palace. Its grand rooms, luscious feasts, and the queen's famous gardens. It'll be like you were there with me."

Meliora cried harder. Of course she didn't believe me. She knew I was a liar.

Mama's door banged open. She huffed—chest heaving and hair hanging lank over her face. The effort that short distance cost her, left her clinging to the doorframe. "What has happened?" She took in the scene, and my weeping wound. "Kirwan, what did you do?"

He sniffed. "The girl's clumsy. She tripped over the table like a one-footed fool. You should be thanking, not scolding me, Olene. Your circumstances will be improving. You'll either have two incomes for the household... or one less mouth to feed."

"Excuse me? What does that mean!"

"It means Kirwan has offered me a job," I rushed. "A housekeeper in his household. I am to leave now for training, Mama, but I'll return in a fortnight."

Her lips drew tight. "If that's true, why is Meliora crying?"

"Because she knows her father as well as I." I gave him a hard look. "I will not be treated well."

"That's not true, faywen," she said, voice sharp. "He will treat you well. He'll care for you better than his own, or I'll know why. Isn't that right, Kirwan?"

He smiled. "I can swear no harm will come to her by my or any fae hands."

Meliora's nails pierced my shoulder. She understood the meaning behind his word choice clear as day.

"In the carriage, girl," Kirwan said. "Don't make me change my mind." *And take Meliora instead.*

I untangled from my sister and bent down, opening my arms to Jaclan. Gisela took that moment to shoot out from behind the cracked door. I hugged the twins tight.

"Be well, my loves. Listen to everything Meli says."

Standing up, I brushed a kiss over Meliora's forehead. She was crying too much. Mama would figure out something was wrong soon. I had to be gone before then.

Chin raised, I walked to the door without looking back at my family. Kirwan's smirk taunted me the whole way.

"Tell Adan I won't be long."

"What—?"

Kirwan advanced on my mother.

"No, you leave her!" I cried, grabbing his arm. "You know she's not well."

Kirwan threw me off. His strength enough to toss me across the room again. I grabbed my siblings as he slammed Mama's door shut, hurrying them out of the house.

We didn't make it far down the path. Meli turned on me, clinging tight and tripping me up. Her weight pulled me down onto the earthen lane. I suffocated under Meli's, Jac's, and Gisela's embrace. The twins did not understand what was wrong, but they knew enough to be worried about anything that made Meliora cry.

I opened my mouth—to give them reassurance. Tell them everything would be okay. Say that their worry was silly.

Nothing came out.

A war wife. The polite, official term for what I would be. The actual term. The one that would be yelled at me in the streets. Branded in the stares I received in the marketplace. Hissed at me as I descended back staircases and crept out of darkened rooms.

Was whore.

Decades after King Kazimir decreed that all women must have their magic bound and rendered unusable by age ten, his son set down another decree. The men who now had to fight alone on the battlefield deserved comfort in the long months and years they spent far from home. They deserved a body to warm their bedrolls, soothe their aches, and sweeten their nights.

Naturally, their actual wives had to stay home and fulfill the only role still available to them in a magical society—raising the next generation of sons to fight and daughters to bear them. Thus, a contingent of women would be sent along with the regiments. The war wives.

Over the years, the soldiers would make more demands of their king—binding the chains tighter around women. A war wife could not be claimed by one man. They were to be shared among whoever wanted them. War wives were not only for soldiers. Nobles and high-powered fae could make use of them how they wished. A noble can take a war wife into their home, imprisoning them with the man who now owned her, and his true wife who hated her. And the law that they fought the hardest for—any children that resulted from their union would be her responsibility.

The men were required to do no more than pay for their sons' education. But if Jaclan went without food, clothing, and a roof over his head, Xandros Waterdancer was not obligated to do anything about it. A sentiment he proved when we went without all three, and I begged him to help the twins—his children—at the very least. He had me thrown away from the carriage and continued on to his grand manor on the hill.

In the end, when a war wife got too old, when they had too many children, when the sickness took them as it would take every woman of Lyrica, all that was left for a war wife... all that would be left for me was to lie ill and broken in a little room, while my children cried outside—covering their ears.

I opened my mouth to tell my siblings that if I survived the beastly men who slaughtered our soldiers in droves, the life that awaited me afterward was nothing to fear...

...and a sob tore from my throat.

I cried—squeezing them tighter than they squeezed me. I had finally done it.

I ran out of lies.

Chapter Two

"Let's go, girl."

Kirwan walked out of my house, his presence imposing and out of place amid our humble home. He tossed a weighty coin purse at Meliora—his final insult upon every exit. Making us take the payments for his time with our mother, even though all payments are supposed to go through the broker.

This is the man to whom you'll abandon your mother, brother, and sisters.

My fists balled. *No.*

"No," I rasped, getting to my feet and taking the children with me. "No crying. I will be back. Nothing will happen to me. I have been there every day since each of you were born. That will never change, faywens." I meant it with everything in me. "I'll return."

Kirwan snatched my wrist, yanking me along.

"I promise."

Meliora, Jaclan, and Gisela didn't speak as I was loaded into the carriage. Adan set off before my back hit the cushion, not allowing me a second's linger in my home. We left Gutter Galley—my faywens becoming still, lonely specks in the distance.

The further we trotted from the Galley, the more noise crowded into the darkened space. Lyrica passed through the sliver in the curtain, warm and alive with the preparations for the royal wedding. The coming faeriken brought fear, but they also brought hope. The hope that the love of a princess and foreign king would save our home and our souls.

I turned away, scooting as far away from Kirwan as the carriage would let me. Shadows danced on the curves and lines of his face, concealing him as well as the unmarked carriage. Kirwan tried to hide his frequent comings and goings from my mother's hut. Not out of shame. The man did not feel such a thing. And not out of respect to his wife. Him respecting any woman was the one skill this master of magic did not master.

He did it to hide his obsession. It wouldn't do for the kingdom to know that Lord Dawnbreaker's weakness was a thin, frail war wife from Gutter Galley.

I once asked my mother why this bitter, hateful man kept coming back when it clearly wasn't for Meliora. There were hundreds of other war wives for him to choose. She gave me another answer I didn't understand.

"Because he loves me, he can't stay away... and because I don't love him back, he hurts me."

No, that did not make sense. If there was one thing I was certain of, Kirwan was not capable of love.

"You will not embarrass me."

I jumped at his sudden speech.

"When we arrive at the palace, you're to speak only when addressed. And when you do, it'll be in a polite, soft tone and not that barking screech your mother should've drummed out of you. You represent all of Lyrica from the moment you step onto the grounds.

"The faeriken are little more than beasts, and yet they look down on us. They see us all as low-powered fae who dress ourselves up in jewels and finery to hide our inferiority."

Are you certain they weren't just thinking of you?

I bit my tongue, holding in the retort. Once, Kirwan hit me and my cheek swelled up like a dalia fruit. Mama broke a bowl over his head, and refused him for an entire year. He returned again and again, offering more money until our empty bellies and blistered shoeless feet forced her to take him back.

Ever since, he was only his most vile where she could not see him. And she couldn't see him then.

"You're an ugly girl." He said it as though it was a simple fact of life. "You're too short, too thin, and too mouthy. And that hair... Only the lowest faeriken with strange tastes will want you. Whatever they tell you to do, you're not to fight or refuse. To do so would disrespect King Salman. I will not stand for shame to be brought upon the crown. Is that understood?"

I tipped my chin, offering no more than that.

Kirwan seemed to accept it because the carriage lapsed into blessed silence once again.

It was a long ride through the winding streets. Every dip in the road sent a jolt through my heart, taunting me the closer we got. This was it. Once my name was recorded and the money was dropped in Kirwan's hands, there was no going back. After the wedding, my details would be passed among the kingdom's brokers.

Any soldier or nobleman looking for a too-short, too-thin, too-mouthy companion would have me offered up on a silver platter. If none of them wanted me, I starved in the streets—denied the right to work in any other profession.

The only thing worse than this being my fate, was if it was Meli's.

The carriage slowed, jolting me out of my thoughts. I chanced a peek outside and frowned.

"What are we doing here?"

"Have sense, girl. You're not fit to enter the palace in that state. You will shower, change, and be here waiting for me in exactly one hour." He climbed out and strode inside, giving no further instruction.

Adan climbed down and waited in his infinite, stoic patience. He was a bit older for his position. Streaks of gray weathered his burnished locks and crow's feet stamped the corner of his flat, blue eyes. But what value was there in replacing a loyal servant who'd never betray your secrets? A faeriken cut out his tongue decades ago.

I stuck my head out, gaze traveling up, and up, and up to the towering chimney stacks—each stamped with the Dawnbreaker crest.

I knew Kirwan's home from the one time Meliora and I followed him back, curious about where he existed outside of our small little hut. He led us to this place with its gold-painted doors; rough, umber sand bricks, and large grand windows that were all shrouded in heavy drapes, giving no hint to the lives of those inside.

Adan led me around the back to the servants' entrance. The least amount of time and kiruna was given to decorating this part of the home, and it was easily grander than anywhere I'd been.

It struck me that Meliora and Mama could've lived here—spending their days in a manor within the richest part of Lyrica, where the floors shone with their reflections and painted hills rolled along the sandstone. This would've been their life, if there had been no me.

Kirwan made such an offer when Meliora was two and I five. He would end their poverty and bring Mama and Meliora into the manor, if my mother put me—the child of another man—in an orphanage.

Mama sent me and Meli out of the room to give her hot, shouted reply. After that day, Kirwan hated me all the more. My mother had no trace of love for him, but she had it all for me. I would always be the one she chose over him.

Adan bowed beside a door at the end of a short hallway. I crossed the threshold and found myself in a communal bath.

I bathed myself, giving special attention to my hair. The water ran brown, shaming me. Of course Kirwan wouldn't let me near the palace as I was. The public baths cost coin, and I saved my share so that Meliora and the little ones were never without a bath. That left the rainwater I collected in buckets behind the hut for me.

Maybe it will be a good thing to have another income to fill the family purse. I sat before the mirror, weaving my shining onyx crown into a web of braids. *It's been hard to find decent work since anything that needs to be done, can easily be completed with magic.*

My reflection tried for a smile. "You will get back to your mother and faywens. All they've known their whole lives is that everyone will let them down or abandon them... except you. That is a promise you will always keep."

The words cheered me, even while tears mixed with bathwater ran down my cheeks.

After dressing in the simple dress and slippers Adan set out for me, I went out to wait next to the carriage. The correct carriage that proudly boasted the occupants inside.

Kirwan returned in his finery. Red slippers with threads of gold, satin tunic, and red breeches. Red and gold—the colors of Dawnbreaker. He flapped an irritated hand at me, ordering me inside.

I climbed up, suddenly hit with the nervousness my anger at Kirwan blanketed. It'd be no time at all until we were at the palace. Forbidden to the likes of me, it would become the place where I would sign away my life in service of a king who'd done nothing to serve me or my family.

It was silent during the jostled ride up the hill. For once I wished Kirwan would speak and distract me from my thoughts, but I dare not voice them to him. *What were faeriken truly like? Were the stories of their unhinged brutality true?*

Letting him know in any way that I was scared would not return compassion or kindness. On the contrary, it would delight him more than the sumptuous feasts and ever-flowing wine on Meya's Day.

All through the ride I repeated to myself the only thing that mattered. No matter what happened, I would get back to my family. I would not leave them alone with *him*.

Lyrica was a monument to fae beauty and advancement in the last two thousand years. Once, we were nothing but slinking, mindless beasts until Mother Meya blessed us and created the fae race. The first pack became a community. Then a small village. Then a bustling town. And finally, a kingdom to rival the human empires in the east.

The stories say the first queen was a traveling farmer. She traveled to different fae settlements, teaching our new species to grow and live off the land. She went far and wide, learning everything there was to know—not just about farming, but about everything needed to prosper. During her travels, she saw how the humans lived. With their frail bodies, stunted lives, and not a trace of magic within them, they built grand cities and made huge advancements with no more than their minds, and many hands willing to turn an idea into reality.

How much more could the fae do? How much more did we deserve?

The not-yet-queen returned from her travels and pleaded to Meya. Begging her to grant her a palace that would be a beacon to fae all over the country. Come and we will build a nation that will last for thousands of years. A shining jewel of this land and the next.

Meya's response was to grant her this.

I stuck my face against the glass, lips parting in silent awe as we passed through the gates.

Soaring spires pricked the sky, boasting whipping flags too high for me to see, but I knew were the multicolored flags of Lyrica. Laced through the columns, stacks on stacks of sandstone were vining, snaking veins of deep-sea-blue coudarian crystals.

Miles away as I knelt in my vegetable patch, weeding and singing to Savia—my gaze would travel where everyone's did, seeking the blueish glow in the distance. Every evening and every morning, the traveling sun would hit the crystals just right and create exactly what our first Queen Wren asked for—a beacon.

The carriage stopped before the palace steps—a riot of stone and crystal leading to two grand doors that could welcome an army. I made to stand.

"What do you think you're doing?" Kirwan shoved me back down. "The likes of you do not enter through the main doors. Adan will take the carriage around back. I've written instructions for him to give to the steward. You will do everything he says. Go where he tells you. Shut your mouth when he commands. Do you understand?"

Kirwan didn't wait for me to answer. Which was good because my reply would not have been polite. He always spoke to me like I was stupid, but that was the single thing I was not. I could not claim beauty, grace, humor, or riches, but I taught myself the theories of magic from the old books Mama's callers once gave her. Well enough that I used to correct the boys from Gutter Galley who did get to go to magic school. Until, of course, they all stopped speaking to the know-it-all kakka.

The carriage door closed, giving me blessed peace. These were my last moments of freedom. The final minutes before nothing, not even my body, could be claimed as my own. The least Meya owed me was the mercy of not spending that time in Kirwan's presence.

The horses encircled the palace, filling my eyes with its wonder. It's said each fleck of crystal had been filled with power by kings past. If the faeriken ever attacked, the palace guards would draw on a millennium's worth of stored power and fend them off for decades.

I wondered how effective that strategy was when they were already inside the gates.

Adan stopped the carriage before a much smaller set of double doors. I decided this was the kitchen entrance going by the baskets of vegetables kitchenhands were carrying inside. Adan opened my door and reached a hand in to help me out—showing the politeness he couldn't when Kirwan was nearby.

"Can I read the note?" I asked as we approached the door.

Adan handed it over without hesitation.

I read it—half expecting orders to flay me when I mouthed off. I would've preferred that.

My teeth gritted reading that I was in debt to House Dawnbreaker, and all the coin I made was owed to Kirwan. If I ran away or tried to steal it, Meliora was to repay the debt in my place.

Of course Kirwan had to come up with some lie for why he should receive the one hundred and fifty kiruna instead of me or a broker. There'd be no point arguing that I owed him nothing. No one would take my word over an advisor to the king.

"As if I would run," I said, handing it back. "Honor and loyalty to family are two things Kirwan knows nothing about."

Adan gave nothing away—in speech or expression. The manservant was a vault of secrets, but deep down I sensed he did not like Kirwan any more than I did. He certainly never hesitated to give us water or sweets on the days Kirwan's visits to the hut forced me and my siblings outside. I knew he brought them just for us.

We stepped inside and were bowled over by a tide of noise. This was nothing like the quiet, chilling Dawnbreaker home. Fae rushed all about—carrying food there, lifting trays here, and nodding and bowing acquiescence to a barking red-faced woman in an apron.

A grand kitchen it was. We could've fit all of Gutter Galley inside, and fed them well for months before another food delivery.

I swept over the feast of ripe fruit, roasted animals, and expensive wine. Who was all this food for? There was only King Salman and Princess Emiana left of the royal family after the death of the queen consort. Did they share this among the advisors and generals too?

Did Kirwan regularly feast on this rich and indulgent food, and yet he attempted to sell his only daughter for some coin? What did he need the money for? A bib?

Adan continued on, so I followed, carrying my anger with me. I would hold on to anger. It was an easier emotion to wrestle than the others lurking beneath the surface.

Adan led me into a small receiving room. I could tell right away this place was for guests, but not for ones the palace respected. Thirty or so women of various ages loitered around the dim, windowless room. A dank, musty smell of a room not often aired out hung over the space.

From the debris and dirt indentations, I guessed the room was used for storage. It had been cleared out and two small benches were placed inside—allowing only six women room to sit. The others leaned against the wall, throwing me horrified glances.

"What are you doing here, shoua!" *Young woman.* "Does Olene know you're here?"

Myrna broke from the pack and bore down on me. A hand on my arm stopped her pulling me away. Turning, I blinked up at Adan as he clasped my hand in both of his, and bowed. The look in his eyes as he raised his head...

"Don't do that," I whispered, throat closing. "Makes it harder for me to believe I'll be okay."

He tried for a smile, and my heart broke in half. Adan never smiled—at me or anyone. He was telling me in every possible way... that he did not expect to see me again.

Releasing me, he held up the note and backed away. He was off to deliver Kirwan's instructions to the steward. That was it for me and Meliora. Our fate would be sealed.

I let him go, penning in all the things I wanted to scream. Honor and loyalty to family. Kirwan did not understand these things, but I did. I wasn't going anywhere.

"Shoua." A woman twenty years my senior and draped in a sheer, crimson dress—her best—tugged me into the center of the crowd. "What are you doing here?" she repeated.

"I had no choice, aya." *Elder.* "It was either me or Meliora."

"Kirwan," Myrna hissed, lips peeling back from her teeth.

I didn't need to confirm or deny, my mother's friends knew what he'd put us through these last sixteen years better than anyone.

I wished I was surprised to see so many women from my part of town here, but who but us would need the money so badly that we'd face faeriken.

"Olene would never let him get away with this," said Nashwa. She was younger than Mama, but you wouldn't know it by the touch of wrinkles on her temples and gray weaving through her reddish locks. "What did he do to her?"

"He didn't have to do anything because she doesn't know, and you must promise not to tell her. She thinks I've taken a position as a housekeeper in the Dawnbreaker household."

"She must know," Myrna cried. "Faywen, do you understand why we're the only ones in this room? Why a dozen more women were here but changed their minds and left too fast to remember their slippers? The faeriken—"

"I know," I cut in, fighting the band constricting my throat. "And that is exactly why I am here. I won't stand for Meliora to be here in my place. Please. Don't tell her. The first time Kirwan hurt me, she refused him and we went hungry. Kirwan spread through Lyrica that he'd ruin any man who touched her, and she didn't see a single coin for months.

"Now that the sickness has taken her, and we have Jac, Gisela, and Savia, I can't risk that happening again. It's better that she believes I'm a housekeeper. I—I can start making real money now," I said, forcing the words past the lump in my throat. "And she won't hurt for it."

Myrna stroked my cheek. "You won't keep a secret like this for long. You can't. When it's discovered, she'll hurt twice as much for all the days she didn't know."

"I—"

Myrna's gaze flicked up. Her eyes hardened. "Get behind me."

"What? Why—?"

Myrna shoved me behind. I swallowed a cry as Mama's friends kept tugging and pushing, dragging me back until I was pressed against the wall and they formed a blockade in front of me.

The door creaked open, inviting a welcome rush of fresh air, and a bobbing golden crown. Rising on tiptoe, I strained to see who came inside.

"Good morning, ayas." A deep, pleasing voice, and it met with a thick silence. "Forgive me for interrupting but Cook got a bit overambitious in her preparations for tonight's alnihaya feast."

Alnihaya. For seven days and seven nights before a noblewoman marries, there are feasts, parties, and celebrations in honor of her last days as a maiden. Princess Emiana's alnihaya had spread through all of Lyrica, inviting those who believed in this marriage to celebrate in the streets.

"Saffron pudding, roasted duck, and shaela bread." Over their shoulders, I saw servants come in carrying trays, tables, and two more benches for us to sit. "Please, enjoy."

No one moved.

Confused, I tried to push between them. Duck and saffron pudding? I could become the highest-paid war wife in Lyrica and saffron pudding would still be a luxury. What was going on? Why weren't they descending on the food?

"I hear from the steward that there's a new addition to your ranks."

What? Could he be talking about me?

"There you are."

I jerked, locking on with twin emerald jewels. Their owner smiled and his whole face lit up, knocking the breath out of me.

It wasn't that I'd never seen a handsome boy before. I'd simply never met one who wasn't sneering and throwing dirt at me.

This didn't look to be his intention—smiling wider until a slight crook bent his lips and dimpled his cheeks. Hair shaved all the way around, he left only the top of his head be, and braided it in one long whip hanging past his shoulders.

"You're quite young. Even more commendable that you'd decided to do your duty for the king and Lyrica. Please," he said, sweeping out his hand. "Come and enjoy. I'd like to hear your story while we eat."

I tried again to get through and the women crowded in tighter around me.

"There's been a mistake," Myrna said. I could barely make out the hem of her sleeve. "She isn't here to do her duty. She's leaving."

"Is she?" I couldn't see him anymore, but his tone hadn't lost its light joviality. "Well, seems the steward was mistaken. I won't take up any more of your time, then. Enjoy your dinner."

They didn't move until the door closed behind him. I fell in beside Myrna while the others gathered around the table.

"What's going on?" I asked. "Who was that man? Why wouldn't you let me talk to him?"

She gritted her teeth, staring at the door like he was on the other side. "He introduced himself my first day here as Kaelan Moontreader. I knew from that moment to stay away from him."

My brows snapped together. "What? Why?"

"Look at where we are, shoua. They keep us in this room all day—bringing our meals to us and only letting us out to use the privy. At night, we're taken to the abandoned servants' quarters to sleep. Despite us stepping up to do our blessed *duty*, the palace has made us a secret. And yet, this young, handsome faeman comes to visit us, welcome every new woman, and bring us treats?"

"Maybe he's kind." My stomach grumbled in need of the saffron pudding. "He feels for you all being trapped in here all day."

Myrna was shaking her head before I finished. "If there's one thing I know to be true above all... it's that a man gives with one hand, and binds with the other."

My lips parted but nothing came out. Myrna suddenly beamed.

"I also know that he has yet to bring us anything poisoned, so eat up, shoua. You could hide behind a broom handle, you're so thin."

I went to eat, but not with the same speed I would've. So soon after the steward received word of a new addition, Kaelan Moontreader came asking for me. Despite Myrna's reply, I was not leaving. My name would go down in a book that would make me available to every soldier and nobleman in Lyrica. Would he come back with smiles and treats then?

I shook the silly thoughts from my head. I was no stranger to men and boys coming around to ogle the war wife. Mama held her head high through many a town market while hooting and lewd offers followed her. When our curves filled out and breastbands grew tight, the same filthy offers came at me and Meliora. Meli more than me. They liked to tell us in disgusting detail what they'd do to us when we became war wives—as if there was no other path we'd take.

Moontreader may have used food and flattery, but he was no different from the rest. He came in here every day to pick his favorite. Once the faeriken were here, we had to be available to them, but no one said we wouldn't be available to everyone else. That was not for me to worry about. There were older, prettier, more experienced war wives to thrill a handsome faeman like him.

I claimed a tray and took it to the far corner to eat. I wasn't alone for long. Myrna and a few of the other women from Gutter Galley came to join me.

I wished they hadn't.

My luxurious, royal meal turned to acid in my stomach.

"You must act as though you're enjoying yourself, but not too much," Shadi warned. She was twenty years of age with dark, shadowed eyes and a smoky tenor that sounded like music. Shadi was far and away the most beautiful of the girls I used to run around the Galley with. Within a month of becoming a war wife, she had three noblemen offering her broker obscene amounts to take her into their home. A month after that, she was back in the Galley.

Mykel Starsinger believed buying women took away her right to say no. One night, he forced himself on her and she beat him with a candelabra. They had yet to take away our right to defend ourselves, so she wasn't punished. Unless of course you considered it a punishment that most of her callers disappeared after they heard what happened, and she was so in need of coin that she was in that room with me.

"If you get too boisterous, they'll take it as an invitation to pump harder. The last thing you need your first time is to have some sweaty, grunting lump flopping and flailing on top of you while trying to shove his reed dick deeper."

I flushed hot. Even the mental depiction of that made the food taste bad on my tongue. Why get mad that Shadi assumed I still had my maidenhood? This would be my first time, and that is what I had to look forward to.

Tamar, another girl from the Galley, nodded in agreement. "Also, if you want it to end quicker. Cup their balls and lick—"

"Thank you," I cried, cheeks on fire. "That's enough for now, I think."

Shadi smirked. "This isn't the conversation you want to avoid." She jerked her chin at the women seated at the table. "See that woman in green?"

I followed her gaze to a slender, blonde woman with pale skin and a long, jagged scar on her cheek.

"Of all of us, she's the only war wife that's gone to war. There's a reason none of the others who've seen the faeriken on the battlefield even thought of collecting that one hundred and fifty kiruna. If you ask her," Shadi said softly, "she'll tell you why."

I gave the woman in green a long look. "Will what she has to say make what's coming easier or harder to bear?"

Shadi didn't answer.

"Then I'll let her enjoy her meal in peace."

I wish I could say they let me enjoy mine. For the rest of the night, I was treated to their collective wisdom of dealing with every unsavory, unwashed, overly aggressive situation. I thanked Meya when a servant came in and said it was time to retire.

She led us down a winding, torchlit hallway. The hustle and noise from the busy kitchen had gone silent. It was then I realized why we were made to stay in that room so long after sunset. We were only allowed to pass through the halls after everyone else had gone to bed.

Irritation beat at my calm. It shouldn't surprise me. All my life I'd witnessed how war wives were treated. I used to dream all the facts and knowledge in my head would amount to something useful. I'd open a shop or give something to Lyrica that could only come from my mind, not my magic. The kiruna would flow, and I'd give my mother and siblings a new life.

Instead, I was another castoff slinking through the back hallways.

"In there." The servant girl gestured at two doors on opposite sides of the hall. "You're not to leave your rooms until I fetch you in the morning."

With that she left, not even offering so much as a good night.

I followed Shadi and Myrna into the room on the left. Fifteen cots were scattered about the stone prison. I wanted to call it something else, but no other word came to mind. There was nothing inside barring the cots and four walls.

"They didn't place a cot in here for you," Myrna said. "I know where they're kept. I'll get another and you can take mine. You're dead on your feet, shoua. Get some rest. The world's better in a dream."

It wasn't until she said it that a wave of exhaustion bowled me over. My knees buckled, dropping me to the stone. I styled my hair to hide the hard lump from Kirwan's attack. Didn't prevent it from thrumming a deep, pricking pain that reminded me with every breath that my life was about to change forever.

Shadi pointed out Myrna's cot and I collapsed, dropping on the thin blanket with my slippers still on.

Life's better in a dream.

It was earlier that day that I told Savia the only happiness for her was in a fantasy. Let there be some waiting in mine.

Closing my eyes, I drifted off into darkness.

***

I woke up.

As simply and abruptly, one moment my eyes were closed, then they were open.

My vision cleared on a figure standing above me. He bent down, beaming his crooked smile directly in my eyes.

"Oh yes. I knew you were perfect," he whispered. "Come with me."

I kicked off the blanket and stood, following him without a word. A calmness settled over my mind. The part of me shouting and screaming not to go with him. Screaming to call for help, was getting quieter and quieter.

Kaelan Moontreader led me out into the hallway and ordered me to shut the door. Then, he started talking.

"You don't know how glad I am to see you, sweetling." He stroked my cheek, his fingers gliding down to take my hand. "All those other hags were useless to me. Too old, too fat, too scarred, too tall, too short. I almost gave up… then you walked in."

We left the abandoned quarters and turned right instead of left down the only familiar path I knew. A narrow staircase invited me up, its walls hugging my shoulders imparting the coolness of its stone—a final kind embrace before he took me somewhere I knew I would not want to go.

"It's a disgrace," Kaelan spat. "That it took me this long to find someone suitable is unacceptable. The king himself sounds the call for you whores to serve your kingdom, and barely any answer. It's our duty—nay, our privilege to do our part to end this war and the threat of the curse.

"Today, you are given that privilege. You will do more for Lyrica and the war effort than anyone in this kingdom. Be proud of that, girl."

A stray thought floated through my head that this faeman was insane. What kind of addled, self-important lunatic believed taking me away to do whatever he was going to do to me, was a grand act in service of the war and kingdom?

The thought crossed my mind and evaporated, unable to summon the shouts, biting retorts, or kicking and slaps that it would if he hadn't bound my free will as easily as they did my magic, all those years ago.

The staircase released us into a space grander than Kirwan's home could ever boast. Tinkling chandeliers reflected dancing rainbows on crème walls flecked with gold. Portraits gazed down on me, the borrowed images of queens past who couldn't help me, and a grave and disapproving look as though they wouldn't even if they could.

Kaelan stopped before double doors and knocked.

"Enter."

Fear and disgust tried to push through. He brought me here for someone… or he brought me to share. Why couldn't I run? How would I get away?

Kaelan got behind and shoved me inside. I tripped over the corner of a rug and dropped to my knees where I stayed, my body refusing the command to stand up.

My eyes rolled in my head, taking in as much as my stiff neck would allow.

We were in a room the likes of which was ten times the size of our modest hut in Gutter Galley.

The finest of furniture stood upon ancient and expensive rugs. I felt their history pressing into my knees. Tapestries climbed the grand windows, allowing the barest sliver of moonlight to grace a bed of silks and downy pillows.

A figure rose from the blankets, concealed in shadows.

"I found her, my love." Kaelan dropped beside me and bowed low till his forehead touched the rug. "The right height and build. Even better, she's a nobody. Nothing. Just another war wife desperate for some coin, and not the child of anyone important. No one will notice her absence."

"Is that so?" A light, almost musical voice floated out of the shadows. "How did such a perfect find land in your lap?"

"It is Meya," he breathed, raising his head. "She sent her to us. Just when we'd begun to lose hope. Our actions are blessed by the All Mother herself. I know it."

"As do I, my love. It is as you say. This meaningless waif was sent to me in my time of need by Meya herself. This is her will."

She stepped out of the shadows, and not a speck of recognition lit in my eyes.

No, wait...

It came to me. Painted flyers in the square. Model figurines in the shops. A name on everyone's lips.

Princess Emiana.

Hair so red it rejected the moonlight fell around her shoulders and brushed the bottom of her bodice. To say she was lovely was to insult her. So simple a word did not begin to describe the beauty of her emerald eyes, bee-stung lips, rosy cheeks, and jewel-cuffed pointed ears. Robes like angel wings floated around her form, revealing more than it concealed.

I instinctively averted my eyes. A finger under my chin drew them back up where she trapped them in her green pools. I would've cringed if my face would've allowed it. No one had ever looked at me with such contempt before, and I endured Kirwan's hatred for years.

She halted in her tracks. "She's moon-kissed. How—? She's disgusting," Princess Emiana spat. "If only Meya had seen fit to send us a comely girl. It sickens me to think I'll be wearing this face for the foreseeable future."

Confusion wafted through my mind and dissipated, not allowing the questions it brought to my lips to come out. What in the name of the All Mother was she talking about?

"Disgusting, my love? I wouldn't say so," Kaelan spoke up. "She has a certain fairness about her that I thought worthy—"

"Don't you dare question me."

The snap closed his mouth.

Irritated, Emiana threw my face away harder than she needed to. "She may be the right height and build, but she is wrong in every other way. I shall be as cursed as her for what we do here tonight. Punishment for dabbling in the unholy arts, but..." She blew out a long breath. "That is how it must be.

"Stand her up."

Kaelan stood me on my feet, gentler in his touch than she was.

"Undo whatever magics you performed on her."

"Your Majesty?"

Emiana spoke to him, but looked deep into my eyes. "Her magic is no less bound than mine. There is nothing she can do to fight back against us. No need to restrain her body and mind too, unless she gives us reason."

Her compassion surprised me for the brief moment I felt surprise. Largely because she was still sneering at me.

Coolness spread down my head and flowed through my body. In the space of a breath, control was mine again.

I lurched back, tripping over my feet and nearly dropping on the carpet. "What is this? What am I doing here!"

"Hey! You address your princess." Kaelan advanced on me. "You will hold your tongue, and speak only when spoken to."

"Fuck you!"

Kaelan's brows blew up his forehead. I suspect it wasn't often a Gutter girl spoke to him like that.

"Kaelan," Emiana said, raising a hand. "I will handle this."

Falling silent, he snapped to the side—ever the obedient soldier. Emiana gave her first change of expression since I was brought into the room. She smiled.

"Fuck you indeed." Her voice was a soft, light brush. "You're angry. You're scared and worried, but just because you stand in my presence, you're ordered to hide what you feel. To lock it away and put on the face of a happy servant. Faemen…" She slid a look to Kaelan. "Cannot understand what it is to live bound by such chains. You may even believe that I don't know either.

"I, Princess Emiana, live in a grand castle high above your problems. How could I ever relate to someone such as you?"

I lifted my chin. "Not to be rude to Your Eminence, but, you can't."

"That," she said, turning her back on me, "is where you're wrong. You see me and think I have wealth, but is that the case when every coin I spend is under the control and permission of others? You think I have power, but is it powerful to sit silently in a room of advisors and rulers, waiting for a single person to ask my opinion. You think I have freedom, and I ask you, what woman in Lyrica does?" she hissed.

"My magic was bound at ten, same as you. My choices were taken from me, same as you. My father *sold* me to warm the bed of a brutish man, just like you!" She whirled on me, stiffening my spine. "In the end, we are all the same to them… whores."

I said nothing. What was there for me to say? To compare our lives was to live in a deluded fantasy. True, I knew nothing of the troubles of a princess, but I doubt she knew what it was to go days without food, weeks without a bath, or a lifetime with no dignity.

"I haven't convinced you," she said, reading my expression easily. "You don't believe we're all the same, no matter the station? Then, this is all I need to say to convince you.

"The royal line passed through my mother, not my father, King Salman. Try as they did, my grandparents were not able to have the son they wished for, leaving my mother to shoulder her birthright. But did they allow her to?

"No." The skin around her eyes tightened. "At ten years old, they bound her magic—the only and rightful heir to the throne—and they married her off to the outsider who sits on her throne. The sickness took her when I was five. The earliest memories I have of my mother... are of watching her die."

Hard and steady eyes beheld me. "You share the same fate as a queen, little whore. What more proof do you need?"

I did not react to her name for me. "Why am I here? You did not bring me before you to tell me I share a queen's fate."

She shrugged lightly, padding across the room to the grand window. "As it happens, I did. You see, a year ago, my father's advisor sat me down and told me history would repeat itself. I would not be allowed to rule the kingdom that is my birthright. As his only child and a female one at that, my father was marrying me off for the good of the nation.

"I expected this," Emiana said softly. "I was raised by tutors and nursemaids. An advisor had to tell me about my impending marriage because my father couldn't be bothered to untangle from the limbs of his harem to tell me himself. Someone who never had a trace of affection to show me, would not grant me the throne. I knew it was coming, but I never expected the name he uttered next to be Alisdair Shadowsoul."

I threw a subtle look toward the door. How close could I get to it before Kaelan struck me down?

"For days, I was in shock," she continued. "I had been ready to do my duty until I heard that name. The truth of him is in the title. King of Wind and Wild. Shadowsoul is little more than a beast. An animal. He will rip me to shreds with the same blood-dripping claws he used to sign the treaty.

"Well, I say no."

I inched toward the door. Kaelan was too fixed on Emiana to notice.

"The one thing they haven't taken from us yet is the right to defend ourselves and fight for our lives," she said to the fallen stars. "That is what I do this night."

I reached behind me, feeling for the wood.

"I would ask your permission, but I do not need it. I would ask your forgiveness, but I do not care for it. My actions are blessed by Mother Meya and I— Stop her!"

Throwing the door open, I ran. "Help! Someone, help—!"

My knees locked. Scream trapping in my throat, I fell face-first onto polished stone. My nose snapped—spurting blood on the floor and in my mouth.

Kaelan dragged me back into her bedroom. He was not gentle that time.

"Forgive me, my princess." He threw me on the floor. "She will not get away from me again."

"It's fine. I did just finish saying it is still our right to defend ourselves. The girl has some sense of instinct." Emiana left the window and knelt down beside me. "She knows she should fear what is coming next."

"What do you want from me?" I forced through gritted teeth. "Why are you telling stories and speaking in riddles? Tell me why I'm here."

She laughed. "That's what I was endeavoring to do before you ran off, but if you desire I should speak plainly, then I will grant your request. You are here because I am not marrying King Alisdair. You are."

A roaring sounded in my ears, muffling the strange nonsense that dropped from the princess's lips. I would've run again but Kaelan did not release the magic he used on my legs.

"Excuse me? I must've misheard you, Princess."

"You misheard nothing," she said smoothly. She sat me up and propped me on my knees. The softness her laugh granted her, washed away under returning disdain. "I will not marry that monster. I will not endure his bed until he rips me apart or impregnates me with his beastly seed. I will not be ripped from my home and forced to live in the filthy den of feces and unwashed animals that he calls his kingdom. I shall do none of those things. They are to be your fate."

I stared at her with no trace of reverence or respect in my raised brows or scowl. "Your Majesty, I cannot marry the king," I said slowly. "You do know this, don't you?"

She nodded at Kaelan—a signal that sent him to her nightstand. "You will permit me one more story," she said to me. "One that we all know.

"Five hundred years ago, the kingdom of Lyrica was a matriarchy. Four hundred and ninety-nine years ago, it was decided the matriarchy would be no more. A lone spellcaster created the spell to bind magic, and it was devastating for us.

"Men do not possess magic within them. They must draw it out of the elements, creatures, nature, and beings around them using runes, spells, and incantations. Then, they must store it in coudarian crystals so they can use it at will. The opposite of women who carry magic in their souls, and draw upon that magic to fight and defend.

"It started small at first," she said, fingers closing over the tome Kaelan handed her. "Whispers of a whisper about a new dangerous spell. By the time Queen Kasra knew it was a serious threat, dozens of women had their magic stolen from them—permanently. She banned the spell of course, but it was too late. Knowledge of it had spread. The incantation itself wasn't hard to perform. Any middle-powered faeman could do it.

"I don't know what makes it worse. How easy it was, or that so many were willing to turn on their mothers, sisters, aunts, friends, and lovers. Just like that, they ripped away everything that made them who they were, and no law or punishment was stopping them."

Laying down the book, she flipped through the thick pages, sadness making her lids heavy. "Faewomen went into hiding or fled the city. They were the lucky ones. The ones who stayed had their last hope taken away from them when Queen Kasra was betrayed by her brother. He bound her magic, then stole her throne.

"During that time of upheaval, he passed the law that said all women must have their magic bound by ten years of age. It was done to prevent her daughters reclaiming the throne when they were old enough. No one knew then that law would condemn us all to death."

"The wasting sickness," I rasped.

She nodded. "The wasting sickness. Our magic is within us. It sustains us like the breath of life. It didn't happen all at once. Some women lived to fifty. Some eighty. Others one hundred. But eventually one by one, losing their connection to magic made them slowly waste away—vomiting, insomnia, fevers, dementia. Illness after illness struck them down until they all died before their time.

"It didn't take long for physicians to realize these deaths were all connected to their bound magic, but was the law repealed? Did they lift our death sentences?"

"No," we said at the same time.

Princess Emiana didn't need to tell me this story. I knew it well.

"Five hundred years," she whispered. "Half a millennium of dying, having our rights stripped away, and being reduced to nothing but breeding mares. In half a millennium, a nation that boasted righteous queens and powerful female warriors of legend, has become a place where a princess and a whore peasant sit as equals."

"The term is war wife, not whore," I sliced in, "and I'm neither."

She went on like I hadn't spoken. "Here it is." Turning the book around, she tapped the page. "The binding spell. It's right there written down in the book of forbidden arts. No one ever bothered to remove it. I— Oh, I didn't ask. Can you read?"

"Yes, I can read. What I'm not capable of doing is understanding why you're showing me this."

"I thought it was obvious. I want you to understand the ever-present and casual contempt they have for us all. They boldly and proudly commit forbidden magic against us, knowing there's nothing we can do about it.

"In the same way my father's pet told me I was to be traded to a cruel and violent brute to spare the lives of a few peasant faemen on the battlefield. He believed there was nothing I could do about it. That would have been true," she said, tapping the book. "If the means to defy him weren't held in the same tome that mocks us."

The soft whisper of pages filled the room, as loud as my echoing confusion. What was this play-acting? She speaks impossible nonsense about me marrying King Alisdair, then goes on about a book that will defy the king of Lyrica. If she had that, why was I here?

"There are spells in here the likes of you could never comprehend. Spells to force someone to fall in love with you. Spells that set fire to cities, cause plagues, set unstoppable fires, and allows you to trade bodies."

The final word pierced my mind. "No!"

"I will become you and you will become me."

"No," I roared, wrenching my body to the side. My legs did not come with me.

"The book doesn't say how to perform the incantation naturally." I was a fly in her presence. My buzzing did not stir her. "Since the day I was told, Kaelan and I have been working to recreate the spell. An entire year, with countless failures in our path. The first several servants died outright," Emiana dropped, devoid of compassion.

"I will not do this."

"The others lived long enough to show us our mistakes. The person I trade with must be as close to my body type as possible, or the agony of my bones breaking to reach or shrink to a new height would stop my heart."

"Are you listening to me? I will not do this!"

"We waited a long time for you. It truly is Meya's will that my life be spared, but what we do is not without consequence—"

I smacked the book and sent it skidding away. "I'm not doing anything. How dare you talk about the right to live and be free while speaking of all the lives you've taken without a thought."

She gazed at me flatly. "Those lives were a necessary sacrifice. I took no pleasure in it."

"I'm sure that's what your father said when he bartered you like land and cattle. A necessary sacrifice."

Eyes flashing, Emiana smacked me soundly across the face.

"The difference is," she said over my ringing ears, "that I am your true heir and sovereign. It is your duty and privilege to lay down your lives for me."

I clutched my cheek, grimacing. "I reject the duty and deny the privilege. I have a family depending on me. My mother is being taken by the sickness. My faywens don't know from one day to the next if they will have food in their bellies."

"A bunch of poor, wailing brats forever clinging to your skirts? How tiresome. I'm doing you a favor." She snapped her fingers at Kaelan. "I'm freeing you of their burden."

I rocked back, her words a worse blow than her hand could ever deal me. "How could you say something so horrible? They aren't a burden. They're my family! The last thing I want is to be free of them."

She looked me in the eyes. "Then I won't be doing you a favor by putting them to death if you don't cease your squawking? Good. It wouldn't be an effective threat otherwise."

Lips trembling, I quieted—sinking back on my heels.

"As I was saying." Kaelan handed her the book. "There are unavoidable consequences to this curse. Try as we did, altering the spell only made those consequences worse. Nature requires balance," she said, smoothing out the pages. "For great reward, there must be great repercussions. This is true in all things."

I barely heard her, my mind spinning. A body-switching spell? Sacrificing myself to spare my *sovereign*? It was all crazed nonsense. Of course the tiny, run-down school I went to in Gutter Galley didn't have ancient forbidden texts. Women were only taught reading, writing, math, and basic subjects, but still, I could not believe magic such as this existed. She was going to kill us both by messing around with curses she couldn't hope to understand, and then what would happen to my family?

They'll be trapped under the grip of Kirwan.

My nails dug half-moons into my palm. I would not let that happen.

I looked around while she nattered on. The princess wasn't the problem. She had no more magic than I, and without it, she was a soft and pampered royal who didn't spend her forming years scrapping and fighting anyone who insulted her mother, or messed with her siblings. I could easily get away from her if not for Kaelan.

I need to find a way to take him out. Maybe if I provoked him into coming closer, I could snatch the book and—

"—once we change, you will not be able to speak things I do not know."

My ears caught alight. "Excuse me?"

"It's here." Emiana pointed to a line halfway down the page. "*You will have their body, their knowledge, and their soul.* It was only by observing our single successful pair that we discovered what this meant.

"You will not only take my face. You will be granted knowledge of my life and mannerisms. You will also have yours stolen from you. Names and stories that I, the princess, do not know can't fall from your lips. Memories that aren't mine will fade from your mind. We will both slowly forget who we are until we become the other completely."

Blood drained from my face. "This is madness."

"Nature requires balance, little whore. There can only be one you, and one princess of Lyrica."

Horror nearly stole my voice. "Why would you choose this? You will forget who you are. Your entire life gone with one selfish curse. How is that any different than getting married? Your life is still over, with mine added to your casualty count!"

"You weren't listening." A strange smile curled her lips. "I said you won't be able to keep memories I do not have. The same holds true for me—"

"Exactly. So why—"

"Have I spent all this time telling you stories and giving you explanations I do not owe you?" She smiled wider. "Because if you know it, I will too. I will remember the night Princess Emiana told me about a curse that switches bodies, and a man she would not marry. I will remember that she is me."

My head spun. "But then so will I. I'll know none of this is real. I'll warn your father and King Alisdair—"

"How do you expect to do that?" She cocked her head. "Do you imagine it's that easy? Mother Meya, Kaelan, you had to bring me a stupid girl. The consequence of every curse is that the cursed cannot speak of their affliction. You will warn no one of nothing. Your lips will part and silence will come out. Your hand will try to form the characters while you glare at a blank page. Yes, you will remember the truth, but you could do nothing about—"

"Olene, Meliora, Gisela, Jaclan, and Savia!" I rushed. "Remember these names. You love them. You promised you would return to—"

"Kaelan!"

He hurriedly touched a crystal on his lapel and an unseen gag stuffed my mouth, cracking my jaw and trapping garbled speech in my throat.

Fury lit Emiana's brow, peeling her lips back from her teeth. I thought she might slap me again.

"So you're not that stupid. But that did you no good. Fine, you will remember the names of whoever those people are, but I will soon know everything about them." She tapped her forehead. "Even if you did manage to tell anyone what I've done this night, ask yourself how many of your loved ones I'll kill before King Alisdair comes for me?"

"Agh!" The rich food spoiled in my stomach, burning its way back up my throat.

"Do we understand each other?"

Stiffly, I nodded. She would have the means to destroy me more assuredly than I could hurt her. King Alisdair would whisk me away to a land of strangers. While Emiana would march my face and body right into my home... with my unsuspecting mother, sisters, and brother.

"Good. I wanted to be civilized about this, but you've left me no choice. Kaelan, keep her silent for the rest of the night. There's much she must know, and I have no time for her interruptions."

"Yes, my princess."

I sat quiet, jaw aching, and chest constricting as she dove into the story of her life and legacy. I was made to listen to everything from her favorite foods and the names of her horses, to her deepest secrets and enemies. She spoke of safe places for her to hide and how to get there. She said in great, terrible detail what to do to the people I loved if anyone questioned her identity or tried to imprison her.

All I could do was sit—trapped and burning with hatred—as she told herself to do something I would never do—abandon my family. Her plan was so insidious in its simplicity. I would lose all sense of myself, believing myself to be the princess, while she ran off with the jewels and gold she spent a year hiding away, waiting until she had a new face that would take her safely out of town.

"If something goes wrong, there is only one way to break the curse," she told herself through me. "True love. A confession of love for your true self and with your true name. He must know and love you, the real you, not the borrowed face you wear. When that love is sealed with a kiss borne of truth and sacrifice, all that you are and once were will return.

"Remember this in case something goes wrong and you have no choice but to reclaim your body. Thankfully, your true love will always be with you." She held out her hand to Kaelan, a smile as warm on her lips as the one beaming on his. "Kaelan will protect you, watch over you, and bring you back when the time is right."

"Yes," he said. "I will. I love you always, my princess. Forever until the end of time."

"And after."

I would've vomited if the bile could escape my throat. Not just for their sickening display, but for the certainty that this was the last night of my life. True love would never free me. I'd spend the last of my days with a man who believes me to be someone else. Even if he discovered love somewhere in the depths of his black, twisted soul... My name. He would never know my name.

"I believe that's it," Emiana said, rising. "Am I forgetting anything, my love?"

"No, my heart. After the change, we'll walk straight past the guards into my quarters. They'll think I took one of the war wives out for a taste. As soon as she's married, we'll both be free."

"Let's not waste another minute. Father has been sending guards to check on me at night to make sure I haven't run."

"Get comfortable," he said. "I'll take care of her."

Getting comfortable for Princess Emiana was stripping naked and lying down on her silky, voluminous sheets.

Kaelan tugged off my clothes and left me on the cold floor—legs locks and jaw trapped. I shook as chill spread through me, tears stinging my eyes.

How did this happen? Only that morning, I was singing in the garden with Savia, smiling at our garden patch's healthy, growing vegetables. Now I was in trouble the likes of which cracked my spirit. Of course this barbaric spell was named forbidden. It was a curse that allowed you to steal someone's life. To rip away their image, memories, and future, take it for yourself, and leave them stranded in the misery you're fleeing. What kind of desperate person created such a spell?

How desperate must you be to use it?

The princess of Lyrica trading lives with a poor, random girl she called "little whore," she wasn't desperate. She was terrified... of Alisdair Shadowsoul.

I knew as much about the ruler of our enemy kingdom as anyone in Lyrica did.

All of faekin lived in harmony until Alisdair Shadowsoul. Peace and goodwill throughout the lands wasn't enough for the peasant faeman. He wanted power, a kingdom, and complete and total dominion over all in his path.

No one knows how he did it, what spell he used, or how he discovered such a terrible spell in the first place. All that was known was that on one terrible day, he tore his heart from his chest, cursed it, and hid it somewhere in the lands that became the kingdom of Wind and Wild.

Our magics—or at least, the magic of those still allowed to use it—were connected to our hearts, feelings, and emotions in so many ways. The explosive destruction of fury. The tenderness and majesty in magic fueled by love. The fits and starts of nerves, and the bubbling, brightness of happiness.

But if all that was taken away, and one was just an empty, soulless vessel of magic who wielded it with cold efficiency? Alisdair Shadowsoul answered that question: you become the most powerful faeman in history... at the expense of everything you are.

Shadowsoul changed.

Without his heart, he began turning into a beast. Half fae, half animal, he became the father of a new race—the faeriken.

On the very spot where he hid his cursed heart, grasping vines, jagged bush, overgrown trees, craggy rocks, and perilous cliffs sprung up surrounding him. A deadly, twisting forest that would one day become the kingdom of Wind and Wild.

If that was the end of his tale, Princess Emiana's madness would not be the start of mine, but it got worse. So much worse, for the cursed heart was not content to contain its evil.

It spread through the soil and into the closest neighboring villages. At first, no one thought anything of it, until they began to change. Warped from reasoned, normal-mannered faekin turned into feral, snarling beasts—half fae, half animal.

That was when the kings and queens of old realized we were in trouble. If the heart wasn't found and destroyed, the curse would continue spreading until it struck down every kingdom and every fae. Thus, they went to war. A war that's lasted a thousand years, with no end in sight.

Shadowsoul did not take well to being attacked. He was certainly unmoved by pleas, treaties, begging, or bribes. Instead, he claimed the faeriken suffering under his curse as his subjects, and set them to fight the very fae trying to save them and themselves.

Our men would come back from the battlefield, speaking of fangs, claws, gills, fur, long ears, and beaks. They spoke of men who lost their souls long ago.

And Shadowsoul was responsible for all of it.

Hundreds of years later, Shadowsoul sat on a throne carved from the land's misery, ruling over a drooling, snarling pack of cursed beasts, and watching my people die in a war we couldn't lose, because we fought for our home and our souls.

It wasn't a choice. Every year, the kingdom of Wind and Wild grew—the cursed land bleeding across the borders of Lyrica, Quatassa, Rajadom, and Sarabai. Even if we gave in and abandoned our crown city, there was nowhere to go.

Across the sea was the human lands, their crown cities were towering death traps of metal and iron—fatal to us. We couldn't live there, and with each passing year, we couldn't live on our natural lands. Defeating Shadowsoul and his faeriken was the only way. If only they weren't proving impossible to beat.

Kaelan sat down beside me, carrying a bowl of spelled ink. I knew not the magics that were performed on the ink to make it able to draw runes of power. Those were the kinds of things you learned in the Academy of Magical Arts. No woman had attended in five hundred years.

Kaelan dipped his fingers in the bowl, then began drawing on my body. Whispering to himself, he repeated the incantations over and over, weaving the spell that would destroy my life.

I screamed and railed against the gag, begging him to stop. Pleading with any trace of goodness in him to let me go.

Kaelan didn't so much as look me in the eyes. I was nothing to him. Just another pawn in their year-long plot to run away together, and leave the rest of us with the consequences.

Only when I was covered head to toe in runes did he leave me on the hard floor. I had to listen to him repeating the process with Princess Emiana, every symbol and word of power bringing me closer to the inevitable.

What am I going to do? I'll forget my family. I'll forget my promise. Mama is getting sicker every day. Meliora's stern face and sharp tongue made it even harder for her to get work. If things got too desperate, what would become of Jaclan? Would Mama have to choose between enrolling him in training or watching all the kids starve?

My breaths picked up, chest rising and falling too fast as my family's ruin materialized before my eyes. Meliora would try her best to take care of Mama and the kids, but she would have something in her way that I didn't—

—her shit-stain bastard of a father.

This can't happen. I fisted the rug. Muscles straining, I flipped myself over, and crawled.

My legs were useless sticks trailing behind me. Slowing me down. But I wouldn't stop.

This was my only chance while he was focused on the princess. She said guards would eventually come to check on her. Let them see a naked girl covered in runes, crawling through the hallway. That was sure to spur them into action.

Come on. I pushed myself up, straining for the handle. *Almost.*

My body seized. Arms jerking, agony racked me—originating from every rune, and they were everywhere.

I was melting.

White-hot heat burned me to ash. Warped my bones. Incinerated my insides. And left me nothing. I was nothing in the face of such terrible, vengeful magic. It wasn't just that this curse was forbidden. The curse was alive. Sentient. It knew its offense against nature, and did not want to be performed. All who dare ignore this, would know pain that had never been experienced.

Hearing Princess Emiana scream louder than the one lodged in my throat was hollow revenge. I was changing.

My sun-blistered skin paled. Callouses disappeared from my hands. My hair—so unique and reviled—lengthened until it tangled around my jerking arms. Another bind restricting me. Dry, tangled ends smoothed out like the finest spun silk, and I felt it all.

I felt the hair grow from my scalp. Felt my flat, round nose both narrow and shrink. Big feet crumpled with the breaking of a dozen bones, becoming the tiny dainty pair worthy of a princess. Everything I was and could be washed away.

I strained for the handle, tears streaking a face that wasn't mine. *My promise... I won't break my promise...*

My hand fell away. Darkness claimed me before I hit the floor.

Chapter Three

"Princess? Your Highness?"

My eyes fluttered open. Light immediately assaulted them, and I snapped my lids shut.

Everything hurt. From the pads of my aching feet to the top of my throbbing scalp. Even my jaw hurt as though all of my teeth had fallen out, then regrown anew in one night. What was wrong with me? What happened?

"Where... am I?"

"Don't be silly." A light giggle tickled my ear followed by the whoosh of curtains. I flipped over as more light pounded my eyes, burrowing my face into something soft and sweet-smelling. "Rise and shine, Princess. You don't usually sleep in this late. Are you well?"

"Why are you calling me that?" I grunted. My head was a mess of pain. If someone told me a spike had been driven through it, I'd say they were lying. This pain was from three spikes. "Just call me... by my name. All the traditions and rules about names... are silly."

"Oh." The person's shuffling feet paused for a beat. "I... That is very kind of you, Princess, but it wouldn't be appropriate. I feel it best I address you by your station."

"Station? What are you talking about? And close those curtains." Why were Shadi and the others being so silly? Who wanted the sun in their face after a night of drinking rich wines? "My head is killing me. I didn't think I had too much wine. The palace stuff must be stronger."

"Wine? But I only brought you one glass with your meal last night," whoever they were replied. "Have you been imbibing in secret? Oh, Your Eminence, the king would not like that."

"The king? Why would he care about the likes of me?"

"Princess, are you sure you're feeling all right?" A cool hand came between me and the pillow. "Hmm. A touch warm. How about I prepare you a rosewater bath? I'll cancel your tutors for the morning, and prepare you tea on the terrace. A cool bath and a little fresh air, I'm sure you'll feel much better, Your Majesty."

"Rosewater? Tutors? Tea on the terrace? What in the name of Meya are you talking about?"

I sat up, and blinked. Large, owlish brown eyes blinked back at me.

"Who are you?"

The stranger laughed, wrinkling her button nose. She looked to be about my age, but that would be where our similarities stopped. She was taller, broader, and wore a plain but expensive tunic, pants, and linen boots. Palace staff.

Girls like her who could get jobs working in the castle were raised nowhere near the Galley. She was likely the daughter of a nobleman, who received the highest-paid work women without magic could get.

Fiona. My mind impossibly supplied the name. How? I did not know the woman.

"That's very funny, Princess. I forget what a lively sense of humor you have. Now come with me." She took my hands, ignoring my sputtered questions.

I was in a room that was both familiar and unfamiliar to me. These floors knew my feet. The bed remembered my frame better than any lover, and yet, I'd never been here before.

"If you're not unwell, you can't be late to meet with the tutors. King Salman was most insistent."

"Tutors for what?" My stomach turned. "Tutors to teach me to be a war wife? Will they show me how to—to *service* the faeriken? That's hideous! Who would think of such a thing?"

She gaped at me. "Mother Meya, no," she cried. "Of course not. They're your usual tutors. Language, history, etiquette, and geography."

"What usual tutors?" I clutched my head, wincing. "You're not making sense."

"Your Eminence, you truly don't look well. I've never seen you so pale." She took my hand again. "Let's put this whole conversation of tutors to bed. You're not meeting with them today. You need your rest. It won't do for a bride to look sickly on her wedding day."

My head snapped up.

"*You are here because I am not marrying King Alisdair. You are.*"

"No."

I ripped away from her, running to an unknown door with steps that were too sure. Bursting inside, I found myself in a wardrobe. What I was looking for stood on the opposite end of a room full of magnificent clothes and shoes. I skidded to a stop in front of the mirror... and screamed.

"No. No, no, no!"

It all came back to me. Every horrible, awful second of it. Trapped, gagged, crawling, begging... and a selfish royal with her besotted lover, offering me up to die in her place. The selfish royal gazing back at me.

It worked. Their evil, twisted curse worked. A mass of red, silky locks covered half my torso. Full, plump lips were dry from just waking up. Lily-pad eyes swam in milky, red-stained ponds, and my too-pale skin bleached whiter than a sheet. This was not me.

"Princess?" Fiona ran inside after me. "What's wrong? Are you okay?"

"Don't call me that!" I snapped, making her jump. "I'm— My name is— My name is—"

I choked, eyes bulging. My name wouldn't sound. Each attempt to say it, and it was stolen right off my tongue.

She said this would happen. I would not be able to voice things the real Princess Emiana didn't know. There was a reason the high and lofty heir didn't bother to ask my name.

"You are Princess Emiana," her companion said slowly. "You're not feeling well today, but that's understandable. You're under a lot of pressure. Come with me and I'll—"

I bolted past her, leaving the shouting attendant in the overstuffed closet. Grabbing the door handle, it gave way as easily as it did the night before. Everything was coming back to me, including how they didn't bother to lock the door. So absolute was Kaelan's ability to control me. I never stood a chance.

I ran out—feet so small and foreign slapping the cool stone. I couldn't voice what she didn't know, but my mind still belonged to me. My memories were intact. How long until that was no longer the case, I didn't know. All I knew was that I'd better act fast.

"Princess? Princess!"

Very fast. The unknown attendant was chasing me, and moving much faster than this soft and pampered body.

I skidded into the back stairwell and flew down the steps. The other women weren't in the little rooms they called sleeping quarters. That left one place they could be.

"Princess, please come back," Fiona called. She was gaining on me fast. "Whatever is wrong, I'll help you."

I threw open the doors to the former storeroom. Over a dozen heads swung to me.

"Help me," I screamed, making four women in my vicinity jump. "I'm not— I'm not—" My mouth refused to utter the rest of the sentence, confessing that I'm not the princess. "I won't marry the king! I won't marry the king!"

The words came out and kept coming. A truth that was real for both me and the princess.

"You have to help me," I cried, throwing myself on a wide-eyed Shadi. "I can't marry the king. I can't marry him."

Hands seized me, dragging me off the confused woman. Guards lifted me off the ground and on their shoulders, weathering my kicks and punches.

"Get off! Get off me! I won't marry the king!"

"Please, calm yourself, Princess," Fiona cried. "New-wife jitters are normal. You'll feel better after you've had some rest."

Sense seized my tongue. "Olene, Meliora, Gisela, Jaclan, and Savia!" I screamed as they carried me to the door. "Olene, Meliora, Gisela, Jaclan, and Savia!"

"Wait," a small voice spoke up. "Why does she speak of Olene and her children?"

Hope soared in my chest.

"Just a minute." Eara, my old friend from the Galley, pushed through the bodies—following after me. "Princess? Princess, do you want to speak to Olene?"

I could've cried. I always liked Eara with her kind smile and a joke always on her lips. She then became my most favorite person in this world. "Yes," I screamed. "Olene. Olene!"

"She isn't here," Eara said, "but I can fetch—"

"How dare you!" One of the guards holding my legs snapped around and shoved Eara, sending her flying into Shadi. "You will not address the princess, nor will you leave this room. All of you, face the wall. Now," he shouted when they didn't move.

They all turned away from him—from me.

"The princess is ill," snapped the guard. "She knows not what she's saying, and you will repeat nothing of what you've seen or heard."

My captors carried me out into the halls—my cries and pleas falling on uncaring ears.

"None of you leaves until the ceremony is over." The guard stormed out, slamming and locking the door on my only hope.

"Don't worry, Princess." Fiona patted my flailing ankle. "I have the perfect thing to calm your nerves and help you sleep. King Salman said to give this to you in case your jitters overtook you. He is as wise as he is kind."

"Olene, Meliora, Gisela, Jaclan, and Savia!" I screamed to all and anyone who'd hear me. "Olene, Meliora, Gisela, Jaclan, and Savia!"

Away they took me—carrying me back to a gilded cage where a delicate bird always sings their pleas, and no one lets them out.

***

"Princess Emiana?"

The door opened, turning my head from the window.

Fiona pushed inside and waved in the trail of servants behind her. I couldn't keep track of all the things they carried in on pillows and carts. Makeup, shoes, necklaces, bracelets, gowns, hairpins, tiaras. The parade of finery was endless, and my eyes crossed trying to follow it all.

Wincing, I turned away, facing the window and the endless garden beyond it.

I'd been this way for the last few hours, days, weeks? Impossible to know. A fog descended on my mind minutes after the guards dragged me away from the war wives and force-fed me a *calming tea* that Fiona brewed.

In the brief moments I could string together two thoughts, I understood exactly why Emiana hated her father.

Memories of a life not mine floated through my head the longer I sat at the window, unable to summon the will to run away. Most of them memories of a man who cared not a whit about his wife, and even less for his only child.

Raised by nannies and attendants. Requests to see and speak with her father were put through a dozen staff and advisors, only for those staff and advisors to relay the message that he was busy and didn't have the time.

Whenever she acted out, spoke up, or tried to exercise the tiniest bit of freedom, King Salman ordered her minders to restrain and punish her—magically. Those bids for attention didn't draw him out as she wished, so eventually Emiana stopped trying, and played the obedient, silent, out-of-the-way child that he wanted.

Raised in a bustling, grand palace surrounded by dozens of people ready and eager to do her will, and Princess Emiana was the loneliest person in Lyrica.

It was my misfortune to know this. Visions, feelings, and memories of Emiana's broken childhood floated through the paved, empty path the tea made of my mind. I almost felt sympathy for her, if not for the other memories that floated through my head.

The marriage negotiations with the representative of the king of Wind and Wild. Like a certain other aloof, uncaring king, Shadowsoul hadn't bothered to be present when he listed his demands for the union—from the twelve children I was to bear him to the highly detailed sexual acts I was expected to perform nightly.

That's who she's forcing me to marry in her place. If only I could get away. If there was some...

I lost track of the thought as a butterfly fluttered past the window. Delicate, purple wings with tiny spots dancing on their tips. The pretty little thing brought a smile to my lips, chasing unpleasant thoughts away.

What was there to be angry about? It was a gorgeous day. The sun was shining. The flowers were blooming. I didn't need to go anywhere. Everything I needed was right there at the window.

"Good morning, Princess." Fiona was suddenly pulling me up and away from my garden. "Forgive me for disturbing you, but it's time."

I cocked my head. "Time?"

"Why, for the wedding, ma'am."

Wedding. The word traveled through my head, incited panic, and screamed at my limbs to run through the open door.

I took a step toward it, then many more as Fiona led me the opposite way.

"Right this way, Princess. Your dress arrived from the weavers this morning. It's radiant," she gushed. "You'll be an absolute vision. The most beautiful bride in a century."

I could say nothing as she brought me into the bath and undressed me.

Protests rose hot on my lips. I'd been bathing myself since a few short years out of swaddling. I did not need their help.

My mouth formed the words, then a bucket of warm water tipped over my head, and my indignation was carried down the drain in a soapy stream.

They scrubbed, washed, rinsed, scented, and scrubbed again every inch of me—including my most intimate places. I was a doll in their hands. A silent, obedient doll. What the princess of Lyrica was supposed to be.

But I'm not a princess, a voice hissed. Was it mine? *You are no one's doll. You're no one's sacrifice. You're a sister and a daughter, and you have people who need you to WAKE UP!*

I jerked up, knocking a scrubbing brush from Fiona's hand.

What was I doing? Fiona left me unguarded for hours? Days? However long, and I hadn't tried to escape once. No wonder Emiana felt comfortable using magic to force her way. She'd been raised to believe it was normal to turn someone into your puppet.

"I... have to... go."

"Oh, yes, you're right, Princess," Fiona said. "You have to go and have your breakfast. The king declared that you'll be leaving the kingdom immediately after the ceremony. It's fourteen days' ride to your new home, and who knows what manner of rotting carcasses those beasts pass off as food."

Murmurs of agreement and scorn passed through the too-filled bathroom. Not even for the sake of the faewoman about to be married off to the beast, would they hide their disdain of faeriken.

Fiona helped me out of the bath and to the dressing room. My mind was coming back in bits and pieces, but my strength wasn't following. I couldn't stop her sitting me before the vanity. Helpless, I watched the buzzing swarm of servants transform the famed beauty of Lyrica into a portrait of loveliness so blinding, I tried to hold on to the urge to look away.

Blemishes were banished from my cheeks. Powder paled my skin nearly translucent. Rouge darkened my lips to glittering, bloodred rubies. My hair was combed until it shone, twisted into a multitude of braids, then woven around my scalp like a crown.

While they transformed me, I planned.

Buried in Emiana's memories was a walk-through of the ceremony.

Fath— King Salman didn't trust Shadowsoul or his men an inch. The faeriken party would be on the other side of the throne room with a contingent of guards between them and the nobles. Salman would stand beside the altar with guards on either side of him, and I would be led through a side door beside the altar.

I'd walk past the king to my waiting soon-to-be husband, and behind him... would be another door that opened onto the palace gardens.

If I made it that far, I'd be free. All the guards would be inside guarding the king and noblemen. They wouldn't spare a single able body to protect the plants. Once I broke out, I'd beat it through the garden, leap over the wall, then make it back to my family.

We'd all have to run of course. Emiana's face was my face, and Salman would have his men hunt this face till land became sea, and beyond.

That was fine. There was nothing left for us in Lyrica. If we have to leave, we'd leave. At least my family would be safe. At least Shadowsoul would slink back into his dark, twisted forest, and find a wife there who was happy to be "seen, not heard" per his contracted request.

I nodded, steeling myself. *This will work.*

I'd never get away from this beastly army, but a quick dart around a surprised and unsuspecting Shadowsoul, and this entire nightmare would be over.

I pictured and plotted every step all through a breakfast that I pretended to chew, sip, and swallow. Every time I asked for this or that to be brought to me, I spat the food out while their backs were turned. There would be no calming teas or scones that morning.

After an unfulfilling breakfast, the servants returned me to the dressing room where my wedding gown awaited.

Gossamer silk fell in soft, wispy waves over ivory satin. Something that glittered like diamonds was stitched on the hem of my gown and the sleeves. Wait— They were diamonds. As priceless and coldly beautiful as the diamond tiara Fiona carried over on a pillow.

I almost spat on the thing.

"You will be the most beautiful bride in all the kingdoms," she whispered, eyes shining, "and... I'm sorry."

I tensed, looking away. "But I thank you," I rasped. The words were coming slow, but they were coming. I didn't speak at all while under the influence of the drugged teas. "Finally, we stop pretending this is a happy day."

No one knew what to say, least of all Fiona. Least of all me. There was utter silence as they helped me into my dress, did up two dozen diamond buttons going up my back, and settled the tiara on my crown of braids.

Fiona is right, I thought as I gazed into the mirror. *Never had there been a more beautiful bride.*

"Would you give me some time alone?" I heard myself say. "This is to be my last day in this room. On my own. I'd like a minute to say goodbye."

"I don't know if—"

"Of course, Princess," Fiona sliced in, cutting off one of the women. "It is the least we, your people, can do for you before you set off to the brutal lands for all our sakes. We thank you, Princess Emiana, as deeply as we love you."

Fiona bowed deeply and the gesture cascaded around the room, bringing all of their heads down. Memories floated through my head of interacting with these women and Fiona throughout my daily routines and before special functions. I had wondered why I couldn't recall most of their names, then it came to me that I never asked.

They all bowed and showed the highest deference to a princess who saw them as nothing more than helpful decoration, because they knew what was awaiting me on the other side of the gnarled, dead trees and perilous cliffs that surrounded the kingdom of Wind and Wild.

I would sacrifice and be put through so much worse than staff forced to serve an arrogant royal.

"Five minutes, if you permit, Princess," said Anice, the dressmaker. "His Royal Highness was most insistent that you not be late for the ceremony."

"Has Shadowsoul and his people already arrived?" I asked.

"They arrived three days ago, ma'am."

Three days. For three days at least I'd been sitting in front of the window like a houseplant, wasting precious time while my family worried, Kirwan tightened his grip, and Emiana got farther away.

"What...?" It wasn't the tea that slowed my tongue. "What are they like?"

Anice's smile wiped away. Looking me in the eye, she said, "They're even worse than we feared."

Her words hung in the air after the servants left, Fiona the final one to walk out and close the door.

Emiana saved me from days of being passed around by feral beasts, only to see me married off to the worst one.

I fixed on all the bits and bobs the servants left behind, most of all the scissors. They—Princess Emiana, Kirwan, King Salman, Alisdair Shadowsoul—believed I could be bought and sold without a fight, even if it meant chaining me down.

"Not quite."

***

I reached for the knob as it opened.

"Excuse me, Princess? We really must go. Are you read—?" Fiona choked, eyes bugging. "Princess!?"

Lifting my chin high, I smiled. "I'm ready. Let's go. We mustn't keep my betrothed waiting."

"B-b-b-but—"

I brushed past her, marching out of the room and into the hall. One of my escorting guards dropped his sword. He swore foully as he scrambled to pick it up, then pointed his gaze over my head—his face reddening.

"Princess," Fiona half-screamed. "You mustn't— You can't—"

"How dare you say can't to me," I snapped, so easily adopting the tone the true princess used on nearly everyone she met. "It is your job to escort me to the ballroom. Do so, and keep your opinions to yourself, servant."

Fiona's eyes darted around, chest heaving. I could tell she was looking for the guards to step in and help her.

Swallowing hard, she faced me. "Princess, if I may, please return inside so that I may help you finish preparing for your wedding. I know it is your desire as well as all of Lyrica's that your wedding ceremony is a beautiful, pleasant affair."

"Why wouldn't the ceremony be beautiful and pleasant?" I asked. "Am I not the famed beauty of the east? Is not my mere presence pleasurable? My betrothed will swoon at the sight of me, and all watching will sing of the wonder and majesty of this day, and the woman who became a bride at the end of it." I stared her down. "Or will you dare to say otherwise?"

Her jaw worked, skin paling. "Please," she whispered. "I beg of you, Your Majesty."

I turned my back on her, marching away. "You begged me not to be late, and now you're wasting time. Let's go. My king awaits."

It was a deathly tense and silent group that followed me through halls I shouldn't know, but that my feet remembered with ease. Assuredly, the king sent all ten of these guards to pen me in like cattle, making sure I had no escape.

Instead, they all walked at least a pace away from me, looking like they'd get farther if they could.

Fiona muttered and fussed on my heels, hissing pleas for me to return to my room, stop this, let her help me—the begging went on.

I'm sorry, Fiona. Rounding a corner, the door to the throne room came into view. *I swear, I will not let you be punished for what I've done, but I must do this. Anything to get back to my faywens.*

I may be a liar, but I never break a promise.

Two of the guards drew ahead and swept open my doors. "Good luck to you, Princess."

"Thank you," I said, and stepped out onto the dais.

King Salman, ruler of Lyrica, champion of the battle of Ryen, and grand sorcerer of the Meya order, took one look at me and choked on his wine.

Hacking and wheezing, he doubled over—clutching his collar and straining as two attendants rushed to help him up and pound his back.

I couldn't blame him for the undignified reaction. For a man who saw his daughter very little, it would still surprise him to see her like this.

Emiana's radiant, fire-kissed hair was gone.

Well, not so much gone as hacked and cut like a blindfolded madwoman went at it with a pair of scissors. Some patches of hair were as long as my middle finger, some were barely longer than the tip. I left myself a few braids to hang over my face and behind my ears, but the rest were on my dressing room floor.

After making short work of her hair, the scissors transformed the wedding dress. I sliced through the bodice, ripped the hem, cut off the sleeves, and scattered the diamonds. I attacked the vanity with equal vigor, snatching up the rouge and face paints, and smearing them all over my ivory gown and ivory cheeks.

It was to compliment me to say I looked like the wild street jesters who danced and jumped around in dirty rags for any coin thrown at them.

My audience went deathly silent at the sight of me, and I went silent at the sight of them.

"Faeriken," I rasped.

An army of guards stood between them, the nobles, and the altar as promised, but they were paper before a flood.

Feathers, fangs, horns, tusks, claws, beaks, whiskers, eyes of every type and color—latched on to me. Seeing straight through me. These people weren't fae. They'd left behind their faemanity a long time ago, giving way to the beast within.

Women with feathers for hair and claws for hands. Men with leathery rhino skin and horns growing out of their foreheads to match. Cat eyes peering above small, wet noses and twitching whiskers. One man hunched over, bent at the waist. The oversize tortoise shell growing out of his back was clearly too heavy to bear. These were the faeriken, and if I didn't stop this. If I didn't get free, I'd be sent away to live with them—to become one of them—forever.

I forced myself to look away and ahead, and our eyes met.

Stories of Alisdair Shadowsoul had been told across the land for generations, and grew more terrifying and frightening with each mass slaughter and unbelievable defeat he won on the battlefield. Mama would croon his story late at night while Meli and I clung to each other under the covers, afraid he'd burst in right then.

Everything Mama said was so horrifically right... and wrong.

Curling, raven locks swept back from his forehead and were tightly bound, revealing the ivory horns poking from his scalp. His pointed fae ears were slightly too pointed, giving away that he wasn't quite the same as us—if the unnaturally long, lethal nails at the tip of strong, powerful hands didn't do a perfect job saying the same. Mama was right. He was half faeman, half beast.

He was also shockingly, heart-stoppingly, breathtakingly gorgeous.

Full, dusky lips set in a small frown, carried by a strong, sculpted jaw. He had a long, regal nose that had never known a pimple or blemish. I didn't know how I knew, but I did. This face had never known an imperfection.

I drew closer to him—captured in his glittering, amber eyes like a bird caught in a sticky, molasses trap. I could go nowhere. I could do nothing... but go to him.

And with every step that brought me closer, his thick brows climbed higher and higher.

King Salman couldn't speak. He'd have to haul his jaw off the floor for that.

"I—I—I have no words to explain this display," Emiana's father wheezed. "Believe me, Lord Alisdair, this is a bewildering mistake." Salman shot in front of me, bringing his half a dozen guards with him. They all got between me and Shadowsoul. "We want nothing more than to see this union through. She will go back and change *immediately*."

"There is no need."

I blinked, confused for a moment. That deep, smooth, honeyed voice could not have come from the monster who haunted my dreams for the last week, and yet it was his lips moving.

Shadowsoul waved his hand, making the guards grab at their crystals. I gasped, eyes bugging.

Mangled, hacked locks flowed whole and new from my scalp. The face paints vanished from my gown, leaving nothing but delicate, gossamer white. Diamonds reappeared at the hem, and the thick, heavy weight of all the goop slapped on my face disappeared.

I was the shining beauty of Lyrica once again, and I could've screamed.

"Let us proceed," Alisdair drawled. He turned on the officiant, who I swear shrunk under his gaze. "Begin."

His command set up a flurry of movement. Salman pounced on me, dragging me none-too-gently the rest of the way down the aisle, and forcing his guards to squeeze and trip over themselves to remain surrounding him. Meya forbid they give the faeriken a clear shot.

"A valiant attempt, girl, but nothing, *nothing*, will prevent what will happen here today," he hissed in my ear. "You think yourself worthy enough to rule? These pathetic antics reveal you. A true monarch knows that to rule is to sacrifice."

My lips parted. *I'm not your daughter. I'm not Emiana! She cursed me. Let me go, please!*

Nothing came out.

"You embarrass me."

My heart panged. Emiana's memories had yet to crowd out mine, but those words I knew. I couldn't recall when, why, or what happened, but King Salman had said those words to his only child many times. For as long as she had memory.

"I don't want to do this," I got out—a truth that was both Emiana's and mine. "I won't marry him."

"You will do as you're told," he snapped, planting me in front of him, and leaving his guards behind. They surrounded me on all sides—boxing me in. Cutting off all chance at escape.

For all the hatred, blood, and tears between our two people, the king honored this joining of our nations and the end to the war with a ceremony beyond compare.

A golden dais rose as high as the arched windows, catching the streaming sunlight in its opulent reflection, and making the entire altar glitter. Rare, red dahlia roses tickled my gown, spreading their sweet, calming scent into the air.

I breathed it in hard, wishing for that calm as I looked anywhere but at Shadowsoul. To be near him was to stand humbled before a mountain, and know that for all your screaming, pounding, and fighting, you would never beat him.

Power radiated off him like heat off the sun—more confusing for the fact that there wasn't a single coudarian crystal on him. What did it mean that this man didn't need to store power, or worry about accessing it quickly.

He towered over me, rising at least a foot taller, and as wide as two of me put together. I could run through him, and break my neck in the attempt.

But you must attempt. You have to do something, my inner voice cried, eyes darting around. *Kirwan told the steward that your fictitious debt would pass to Meliora, forcing her to become a war wife in your place. Emiana will not take care of my family. It'll look like I simply disappeared, and Meliora would be left to the horror I tried to save her from.*

The officiant cleared his throat. A short, stooped man with thick, broken veins in his nose, and hands that shook too much. He somehow looked even more uncomfortable than me. "Let us begin," he said, opening his tome. "One and all, we are gathered here in these hallowed halls to witness the joining of Princess Emiana Graycloud and Lord Alisdair Shadowsoul."

Hands reached out and took mine, making me jump. I stiffened as Shadowsoul laced our fingers together. It was such a sudden, intimate gesture, I couldn't hear for a full minute for the sudden roaring in my ears and blood rushing to my face.

"Meya, we ask your blessings for this union." The officiant brushed an oil-covered thumb across my forehead, then made a gesture in Shadowsoul's direction. He couldn't summon the courage to touch him. "Princess Emiana, it is time," he intoned. "Make your vows before the All Mother.

"Do you, Princess, vow to care, honor, and obey his Lord Shadowsoul?"

"I do not."

"D-do— Excuse me?" He blinked at me, trembling harder. He wasn't expecting that. "I said, do you, Princess, vow to care, honor, and obey his Lord Shadowsoul?"

"Not a chance in hell."

He choked, whipping around to King Salman while cries and gasps filled the room.

I didn't know Shadowsoul's reaction. I couldn't seem to lift my gaze higher than the firm, muscled chest barely concealed by his ceremonial wedding uniform.

"Continue," Salman barked, striking fear that didn't belong to me in my chest.

Emiana was afraid of her father. I hated that I would eventually know why.

"Do you, Lord Shadowsoul, vow to care, honor, and obey Her Eminence, Princess Emiana?"

"I do solemnly vow," he said easily.

"Do you, Princess, vow to give your title, your love, and your life to the king of Wind and Wild and his people, forsaking your claim to successor of Lyrica with hope it will pass to your son and heir?" He leaned in. "Repeat after me. I do solemnly vow to give my title, love, and life to the king of Wind and Wild and his people."

"I don't vow any such thing," I said, lifting my head and looking Shadowsoul straight in the eyes. "I'll be keeping my title, my life, and my love, thank you very much. You can fuck off back where you came from."

The officiant swayed on his feet. I thought he might faint.

"What is she doing?" my side of the ballroom cried.

"She's going to ruin everything."

"We were finally going to see an end to the war."

Lamentations sounded behind me, but behind Shadowsoul, was nothing. The faeriken didn't twitch, speak, or acknowledge in any way that something out of the ordinary was happening. They were as silent as their ruler—staring at me like I was an uninteresting bug that would soon enough be caught in his web.

"And—and do you, Lord Shadowsoul, solemnly vow to give your life and love to the princess of Lyrica?"

"I do solemnly vow."

"Do you, Princess, vow to take this man as your lawfully wedded husband, forsaking all others, for as long as you both shall live?" The loose-jowled, shaking old man turned on me with a hard set to his weak chin. "Princess, you will repeat after me: I do vow—"

I slapped the book of vows out of his hands, sending him flying after it with a cry. "I'll take over from here," I dropped. "I vow to be nothing but a nightmare, a festering sore, a gnawing ache, a splitting headache for the rest of our *short* union.

"I vow to spend every day and night running from you—fighting to get back to my true home and freedom." Visions of my family spun in my mind. "I vow that I will never love you, want you, or delight in a single peaceful, pleasant moment with you.

"I vow that I will make this enduring Thousand-Year War seem like child's play," I said, loud and clear. "Every day with me will be a battle to the end. I will gray your hairs, wrinkle your eyes, hunch your back, and grind away your will.

"I vow, Lord Shadowsoul, High King of Blood and Evil, to kill you."

You could hear a mouse scurry across the floor of a room on the other side of the castle, it was so deathly quiet.

This is it. The moment he takes his court of half-beasts, gets into his carriage, and rolls away for good. Emiana thought her only way out of this marriage was to flee with my face, but there was always another way, I thought, smile tugging to my lips. *Make Shadowsoul dump me at the altar. Let him be the one doing the fleeing.*

Shadowsoul's expression suddenly changed, and I reeled back—heart jumping in my throat.

He smirked.

"A festering sore, you say? A splitting headache. An enemy to my peace, youth, will, and eventually, my life. You claim these as your vows?"

I didn't break. I didn't look away. "I do."

"Well." He released my hands, knocking me off-balance. "I won't stand for my wife to break her first vow to me, so..." Shadowsoul unsheathed his sword and presented it to me—hilt first.

My mind spun in the split second it took his and Salman's guards to move. I'd never killed anyone before. I'd never even seen anyone be killed. It was a hard life in Gutter Galley, but a peaceful one. Everyone was too tired and hungry to stir up trouble.

What life in Gutter Galley is... is mine. It's my life, and Emiana sought to steal it from me to save herself. If I let this monster marry and whisk me away, she'll have succeeded.

I had to get back to my family. I just had to. This was one promise I would not break.

I snatched the sword. Without pausing for breath, thought, or regret, I plunged it in his chest.

"Ahhh!"

Screams rang out in the ballroom. Shadowsoul folded over like a puppet with cut strings—his mountainous, head-scrambling presence disappearing in a blink. The faeriken ended their silent vigil—snapping, snarling, and barking as they madly climbed and stampeded over each other, surging toward me.

"Guards," Salman bellowed. "Guards! Take her away!"

A noise sounded high above the calamity, striking fear the likes of which neither me nor Princess Emiana had ever known.

Alisdair Shadowsoul *laughed.*

Shoulders shaking, chest rumbling, breath catching—he laughed out loud, striking a dong for stunned silence over fae, faeriken, and me.

Straightening, he pulled the sword out of his chest—unharmed. "You, little bird." My breath caught when he cupped my cheek—a smile as beatific as it was terrifying stretching his full lips. "I must have you."

Shadowsoul snapped his fingers. The book of vows flew off the ground and dropped on his outstretched palm. "I do vow to take this woman as my lawfully wedded wife—"

"No," I rasped, scream trapped between my teeth. What was he doing? He couldn't do this!

"—forsaking all others, for as long as we both shall live." He snapped the book shut, smiling wider if possible. "This I vow to you, little bird. Not peace, or happiness, or love, or friendship, but I do vow you will never be bored... and you will always be mine. This I promise for the rest of my days—may they be many or few." He swooped down and kissed my lips so fast, he was already pulling back when I squawked and jumped away. "I leave that up to you."

"No, y-you can't do this." My lips were numb. Did I speak out loud? Because I couldn't feel them move.

A weight settled on my wrist. My head wrenched down to see a silver bracelet clutching a sparkling black stone. *The first gift bestowed to his bride.*

That meant there was only one thing left to do. "I don't accept this." I threw myself at the wall of guards, my hands straining and flailing through the gaps of their bodies. "I will not marry y—!"

"By the power granted to me by the All Mother, Meya," the officiant cried, scrambling up. "I name you husband and wife." He sliced his hand down between us—a coudarian crystal clutched in his hand.

"No!"

It was much too late. Magic washed over me, searing into my skin. I cried out as a black symbol etched into my pores—burning the rune for married deep into my forearm where it would always be, denoting me as the very thing Shadowsoul named me—*his*.

I lost it.

Screaming, I rammed my head into their armor—opening a dozen cuts on my forehead and cheeks. I pounded every hand that tried to grab me. I kicked and flailed as I was lifted into the air, catching two guards across the face.

Shadowsoul couldn't take me away or Meliora and my family would lose the only thing they had left to lose—freedom from Kirwan's iron fist.

"I won't go!" Running at Shadowsoul, I fell on him, and gripped his sword.

I turned on my attackers, weapon held high. I wouldn't let the last thought my family had of me be that, in the end, I was nothing but a liar. "I promised," I screamed, slicing the air and sending my chargers scattering. I darted through the space they stupidly provided me, racing for the doors. "Olene, Meliora, Gisela, Jaclan, and Savia!"

The guards stumbled over themselves chasing after me—torn between stopping me and blocking the cursed faeriken from the royal and noble fae.

I seized the door handle. "Olene, Meliora, Gisel—!" An unseen force hooked me around the middle, lifting me off my feet. I flew back and slammed against a hard chest—the wind whooshing out of me.

"Little bunny might be a more apt name for you." His deep tremble sent a chill up my spine. "Dangerous little thing, aren't you?"

My face hardened. "You have no idea."

Spinning around, my stolen sword fell in an arc, swinging straight for his neck. The bastard may not have a heart to stab, but cutting the head off a snake always worked.

Alisdair was the slaughterer of millions. His selfish and greedy bid for power warped innocent fae into feral beasts, and the curse spreads farther still—dragging us all into his hatred. Every kingdom of the fae would rejoice and honor me for getting rid of our greatest threat, and even so... I wasn't doing it for them.

Kingdoms had warriors and soldiers to fight their battles. My family only had me. I would not be Shadowsoul's queen of the beasts. This was always going to end one way—either he left this palace a widower, or I left a widow.

Shadowsoul lazily threw up his palm, and the bronze blade halted just short of it—hanging still and obedient in the air. I tugged, wrenched, and pulled with all my strength. It didn't budge.

"That is enough!"

Rough hands hauled me around. I had time to see Salman's furious, purpling face, and the shadow of his backhand falling across it, before it fell.

Movement flashed out of the corner of my eye.

Shadowsoul's claws shredded Salman's sleeve and pierced his skin, staining the fine fabric with pinpricks of blood.

"That is the last time you attempt to lay a hand on my wife." Alisdair struck his chest with an open palm, and Salman blasted off his feet and crashed through the wall.

Someone screamed. I think it was me.

No— It was everyone.

Through the man-sized hole, the palace harem wives bolted from their beds and lounges, running screaming for the door. Their cries were the only sounds coming from the room. The floating mound of silk, blood, and plaster in their bathing pool didn't speak or move.

"And for your sake and the sake of that worthless parchment the treaty is written on," Alisdair finished, "it'd better have been the first time."

"Argh!" Guards, nobles, and Lyricans roared to life.

Coudarian crystals on their clothes, weapons, and staffs blazed with power, and the world lit on fire.

I stood stock-still as explosions burst and danced all over me, greedily headed for us, then forced away—streaming around an invisible barrier.

"Ah," I cried when the world spun.

Shadowsoul tossed me over his shoulder. "Let us away, little bird. We've overstayed our welcome."

"Put me down!" I clasped my fists and smashed them against his spine—kicking and fighting with all my might. "I'm not going anywhere with you! Let me go. Let me go!"

"No."

He spoke so calmly and with such finality, my protests clogged in my throat. I could not make this man do a single thing he did not wish to do. I knew that as surely as the explosions crashing over our heads, repelled by an invisible barrier.

Alisdair Shadowsoul could not be touched. He could not be stopped. I was a dandelion before a storm. My only hope was for the soil to remember me after I was washed away.

A wave of exhaustion bowled me over. My lids drew heavy over my eyes, begging to close. This was no one else's doing but his.

"And to think," he said as black crept into my vision. "I had every intention of leaving you at the altar..."

I flopped against his back—gone.

Chapter Four

"Meli!"

I bolted upright and tipped over—my head bumping against the curtained window. Hurriedly I ripped it over, and gazed out over the vast, rolling fields.

I wasn't in Lyrica anymore. By the gnawing in my stomach and the bright, morning sun creeping over the horizon, it seemed I left Lyrica some time ago.

"No," I whispered, throwing myself against the door. "No, no, no!"

I scratched, screamed, pounded, and kicked at the door panel. The frame didn't bend. The handle didn't bother to move. I was locked in, and not going anywhere.

How could this happen? Without me to stop him, Kirwan would force Meli under his thumb all to have sick, bedridden Mama under his thumb. Without them to take care of the little ones, Kirwan would ship Gisela, Jaclan, and Savia to an orphanage without sympathy or hesitation.

Just like that. One selfish princess and a beastly bastard of a king—ruined our lives forever. And to think, that morning, my biggest worry was finding a shop owner who'd let me do some sweeping for extra coin.

Sinking to the floor, I cried.

Chest-heaving, lung-shredding, hiccupping, bawling wails ripped from my throat and spread throughout the countryside.

"There, there, little bird." I jerked when a warm hand brushed the back of my head. "Don't cry." His slow, steady crooning was as gentle as the fingers tangled in my hair—soothing me more than I wanted them to.

Slowly, achingly, my tears stopped falling.

"See? Much better," he said. "No sense crying now when things are about to get much, much... worse."

I flung back, slapping his hand away. Alisdair's laughter filled the small, darkened space.

Pressing my back to the cushioned corner, two strange, shining eyes beheld me through the gloom. Sometime between my abduction and waking up in the carriage, he had time to change out of his wedding robes into a casual, almost peasant-like outfit of a tunic, trousers, and simple leather boots. His hair had been released from its confines, and fell in soft, curling waves around his ears, and horns.

I glanced at his hands, then doubled back. There was no doubt. His claws were shorter than they were the day before. Had he trimmed them? Did he do that... for me?

So it wouldn't hurt when he mounted me—

I cut the thought off at the knees, put it in a box, set it on fire, then buried the ashes. In no reality—alternate or otherwise—would this man enter me.

"Take me back."

Alisdair didn't move. He didn't speak.

"Take me back now," I repeated, raising my voice.

Nothing.

I swallowed hard, absentmindedly tugging on the symbol of my oppression—the charm bracelet. Once, a hungry, ragged wolf wandered into the Gutter Galley and cornered me in an alley—growling and salivating for the coming meal that was me.

I'd have given anything right then to be back in that alley.

I was being assessed by another predator, and this one was more terrifying than a starving wolf would ever be.

Stop it, I snapped at myself. *Stories and legends are just that. Whatever he's done, Alisdair Shadowsoul is not invincible. He's flesh, blood, and fae like the rest of us. A very powerful faeman, but still, just a man.*

You've been around enough men to know what they want, and what they don't.

Straightening, I wiped my tears on my sleeve and set my jaw. I was done crying. Crying never solved anything. The only way to get home was to go through him, and I was more than up to the task.

I cleared my throat. "You should, you know. Take me back, that is." My tone was even. Almost cordial. "It's in your best interest to end this sham of a marriage now."

His only reaction was a slightly raised brow.

"Come now. Didn't you wonder why King Salman offered his daughter and only child to his worst enemy? Did you really think it was to get you to sign that silly little peace treaty? Aww, you did, didn't you?" I clicked my tongue, mock-pouting. "So cute."

His brow rose higher. One thing men like Shadowsoul didn't like—being made to seem naïve and clueless.

"It wasn't about you," I went on. "It was about me. My father"—my throat burned to call him that—"knew he'd never be able to arrange a real match for me, so pawning me off to you was his last hope of getting something out of the deal."

I took a deep, exaggerated breath and released it slow. "You see, I was born with a tragic condition. Very rare. Very real. You can learn about it yourself."

"I am on the edge of my seat," he drawled, startling me. Would I ever get used to his unnaturally deep, honeyed tone. "What is this condition?"

"My pussy," I dropped, raising that brow as high as it could go. "It has teeth. Rows of them all up my walls. Very sharp."

A strange noise came from his side of the carriage. Was he...? Was he *laughing*?

"It's true." Laughter pealed from his lips. "It is! This is no laughing matter. Any attempt to consummate the marriage will result in your cock being horribly mangled. See for yourself." I held up my hands. "I got these cuts from my unwise attempts to play with myself."

I revealed the many slash marks on Emiana's fingers. They were from my escape attempt. The lone day Fiona went too long between administering the tea, and I cut myself trying to hop through a broken window.

"And of course, since nothing can go in, nothing can come out." I had to raise my voice to be heard over him. "That means no children. None. So, do you see? Do you see how King Salman tricked you? He saddled his enemy with a wife that will never fuck him or bear his children. You might as well take me back now because— Stop laughing!"

If anything, Shadowsoul laughed harder.

"Oh, my queen. When that odd, foolish little man"—he described the king of the most powerful fae nation in the land—"told me he had a little bird he wanted to give me, I was skeptical. Especially when all reports declared you a meek, decorative, pointless creature."

I bristled, and he wasn't even talking about me.

"But alas, I shall have to slaughter every one of my Lyrican spies. You are far from meek or decorative, my crude, court jester of a bride. You are what no one has been to me for a very long time." He smiled, revealing true rows of sharpened, lethal teeth. "Entertaining.

"So, bite me, little bird. Mangle me." His eyes flashed. "I dare you."

The conversation had taken a strange and terrible turn. I did not understand this man. It seemed everything I did to repel him, only increased his fascination of me. What would it take to make him open the cage and let the little bird fly free?

"You needn't be afraid of me, little queen."

"No?" I straightened, pushing down my fear. "So all the stories weren't true? About your cruelty? About your palace being a den of nightmares? About the things your people do to their mates on their wedding night?"

He smirked. "No. All of that is true and more, but you still needn't be afraid because now my cruelty will defend your honor. My den of nightmares will be made into your home. And the things I do to you tonight will create their own legend. The only thing you'll fear is that I'll stop."

His grin widened. "Don't worry. I respond well to begging."

I leaned forward, getting as close as I could stand. "Teeth or not, I will never *ever* lie with you. For the rest of our short marriage, your bed will be as cold as the splinter of ice where your desiccated heart used to be."

"You will lie with me every night and twice in the mornings," he replied, tone flat. "Our bed will slide across the floor, riding the river of your sweet, flowing juices, while I plunder your hole to the music of your ear-shattering screams for more."

I choked, eyes bugging. What did he say? He could not have said what my cursed, ailing mind thought he said.

"Not only are these facts written in your future, but I will have you every night with your complete and willing consent. You will beg, little bird," he hissed. "And I will be only too happy to oblige."

I stared at him for a long time, eyes huge—heart racing to get free. Shadowsoul didn't break. He didn't even blink.

I whipped around. "Help!" I threw myself against the window, screaming my throat raw. "I know you hear me up there! Let me out of here! Let me out!" My magic surged up inside of me, heeding my distress, and smashed against the internal barrier forced on my soul on the day I turned ten years of age. It wasn't going to help me—nothing and no one was.

"I don't accept that," I bit through clenched teeth. "I'm going home."

Tearing off the curtain, I wrapped it around my fist and prepared to strike under another amused smirk.

Shadowsoul could smirk his ass right to hell. When they locked Emiana in her chambers, they didn't think that pointless, decorative princess would throw a chair through her window and climb out of that either. I was getting back to my family. Nothing would stop me.

I descended on the glass, preparing to—

Something flew across the horizon, soaring straight at my face. I shrieked as a flash of scales and teeth roared past my vision—snatching whatever it was out of the air.

"What was that!"

"An assassination attempt, most likely." Alisdair couldn't have sounded more bored if he tried. "There were many who opposed the treaty and are taking this opportunity to ambush me while I'm away from my kingdom. It is no matter," he said. "My guards will protect you, little bird. Most fervently from the ones who did want this peace treaty. They will not be pleased to know you've broken it not ten minutes after it was signed."

"*I* broke the treaty?" I gaped at him. "Oh, how terrible it is when age addles your mind and rots your memory. If you think real hard—really strain until you hurt yourself—you will find, *old bird*, that you broke the treaty when you threw the king of Lyrica through a wall."

He grinned. Once again, I was amusing him, not irritating him. Certainly not enough to force him to turn the carriage around. "The terms of the treaty were that all acts of aggression between my kingdom and yours cease—"

"Exactly. You—"

"—therefore, plunging a sword in my chest, unprovoked and before a hundred witnesses, counts as an act of aggression, wouldn't you say?" His grin was terrible to behold. "Do tell me, my queen. You know how age rots the mind."

My lips pressed into a thin, numb line. "What does this mean? What will you do?"

"Now you ask?" He cocked his head. "Now you inquire about the treaty? Only now you mention your father, and not even to ask if he's still alive? Why is that?"

"Because I'm not—!" I choked on Emiana's name, strangled by curse and frustration. I sighed. "I don't care what happens to that man. In the end, he was no better than a broker—selling his own daughter to warm his enemy's bed. That's all I was to him in the end. A pawn to sacrifice."

He gave me a long, leveling look. "I see. So that was not the first time he's struck you."

"I—" I started to say I don't know, then memories that weren't mine rose to the surface. "No, it was not the first," I replied, knowing it to be true. "Nor was it a common occurrence. He'd have had to spend more time in my presence for that—barring the one night a month I was allowed to sit beside him during the Meya's Moon feast."

Impossibly thick lashes cast long shadows over his unnatural eyes. They were beacons that kept drawing me back to them, no matter how much I wanted to look away.

"Take heart, my queen, for your plan worked."

"My plan?"

"To break the treaty and therefore remove all barriers and excuses... for me to kill him."

My eyes narrowed. "That's not going to work. Although I will say, your seduction techniques are quite unique and advanced. Pretending that you care so much for my honor, you'd kill the man who hurt me, is a nice sentiment, but it doesn't erase the fact that if you truly wanted my happiness and freedom from a man who'd rule and control me... you'd turn this carriage around right now and take me home."

"No."

Anger welled in my throat. It was everything in me not to leap across the divide and claw the boredom off his face. "Why?" I cried. "Why do you want me? I know of you. I know kings, queens, and emissaries from the four kingdoms have offered you money, land, brides, and grooms all in hopes of you lifting the beast curse off the land.

"You turned them all down by way of severed heads and mangled limbs sent back to where they came from. Why now? Why say yes to this marriage? Why force me to go back with you when you want this marriage even less than I do?"

"I have answered this question, but if you wish to hear it again, I will oblige," he replied. "I have mastered the magical arts, created a superior race, conquered my kingdom, and amassed wealth that rivals the coffers of this and the human lands. But..."

"It's not enough." He snapped his fingers and the torn curtains vanished from my grip and reappeared whole and intact over the window. "There was one more horizon to conquer. One that's always been out of my reach... until a little bird plunged a sword through my chest."

He smiled, and for the first time, I felt I'd done something very wrong.

"There is something we must do, and at first, I did not believe you were the one to stand at my side. But I see now I was wrong. When you're in my presence, there's no fear in your eyes, tremble in your chin, or deference in your speech. You do not fear me, though you do revile me, and yet, arousal wafts thick and heavy from your lethal pussy—telling of your desire for me."

My face heated. "That is not—!"

"That wasn't a question," he growled, slicing in. "Merely a fact that ever more intrigues me. I demanded the All Mother aid me, and she gifted me you." His voice was barely more than a whisper, lulling my lids heavy once more. "A beautiful little enigma wrapped in venom and violence."

He laughed—full and free. "Of course I'm not going to give you back, little bird. I'm going to trap you within my cage and watch you squirm. Listen to you scream. Delight as you buck and fight and defy until I have conquered the most interesting challenge yet—claim of your life, your soul, and your heart."

I wanted to rage. To give him exactly what he asked for—screaming, fighting, and bucking—but I could do no such thing. Darkness claimed me again, dragging me under to where I would not wake.

***

The carriage bucked, jolting me out of sleep and off my seat. I fell flat across a hard, sweet-smelling body and was immediately captured in his arms.

"Good evening, my bride." Fearsome claws trailed a shiver-inducing path up my spine. "I trust you slept well."

I shoved off his lap, escaping those tickling claws. He took no notice as he leaned over, sweeping back the curtain.

"Welcome home."

My lips parted, but nothing came out. I'd seen many maps of the fae-lands, and all of them had a huge, looming shadow where the kingdom of Wind and Wild should be. There was nothing else there could be for every cartologists who crossed the border never made it back alive. I understood why in that moment.

"It's dead," I breathed. "Everything... dead."

There were a million words to describe the frozen wasteland surrounding me—smothering me. But none would capture the sight so completely as *dead*.

Snow blanketed the hills and mountains, wiping away any trace of greens, browns, reds, oranges, or any sign life once existed beneath the ice. Twisted, snarled, bare stumps reached for the skies, their skinny frozen branches beseeching the sun for warmth.

That was it. The world had washed away. Summer, light, laughter, and warmth disappeared, and all that was left were dead trees, mountains, and ice.

"Is this the curse?" I pressed my fingertips to the glass. The cold seeped into my bones, chilling me to the core. "This is what it does? It sucks the life out of... everything."

Alisdair didn't answer. I couldn't be certain he heard me. That was fine. He didn't need to explain himself. My supposed new home said all that needed to be said.

This is what we've fought a thousand years to prevent. This land of winter and death, where we'd roam forever as mindless beasts. And somewhere, buried under the unmarked ice, was Shadowsoul's wretched, still-beating heart.

No wonder our fae forces couldn't find it. No wonder we could never stop trying.

"Enough," I announced, facing him. "No more games. No more stories. This is not my home. It can't be. I need to get back to Lyrica. I have—" *people who need me.*

The rest of the sentence wouldn't come out. Seemed Princess Emiana did not have anyone in Lyrica who needed her. Well, I did, and I wouldn't be a bird in Shadowsoul's cage any more than I'd be a pawn in Emiana's escape.

"—important things to do," I finished. "Take me back, or Meya bless it, open the door and throw me out here. I don't care. I just need you to let me go. What will it take for you to dub this the shortest sham marriage in fae history? Name your price."

"To make such a statement one must have something to bargain." He leveled that hated smirk on me—the one that said I was being a funny little bird again. "What will you give me if I let you go?"

"You can tell everyone—all the nations—that I, Princess Emiana, am responsible for breaking the treaty. I have let down my people—nay, the entire fae race, and I should be named and condemned for the selfish, manipulative witch I am." Of course the curse let me say that. Every word of it was true.

"Hmm," he vocalized, tipping his chin. The act drew my attention to how full and chiseled it was. A sharp fist clench and nails piercing my palm made me stop. "This is awkward for you, little bird, because I already ordered my people to spread that very truth throughout the kingdoms. Nearly word for word." He cocked his head, studying me in that unsettling way. "What else?"

"This can be your chance to prove the whole world is wrong about you. Deep down, there is goodness and kindness in your soul. What price can be put on your redemption—?"

"No."

I bit hard on my lip, penning in a stream of foul words. Something about his nos put me in a chokehold. My survival instincts sensed pushing him would have dire consequences.

"I—I will..." I cast my mind for something—*anything*. "Lie," I blurted. "I will lie to King Salman, assuming he still lives, and tell him the heart no longer resides in the kingdom of Wind and Wild."

His grin melted away, but mine widened. I had his attention now.

"I'll say I witnessed you unearth it, put it in a chest, and tossed it in the sea. It now lurks at the bottom of the ocean, never to be recovered." I leaned forward in my eagerness, bumping my knees against his. "One lie from these lips will end the war and grant peace—true peace—that your kingdom hasn't known in over a thousand years. What say you?" I held out my hand. "Do we have a bargain?"

He eyed my hand, expression unreadable. "What you speak of is treason, my queen. Deliberately misleading your former king, acting as spy, and spreading false information to the detriment of their war effort. If discovered to be untrue, you will be tried and executed in a cauldron of molten iron."

My throat seized. I was not aware of the punishment.

"Knowing this, you'd make such a bargain all for the sake of returning to Lyrica to attend to *important things*?"

The most important.

"Yes," I said clearly. "I will."

I thrust my hand out farther. "Do we have a bargain?"

"Well, well, it appeared you did have something to trade. You are not to be underestimated." He firmly clasped my hand. "I will remember that."

"No need." I looked him in the eyes. "We will never see each other again after today."

He laughed. "So it is."

I broke free, ignoring the odd tingling going through my fingers and up my arm. "You can stop the carriage here."

"I wouldn't dream of it. You have no food, water, or proper clothing. You'd never make it." Alisdair pounded the roof of the carriage. "I will bring you back to Lyrica, and you will tell your lies. As agreed."

The carriage jolted, nearly throwing me off the seat again, because we were turning. We were going home.

A happy noise burst from my throat—warped from a stolen voice, but still real and true. I couldn't contain my happiness. Beaming, I said, "As agreed."

Relaxing for the first time in over a week, I sank back into the cushion, settling in for a long silent ride.

After a spell, I closed the curtain myself. It made it easier to stare at him without him noticing.

He wasn't what I was expecting in so many ways. His anger at discovering Emiana's father hit her seemed genuine, but with the same breath he'd sworn to slaughter his Lyrican spies for relaying incorrect information. How did one who disregards life as casually as he did turn around and threaten someone else for their treatment of women?

Was he more than what I'd been raised to believe? Was there a side to him that wanted his war to end, peace to reign, and the violence to stop?

He shifted and his tunic fell open, flicking my gaze to his hard, shadow-dusted chest. All those men who came back from the battlefield speaking of yellowed eyes, a foaming maw, fur and scales where none should be, and a face so hideous it made you weep—I cursed them all as kakkas for telling such terrible lies.

Alisdair was dawn breaking over the horizon. A rare flower blooming under a midnight moon. Rainbow eels dancing in a clear, placid lake. No matter who you were or what you were doing, you simply had to stop, stare, and bask in the sight of him. Although, sunrises and rainbow eels were bright, joyous sights. Alisdair was different.

There was something dark and feral about his beauty. More like the inherent fear clinging to your shivering spine when you ventured deep into a dark cave glistening with silk worms. To be in that wondrous, quiet space was beautiful, but you'd never shake the sense that something was lurking in the dark—waiting.

Even so, it did not make him any less gorgeous. I said I wanted to stop thinking of Kirwan as handsome. My wish was granted for all fae-men were the hideous, bloated hindquarters of a *skletmacca* compared to Shadowsoul.

"So soon?" he said, startling me. He breathed deep. "Already you're on the edge of begging."

It took my last blissful, ignorant second to realize what he was talking about, and what he was scenting.

My face lit on fire. "I can assure you, Shadowsoul. One way or another, if that thing comes near me, it will be bitten off."

"Oh? Shall we make another bargain? You do so enjoy those."

"What kind of—?"

He ripped his tunic clean off his body.

"What are you doing!" My scream was two octaves louder than it needed to be. I couldn't help it. Of all the things I anticipated he'd do—and slaughtering me and drinking the blood from my corpse was high on the list—I never expected him to do that.

"Nothing that should concern you." Those claws moved down and found his waistband. "You do not want me. You do not ache for me. Your arousal does not hang heavy in the air, betraying your flushed skin and quivering lips." He sliced through his pants, his claws a knife through butter— No, a blade through fabric, revealing him from top to tail.

My jaw clenched tight, clamping down on a high-pitched squeak before it left my lips. The remains of his trousers hit the carriage floor, leaving nothing behind but every bare, breath-stealing inch of him.

Roaring sounded in my ears. Bright lights blinded me—impossible for we were in a darkened carriage, but I was blinded all the same. I had no experience of being alone with a naked man, and this was the worst of all men to be alone with.

Losing one's maidenhood was a risky prospect for girls from the Galley. All a devious suitor had to do was lie and say they paid me for our evening together, and just like that, I was branded a war wife for the rest of my life. Of course, I could say they were lying, but the word of a poor woman from the Gutter didn't amount to much.

Two of my childhood friends had been caught in that very trap. After months and years fighting it, and starving, they both now lived in the homes of the noblemen who tricked them—circumstances left them little choice.

I swore that would never be me. No sweet words, muscled arms, charming grin, or promise of forever would tempt me to bed a man I didn't trust absolutely. No man was that handsome. No man was that alluring. No man... was Alisdair Shadowsoul.

There wasn't an ounce of fat on sculpted thighs, or indeed anywhere else. All of him was lean, hard muscle. Inky-black runes covered him from neck to shin, finding a home on every part of his body—including the part I was doing everything in my power not to look at.

"Resist me, little bird." His words washed over me—spell-binding. Head-scrambling. "Deny what your body screams for even now, and I will not give it to you."

That was hardly a bargain. I would've laughed at the absurdity, if I could've done anything at all.

My gaze glued to the hand traveling back up his leg. Before my eyes, his claws shrunk, reducing to the size of an average faeman. The sight so baffled me, I hung on too long and didn't look away before he gripped his length. Looking me straight in the eyes, he started pumping.

A low, deep hiss leaked through my gritted teeth. I was choking too hard on my groan to let that through—though my body betrayed me all the same.

I had no one to compare him to and still my mind supplied, *Huge. Big. Powerful.* All that and more described the massive, smooth cock rolling over his palm. Alisdair widened his legs and mine snapped shut—knees knocking together hard.

It wasn't just the sight of his muscles clenching, toes curling, or lips parting. It was the unabashed shame of him. The pure truth that he didn't care. Trapped in a carriage with a forced wife who hated and bargained to leave him at the earliest opportunity, he stretched bare and bold before me with no hesitation. No nervousness. No fear of rejection.

I'd never been so free and confident in all nineteen of my years.

My inner voice shouted for me to look away, but I couldn't. Shadowsoul wouldn't let me.

A mad statement, but true all the same. His heated gaze trapped me. His body held me in thrall. I could look nowhere but where he wanted me to.

Slow, firm, steady strokes milked his length, teasing the tiniest bead of seed to the tip. A strange noise filled the carriage. It took me a minute to realize it was my fingernails ripping through the seat cushion.

"Who are you putting on a show for?" he barked, making me jump. "No one can see you but me."

My lips parted to ask what he meant, but I knew.

My hand pried off the cushion, taking a handful of goose feathers with me. I was still dressed in that obscene wedding gown with voluminous skirts. They were as cumbersome to put on and cut up as they were to lift.

They bunched up around my face—tickling my chin and nose. I couldn't see my own hand traveling down, but he could. Alisdair furiously picked up the pace when my fingers slipped inside—an impossible speed that I couldn't hope to match, but tried.

My fingers worked my toothless pussy, spreading lightning-charged heat zinging through my body. I felt hot and cold at the same time. Chilled but feverish. Disgusted but dirtily lustful like I'd never been before. So this was why sex was worth the risk—huh.

"Legs open," Shadowsoul ordered. "Feet on the seat."

My lips peeled back from my teeth—only partially because I was moaning. "You don't tell me what to do."

He stalked over, a coiled serpent narrowing in on his prey. My head fell back as he leaned over me, like a lover waiting to receive a kiss, or a caged animal readying to bite.

"No, I don't tell you," he whispered. "You tell me. You *beg* me down on those soft, supple knees—spilling the name you once cursed from your lips. Harder, faster, deeper, *more.*" Fingers trailed a slow goose pimple-popping trail down my forearm, giving me a chance to stop him—daring me to. "You teach me all the ways to make your nipples hard, your pussy wet, and heart race."

Alisdair was so close, I could count every one of his lashes. He brought his hand down beside my head, overwhelming me with his heady scent of cedar, pine, and something exclusively *him*. I didn't fight it when his palm cupped the back of my hand. Nor did I stop him slipping two fingers past my folds to join mine.

"Tell me your secrets, little bird." He pushed in deeper than I'd ever gone and spread his fingers—spread me—wide.

"Ah," I moaned, eyes rolling back in my head.

"Sing."

Sing. That's what Mama used to do when I was young and she was well. She'd sing sweet, happy, beautiful songs to me, and a man whose laugh I only remembered in my dreams—Papa.

Mama didn't become a war wife out of desperation, starvation, or boredom. She did it to be with my father. Son of a wealthy nobleman, his father forced a respectable, wealthy bride on him the minute Papa was of age. No one cared that he wanted to be with his true love. The girl he loved since she first set foot in his home, clinging to the skirts of their new housekeeper.

When Father was called up to fight, Mama seized her chance to be with him. Possibly her last chance if the All Mother called him home off the battlefield. She went to war with him. They were together, they were happy, and they had me.

Then, the law changed. It was decided that men were free to abandon the children fathered with war wives, and after Papa died—struck down near the Rajadom border—that's exactly what his father did. My natural grandfather claimed my mother and I were no responsibility of Papa's and refused to give us the home, money, and land he willed to my mother.

Left with nothing and now unable to take any other work, we moved to a tiny, broken-down pit in the Galley, and Kirwan entered our lives.

"Ah, Alisdair," I breathed. "Yes, more, please."

A deep, primal growl rumbled from the depths of his throat. The erection digging into my thigh got impossibly harder—begging for entrance.

"Oh, that's so good," I panted, chest heaving. "Alisdair, yes."

"Louder," he ordered, picking up the pace to my rising cries. "Tell me what you desire. Beg for it."

"I want— Oh, Alisdair, I want—"

The choices my mother had to make. The pain she went through. The father I never got to know. Our lives were ruined before our very births—

I moved down, fixing on a faint, half-moon scar on his chest.

—all because a thousand years ago, a selfish, power-hungry bastard ripped his heart out, and now... my mother didn't sing anymore.

"—to drive the next strike through your real heart." My smirk mirrored his own— Or it did. His triumphant grin melted away. "I want to know why men such as yourself are so easy. So simple." My laugh was loud and harsh. "You truly believe all it takes to control a woman is a flaccid cock and a few fake orgasms."

My foot came up and kicked his shoulder. Alisdair smoothly ducked the strike, pulling out of me in the process. "Let that be a lesson to you, King of Blood and Pain. You cannot use sex to get what you want from me." I threw my skirts down, straightening in my seat. "This bird won't sing for you."

"Hmm." Alisdair reclaimed his space. In a blink he was dressed. Truly, within the space of a blink, his clothes vanished from the floor and reappeared whole and new on his body. "You are a mystery, Princess. One I intend to unwrap."

I heated under the obvious double meaning. "You have the length of this carriage ride to do so. Good luck."

He didn't rise to the challenge, or if he did, he didn't see fit to tell me. We lapsed into a heavy silence; the air charged with the memory of what happened between us. Yes, Alisdair Shadowsoul was the handsomest of men, and he knew exactly what to do with the face and body the All Mother gave him—but I wasn't a fucking little bird.

No man would ever put me in a cage.

We lapsed into an uneasy silence. More so uneasy for me since Shadowsoul fell asleep half an hour in.

He is no concern of mine. What I need to do is figure out how I can get back to Meli, Mama, and my faywens, and explain to them that we need to track down the crown princess of Lyrica and force her to give my body back.

That was the only path available to me, because getting Alisdair Shadowsoul to give his heart to me—the real me—and speak my name was the impossible nonsense of a curse that didn't want to be broken.

How was he to speak a name I couldn't tell him while living in a kingdom of people who didn't know it? Your first name is given by your parents, but your second is given by your fame, acclaim, or reputation. The name Shadowsoul was given to him by the world. It was obviously not a second name he would've chosen.

As for me, I have done and achieved nothing in my true life. I did not yet have a second name for him to speak, and as for my first, the name given on my day of my birth—my parents saw fit to choose an old, ancient fae name that fell out of favor centuries ago.

It was not a name that was guessed, stumbled upon, brought up in casual conversation, or heard on the wind while walking through the market square. He was never going to speak my true name, and that was just the practical reason why the curse couldn't be broken the way it was intended.

The harsh and brutal reason was I couldn't win the heart of a man who didn't have one.

No, my only choice is to go home, protect my family from Kirwan, and then together Mama, Meli, and I can find a way to track Emiana down and get my body back.

I nodded to myself—satisfied. *Don't worry, faywens. I'm coming home.*

My forehead pressed to the window, watching the endless, unchanging landscape. Something appeared in the distance, tightening my brow.

Dark, ominous clouds rolled over the horizon, blotting out the sun, and we rode directly toward them.

Shadows and gloom bled inside, making the solitary corner of the carriage, and the man reclined in it, all but disappear except for his too-bright eyes.

The endless sea of white began to break up, giving way to an overgrown barrier of wood and death that stretched as far as I could see.

A forest.

Tangled, knotted, weeping trees pushed and grew over the other, allowing no entrance to fae or animal. The carriage jarred—throwing me roughly to the side when we forged through anyway, slipping through the trees on a path I couldn't see.

"What is this?" I squinted through the branches but there was nothing to see. The scant view of the sky granted through the bare branches revealed nothing but black clouds. "Is this a shortcut to Lyrica?"

No reply came from his side of the carriage. My throat tightened—anxiety rising.

"What's going on?" I demanded. "You said you were taking me back. Is this the way to Lyrica or not?"

Noise came from him then—a deep and clear laugh.

"You liar!" I pounded the glass. "Take me back. Take me back n—!"

The carriage put on a burst of speed, throwing me back and burying me under a mountain of tulle and silk. Wildly, we raced through the forest—hitting every stone and tree root. I screamed under the wild jostling—trying and failing to hang on to something. Anything.

Another bump and my face smashed against the window... that's when I saw them.

Rapidly shifting, racing figures moved through the trees, heading straight for us.

For as long as I lived, I'd never find the right words to describe the sight before me. *Fangs.* That was what I saw first. Horribly overgrown, lethal yellowed fangs forced from a jaw that couldn't hold them—dripping with drool. Tufts of fur grew in tangled patches on their skin. Claws the lengths of their forearms erupted from their fingers, and their eyes...

In their eyes lived pure madness.

"What are they!"

"The Taken."

I was shocked to hear him answer, then even more surprised when he pounded the top of the carriage.

We began to slow.

"What's going on? Why are we slowing down? We can't stop here, those things are coming." My cries fell on uncaring ears above and below. "We have to get out of here!" I turned and made eye contact, locking on to the beast's rage-filled orbs. Doubling over, I threw up.

The carriage rolled to a dead stop—a lone beacon amidst the oncoming storm. Shadowsoul grasped the handle.

"Don't," I rasped. I couldn't say how I knew. Call it instinct. Name it a being's deep-seated will to survive, but those creatures weren't meant to be faced. In their presence all had to run. Run and run and run, and never stop.

Alisdair stepped out, uncaring of my pleas. I crawled through vomit. Snatching the handle, I slammed the door closed after him—scream leaking through my teeth. I was afraid. Whatever those things were. Whatever unholy demon had created them, I'd never been more afraid in my life.

I yanked the door shut just in time. The world set on fire.

Bright white heat exploded in my eyes, burning through my retinas and imprinting its power in my brain forever.

I swayed—blinded—and tipped over, falling against the door which did not bother to hold me. I dumped out on the frozen ground, eyes huge as the sight looming over me.

The creatures—the Taken—thrashed on the ground, slowly consumed by the flames. Their screams pierced the dead forest and my gut, nearly causing me to be sick again, and above it all stood Alisdair Shadowsoul—laughing loud and free as fire rained from his palms, consuming all, and everyone, in its path.

Something flickered out of the corner of my eye, drawing my head up.

A flower?

I questioned but that was all it could be. Beautiful, delicate, and out of place, a small purple flower pushed through the frozen earth—unfurling satin-kissed petals before my eyes.

Alisdair's laughter cut off with the heat. He ceased his magic, dropping his hands, and the cold raced in—shredding through my dress.

Huddling on the ground, I held myself—fighting not to look at the dying creatures, but unable to look anywhere else. Shadowsoul killed them so quickly and easily, and with such enjoyment. That was a good thing. There was no question they were racing to kill us all but...

"Such power," I rasped, lips trembling as I met his eyes. "What are you?"

He smiled. "The flowers," Alisdair said. It took me a second to realize he wasn't speaking to me. "Take care of them. Now."

"Yes, my lord." The carriage driver jumped down.

I didn't have a chance to ask what was happening before he raised his hand, and the beautiful purple flower wilted into dust.

"Let us away." Alisdair reached for me. "It doesn't do to dwell in the Taken's territory."

I smacked his outstretched hand. "Get it through your fucking head! I'm not going anywhere with you!"

Pushing up on my feet, I ran. Past the carriage driver, the lead carriage, and a host of guards.

"But, my sweet little bird," Alisdair called.

I darted around the watching, still guards—jumping over the rising roots and frozen dirt that made the beginnings of a forest path.

Up ahead, the trees grew closer together, their branches reaching to embrace each other for warmth. They cut any chance for the carriages to get through, or pursue me.

"Olene, Meliora, Gisela, Jaclan, and Savia," I shouted. I shot through the trees, opening cuts on my face, neck, and hands forcing my way through. "I'm com— Ahhh!"

I pitched forward, teetering on the edge of a sudden cliff. Bugged, wide eyes beheld the long, long... long drop.

My foot slipped, and I fell. "Ahhh!"

Claws snagged my collar and bits of my skin. My dress stopped dead while the rest of me kept falling, pulling my bodice sharply against my throat. I choked—cutting off my scream.

Alisdair pulled me up and to him, crushing me against his chest. Instinctively I threw my arms around him—holding on to the only sure, steady thing as my sudden brush with death crashed over me.

"We're here." I shook with his laugh. "Welcome to Lumenfell. Your new home."

"No," I whispered, taking in the sight before me. *It can't be. This simply can't be real.*

Falling to my knees, I slid out of his grasp. Vomit rose up my throat again, ejected from my heaving stomach. "Oh, Meya... What have I gotten in to?"

Chapter Five

The carriage traversed the treacherous cliffside road, carrying us down, down, down into the kingdom I only knew of in stories and nightmares. Proximity only confirmed what distance revealed.

It was beautiful.

My eyes were as wide as they could go pressed to the glass, and it still wasn't wide enough to take it all in.

Snow fell in a light angel's dusting, sprinkling on the sleepy village like sugar on a pastry. Perilous dark clouds held back the sun, but that didn't stop them. Brilliant, softly glowing orblights shone on the frozen streets, reflecting through the ice and making the entire town seem as though it fell into a star.

Traditional Lyrican homes were tall, tightly packed, and bursting with activity. The complete opposite of the simple stone and wooden retreats spread out before me. The space between the hut-style homes afforded wide roads for little, skating faeriken—the children's giggling bounced up the cliff-face. Behind every home were see-through dome structures.

"Greenhouses," I whispered.

Once, back when he fancied himself in love with Mama and wanted to pretend to be a gentleman, Gisela and Jaclan's father invited us to his home to see his greenhouse. I remembered walking through the sea of colors, breathing in the scent of fresh dirt, and thinking one day I would have this.

I'd learn to grow every kind of fruit, vegetable, berry, and tuber that Lyrican soil would produce. Most of it I'd sell in my produce shop, but a significant portion would always be free and available to the poor and struggling in Lyrica. No one in Gutter Galley would go hungry again.

Impossibly, it seemed that dream had already been achieved in the kingdom of Wind and Wild. No one we passed looked like they'd been hungry a day in their lives.

Laughing men and women strolled, skated, and weaved through the streets, wearing a simple but sturdy style of fur-lined tunics, long woolen gowns, and thick boots. The complete opposite of the dazzling finery and shining, prominent coudarian crystals I passed on the main streets of Lyrica.

We passed by the crown jewel of the town—a square just beginning to wake up as people filled it, visiting the merchants, food carts, and a frozen fountain. A massive, intimidating statue of Shadowsoul glared down at mothers and fathers while they placed their little children in the fountain to skate upon the frozen water.

Those mothers, fathers, merchants, and couples all stopped their business to watch our carriage go by, gifting me a view of cockscombs where hair would be, beaks for noses, leopard fur, and—

I frowned, narrowing on a young fae manning an apple cart. He had neither beak nor fur nor wings. Every bit of him poking out from under his wool cap was normal fae. In fact—

I know him! I tried to speak the words, but they wouldn't come out. All the same, the recognition was undeniable, even though I couldn't recall his name. That guy was from the Galley. His family signed him up for the war college and he left years before, but I remembered playing marbles with him on the steps of my home the day before he left.

I remembered because he came over specifically to play with me, saying it was his last chance to do so before he was gone.

Mama teased me after—saying he had a crush on me, and maybe one day when we were older, fate would bring us back together again.

"Looks like it has," I whispered, feeling small before the uncomplicated beauty before me.

No dirty, long-faced children chasing after the carriage, begging for the smallest scrap to be tossed out the window. No noses high in the air. No sneers or avoided eye contact between passersby. Everything before me was the opposite of Lyrica—apart from one.

A huge, decadent castle loomed over us all—its towers and soaring cornices rising higher than the craggy cliffs. The palace of Lyrica was a shining jewel, but this monument before me was an obsidian saber. A strange comparison, but the only one that fit.

There was something sharp and deadly about the pitch-black sandstone, and bronze slats on every window my eyes could see. Light and color attacked the castle, and was soundly beaten and drowned—never taking up the fight again. And yet... it was magnificent.

"What is this?" I croaked. "How can all of this be here? Is it a trick?"

"It is no trick. That is your home," Alisdair said, speaking of the castle though he did not look at it or me. "This is your kingdom. Your people."

I swallowed hard. "How did all of this get here? Nothing I ever heard of Wind and Wild said it was... this."

"What did you expect, Princess? A dirty cave hovel where we ran around naked, bayed at the moon, and picked the blood and bones of fae from our maws?"

I looked him straight in the eyes. "Yes."

He chuckled. "What a relief this must be for you. The rest of your life will be nothing like the nightmare you imagined."

I clenched my teeth, hearing the threat loud and clear. "Why did you do this?" The carriage jarred to a stop. "Why bring me here? Why lie? We had a deal. I was going to lie to the king of Lyrica for you. The greatest threat against you and—"

"Ah, but that's where you failed in your calculations." His smirk was a living thing, reaching across the carriage to chase the chill up my spine. "That old fool is no threat to me. None of you are," he hissed. "You waste your time, your coin, and your lives on this silly little war, because it delays your accepting the inevitable—that your unimpeachable lord and master *is me.*"

He leaped across the divide, trapping a scream in my throat when he slammed his hands on either side of my head—trapping me in. "Let them come. Let them water the earth with their blood and the soil with their bones. When all the fighters and the defiant are gone, I will stand above as all you see before you spreads from sea to sea, consuming the faelands.

"Soon, all will be cursed, everyone will be faeriken, and everything will be mine— Oh, excuse me. I meant *ours.*" My heart curdled in face of his grin. "The worst part is, my queen, after all you've been raised to believe, and hate, now that you've seen what I've created, a part of you is thinking *that might not be so bad.*"

"I— You— No!" I cried, even as shame filled me. There was a brief and terrible moment when I thought this might be a better life than Lyrica's. "Your horrid, lunatic's rant aside, why didn't you simply tell me you didn't care about the heart or ending the war? Why lie when you were never going to take me home!"

He shrugged. "Turnabout is fair play, little bird. You lied to me first."

"I did not—"

His hand flashed, snagging mine from my lap. My jaw cracked in a silent cry as he took the fingers that were inside me, wrapped his lips around, and sucked them clean.

"No blood," he whispered. "No teeth." Shadowsoul flicked my nose like a child, further humiliating me. "This is the deadliest game you'll ever play, Princess. You'll either need better lies, or better aim."

"I—"

He climbed out of the carriage—done with the conversation and me.

"Wait. Come back here!" I tumbled out, chasing him down.

This wasn't over. I was getting back to my family no matter what I had to do. Better lies or better aim? I chose better aim.

"Argh!" I leapt on his back and climbed him like a spider monkey. Hooking around his neck, I squeezed and wrenched—bellowing my war cry. "You're going to take me back! Now!"

Alisdair didn't slow his stride. He was as unbothered as the contingent of guards following us over the drawbridge. What were they for? Because protecting Shadowsoul from threats wasn't it.

"Surrender, beast!" I got my legs over his shoulders and grabbed his horns. Holding on tight, I squeezed, straining to tear his wretched head off his shoulders. "One thing I said wasn't a lie. I vowed to be your nightmare, your poison, the sword in your side." I threw myself back, yanking him with me.

The castle doors opened for us, releasing a blast of heat and light.

"You won't know peace for a single day in your life! While I breathe, I'll see to it that you don't! I'll never—"

Claws seized me and the world spun. "Take this."

Shadowsoul dropped me and I fell on a hard body. Many hard bodies. They barely caught me and stopped me taking us all down.

"Feed her. Bathe her," Alisdair barked. "I want her ready for the ceremony within the hour."

"Yes, my lord," said a deep, smoky voice.

I burned watching him leave. The way he spoke about me. As though I was already the animal this place would turn me into.

"Are you all right, my queen?" I was set back on my feet, and finally given a chance to gaze upon the line of women waiting to greet us. One had thick, dark fur poking her pants and sleeves, and large beaver teeth down to her chin. Beside her was a horse faeriken. With the long muzzle and ears on her crown, she could be nothing but.

On the other side of the woman setting me on my feet was a tiger faeriken. Striped, fuzzy fur and unsettlingly long canines gleamed between her whiskers.

I tried to stop staring at them, and ended up staring at my catcher's plume of black feathers and slitted eyes. She beamed at me.

"Welcome, Queen Emiana, it is our pleasure— Nay, our honor, to welcome you."

They bowed low.

"Um, thanks." I cut a look at the door.

The guards were drawing it closed. Gazing up, I saw the massive, thick slab of wood waiting to slam home on metal hooks, sealing the door, and me in.

"Will you allow me introductions?" she asked.

I turned away to face her. It occurred to me to make a run for it, but I'd breathe fresh air for all of a second before his guards tackled me. There has to be another way out of the castle.

Like through a servants' entrance. My interest piqued. *Servants like the ones before you. They are who I need.*

"Yes, please," I said, putting on a smile to match.

"I am Aeris. Head servant and personal attendant to you, my queen." She bowed again, then kissed my hand on the way up. I would never get used to that. "This is Mavourneen." She pointed to the horse-faced girl. "She is your royal dresser.

"This is Talulla." *Beaver girl.* "She is your official taste-tester.

"And this is Eadaoin." *Tiger girl.* "She is your companion. She will be by your side always, providing for your every need—recreational and sexual."

I blinked. "Excuse me?"

Aeris's smile still blinded. "This is Eadaoin, your companion."

"I heard that part. What was at the end of your sentence?"

"She is here to serve your sexual needs," she repeated, blowing my eyes wide. "That is, of course, when our lord and master is not available to satisfy them for you. Eadaoin is quite skilled." Grasping the woman's shoulders, she brought her closer. "She was chosen just for you."

"Nope." I tossed my head. "No and nope."

"My lady?" Aeris's smile slipped. "Is something wrong?"

"Eadaoin will not be serving my sexual needs. That has been removed from your duties."

"Oh." For some reason, Eadaoin slumped. "It is because I am hideous to you. I knew it. I'm so sorry, my lady."

"No, that's not—"

Aeris sighed, nodding. "Of course, I should've known. My queen, I will find your next companion myself. One who has yet to undergo the change. She will be the epitome of Lyrican beauty." Another deep bow. "But she will not hold a candle to you."

"There will be no she!"

"No she?" Talulla made an odd sound, clicking her teeth. "Ah, I see. Our queen is saying she wants a man."

"A man?" Aeris said the word like it was foreign. "You wish for a male companion? But, my queen... you're a married woman." Reproach was so heavy in her eyes, I almost shrunk. "Our lord will not like this."

I threw up my hands. "Let me be clear. I have no wish for a sexual companion of any gender. At all. Ever. However, a regular companion who—once again does not perform any sexual acts—would be wonderful." I tipped my head to Eadaoin. "I'm sure you're perfect for the job."

"Thank you, my queen." Eadaoin's smile returned. "It is my honor to serve."

She truly sounded it. Rolling through that exceedingly normal, quiet town was enough of a shock to my system, but now this? Faeriken were mindless, bloodthirsty beasts. A scourge on our land, and the cursed shame of our race. Never did I think I'd be this close to faeriken, let alone allow one to take my hand and lead me somewhere that wasn't to my death.

"You will not be serving tonight," Aeris told Eadaoin. "Our lady doesn't require you. You may have the evening off."

"Thank you, Aeris." Eadaoin's gaze flicked over my shoulder.

That was all the warning I got before a tall, pine-scented figure brushed past me, and tore her clothes off.

"Ahh!"

The armor-clad guard shoved Eadaoin against the wall, unheeding of my screams. Kissing down her neck and chest, he sucked her nipple in his mouth, tearing a moan from her lips.

A flush rose to her furry cheeks. I expected her to kick, slap him, demand he carry her somewhere private!

Her legs spread—both knees touching the wall. "Ah, yes, fuck me!"

That was all the permission he needed to tear his pants off too. One look at his gray, leathery bottom, and I was gone.

I had no idea where I was going. I simply needed to be somewhere I understood.

What is this cold, strange place? Why is nothing as it's supposed to be?

I took off down a dark, rounded hallway. It reminded me of an owl's undergrown burrow. Or the burrow of a creature much less cute. Somewhere in this rat cave there had to be an empty room with a door I could slam shut and lock. This was all too much for me. I needed a quiet place to think.

Rapid footfalls chased me down. "My lady, you're going the wrong way, silly. Your chambers are this way." Aeris grasped my shoulders and spun me around. "Don't worry. Talulla has gone ahead to prepare your feast. It will be waiting in your chambers, along with a fresh change of clothes. I'll take you to your bath now."

I didn't know what to say as she led me past Eadaoin and her lover. He now had his sheathed sword in his hand, and was furiously fucking her pussy with the hilt. Something told me that wasn't his commanding officer's intention for the sword when they issued it to him.

Aeris led me down another circular hallway to a pair of double doors. Sweeping them open, she wasn't there to catch my jaw when it fell.

"What... is this place?"

"Welcome, Queen Emiana." Aeris passed through, holding her hands to the ceiling. "To Castle Riagin."

I took a step, then another, then one more. Getting closer didn't make it more real.

Days ago, I was forcibly confined in the most opulent, beautiful, richest palace in the faelands.

It was a steaming pile of dog shit next to Castle Riagin.

Everywhere I looked, were diamonds and gold.

Diamond chandeliers clung to the domed ceiling, raining rainbow rain on my slippered feet. Golden statues lined the wall—each a different immortalized fae-beast. Were they important people in Wind and Wild history? Did they have a real, documented, and celebrated history?

The strange, dark walls remained in this place, but somehow, it was a perfect contrast to the gaudy golden lounges, diamond pedestals, and deep plush carpet. It was normal and simple beside the obscene and jaw-dropping.

"What is all of this doing here?" I wheezed. Did Alisdair steal it? When? For a century, we've brought the fight to him. He's never had the chance to raid Rajadom, Sarabai, Quatassa, or Lyrica. There's never been a report of him plundering our wealth.

"All of this? Oh, you mean all of the statues and diamonds and gems? It is a bit much, but it serves a purpose. Castle Riagin is the exclusive employer of bird faeriken."

"What does that mean?" I asked as she led me off again.

"They— Well, we," she corrected. "Are overly attracted to shiny things. The urge to possess them only gets stronger as we—" Her jaw worked, but the words didn't come out.

Of course. The cursed can't speak of their affliction.

"Anyway, it led to a lot of thefts and tensions in the village, so in his wisdom, our lord and master brought all of us here, and hired us as his servants with free room and boarding. Now, when something shiny goes missing, it is no matter. It is still somewhere in the building."

It was my turn to open my mouth, and say nothing. I had to admit that was an elegant solution. Also, a diplomatic and bloodless one. No other king would consider hiring a race of thieves to work in his palace, but he more than anyone should know they were suffering from a curse not of their making.

Aeris guided me down another hallway and up a set of stairs with golden banisters and cold, shiny marble pressing back against my feet. I didn't know where she was taking me until we turned a corner, and found the door already open.

Hot, vanilla-scented steam wafted out, filling my nose and my mind with the memory of how long it'd been since I had a bath.

I crossed the threshold, stepping into a porcelain paradise. Waterfalls escaped from the ceiling, all feeding into a huge water basin sprinkled with rose petals. Candles flickered from dozens of golden perches, casting a warm glow over the sun-shielded space. A small half-wall designated the privy, and a large, porcelain lounge dominated the middle of the room. I assumed that was the place for me to stretch out and luxuriate in the heat and steam.

"This, Queen Emiana, is your private baths."

"Please, don't call me that. Emiana," I clarified. "Call me—"

I tried saying my name. *Nothing.* I attempted a version of my name. *Nothing.* I even attempted my siblings' names, but the clever, wretched curse didn't let that leave my lips either. Too much of a giveaway to my true identity.

"Ana," I burst out in frustration. "None of this my queen or my lady stuff. Just call me Ana."

"I am deeply flattered, my lady, but I could never address you so informally."

"But—"

"Come," she barked, clapping her hands. "My lady requires her bath."

That was the cue. Half a dozen attendants flooded the room, and descended on me.

My cries fell on unheeding ears as they stripped me, unwove the tiara from my borrowed hair, took my shoes, pulled down my underclothes, and deposited me on the lounge.

One of the attendants ran for the bucket beside the water basin, filled it, grabbed a bar of scented soap, and they commenced with scrubbing.

"Whoa, hey!" I scuttled away when Aeris slipped her scrub pad between my legs. "I can bathe myself— Actually, I insist on bathing myself."

She just laughed. "Don't be silly." Deceptively strong arms pushed me right back down. "I know you think us savages, but I swear to you, Queen Ana, you will want for nothing while you live in this castle."

Two men in light armor walked into the room.

"What the fuck!" I snatched a water bucket, using it to cover Emiana's bits as best I could. "What do you think you're doing just walking in here? How dare you. Get out!" The shock was mine, but the imperious tone wasn't.

I sounded like an outraged princess, instead of a regular outraged girl. Was that how quickly the curse took hold? How long until I forgot my family's faces? Two days?

"Forgive us, Your Majesty." The fore-man dropped to his knees, bending his head low. His wings crowned to stabilize him—a curtain of beautiful, iridescent black feathers.

Raven feathers, if I was correct. It was hard to be sure, because the curse had yet to reach his face.

He straightened, giving me a proper look at his face, and I near gasped—clutching my bucket tighter.

Inky eyes trapped me, sucking me down into bottomless depths where the sun never shone. Shocking, haunting, unnatural—but that wasn't what cowed me. From one look, I knew why the curse struggled to touch more than his eyes.

Even it knew to mar such a face was a crime against Meya and nature.

Hawk nose; rock-hard, dimpled chin; long, black locks framing an unblemished face; and that smile. He had a smile like he'd just done something naughty, and no matter what it was, he was going to make you do it too.

The second-most handsome faeman I'd ever seen, solidly throwing Kirwan from the spot.

"We welcome you to Lumenfell, Your Great and Wonderful Majesty." He bowed deeper, his forehead touching the wet tile. "I am Bradach. This is Foalan."

Say hello to number four, Kirwan, you ugly bastard.

Foalan tipped his head to me, and silver strands fell over his golden eyes.

I didn't know where to direct my stare. At the wolf ears perched high and alert on his head. His rounded, almost snout-like nose. Or his broad shoulders; trim, masculine beard; sharp, glass-cutter's cheekbones, and full, cherry-kissed lips.

How did the curse choose their animal? Why was Foalan becoming a wolf, and Bradach becoming a raven? Was it even polite to ask?

A deep, soothing baritone rolled from Foalan's throat. "It is a pleasure, my queen."

"It is our pleasure to serve you," Bradach said from the floor. "We are your royal back scrubbers. At your service."

My eyes bugged. "Really? You are?"

"Fuck no, *keva*." He popped up, dropping that subservient tone so fast, I looked for it on the floor. "Damn, they say you Lyricans are a pampered, high-nosed lot. Royal back scrubbers? What's wrong with you?"

I gaped at him—both for plopping down next to me bold as day, and calling me a *keva*—otherwise translated from High Fae as strange person, odd, or freak. "I didn't say that, you did, and— Hey!"

Bradach tugged on my bucket, making me cling on for dear life. "Why are you hugging this? They need it to wash you."

"I'm hugging this because two strange men just walked in on me taking a bath."

"What? Where!"

No word of a lie, Bradach and Foalan both spun around, clutching their hilts and looking for the strange men.

"I meant you two," I hissed through gritted teeth. "Please, leave."

"Us?" Bradach's brows snapped together. "Why?"

"Because I'm naked."

"Oh, that?" He waved that away. "We don't mind."

"I do."

"Do what?"

"Mind!"

Understanding finally dawned on his handsome face. "Oh, I see. Forgive us, my queen. Aeris told us to study your customs, but we thought this one was a joke," he said. "Lyricans can only be naked in the same room if everyone is naked."

"Oh, right."

"Of course."

"I can't believe I forgot," Aeris cried. "Queen Ana, please, forgive me. No wonder you're uncomfortable."

Bug-eyed and slack-jawed, I didn't have words as they all stripped off their clothes, leaving me and my bucket in a room full of naked faeriken. What was even worse... Bradach was right. It was socially acceptable in Lyrica for me to be naked in a bathhouse with other women—

The key word being women.

Bradach sprawled across my stone chaise, making himself comfortable. Foalan sat straight-backed and crisscrossed beside me. I sat like a folded-over pretzel, using all of my limbs to cover all of my parts after Aeris finally wrestled the bucket away.

"Once again, introductions," Bradach began. I hyper-focused on his face and didn't let my eyes drift an inch lower. "Foalan Volk. He is commander of Lord Lumenfell's army."

"Lumenfell?" I broke in. "Who is Lord Lumenfell?"

"Who is Lord Lumenfell?" he repeated slowly. "He's your husband. You married him a few days ago, keva. Don't you remember this?"

My face flushed from more than steam. "I wasn't informed that he... went by another name."

"As in, you thought his subjects referred to him by the insulting, blasphemous slur, *Shadowsoul*?" Foalan growled. "To even let that title leave my lips is offensive."

"Oh, I didn't mean—"

"He is Lord Alisdair Lumenfell here," Aeris said in a kinder, more patient tone. "A name as fitting for him as it is for our kingdom: the land the stars forgot."

I hummed quietly. Strangely, I agreed. Lumenfell did suit the dark, brooding figure I was coming to know too well. A man forgotten by the stars, the light, the radiance and wonder of the world. Outside was mesmerizing beauty, but inside... was darkness.

"As for my true title," Bradach continued. "Why, the list is endless. I am Bradach Arasu, my lord's right hand, his most trusted advisor, his sage counsel, his closest companion, his truest comrade."

I stilled, alighting on one word: *companion.*

"Oh," I breathed. "I see."

Aeris heaved a sigh. "Bradach, how you overreach." She had moved on to washing Emiana's hair. Long, glistening red strands sluiced off the chaise, and hardened my heart. I dropped my hands and legs, sitting up bold and straight. Why was I being protective of a body that wasn't mine?

"There is no overreach." I stretched out my legs and Bradach immediately slid away. Was he avoiding my touch? Did faeriken dislike their normal fae counterparts as much as we disliked them? "My lord trusts me. He confides in me. I am his friend."

"Preposterous," Foalan spat, drawing my eyes, then blowing them wide. I'd never seen such fury on someone's face, but then, no one I knew had fangs. "I would never presume to claim such titles, but if my lord were to bestow them on anyone, it would be me."

"Do you think so?" Bradach's grin was smug. "Then tell me why my lord asked me personally to stay behind and protect Lumenfell while he traversed the summerlands to acquire his bride?"

"He asked me, you fool," Foalan replied through gritted teeth. "You were merely in the room."

"You are recalling that incorrectly," Bradach breezed. "One too many hits to the head with a sword hilt will do that to an old man."

Foalan's lips peeled back from his teeth. "A mere two weeks ago my lord threw his favorite coat in my direction, entrusting it to me."

"Ah, but the day before he tore off my coat to wipe his bloody sword," Bradach shot back, "*entrusting me* with the care and cleanliness of his weapons."

My gaze bounced between them, brows high in disbelief. Was this real? Were they truly fighting over the cold and withheld affections of that cruel man?

"Last moon an intruder broke into the castle, and my lord had me flogged only a hundred times, instead of the thousand I deserved," Foalan said, smiling his triumph.

Bradach smiled wider still. "When my lord arrived this eve, he told me to have a meal prepared and sent to his study because he was... hungry."

Two attendants gasped.

Aeris halted sudsing my hair. "What? He said this to you? Truly?"

I pulled a face at the lot of them. "Is this a jest? Surely it doesn't matter that—"

"No," Foalan sliced in. His expression was terrible. "The jest is that I believed myself higher in my lord's esteem. Bradach has bested me. My lord has never shared such intimate knowledge of himself with me. Clearly, I have displeased him." Foalan hung his head.

It was like looking upon a man in mourning, but the one mourning should be me. What kind of person was so closed off, it was a shock and delight for him to tell you he's hungry?

My husband—that was who. I would never get a being such as him to fall in love with me. Which was why my only option was to run.

"So it's true."

I flicked up to Bradach, but he wasn't looking at me. Following my gaze, I saw one of the attendants carrying a large, blue crystal bowl. She waved her hand over it and it filled with white, milky liquid.

I was so shocked, my brain froze—senses fading out.

"...true. My lord honors his bride with the full and true mating ceremony," Aeris said. "The ceremony is nigh."

"Fuck it to Meya, Princess," Bradach cried. "Lord Alisdair intends to bond with you and make you his eternal mate? What'd you do to piss him off?"

If anything could've torn me from the miraculous sight of a woman performing magic, it was that. "Eternal mate? What are you talking about?"

"She rejected the marriage vows and plunged his own sword through his chest," Aeris dropped.

Bradach whistled. "That'll do it."

"Excuse me? Hello," I said louder. "What does that mean? What eternal mate?"

"The ceremony they're getting you ready for." Bradach moved aside as two women approached me with towels. "It would seem you're to be married again. Properly, this time."

"Properly?"

"The faeriken respect the old traditions of marriage and bonding." Aeris's voice reached me from underneath the vigorously rubbing cotton. "Your people threw those traditions away to allow for the travesties they commit against their wives and women. Vows of fidelity? I think not.

"Our lord honors you, Queen Ana," she gushed. "He means to make you his mate and bonded for eternity. Only death will separate you."

I whirled on Bradach. "If this is such an honor, why did you speak of it like a punishment?"

Bradach shrugged. "Because when my lord left, he made it clear in no uncertain terms that he planned to leave you at the altar. This whole arranged marriage nonsense was obviously a brazen attempt to get a spy across our borders," he said, black eyes pinning me through. "You.

"He played along, signed your worthless treaty, accepted the many crystals, jewels, and money bestowed upon our kingdom as a wedding gift, but in the end, there was to be no marriage between Lord Lumenfell and Princess Emiana of Lyrica. But then—"

"I put a sword through his chest," I whispered, lips numb.

"Exactly, keva." He made to clap me on the back, then stopped—pulling back. "With one simple, insane move you proved beyond a doubt that you are no spy. In fact, you have no subtlety at all. There couldn't be a worse spy than you."

I choked. "And for that he went through with the wedding? For that, he ripped me from my home and dragged me from the faelands!? It is your precious Lord Shitsoul that's insane!"

Growls peeled from Foalan's lips, standing my neck hairs on end. Suddenly I was back in the alley with the wolf.

"I humbly insist, my queen," he said, his even tone at odds with his bared fangs, "that you do not speak of our lord in such a manner."

Aeris screeched, shooting my heart in my throat. "How dare you, Foalan! Do not threaten our queen."

That was a threat?!

"After these many long decades, Lord Lumenfell has finally chosen his mate, and he's chosen her." She took my shaking hand. "It truly is an honor. He must see something special in you."

"Or." Bradach's voice grated on my ears. "He sees a special and honorable opportunity... to draw out your punishment. You thought yourself his assassin, now you find yourself his pet."

Silence fell over the room, smothering me. What did it mean that no one was arguing with him? Not even Aeris.

I was quiet for a long time—long enough for the attendants to guide me to the vanity and begin braiding my hair while Aeris left and came back with a plate of food for me. I barely glanced at the shaela bread, grapes, roasted chicken, or wine. The food grown and bred from this cursed soil would turn me into one of them. Not a morsel of it would cross my lips.

I won't be here long enough to need to. Eventually, all of these hovering servants will leave my side and I'll have a chance to run. The question was when?

"What is about to take place?" I spoke up. "I've heard things. Legends. Stories. About the old ceremonies. The customs were done away with for more reasons than war wives. What does my dear husband believe he's going to make me do?"

There. In the mirror. Bradach and Aeris exchanged a look.

Aeris cleared her throat, making the feathers on her neck puff up. "It is very simple. You will both be painted with the traditional marriage runes, you will make your vows to one another, and in the morning, after consummation, the runes will take root in your skin and in your soul—binding you before Meya, in life and death."

She stood me up and draped a black, sheer gown over my body—covering everything and concealing nothing.

"Will we be alone for the"—I forced the word out—"consummating."

She blinked. "Of course, my queen. Why? Is it your preference to have an audience? My Lord Lumenfell doesn't care for such, but if that will stoke the flames of your desire, I'm sure I can convince—"

"No," I bleated, louder than necessary. "That is not how my desire flames are stoked. I merely asked because we've not had a true minute by ourselves since we married. I should like to finally be alone with my husband." *To get rid of him for good and make my escape.*

"Why?" A hand snaked across my vision and helped itself to my grapes. "To try your hand at another assassination attempt?"

My face heated. The power of mind reading wasn't possible through magic or curses, but right then I would've sworn the raven man did.

"That would be very stupid, keva." He tossed a grape in the air and caught it between his teeth with a strange, rapid, head-jerking motion. Rather like a pecking bird. "Do you see this palace with its high walls, barred windows, and battalion of guards? They all exist to protect *them*," Bradach said, pointing to the attendants. "Not Lord Lumenfell. He doesn't need walls, weapons, or guards. He is the Lumenfell Army. We are merely his toy soldiers, brought out to play when he's bored."

His smile sent goose pimples down my spine. "Alone or before an entire wedding party—your sword will never strike true."

I glared into those glittering orbs. "Has anyone told you, Bradach Arasu, that you are a tiresome man?"

He grinned, chuckling. "They never stop."

The candles flickered—the one beside me whooshing out. I knew even before Bradach's grin melted away and he shot up, straightening tall and proud before his king.

I turned to face him. Even then, I couldn't help but be struck by his presence. His heavy black coat should've swallowed him, but he swallowed it. Alisdair filled that coat to bursting, stretching his seams, and its ability to conceal the naked form underneath.

I blushed for no good reason. I had already seen what was under there, although if I was honest, it would be a long time—possibly a century—before Alisdair Shadowsoul stopped being the man to which I compared all other men. His sculpted form, muscled thighs, ridged abdomen, and obscenely large cock had no equal.

Foalan dropped at his feet. "My lord, forgive me. I don't know what I've done to fall in your estimation, but I apologize utterly, and accept my punishment. Please, my lord, lift my shame and bestow the cleansing fire of pain—"

Shadowsoul kicked him in the teeth. My surprised scream echoed off the wall.

Burying his foot in his gut, Alisdair lifted the commander off his knees and kicked him across the room, smashing a dent in the marble wall, and his head. He broke no more a sweat than if he kicked a feather.

Foalan coughed and wheezed, spitting up blood. "Th-thank you, s-sir."

No one went to him. Not even his supposed friend, Bradach. He didn't so much as glance in his direction.

"Come," Alisdair barked. "The ceremony begins."

He turned his back on me, sweeping out.

I bristled. "Is that how you summon your wife to the ceremony that will make her your eternal mate? One would think you can do better than that."

Alisdair halted in the entrance, his back to me. "One also would've thought this harem of clucking hens would've disabused you of the notion that it's wise to speak to me this way."

"Fuck you. I'll speak to you any way I please."

Aeris, Bradach, and the attendants were finally gaping at a wretched sight—me.

The washing girls backed away from me so fast, they were across the room before I could blink.

Slowly, he turned, and the smile on his lips... I nearly ran away too.

"The clucking hens have told you." He laughed—a deep, flowing sound. "You know what awaits you at the end of this walk, and you believe a foul mouth will change my mind." He tsked. "Think it through, little bird. What man in his right mind wouldn't want your dirty mouth all the more?"

I flushed hot.

I knew what he was doing. I stepped on his overconfidence by using sex to toy with him. Shadowsoul was proving he could do the same to me, but better. Yes, I knew this tactic.

Didn't mean it wasn't working.

I stood as tall as my shaking, naked knees would let me. "You mistake me, husband. I'm not trying to get you to change your mind. What I want is for you to do what no one has done since this all began.

"Ask me," I stated. "Ask me to take this walk with you. Ask me to become your eternal mate. Ask and I will. Ask... on your knees."

All eyes shot from me to Shadowsoul, awaiting his answer. No one moved. No one breathed.

His eyes locked on mine—dragging me under the depths and drowning me. I almost didn't notice when he took a step, closing the distance, bringing those impossibly bright pools closer.

Alisdair stopped before me, and knelt.

My eyes widened. *He's doing it? He's truly doing it. What does this mean? Is this not a cruel, sick punishment to him? Does he truly want me to be his—?*

Strong arms seized me, tossed me over his shoulder, and carried me off.

"Hey! Put me down!" I pummeled his back, hitting harder for every raucous laugh belted from Bradach's throat. "Put me down this moment!"

Shadowsoul didn't pay me a lick of attention. Carrying me through the shining, gilded halls, he ignored my ranting, kicking, raving, and my bluff.

Of course I wasn't going to follow him to the ceremony if he proposed. I only wanted him to drop his head, so I could break the basin over it.

Mind reading did not exist, and still he remained twelve steps ahead of me.

"Put me down!"

Alisdair carried me through double doors and a blast of cold burrowed into my bones, banishing the lingering warmth of the steamy bath. The world spun and I was right way up, gazing at an impossible sight.

Roses, violas, poppies, and primrose. Bluebells, snapdragons, witch hazel, and hellebores. Flowers of every color and type surrounded me, fighting to spread their loveliness among blanketing, smothering white.

"A garden?"

A beautiful, snow-covered garden spreading as far as the towering woods would allow. It was amazing. Dare I say, even more amazing than the Lyrican palace gardens. That place was taken up by gaudy, large statues of past kings while here, there was nothing but the natural beauty of nature's prize.

"What is this place?" A white-dusted path lay before me, leading to a silver cauldron nested among a frozen rose bush. I went closer, gazing down into dark, inky liquid like the white stuff Aeris carried out behind us—followed by four other servants. Two of them men, and one carrying a bowl identical to hers. Bradach and a limping Foalan came outside behind them.

Somewhere amid the time I was being carried around like a child, Aeris, Bradach, Foalan, and the attendants dressed themselves in similar sheer black cloaks.

I scanned my mind for trace knowledge of ancient High Fae marriage customs, but returned nothing. Not only did I not know, but it seemed Emiana didn't know what was about to happen here either.

"Not that it matters," I said, stepping back and facing him. "I had no wish to marry you in the first place. I am hardly going to marry you *more*. You can force me into that cauldron. You can make me repeat my vow to make your days a nightmare, your nights cold and barren, and your life short. But what you will not do is make me your mate in any way that matters.

"The wife you *never wanted* is going," I said, walking off. "This time, I leave you at the altar."

"Another bold speech," he replied to my back. "Do hang on to that bluster after you've fallen off the cliff you're headed toward, and land in the nest of Taken living below."

I ground to a halt—the cold leeching the feeling from my bare feet. Sharp, naked fear choked at the very thought of seeing those terrible creatures again.

"Or," he drew out, grinding my teeth. "You come back, willingly step into this cauldron, recite the proper vows, and take your place as Queen Emiana, High Lady of Lumenfell."

"Why in Meya's name would I do that?" I snapped.

"Because then and only then... will I accept your deal."

"My deal?" I turned around, interest piqued despite my instincts yelling at me to run. "What deal?"

He threw off his cloak, exploding heat in my treacherous, stolen body. I thanked the cold. That I could blame for the unfortunate effect he had on me.

"I was more than clear," he said, stepping into the cauldron. "My little bird flying away to whisper lies into the ear of a pompous, old fool is no boon to me. What I want is you."

"Me?" I cried, stepping back.

"I want you as my queen and my wife in every sense of those words. Your body mine to plunder. Your lips mine to plump. Your hand mine to hold as you take your seat beside my throne. I want to bend you over and take you like the beast you believe me to be—making you cum so hard, your screams pierce the veil and Meya strikes us down from sheer jealous—"

"Stop!" I shrieked, face on fire. Did this man know shame? How could he speak to me like that in front of his servants, *companion,* and the commander of his army! "Why would you want these things? Your man, Bradach, told me the truth. You never wanted me here. You had no intention of marrying me."

"I want these things, my queen..." His smile stretched over his sharpened canines. "Because you don't."

I chilled, lips pressing into a thin line. With that, the question of who was right—Bradach or Aeris—was answered. This wasn't about love, attraction, or honor.

This was punishment.

"You say such a thing and then expect me to willingly get into that cauldron? You're insane."

His smirk went nowhere. "If you do not willingly step into the cauldron, I'll have to assume your desire to return to your homeland was not as strong as you led me to believe."

I stilled.

"Seems those *things* you needed to do were not important after all."

I licked my lips, swallowing hard. Just like that, he had me. "You're saying you'll let me return to Lyrica?"

"Circumstances will say, Princess, not me." He swept out his hands. "Within this cauldron, we will name our true vows—yours to do everything in your power to be free, and mine to do all in my power to keep you caged.

"As the runes dry on our skin, you will run," he hissed. "Run as fast and as far as you can. If you elude me until daybreak, the die is cast and you will have won. I will be rune-bound to let you leave without a fight."

"I—"

"But," he sliced off. "If I catch you, little bird, I will ravage you where you fall—consummating our unholy union before Meya and all who've gathered to see. And so it will be every night until you've either escaped your fate, or accepted it."

I took a step toward him, then another. "How do I know you're telling the truth? This could be another trick. A lie. Elude you until daybreak and you'll let me ride away from you and this frozen wasteland forever? There's nothing to hold you to your word."

A soft cough drew my attention away from him.

"Excuse me, my lady, but he can be held to his word." Aeris stepped up next to the cauldron. "I told you your people abandon the ancient ways for this reason. They couldn't step into the cauldron and promise fidelity if it was a promise they never intended to keep. The runes of bonding and marriage hold all to their word—even a being as powerful as our lord."

I eyed the bowl of viscous soup in new light. I couldn't be blamed for not knowing much about rune magic. Even if my poor little school had been allowed to teach us, it wasn't something women needed to know.

Our magic was inside of us. A part of us. It bent to our will by command alone—before it's taken from us. We didn't need runes to make magic obey us.

"Hmm." I took another step. "Will... Will the runes work on me? With my magic bound as it is?"

"They don't need to work on you, my lady. As you said, they only need to work on him," Aeris replied. "And they will."

I met Alisdair's gaze. "You would do all of this just—"

"—to ravage that sweet, toothless pussy to my heart's content," he finished. "Of course, my queen. As any man would do, and more. Don't underestimate yourself."

"Stop it," I barked, covering my chest. As I said, I knew what he was doing. That didn't make me able to stop my body's reaction to him.

"Toothless?" Bradach muttered, clenching my teeth tighter.

Alisdair held out his hand. "Have we a bargain?"

I hesitated. My hand drifted down and stroked the bracelet he gave me on our wedding day. Our *first* wedding day.

Am I truly doing this? Bounding the chains to him even tighter all for the hope he'll let me leave this place?

This may be your best chance, another voice said. *Escaping this smirking, pampered fae-beast is only the first step. You'll still need to traverse miles of snow, then the miles of a barren desert battlefield to get home. You'll need food, supplies, clothes, transport, allies. You'll need a way to get past those horrible creatures lurking around the town. All much easier to collect if I'm not doing it in secret.*

I will plan my escape right in front of him, but by the time he sets off on the chase, I'll already be gone.

To make a deal, you have to have something the other wants. Shadowsoul wanted to watch the little bird screech and flap in its cave while he laughed at the silly creature's attempts to escape. And I wanted to go home—more than anything.

"We have a bargain."

"Wonderful." Aeris clapped, bouncing on her heels. "Come, come, my lady. Allow me the honor."

I chanced one more look at the trees, wondering at my chance of taking off and running right then.

A vision of the Taken flashed in my mind and I turned back, taking Aeris's hand. She helped me up and into the basin. I hissed when the liquid touched my skin.

It was warm and slimy like slipping into a vat of nose leakings.

"What happens now is quite simple," Aeris said for my benefit.

I tried to look at her, but Alisdair's eyes held me fast—refusing to let me look anywhere but at him.

"There is no officiant because this ceremony is between you and Meya," she continued. "You will paint your vows on each other with runic ink, then we shall bathe you in the pure sealing magic of Meya. If your promises are true, the rune will bind to your skin. If you lie, the ink will scald you until you burn alive and die."

"What!?"

Aeris was already off and rushing to get everyone into position. For the life of me, I didn't understand her excitement. She was like a proud mother on her son's wedding day. Was it a birdlike innocence that prevented her from seeing this was not a happy occasion?

"Why do this?" I asked softly. "Why offer me any deal?"

"I have answered this question."

I tensed. "Tormenting me cannot be the reason you're enduring this ceremony. We could've made the same bargain without all of th-this." My voice cracked as one of the servants removed my robe, leaving me naked before his feasting eyes. "In fact, you could've countered with your true terms in the carriage, instead of making me believe you were taking me home.

"Why are you doing all of this to bind yourself to a woman you never wanted to marry?"

"Very well. If plain words do not suffice, I will tell you a story." His gaze drifted off me to someone over my shoulder. He nodded and Aeris took her place beside me. Bradach took his place beside him. Both held those bowls of strange, white liquid.

"You may begin painting your promises on your mate," Aeris said.

"How?" I asked. "I don't know runic mag—"

Alisdair laced his fingers through mine. "Once upon a time, a century ago..." Dipping our hands in the cauldron, he laid my palm over his heart—stopping my breath.

Runic ink dripped down my skin onto his and spread, and kept spreading, skating down his chest in odd, twisting lines that grew and spawned more.

"How is it doing this?" I whispered. The runes were forming before my eyes, borne from words I didn't need to speak to be true. Although my knowledge of runes was limited, I read one clear as day: *betray*.

I jumped when a light touch brushed my shoulder.

"There was a brash, young faeman from Sarabai," Alisdair began, tracing his promise with surprising gentleness. "He staggered off the battlefield and found himself lost in the wilds of Lumenfell, cornered by the Taken.

"Desperately, he screamed for help, summoning his enemy to save him from a worse fate, and as his luck would have it, his cry was answered." Alisdair traced a path along my shoulder blade, popping goose bumps in his trail. "A young woman—a faeriken—came to his rescue. She saved him from the Taken, then saved him again by hiding him from me."

My lips parted to ask why he was telling me this, but the words didn't come out. There was a seriousness belying his tone. One I was hearing for the first time. I wanted to know where it would take him.

"She stashed him away in an abandoned shack far from the village. She nursed him, fed him... and fell in love with him." His fingers skated around my hip. The rune for possession drew just above my middle. I knew that one. Kirwan drew the same one night above Mama's door. "When he was healed, she came to me. Begging me to let them go and build a life far from the war, the fighting, the prejudices. Far from the faelands of Elva.

"I said no."

Alisdair pulled me close, erasing the scant distance between our bodies. I held my breath as he touched his cheek to my chest, peering over my shoulder to draw a rune on my spine.

"A fae and a faeriken? There was no life for them outside of Lumenfell. All that awaited them was pain and struggle. The gratitude of the faeman that turned into love, would morph again, becoming resentment and hate." His grip tightened on my thigh. "She did not believe me. Convinced their love was true, she ran off with him in the night.

"It's possible she did get to live her blissful, fairy-tale life for a short time. I'll never know for certain," he said, "because Gorban Salman murdered her a year after they fled."

I froze. "What? Did you just say Salman?"

"That's right." His voice was a low, dangerous hiss. "That man was your father. He loved Raelina. He was desperate to be with her. That was until your grandparents announced they refused to give the throne to their daughter, and would instead bestow it on the man who wed her. They decided it should be the *hero* who survived the cursed lands, and faced me and lived to tell about it.

"They didn't know he was already married. More so, that he was married in a ceremony like this one—bound by runic magic and blessed by the goddess Meya."

I couldn't move. I couldn't speak. If I could've done either, I would've run screaming. Something was happening, and it was not good.

"Divorce cannot end a marriage such as that"—he smiled—"or a marriage such as this. He was ineligible to marry the princess, become king of one of the wealthiest nations in Elva, or hold more power in his pinky than the strongest fae in the land. All because of Raelina."

"No," I whispered. "Please."

"So he made a terrible, brutal choice to slaughter the wife no one knew about. No one but me."

"Who... Who was she to you?"

His eyes flashed. "She was everything. Our last hope. My last chance. And he took her and threw her away like she was nothing."

I squeezed my eyes shut. "That's why you wanted to humiliate him by leaving me at the altar."

"No, little bird," he said, surprising me. "My subject was quite wrong on that score. I never intended to leave you at the altar." His glare pinned me through. "I was going to slaughter you on the altar."

Noise, breath, people, everything. It all stopped.

"I was going to slaughter his precious heir—famed beauty of the east—right in front of him while he stood helpless to stop it. But then..." Alisdair moved up to my shoulder, covering me with ink as promises I couldn't name spelled out on him. "You trumpeted my vow before the whole of the Lyrican court—swearing our marriage would end in death."

"Why?"

Did I speak? My ears were roaring. My lips were numb. I couldn't be sure they moved.

"Why did you change my mind?" He wasn't drawing anymore. His fingers were gliding over my body, but leaving no ink behind them. He was simply exploring me—

His new possession.

"Because I saw in that moment that you hate him as much as I." Laughter rolled out of his chest. "Not only do you hate him, but you openly and blatantly defy him—destroying his bid for Lyrica's peace and your subjugation—it was you who tried to kill me in front of him. It was then you and I came up with a much better plan.

"Killing you would solve nothing. If the hatred between you and your father is mutual, he would care for you passing only long enough to shed fake tears at your funeral," he dropped. "No, if I was to truly hurt him, how much better would it be... to keep you?"

His words reached me from far away.

"To corrupt you. To make you mine in every way—including becoming the natural successor of the Lyrican throne."

"What?" I whispered. "But—but you can't—"

"No, you can't," he barked. "A woman cannot take the throne, so in the case of your parents, it passed to an outsider. Your father threw you away so easily because despite only having one child with your mother, he has half a dozen bastards out there, waiting for the day one is tapped to rule."

I choked, eyes bulging. The surprise wasn't mine. Seemed Emiana didn't know about these half-siblings.

"Or I should say, he used to have half a dozen bastards out there." A slow smile stretched his lips. "Do forgive me for having to put you to sleep so many times during our return home. I couldn't have you interfering in their ends."

"Their ends?" I cried. "Are you saying you killed them?"

"A mere precaution. We don't want anyone with a legitimate claim to threaten my ascension to the throne."

"Stop saying we!" Or at least, I tried to scream it. Panic had such a stranglehold on my throat, nothing but a hoarse rasp could get out.

"Naturally, when I signed the treaty, I relinquished any claim to Lyrica and swore it on Meya's name, but then, you, my dear one, broke that treaty." He caressed my cheek with the back of his fingers. "Your rights remain intact, and through this ceremony—binding us as one—your rights are my rights. The throne denied you, will be mine."

My body came alive. I shoved his hand off. "You bastard."

He growled, lips peeling back. "You believe you hate me, little bird? I assure you the feeling is decidedly mutual. You are nothing. Less than nothing. Just another sniveling, insipid, pampered child who thinks if you scream and shout loud enough, you'll get your way, but a marriage doesn't require love, and a partnership doesn't beg respect.

"Thanks to you, I will take away everything your father truly loves. His wealth, his land, his honors, his throne. You will watch the man who threw you away reduced to nothing. All that he greedily gobbled on Raelina's sacrifice will vanish into vapor, and right as I plunge my sword into his chest, he'll know the reason why."

He stepped back, beholding me with something akin to pride. "I told you, my queen. I answered this question already. I made you mine because you and I will stand atop the world, claiming the faelands for our own, and crushing the beast who spawned you under foot."

I gaped at him, body shaking. "What is wrong with you? Why do you keep saying we? You can't possibly believe I'll allow any of this to happen."

"Oh?" Alisdair said, cocking a brow. "You think you're going to stop me?"

"Of course!"

"Then, you've decided to stay."

"I—" I cut off, jaw clenching. *Oh no.*

I agreed to this with the promise of fleeing from him. A promise I burned on his skin. I either stayed and fought to save all of Lyrica, or I ran to save my family.

"You wanted this," I hissed. "You tricked me!"

His expression was flat. Bored even. "I did not. There can be no tricks in the cauldron. I offered you what you truly want—to leave—and named what I truly want—for you to stay. From this point on, we will fight for our wish. But I say to you, my queen"—flicking off me, he nodded at Aeris—"I intend to win."

"Wait! No!"

Aeris and Bradach tipped the basins over our heads, shocking my system with a blast of freezing cold. Even colder than the elements.

The white magic rushed down my body like water, washing away ink like it was never there, and leaving only the runes behind. I gasped as the cauldron of ink went ghostly white.

"In honor of the gift your sword through the chest has given me," Alisdair said, wrenching my head up. "I shall give you a gift. A head start."

I stared at him, eyes unfocused and shivering in a vat of my greatest mistake. *What...? What was... going on?*

"Nine minutes fifty-one. Nine minutes fifty—"

"Run," Aeris hissed. "The magic takes hold at daybreak. My queen, you have to run!"

I hefted over the rim and hit the ground before she finished her sentence. Snatching up a cloak, I blew past Bradach and darted into the trees.

There was nowhere else for me to run. Castle Riagin was home to Shadowsoul and a maze to me. He knew all its twists, turns, and secrets—what hope did I have of losing him in there? My only chance was the woods. All I had to do was elude him until daybreak. I could do that.

I will do it!

Stupidly, and unwittingly, I promised before Meya and under the threat of magic to act as his true wife and queen for all the days I remained at his side. Now I knew exactly what he wanted his wife and queen to do.

I raced through brush and reaching branches, collecting bruises—opening cuts on my cheeks.

I ran faster.

I cared not what happened to King Salman. Just like he cared not what happened to me or those of us living in the Galley. Pleas to him for more food, help, wages, and protection were met with more taxes—tightening the noose of poverty further. What did I care if Alisdair avenged a wrong it sounded like should be avenged?

Salman was a particular kind of loathsome monster to murder his wife and the woman who gave up everything to protect, care, and be with him—all so he could be king of Lyrica. Let the two rivals battle it out and kill each other in the process, but what Shadowsoul wouldn't do is take us all down with him—plunging all of Elva into this frozen, rocky hell.

The terrible irony was that if the true Emiana had known what Shadowsoul wanted to do to her father, she'd never have run from him.

Run.

Frozen stumps that used to be my feet pounded the snow, leaving a trail that was quickly swept away by swirling winds. No moon. No stars. No light.

Darkness wrapped around the trees, blanketed the snow, and smothered my vision. I could barely see two feet in front of me, and the further I left the glittering town behind, the closer the shadows moved in. If I'd been thinking, I'd have snatched a torch, clothes, shoes—anything to get me through the night!

No, sense said. *Torchlight would be easily tracked in his darkness. Fetching clothes and shoes would've wasted my scant head start.*

I had minutes to get away from a rich, overindulged king who stopped relying on his body and physical strength long ago, and now did everything by magic.

He'd never be able to catch up with me, especially—

I slid to a stop, sucking in deep, freezing lungfuls.

—if I'm clever.

He's expecting me to run around blindly, crashing and stomping around the forest—kicking up noise and fuss.

I didn't need to be fast. I needed to be slow and quiet. I needed to be another looming shadow in the darkness, bypassed without a second glance.

Pulling my useless covering tight, I stepped lightly over a black mass that looked like a tree root. All these mountains, cliffs, and crags, there had to be a cave somewhere nearby. That's where I'd tuck myself away to hide for the night, and in the morning, when I returned triumphantly to that monster after the runes faded away, I'd demand he personally drive the carriage taking me home, then kissed my feet after they stepped on my homeland, begging for my forgiveness.

He thought me a spoiled, pampered princess. He thought me a pawn in his thirst for revenge. I was neither.

I was his match.

A twig snapped in the distance, whipping my head around. I squinted through the gloom, but saw no one. Nothing but shifting black under layers of white.

Crunch.

I twisted, and locked eyes with two, red glowing orbs.

"Ahh!" I took off running.

Crashing through brush, colliding with trees, kicking up a flurry of snow, screaming my lungs out. I cared not for Alisdair, or if he caught me. All that mattered was getting far away from that creature.

Light emanated ahead, drawing me back toward the village. I huffed and wheezed, making for noise, people, and protection with every last bit of strength in my numb legs. There'd be places to hide in the village. Crowds to lose myself in. Possibly people to take pity on me and give me clothes and shelter until dawn. And, most importantly, there'd be no Taken.

I shoved through two trees and staggered to a stop. I wasn't in town. On the contrary, I didn't seem to be anywhere near it, but where I was... was beautiful.

My lips parted, awe stealing my breath—drawing me closer.

Water streamed down the riverbed, making them dance.

"Stars."

I dropped down at the edge of the bank. Small, glowing, impossible flowers brushed against my knees—their long, delicate petals so featherlight, I barely felt them. They almost resembled sun flowers, though their petals were as long as their stems.

"Starflowers," I whispered, touching one ever so lightly. Pulling away, I gasped, wondering at my glowing fingertips.

Their gentle light emanated from seeds to stem, and carried down into the roots—making the bank shine. Was this the work of magic, or were these beautiful things made this way by the goddess herself?

Sitting back on my heels, I swept the calm, still clearing.

The trees curved around the river and reached for each other overhead, their branches stretching, reaching, tangling into a natural roof that blocked the falling snow. It was a quiet, pocket world outside of time—outside of war, harm, and the dangers of the night. I don't know how, but I knew the Taken wouldn't come here. Such a place was too beautiful for the likes of a beast.

I lit on something to my right, rising at the edge of the clearing.

A bridge.

Carefully, I ripped the hem of my cloak and used the cloth to gather up a handful of starflowers. "Goodbye," I whispered.

Holding out my natural lantern, I crossed the bridge and stepped onto a path.

I was torn. Wouldn't Alisdair search for me along the routes that he knew—like this very path? Or did I heed sense, and stay on a path that clearly led somewhere, instead of wandering through the dark and night until I tipped over the cliff into that nest of Taken?

My mind was made for me. Lifting my feet, I stayed on the path.

Where is he? Have I truly lost him? The most feared man in Elva—No, in all of Elvan history, and he couldn't track down one sniveling, insipid, pampered princess who was lost in the woods.

I couldn't help but smirk.

A shadow jumped out of the trees. "Ahh!" I flung back, landing hard on my tailbone, and harder still when it landed on my chest—shoving me down. We blinked at each other.

Curious, the rabbit sniffed me—its twitching, little nose tickling my cheek. Was it not used to people, or was it not used to normal fae? It certainly inspected me like I was a new and interesting discovery, and wanted to know if I was edible.

"Hello to you too," I said softly. Gently, I stroked his soft, fuzzy head—almost smiling when I heard his sweet, grinding purr. "Would you like to come with me? I'm in search of a place to hide from a monster."

Wings sprouted from his back, trapping another surprised cry behind my teeth. He took off, shooting into the air.

I held up my starflowers to follow him and came eye to eye to eye with a herd of white and gray rabbits, all gazing down at me from the trees. My new friend was clearly the brave one—putting himself forward to check if I was a threat.

He dropped down on a branch, chittered to his friends, then took to the skies—leading his colony away.

I gasped at the sight—eyes wider than they'd ever been. "What is this place?"

A soft, scratching sound tickled my ear, wiping my smile away. Was it the Taken? Another impossible creature? Or him?

I paused—scanning the limits of my starflower-light. I grew up in the city. A city surrounded by forest, yes, but a forest Mama forbade me to step foot in alone.

The forests of Elva were tricky, living, magical, *mischievous*. They liked to obscure paths, confuse travelers, and mimic the voices of desperate, calling loved ones. Many a young fae entered the forest and never returned.

But not this place.

I could feel it. Sense it within the well of magic inside my soul that was forever out of my reach. There was no magic or mischief in this forest. It was dead.

Which meant that noise was not a trick to scare me. Something or someone made it, and I needed to move.

I hurried on—bursting into a near run. The flowers lit my way, illuminating tufts of fur and flashes of feathers as critters fled from the strange, charging giant clomping through the woods. Something appeared ahead of me and I pulled up short, skidding to the edge of the cliff.

Heart in my throat, I peered down. *No, not a cliff.*

It was another sharply inclined path like that one that carried our carriage down into Lumenfell, but this one led to—

I frowned. "What is that?"

I held the flowers higher, squinting to see. About eighty feet below, something—many somethings?—shifted in the dark. A soft, humming noise lifted up on the backs of the howling wind, and furrowed my brow. It almost sounded like... snoring.

Shuffling sounded behind me, turning me in time to see another tuft of fur flit into the dark.

I smiled. "Come now, little one. There's no need to be afraid of me. I won't hurt you."

"I'm pleased to hear it."

Screeching, I clapped my hand over my mouth—dropping the flowers. They fell at the feet—two proper, non-rabbit feet—of the man who stepped out of the shadows.

"Although, calling me *little one* is quite insulting. I was far from the runt of my litter."

I choked, eyes flinging up and off his bare and bold nudity. There wasn't a stitch of cloth on his bronze skin, and the flowers were only too eager to prove it. I landed on his face, and started.

"Foalan?"

As soon as the name left my lips, I knew I was wrong. This man had undoubtedly stolen Foalan's cherry-kissed lips, sculpted jaw, and glass-cutter's cheekbones, but he left the commander his beard.

This faeriken didn't have facial hair. His fur was also snow white—much like the rabbit I had mistaken him for.

"Not Foalan." I stepped back and his eyes tracked me, moving in time like a dance partner. "Who are you? Why are you naked?"

"Who are you?" he mocked, cocking his head. "Why are you naked?"

I flushed, clapping my hands over my body. "Fair enough. I am—" I fought the futile struggle to say my name. "My name is Ana. You must be Foalan's brother."

"I don't know that I must be his anything." He sniffed the air, coming closer. I couldn't say why the hairs on the back of my neck stood on end. "I am Meallan. Why are you in my woods, Ana?"

"I'm running from someone."

Inexplicably, he smiled. "We're all running from someone. Be more specific."

"This someone is the king of Wind and Wild."

If anything, his grin widened. "Ahh. You must be his fresh, young mate."

I bristled. "I don't know that I must be his anything."

Meallan laughed—loud and free. "Well said."

Nodding, I inched to the side, skirting the cliff. "Okay, well. I should—"

"If you're running from him, you are not his mate yet." Still his eyes didn't leave me—tracking me through the snow, taking in my drying runes. "Would you like my help?"

"Your help?" *Why is he staring like that?*

I moved to the left, then the right, then I darted side to side quickly, spun around, and jumped. Meallan's orbs bounced in their skull following me around, though he said nothing.

"What? You're not going to ask why I burst into dance?"

"It's not polite to remark on one's madness."

My face heated. "Well, then why would you want to help a mad-woman?"

"Just because you're mad doesn't mean you aren't wise. Running from Alisdair Lumenfell is exactly what you should do." Meallan held out his hand. "Come with me. My people and our home are below you. Lumenfell cannot cross into our territory. You will be safe from him."

"Your home?" I glanced down into the darkness, the shifting masses, the rumbling snores. "Why is it so dark down there?"

"Come," he repeated, his hand hanging in the air between us. "We will shelter you."

"No, thank you," I said, backing further away. "This is between me and Alisdair. I wouldn't want anyone to get hurt because they stood between us."

His hand returned to his side. I only relaxed a fraction.

"Nothing is standing between you and him. He knows exactly where you are. He will find you in moments," Meallan dropped. "It's a wonder he isn't upon you now."

"What? Why would you say that?"

"Your scent." He breathed deep. "I smelled you the second you entered my woods and have been following you ever since."

I tensed. My senses were right. There were unseen eyes in the dark.

"If you will not accept my protection, then take my advice." He picked up the flowers and gave them to me. "Use these. Rub them on yourself. The smell of the flowers will obscure your scent."

"But if I do, I'll glow."

"A glow is easily hidden by a large tree. A scent is not."

That logic could not be argued. Quickly, I crushed the starflowers and rubbed them over my face, arms, stomach—everywhere.

"Thank you, Meallan."

"You are most welcome, Princess Ana. Hopefully when the opportunity arises, you will return the favor and lend me your aid."

"I can't," I said bluntly. "I'm not staying. That's what all of this is for. If I avoid him until daybreak, I'm free. I'll return home."

He shrugged. "The path of freedom leads one down many roads. By Meya's fate, ours will converge once again."

"Well, if it does, then sure. I'll return the favor."

"Thank you." Meallan moved back, returning to the shadows. "Goodbye, Lady Ana, Queen of Nothing, owned by no one."

I blinked and he was gone, leaving me unsettled. I wasn't sure if his parting comment was an insult or a compliment. I had a feeling it was a little of both.

"Strange place," I muttered, heading far away from the cliff and the dark pit Meallan called *home*. "Strange people."

I had no flowers to light my way, and didn't need them. My body was one big starflower, casting back the darkness as I stepped lightly on the path, heading deeper into the woods.

It wasn't long before I found myself in another clearing, this one more beautiful than the last.

Starflowers gathered around a pond, dancing a merry shake as rabbits chased each other along the bank and through the glowing reeds. The long stems reached high, tickling the backs of two fawns gently lapping at the water. Large, graceful wings sprouted from their backs.

The deer raised their heads when I approached, took me in, then returned to their drink.

A heavy weight landed on my shoulder, almost startling a cry out of me. My brows blew up when a small, furry head stuck its face in mine, inspecting me closely.

The little monkey must've been satisfied because he chittered at the trees, and the trees chittered back—proving he had a couple friends up there waiting for the verdict.

Unlike the impossible rabbits and deer, I saw no wings on the monkey, but he was still different. His coat was much thicker, heavier, and warmer than the monkeys of the Beharra Forest. This little critter was built for the cold.

"What is this place?" I breathed, stroking his soft fur. "How can this forest be dead, bleak, and desolate, while also being beautiful, enigmatic, and wondrous? How did you all get here?" A rabbit flew up to the trees. "How did you become... this?"

The monkey screeched and leapt off my shoulder. I assumed that was his answer.

Laughing, I took a seat in the amazing place, deciding then to make it my hiding place. I was surrounded my more starflowers. They'd further obscure my scent. "My"—the word wouldn't leave my lips—"won't believe when I tell them of this. No one will."

"So much beauty in a nightmare."

"Poetic."

I bolted upright, moving only half as fast as the animals. They bolted out of the clearing so fast, they kicked up a wave of snow that showered my back.

Alisdair slithered out of the dark—the trickster's smirk baring his fangs. "Oh, my dear, you're glowing. I'm flattered."

I moved as he moved, maintaining our distance—edging around the pond.

"How did you find me?" I croaked. Did Meallan lie? Did I cover myself with a beacon instead of a barrier?

"Of course, I found you. You are just like these flowers…" He bent slowly, eyes fixed on me as he plucked one off its stem. "Meek, pointless, decorative, and so terrified of the dark, you cling to the light." He flung the pretty thing over his shoulder.

"Come to me," he growled like a wild animal. "This will be neither quick nor gentle nor loving, and still you will enjoy nothing more."

I choked, knees knocking together. What a way to describe our first joining as faeman and wife. "You haven't caught me yet," I replied when I found my voice. "And you won't. I will never—"

I dropped down, grabbed a fistful of snow and mud and flung it in his face. I was off before his roar hit my ears.

No sneaking, no hiding, no flowers, no time. I ran as fast as my borrowed legs could carry me, crashing through brush and scattering every critter in my path. He couldn't catch me.

No matter what it took, I would outlast him until the dawn, and get back to my family.

Heavy footfalls thundered behind me, trumpeting his pursuit. Snarling, I ran faster.

Shadowsoul looked at me and saw a pointless, decorative princess. That night would be the night he learned to never underestimate a woman inside for the pretty wrapping outside.

I was no princess. I was the girl who ran from bullies nearly every day of her life. There was a reason they all slunk home at the end of the day, cursing their failure. A slipperier girl than I did not exist.

A low-hanging branch loomed ahead. I grabbed it without hesitating, flipped, and landed on my toes. From branch to branch I climbed, scrabbled, and skittered up the tree as easy as a monkey.

There was a reason the forest animals did not fear me. They knew I was one of them—a child of the forest. The forest was where we fae belonged, if not for our ancients envying the humans and wanting cities, gold, and government for ourselves, we'd still live in the forests and they wouldn't have turned against us for the slight. But not this poor dead and withered place. It carried no ill will.

"Argh!"

Not like the enraged beast coming after me.

The tree shook with his pursuit, almost shaking me off its side.

Snap!

I smirked at the hard, unforgiving *thud* echoing off the ground. The fae were natural climbers and children of the forest. The same could not be said for that too-handsome, faeriken monster below.

Right then, I thanked the terrible curse that made these trees grow wild and too close together. It made it all the more easy for me to flit from branch to branch—out of reach of Alisdair.

His roar echoed through the night, and faded in the distance.

I flit from tree to tree until I lost him. Silence reigned as I climbed down, dropping lightly on my feet. I could barely hold in a laugh. The silly man thought he had me. I bet he was proud of himself, finding me in the starflower clearing right where he expected, sneaking up on me with his snark and sneer.

All that to get a fistful of mud in his face, and a sore bottom from falling on his ass.

This will be easy, I thought, leaning against an oak. *All too easy.*

"Tired already, little bird?"

My head snapped up, locking on the naked and hard figure reclining on the tree branch above me.

"We're just getting started."

"How!" I cried. "You were behind me. A mile behind. How are you here!"

He only chuckled. "Shall I take you now, or should we continue our dance a little longer?"

"Please." The truth raged and battered against my lips, desperate to come out. "You don't understand. You don't want me."

"You..." Alisdair reached down and stroked my cheek. "Are all I want."

I ducked him and backed away. Alisdair dropped out of the tree and followed—a predator tracking his prey.

"Listen," I began, forcing a laugh. "We've said and done a lot of things to each other in this short time, but I know deep down, you don't want our first time as man and wife to be—"

"Argh!" He tore the scant robe from my body.

I was wrong.

My back collided with rough, cold bark. Alisdair slammed his hands down on either side of my head, penning me in. Seemed continuing our dance was off the table. He was taking his prize.

Now.

"Not here," I tried. He plastered against me, heating my chilled body to life. "You have a castle. Chambers. A bedroom. Take me there."

"I could never dishonor you so, my queen. Mating is raw, dirty, and primal. We lock it away behind closed doors out of shame, but you, should never be hidden." He tugged sharply on my hair, snapping my chin up and ripping free a cry. Or was it a moan?

"Let the clouds part and the moon finally shine its light in greed to see me bond with my true mate... and fuck her like a common nightwalker."

"What non-sense are you spouting!" My voice cracked, breath hitching at the seeking, stroking hand climbing my thigh. "You have to listen to me. I'm not—not—not— Agh!"

"Our promises are inked on our skin, little queen. For as long as you run, I will chase. Tell me"—deep, treacherous pools drowned me—"have you stopped running?"

My chest heaved, pushing against him. I knew what he was asking.

I rose on tiptoe, digging my chin into his scruffle—baring my teeth like fangs. I spoke, strong and clear, "Never."

His lips crashed on mine, swallowing a cry that was undoubtedly a moan. I couldn't help it. His fingers had ended their exploration, and found their destination between my legs.

This couldn't be happening. Was I truly to lose my maidenhood in the forest, against a tree, while trapped in another's body? For all my caution with love, lust, and young men's promises. For all my mother's warnings. Nothing could've prepared me for this.

And even less could stop it.

Alisdair caught me fairly, and laughably, easy. He was one hard, punishing thrust from completing the ceremony, and making himself the rightful heir to Lyrica and the eventual destruction of Elva as we knew it.

He was also one thrust away from binding himself under my demands. For as long as the runes were in power, he had to repeat this dance every night—giving me a chance to run away, and honoring our deal if I succeeded.

Open, glaring eyes burned each other even as his mouth devoured mine.

It was there underneath his pet names and teasing, lust-filled taunts. He hated me.

He wanted nothing to do with the useless spawn of the man who stole Raelina from him. I was nothing but a reminder, a torture, a pawn. Alisdair Shadowsoul would see Emiana corrupted and all that should've been hers, made his. All in the name of revenge against her father.

"Agh," I cried, eyes rolling as two fingers pushed past my folds, burying deep to the knuckles.

I could stop this now. To break our deal was to have no deal. We could live in this impossible winter wasteland together—living out days knowing we came so close to what we wanted, but close wasn't close enough.

I could save Lyrica right then. With one word.

But that wasn't my duty. There were five people depending on me. Waiting for me. I could save Elva, but no one would save them. No one but me. Let the true princess of Lyrica clean up the mess she created.

I was going home.

Laughing, a smirk twisted my lips. "Is that all you got, pretend king? Who knew you were so... gentle?"

A huge, terrible grin split his face. "Oh, yes. You'll do just fine."

Alisdair hefted me up, scraping my back against the tree. My cry choked on a groan, caught in my throat as he closed over my nipple. I assumed only faeriken women shared the experience of a man with fangs ravishing your breasts. I envied them for discovering the experience long before me.

His tongue teased and tortured the little nub to a hardened pebble, standing it to attention, then punishing its wantonness. Sharpened canines scraped the delicate flesh—shooting equal parts pain and pleasure straight to my lower belly.

"Oh, Meya," I rasped. I tightened, legs clamping on him. "Do you... really think— Oh!"

He snapped my legs open, pushed in deeper still, and spread his fingers wide—spreading me like a Meya's Day turkey.

"—that," I breathed, straining to keep hold of my senses. "It's going to be this easy?"

I hauled back and slapped him across the face.

He growled, head snapping around. The distraction gave me a chance to get my feet between us, and kick.

I threw him off me and took off running, bolting for the trees. They helped me lose him once, they'd help me lose him again. I accepted this deal was my only chance for getting home, but I hadn't accepted defeat. Not by a long shot.

"Argh!"

I threw my body to the side, and he pounced on the spot I'd been standing in—tackling nothing but air and snow. A strange noise came from him.

Was he... laughing?

Loud, hearty guffaws echoed through the forest. By the goddess, he was enjoying this. Every second of his hunting me down like a wild animal and trying to claim my body like a prize to be won. To him, all of this, was nothing but fun.

He can have his fun eating my snow!

Leaping off the balls of my toes, I jumped, seized a branch just within reach of my fingertips, heaved myself up and—

Snap!

"Ahh!"

I collapsed on the ground, pinned under the branch. A shadow fell over me.

"Seems it is this easy." Alisdair moved around me, the stalking panther. "Are your wings caught, my pet?"

I shoved against the wood. The answer was unreservedly, humiliatingly, yes. "Get this off of me."

"Now why"—he flicked my knees apart—"would I do that?"

My pulse raced as his fingers found themselves between my legs again. As they found my clit. "B-because," I gasped. "You don't want the fun to... end too so-on— Ah!"

He rubbed the bundle of nerves between my legs like he was rubbing out the spot of damnation. Hard, fast, rough—spots danced before my eyes that made me think I was seeing stars.

I wriggled, kicked, and flailed under the branch—body hot and cold. Shivering and shuddering. How could someone I hated so much make me feel this good?

"Let me... run for you," I cried, desperation filling my voice. One thrust and the marriage was consummated. The bond was sealed. One thrust, and I woke up the next morning a failure, and prepared for another night... as his prey. "You said I was your entertainment. You said this is our dance. Let it go on for a little long—"

Alisdair dropped between my thighs, and devoured my pussy. My back snapped up—mouth open in a silent, jaw-cracking moan.

He growled, snarled, and snapped—a feral beast going down on a ripe peach. In all my life, with all the books, and all the poems, I'd never find the words to describe this. Of course no book or poem could help me—no other woman had ever been fucked in this manner.

Alisdair's tongue plunged into my entrance and kept going, going, growing.

I didn't know what type of magic this was. I didn't know if it was magic, or simply how the curse changed him. But an infaeman tongue, probed and *streeetched* me—pushing this borrowed pussy past limits it'd never gone before.

He bobbed and shook his head side to side—both drilling me and tormenting the bundle of nerves at my apex. Crashing, surging waves of pleasure flooded my body over and over again. I couldn't catch my breath from the first wave before the next was bowling me over, dragging me back down into ecstasy my life of sensible maidenhood had never known.

"Oh, fuck," I screamed when his tongue struck a head-scrambling, fire-igniting spot within me. Where had that been all my life?! Did other women know about this? Why didn't they tell me! "Meya, save me!"

From what? I had no idea. Save me from his tongue, or how incredible it was making me feel? Either way, if he struck that spot again, I could not be held responsible for my actions. My melting mind wouldn't even remember them.

Get a hold of yourself, woman! You have to keep running! Why end tomorrow what we can end tonight?

Alisdair's hand slid under the branch and palmed my breast, taking my poor nipple between two claw-tipped fingers. I had a passing thought that his claws looked longer, then a finger disappeared inside my ass.

My eyes blew wide—wider than the gaping "O" that became my mouth.

Why hadn't I listened to Shadi and my friends when they tried to tell me what was coming? The only thing I recalled was the warning not to get too loud, or he'd go faster, deeper, and longer.

"Uh, uh, uh! Oh, fuck, AH!" That ship had sailed, taken on water, and wrecked on the seafloor. I couldn't shut myself up, and Alisdair was all too happy to take on the encouragement.

His finger stretched my puckered hole. His tongue plundered my pussy. His thumb rolled my nipple, and his fangs tortured my clit. Branch or no branch, I never stood a chance.

Tension rose to a fever pitch, boiling over with hot, sweaty, limb-trembling pleasure, and I exploded.

Screaming myself hoarse, I came so hard, I bore down on the branch and snapped it in half.

"Holy Meya fucking shit, Meya fuck," I groaned, chest heaving—fire spots dancing above my eyes. "What... did you... do to me?"

"That?" Derision laced his voice. "That was nothing. I was holding back."

Yes. Everything every war wife, Lyrican, and fae said was true. Having sex with faeriken would kill me.

Alisdair licked my juices off his lips. "The time for dancing is over, little queen. I confess, you and your trickster's lips have had a stronger effect on me than I was anticipating."

My eyes bugged glancing down. By the All Mother, his cock was already a force to be reckoned with, but seeing it then, painfully hard and engorged to five times its size, I knew why he was balancing on the edge of an apology. That thing would destroy me.

"I'm going to fuck you so hard," he dropped, "you'll die."

I gaped at him, bulging eyes huge. There wasn't a trace of irony or teasing in this tone. He spoke as though this was simple fact.

"You're going to slip beyond the veil and gaze upon the face of Meya herself. The dawn will rise on the shell of the innocent, pampered princess you used to be, and then I'll fuck the wanton whore you've become all over again."

"Oh, gods," I rasped, lower belly contracting so painfully, I came again.

Alisdair cracked my legs open like an egg, positioning himself at my entrance.

I grabbed half the branch and smashed it over his head.

He snapped around, hands flying off me, and I took off running.

"*Huh, huh, huh.*" At least, in my mind, I took off running. In reality, I staggered and stumbled through the snow—panting like an animal and trying to will urgency into my relaxed limbs, and loosening into my tauter-than-a-bowstring core.

Shadowsoul was on me in a heartbeat, throwing me up against a tree. Rough, unforgiving bark fought back—digging into my cheek and stomach. Alisdair's laugh was warm, tickling breath on my ear. He thrust inside me with one smooth move.

We both groaned so deep and guttural, it shook the tree.

I couldn't believe I marveled at his impossible tongue. It was nothing—nothing compared to the monster between my legs.

"Oh," I cried out. "Ah!"

"Say it," he hissed. He licked a stripe up my cheek and grumbled. I tasted good. "I will have no more of your blustering. Your holding back. The lies on your lips and the truth in your pussy. Scream my name." A hard snap of his hips drove him deeper, rolling my eyes up in my head. "The name you curse. The name that haunts your nightmares. The name that burns your tongue. *Scream* it, little bird.

"Sing."

My eye rolled in its socket, meeting his straight on. "Fuck. You."

He smirked—wide and terrible. "Close enough." He pulled all the way out and thrust in, impaling that spot with one strike.

I died.

No dramatics. No exaggerations. No bluster. No lies.

Alisdair started pumping—*pounding*—my pussy, and the person I was, was no more. It was simple fact, as he said. One simply could not know such filthy, dirty, shameful, *amazing* pleasure, and emerge the same person.

"Oh, gods, yes," I shrieked. "Ahh, fuck!"

Alisdair was no less quiet than me. His beastlike snarls and growls increased with his pace, filling me with a feeling that should've been fear. Oh, how I wished to Meya it was. But no. The only thing I felt at hearing him come apart at the seams, losing all sense of himself and his hold on his faemanity for want of me... was turned *on*.

I tightened my walls, clamping down on his cock.

"Agh," he bellowed, falling on top of me. "Fuck's sake!"

I smirked. "You scream my name, oh Lord Shadowsoul, King of Beasts. Enough of your lies and bluster. I am a pointless, decorative creature, and you still can't resist me."

His eyes flashed. "Oh, dear. I'm going to reach a new level of savagery with you."

"Are you?" I yawned, and had to snap my jaw shut when a ragged moan tried slipping out too. "When does that start?"

I knew instantly I made a mistake.

The forest spun. Blinking, my mind couldn't connect how I came face-to-face with him, and the vicious cut I opened on his forehead. My back pressed to the tree within the space of a breath. A small *eep* escaped me, undercutting my bluster, when he dropped my ankles on his shoulder.

"Starts now."

Alisdair lost control.

There was no other way to describe it. No word more flowery. No adjective more accurate. The man buried deep inside me, and all sense of civility and control snapped.

My cries were straight screams, echoing into the whistling, frigid forest. Alisdair pumped so hard and fast, he was barely out before he was thrusting back in, hitting heretofore undiscovered angles, and exploding heat and fierce, fiery arousal deep within a core long ignored.

I kicked and slapped at him. Somewhere in the part of my mind still functioning, it was screaming I still had a chance to break free, and stop this before the ancient rites took hold.

My hand came up to dig into his cut, but he threw his head back at that moment—ragged groans ripping from his throat, and baring his fangs to the sky. Fangs that were... bigger?

Alisdair snapped his head forward, and my head back—tangling in my hair and wrenching a cry out of me. It was all the things he'd said it'd be. Not quick, gentle, or loving but—

"Ahh," I moaned. "Ohh, so deep. You bastard, I—"

"Hmm. You're moon-kissed..."

Heavy-lidded eyes snapped open, and landed on the strands of snow-white hair woven through his fist. I looked up.

The ever-present clouds parted the barest bit, letting through the scant glow of moonlight that fell over me, revealing my great shame.

I tripped over my tongue. "I—I can—"

"You continue to surprise, little bird." With that, he latched on to my neck, sucking and teasing my skin.

That was it? People who found out I was moon-kissed usually had much harsher, insulting things to say. Why wasn't—?

"Ow!" I cried out more from surprise than pain. The madman drew back, admiring the small nip he left on my neck. Palming my breast, he gave the sensitive, heated mound another to match.

"Hey, what are you—?"

Alisdair broke the limits of possibility and pumped faster still, hammering that spot like it needed to be punished. My ability for speech flew up into the trees with the rabbits, abandoning me for good.

I was filthy, raw, and wet. Gravity pulled me down, making me meet him thrust for thrust—bouncing as he bucked. Alisdair nipped me all over my neck and chest, and my swats were landing softer. The sharp pinpricks of pain anchored the pleasure, making it sweeter still.

Too sweet.

My muscles coiled like a viper, bending my back off the wood. Alisdair sank deep and his chest tightened against my thighs. Explosions burst in my mind, throwing me to the edge—tumbling, falling, screaming—*gone.*

He spilled inside me, filling me to the brim with seed as my pussy gushed its own warm arousal.

Alisdair dropped to his knees—the great and shadowed evil of the faelands brought low because of me. I might've crowed about it if I could catch my breath, or take my eyes off my shoulder.

"The rune..."

It was glowing.

I slid down the bark—transfixed. All over our bodies, our runes—our binding promises—lit like the glow from the moon.

And was that it.

I was Shadowsoul's wife. His mate. His queen. His stepping stool to the throne, then all of Lyrica. I was his to own, command, taunt, torture, and fuck.

I was his... until I learned to run faster.

Alisdair grasped my chin, lifting my gaze to him as the glow faded. "You must forgive me, my queen, for I lied to you once again.

"It actually starts now."

I didn't know what he meant, until I did.

"Wait—"

That was the last intelligible thing I said for the rest of the night.

Chapter Six

I cracked a lid open, groaning before my eyes were all the way open. I felt around for the ice and wood that would be my rude awakening, and my fist curled around silk.

Grimacing, I pushed up—vision clearing on my surroundings.

I wasn't in the woods anymore. I didn't know where I was.

Fresh, sweet-smelling red-and-gold sheets and tasseled pillows covered me, cocooning me in warmth. Long-stemmed candelabras loomed over me, casting soft candlelight on the bumps, cuts, and bruises on what used to be the fairest, most unblemished skin in the east.

My face heated as memories tumbled through my head, each more shameful and scandalous than the other.

Alisdair Shadowsoul ravished me. I wished there was another word I could use. One that didn't make me sound like that soft little peach torn apart by a beast. But there was no other word, because that's exactly what he did.

Alisdair took me like an animal against that tree all night long. Pounding me in every position known and unknown—extracting so many orgasms out of me that my well ran dry. His did not.

Nothing slowed him, tired him, or filled him with mercy.

I rolled out of bed, biting hard on my lip. My whole body was one big ache. My only saving grace was that even though I was a maiden, Emiana obviously was not. If it had been her first time too, neither of us would've walked for a week.

I waddled across the room, wincing and bobbing side to side. "I'm barely walking now."

With difficulty, I made it to the wash basin. One touch confirmed what the steam told me. It was wonderfully hot, proving someone had brought it in minutes before I woke. Was this the life of a prin— No, a queen? To have my needs anticipated before I opened my eyes in the morning?

If only Emiana hadn't let fear and ignorance drive her to ruin my life and run away. She would've found herself no less pampered and catered to in Castle Riagin.

Gazing around, I wondered at this life I'd fallen into.

High ceilings painted with scenes of battle looked down on me. All the gaudy golds, diamonds, and silvers adorning the castle hadn't made it into this room. The simpleness of the small wash basin, black-stain nightstand, and a bed half the size of Emiana's—made it all the more grand.

Next to the wash basin was a stand with towels, soaps, scents, and oils. Beside that was a tall clothing rack carrying no less than four dressing robes. I chose the longest and fluffiest, wrapping myself up tight.

Of course I was freezing, the bedchamber only had three walls.

I crossed the room, padding over red tiles with flecks of coudarian blue. The wall gently sloped down, giving way to a small ledge that tipped off into the free, cold air.

Slowly, I inched as far as I dared, gazing down, down, down to the sleepy town and thick forest, and rolling mountains spreading out before me.

Amazing. Truly, the most amazing view, and still not worth the sacrifice of a wall.

I scrambled away, heading straight for my bed and warm sheets. I would have to tell Aeris, or anyone, that I needed a new bedchamber. Or even a cot next to a fireplace would do as well. The people of Elva were summer fae. The cold wasn't meant to live in our bones.

I rounded the headboard, getting the first proper look at my bed, and screamed.

Clapping my hand over my mouth, my eyes were huge, looking upon the—

"Monster."

Thick, black horns burst from his scalp and curved down to his shoulders. Long claws sunk into the remains of a pillow, and a large, furry mass slung over his leg. *A tail.* Its nose was smashed in, but its maw the size of the basin—terrifyingly long, lethal fangs refused to be contained in its face. It's hideous, disfigured face.

It was huge. Twice the size of a bear with half the fur. Most of it covered its back, legs, and forearms, leaving its chest bare.

I stilled, fixing on a familiar rune on his stomach.

"Shadowsoul?" I whispered, backing away.

I hadn't imagined it. All those times it seemed like his claws were smaller, or his fangs were longer. The reason why he looked so close to fae while his subjects were succumbing to the curse. He was using magic to hold the beast at bay. This was the true him, and he looked like...

"Taken."

I ran.

Bursting through the doors, I collided with a hard body.

"Oh, Queen Ana." Aeris set me back on my feet. Nose wrinkling, she backed away a pace. "Are you all right? I was just coming to fetch you. Your baths are read—"

"Let's go," I ordered, already brushing past and leading the way. "A bath is exactly what I need."

I spared only one glance back at the monster I'd bound myself to till the end of everything.

***

"I see you did not last until dawn."

My face flushed at the burst of giggles that sounded behind me.

We were in my baths again. Aeris combed and braided Emiana's hair—all traces of white leaving with the sun's arrival.

I couldn't believe that even while cursed to wear another's skin, I couldn't escape my other curse. My first one.

Since the day of my birth, my hair has turned white in the moonlight. No one—not my mother, not our neighbors, not the healers knew why, or how, I came to be this way. I couldn't even say if it was a curse, because no such curse was known by fae. But then of course, one did not need magic to be cursed.

There was a reason that although we were all struggling, all poor, and nearly all the children of war wives, I was singled out for chasing, beating, and bullying. Only I was the keva with the strange, color-changing hair. Only I the freak.

But Alisdair said nothing of it, and he said a great many things last night while fucking the sense out of me.

I wasn't certain of half of the filthy things he called me. I only knew it was filthy because of how it melted my core when he growled the words while drilling me into the snow.

"—try again?"

I snapped to, returning to reality. "Yes," I replied. "Of course I'm trying again, and I will every single night until I'm free of this place, and him. Speaking of, Aeris, there's another way out of the castle, yes? Other than the front and garden entrance." I took her hand, squeezing it. "Tell me where it is, please. Lord Alisdair can have his midnight run—hours after I've left."

Aeris smiled at my reflection. "My queen, did you forget your end of the bargain? By night you run, during the day, you reign."

My hope dimmed. "He meant that? He truly expects the unwanted wife he narrowly killed to play pretend at his side? For what purpose?"

"It is not pretend." She pinned the final braid to my crown, then snapped her fingers. A feather fell from her hand and hadn't yet hit the ground before three attendants were beside us, holding out three tiaras. "This is a real kingdom, and you are our queen. Your day is full, Lady Ana. In truth, you're already behind. You shall have to eat quickly."

I ate nothing, and did not despair for doing so. I wasn't worried about finding safe food to eat before I starved. I'd be home in Lyrica long before that happened.

"You can take this back, Talulla," I said, returning the tray to my taste-tester.

She took it, wrinkling her nose as she did. She looked like she was holding her breath.

"What? What is it?" I asked. "Do I smell?"

"Of course you don't," Aeris rushed. "Come now, my queen. Your lord awaits."

She helped me up and tried to tug me away. I stopped short, catching the eye of the woman in the mirror.

It wasn't me, so I couldn't marvel at the crown of shiny, copper braids—winding around the glittering gold, diamond-encrusted tiara. They weren't my lips plumped and shining to perfection, still carrying his punishing kiss on my lips. It wasn't my neck, framed by the intricate beadwork clinging to the slivery-white gown's collar, and clashing boldly with the red and purple marks on my throat and skin. It wasn't me that looked more beautiful than I ever had in my entire life.

It wasn't me who looked like a queen.

I followed Aeris out through winding hallways and hidden staircases leading down into the bowels of the castle. The further we went, the more the rich décor, jewels, antiques, and heavy tapestries disappeared.

Aeris stepped off the stairs, entering a large antechamber with nothing on its gray walls but flickering torches. Two large double doors loomed over us, calling us inside.

My feet didn't leave the bottom step. "What is this place? Why are we down here?" I backed away. "Is this a trap?"

"A trap?" She cocked her head too far to the right. "Why would our lord need to trap you, Lady Ana? He already has you."

Indignation rose up in me hot and heavy, and reality drowned it out. She had an awful and accurate point.

"Not for long," I warned, and stepped off.

Aeris knocked sharply on the wood. The doors swung open, revealing the scene on the other side.

I turned and left.

"Lady Ana?" Laughing, Aeris chased me down. "Where are you going, silly? It's this way. This is where our lord, and now you, hold court every morning. The people come to you with their issues and disputes, and you hand down your wisdom."

"Are you kidding me?" I barked. "That is not what's going on in that room!"

Aeris dragged me into a large, gray room much like the one we were leaving behind. Torches hung high on the walls, stretching the shadows basking in the windowless space. A long, black rug adorned with the phases of the moon led the path to a stone dais, with two thrones upon it.

Alisdair stretched out across the silver throne—his elbow propped on one arm, and his leg hanging over the other. Standing at his side was Foalan. Propped against the throne that was presumably mine was Bradach.

No trace of the beast I found in my bed remained. His claws shortened, his fangs shrunk, his horns were small ornaments poking from his raven curls, and his handsome face *handsome.*

I couldn't believe it, but focusing on him, and his smirk, was helpful in that moment. He gave me something to look at other than the massive, temperature-heating, lust-soaked orgy happening all over the floor, carpet, walls, and for a couple bird faeriken, in the air.

Three faeriken with leopard faces and spots contorted themselves over a lounge—one man plowing into the young lady from behind while she swallowed the other's cock to the hilt. My sweet taste-tester Talulla was also being tasted by a furry-faced faeriken with twitching whiskers. I assumed she was part cat, because she was certainly lapping her pussy up like one.

Something *splatted* down beside me and I picked up the pace, practically running up the steps to the only safe place not taken up by an amorous couple, or five.

"What is this?" I hissed at Alisdair. "Why are you allowing this?"

"They're in heat," he drawled back. "They cannot stop themselves. The drive to mate is too strong. They're also your subjects now, little queen. You'd do well to stop judging and looking down on them."

I lifted my chin. "I am not judging them. I envy them." I jerked my chin at a group of six that was getting very rough, and very loud. "At least they're having a much better time *mating* than I did last night."

"No," he replied, light and calm. "They're not."

I felt my cheeks brightening. "Last night was awful for me. Worst sex I've ever had."

"No, it wasn't."

"I didn't complete once. I faked it each time."

"Seven times," he corrected, "and no, you didn't."

Irritation bloomed in my chest. His calm dismissal of me was a hundred times worse than bluster or arguments. He saw right through me, and to the mess he made of me, and it made me hate him all the more.

I sniffed. "I don't know why you're so confident of that *tiny* little fella in your pants. I doubt it's ever pleased a woman."

"It pleased the woman who had to limp onto her throne. You're welcome."

"You—!"

"My queen." I jumped to find Bradach leaning over my ear. "May I humbly suggest you stop while you're behind? You're humiliating yourself."

"I do not recall asking for your input," I snapped, whirling on him.

Bradach lurched back, nose wrinkling even as he smirked.

Why does everyone keep doing that? The attendants scented my bathwater with rose and jasmine. I cannot possibly smell bad.

Bradach fixed on Aeris. His smirk melted away, replaced by an expression I sensed rarely graced his face. "Hello, Aeris. You look well."

She sniffed. "Why would I look unwell, Bradach? I am not ill."

"I meant you look beautiful." He dipped, bowing his head to her—wings fluttering. "Should you find yourself in need of a mate this heat cycle, I'd be more than happy to fertilize your eggs."

My brows shot up. What did he just say?

Aeris gave him a flat look. "You're an idiot."

Yes, that was the response I expected.

"I do not lay eggs, and bird faeriken do not have heat cycles—as you well know."

"Ah, must have slipped my mind. Even so, the offer still stands."

She was walking off before he finished his sentence.

"And you say I'm humiliating myself," I muttered.

He muttered right back. "My queen, your tongue is as sharp as you are beautiful."

I hid a smile. Far be it for any of these fae-beasts to think I was fond of them. Far be it for me to think it either. I was going home. I would never belong in Lumenfell.

Alisdair flapped a hand at Aeris. "Send them in."

Aeris clapped and a door off to the side of the dais was opened. My brows lifted as dozens of faeriken of all types and sizes streamed in—my count lost at thirty. This wasn't for show. This twisted, smirking beast actually held court like a proper ruler in a proper kingdom. Despite what Aeris said, the free-for-all orgy in the dark, windless cave better fit the picture I had of the kingdom of Wind and Wild.

I tried to stop looking at said free-for-all orgy. "Shouldn't we make them finish?"

"They do that on their own."

"Humorous," I deadpanned.

"Line up," Aeris ordered. She ushered them into an orderly line, feathers dropping in her wake. "One at a time. Address our lord clearly and be concise."

I snuck looks at him out of the corner of my eye. How was I supposed to make my arrangements to escape if I was forced to sit under his watchful eye all day? The night before he gave me only a ten-minute head start. Not nearly enough time to arrange a way home. And even if I did, he had all night to catch me... which he did... easily.

He's quick, strong, and powerful. What hope do I have of slowing him down, or hiding long enough to make it to daybreak? What did I used to do to outrun bullies faster than me?

An idea occurred to me.

"What? No, Alisdair, don't say that," I blared. "There's nothing wrong with bursting into tears when you reach completion. I thought it was very sweet. Adorable even. I do think, however, that you didn't need to sob quite so long, or so loudly."

Aeris cut off with a squawk, gaping at me.

Slowly, dangerously, Alisdair's narrowed eyes turned on me.

Bold as ever, I patted his hand. "Oh, my poor husband, you needn't feel bad for not being able to satisfy me. With time and practice and less crying, you'll improve."

"Uhh, Queen Ana," Bradach whispered. "I once again must say—"

"Thank you for asking, Bradach, the answer is many." I was so loud, I drowned out the moans. "I've had many well-endowed, fierce, passionate lovers, so you're right, my lord never had a chance with that tiny, little cock, but trust me, with practice, he can at least make it so I'm not so bored." I beamed at Shadowsoul's darkening expression. "Does that make you feel better, darling?"

He was staring hard at my mouth, like he wanted to rip it out. "You shame only yourself with this display."

"Shame? No, it isn't shameful to have a mole on your cock that is bigger than your cock itself. All bodies are beautiful and wonderful in their uniqueness." My smile was sweet. "I only ask that you do not make me suck on it again. I know you get off on that, but it's so hairy. It was like licking a cat."

I wanted the fucking couples to cease their activities, and they most certainly had. I claimed the wide-eyed, gawping attention of everyone in the room. *I* did. They were all—townspeople, guards, servants—blinking at me.

I swallowed hard, keeping my chin high. I didn't know this face. Did it blush as easily as my true one? Because if it did, this scene was even more embarrassing than it felt. Even so, I had to keep it up. I vowed to stay by his side during the day, learning how to rule. I may not be able to leave, but our promises said nothing about him getting fed up with me and sending me away.

I will make him despise me so much, he wants me nowhere near him before moonrise, and he runs much slower after it.

"Um, my lady?" Aeris ventured, nerves lacing her tone. "Have you finished? May we begin now?"

I laughed. "Oh my Meya, I said the same thing last night! The tragedy was that he had finished, and I didn't even know we'd begun—"

Alisdair snapped his fingers. My lips kept moving, but nothing came out.

"Proceed," he ordered.

I cursed foully with no one to hear it. Magic. My plan did not take magic into account.

Two men stepped forward. Thick, scaly bumpy skin covered their faces, hands, and elongated jaws. They looked about with strange, slitted eyes, flashing teeth too long for their mouths.

"State the issue that brings you before our lord and king," Aeris ordered.

Both men snapped their hands up, pointing at the other. It was only then I noticed their arms were shorter than they should be—as if they were shrinking back into their bodies. I couldn't begin to guess what kind of animal was taking over them.

"Lorcan, my lord. We have shared the waters of the Lumenfell River for three generations," Lorcan said. Beyond his odd reptilian skin, I noted his trim beard, broad shoulders, and quivering jowls. "His bask has taken over the northern marsh, and are refusing our bask entry. They killed two of our own who tried!

"Most of the prey have taken to the trees," he said. "We have only the fish in the northern marsh to eat. They're driving us to starvation."

Alisdair turned on the other man. "Is this true, Arin? What have you to say for yourself?"

Arin flashed Lorcan a contemptuous sneer. "He paints himself as the innocent when, in truth, his bask ceased all trading of goods, which is why we needed the northern marsh in the first place. It is *us* who are starving! He only comes to you now with his bleating because the prey took to the mountains two months early, and their food stores are low."

"I see." Alisdair's expression was unreadable. I couldn't guess what was going on behind those unfathomable pools. "Have you made every effort to solve this dispute among yourselves?"

Growls and snaps were their reply. Compromise and diplomacy had clearly broken down between these two.

"Very well. What say you, my queen?"

It wasn't until I noticed everyone staring at me did the words penetrate. "What? Me?" I said, shocked to find I could. "What say me?"

He nodded, clearly irritated. "What is your suggestion for them?"

I blinked at him. We settled on the fact that he was indeed speaking to me, but for the life of me I didn't know why. Women in Lyrica weren't asked their opinions on any topic—least of all the runnings of the kingdom and the needs of our people. He truly wanted to know what I thought best?

"Uhh, okay," I said, sitting up straight. "First, I—" I twisted around to Bradach. "Bradach, what is—?"

"You will address your questions to me," my husband stated. Had I imagined it, or had something other than flat disinterest entered his tone?

"Very well." I faced him. "What is a bask?"

"A bask is a group of crocodiles," he replied, surprising me again.

I couldn't remember the last time a man answered a question I asked without mocking, scoffing, or calling me stupid. It had been that long.

"They are crocodile faeriken."

I nodded slow, taking that in. I didn't know much about crocodiles. One didn't encounter them in a big city like Lyrica, but Mama did a few times, when she went to battle with Papa. She compared them to big, angry lizards.

That explains why their limbs don't match the size of their bodies. As the curse takes hold, it must be getting harder for them to hunt. Certainly too hard to chase a flying rabbit up a tree.

I kept my voice low. "But why would they be starving? They don't have to hunt. Our carriage passed through a bustling market only yesterday."

"We are cut off from the other kingdoms," he replied, matching my tone. "We must survive on what we grow and hunt here in this land of winter. Our people must be self-sufficient."

I wondered if I'd ever get used to him referring to them as *our* people.

I don't plan on staying long enough to need to.

"When they have a surplus of food, they bring it to the market to trade," Alisdair said, continuing the longest civil conversation we had since we met. "But no one could hunt enough to feed forty basks."

"Forty?" I squeaked.

He inclined his head.

"So," I drew out, putting the pieces together. "Like everyone else, they must rely on themselves for hunting. But then their prey took off to the mountains earlier than expected. Is there a reason? Did something happen?"

"This land has been cursed for a millennium. All living beings had to adapt or die. The plants and flora learned to grow without sunlight. The woodland animals evolved new ways of escaping predators in the dark," he said. "And the predators in that darkness..."

I knew without him saying so. *The Taken.*

"As their numbers grow," Alisdair went on, "the animals flee. Soon it will be only us, and them."

The hairs on my skin stood on end at the very thought of being trapped in this place with only the Taken.

"What are they?" I whispered, voice shaking. "Are they your people? The faeriken? Is the last stage of the curse becoming... that?"

He gave me a long, unreadable look. So long, discomfort tightened my skin. "Oh, little bird," he said softly. "It's much worse than that."

"My lord? My lady?" Aeris spoke up, saving me from trying to force a reply from my suddenly dry mouth. "What is your decree?"

All eyes were on me—Alisdair's included.

Drawing back, I blew out a breath. "All right, I believe I understand the problem, and that problem is any solution that utilizes our current resources would be temporary. We'll all be right back here within a week. What we need is to open trade between the other kingdoms."

"Well, there was a certain treaty that ended the war and allowed for the very trade you speak of," Bradach sang. "But a certain princess saw the end of that."

"Thank you, Bradach," I forced through clenched teeth. "As always, your unasked-for interruptions are most welcome and not in the least bit irritating."

Winking, he bowed deeply. "You're welcome, my queen. I am your eternal servant."

I rolled my eyes. "The truth is, you never need a treaty to trade. All you need is a fake merchant license, and someone who blends in with the n—with the fae," I corrected, leaving out the word *normal.* "I will forge the license and teach our chosen merchant what they need to know. You"—I turned on Alisdair—"will provide the coin.

"This palace is rife with riches. A few trinkets from the front entryway, and you'll have fifty cartfulls of fish, chickens, turkeys, and flightless bunnies," I said. "In the meantime, we will work out a schedule that gives both your basks equal access to the marsh. That should tide you over until..." I glanced at Alisdair. "How long is the journey to and from Lyrica?"

"A fortnight."

"Two weeks," I announced to the bask leaders. "If you both can get along and abide for the schedule for two weeks, you'll soon have all the food you need. Agreed?"

The men stiffly turned in each other's direction, as if having to look at each other was torture itself. Snarling, they both said, "Agreed."

"Very well."

Noise sounded in the throne room. It was applause.

"Well done, Queen Ana," Aeris gushed. "Of course you would know exactly what to do."

"She's amazing."

"Our queen. Beautiful and wise."

I blushed in spite of myself, preening a little in my seat. I didn't want to admit it, but their praise felt good. As good as it felt to come up with a solution to a real problem, and be heard. The only hope of a future I had was selling vegetables in a market square. The only thing anyone would ever ask of me was the price.

But now here I was, solving food shortages and ending territory disputes. Me, the queen of nothing, and owned by no one.

"Yes, very well done," Alisdair remarked. "A fair and reasonable plan that solves their issue and a great many more. I like it."

"You do?" I hated immediately that I asked that. Hated even more that a small, lonely, pathetic part of me was pleased at his approval.

"I do," he replied, rising up. "I like it so much that I will have this schedule drawn up immediately." Alisdair nodded at Aeris. "Aeris, share it with their widows as soon as it's complete."

My smile twitched. "Wait. Their wid—?"

Alisdair roared. Launching off the dais, he changed in mid-air. The handsome king melted away, and the ferocious beast took over.

Lorcan had just time enough to shout before his throat was ripped out.

I screamed.

Gurgling, hacking, spurting blood, Lorcan thudded on the ground and Alisdair pounced on him—ripping him apart.

Arin turned and ran on legs too short to take him far. Three bounds, and Alisdair was on him.

Something flew through the air, smacking me across my screeching mouth. I looked down on the bleeding remains of a foot.

"Ahhh!"

Slapping it off, I ran.

I bolted out the side door, skidding out into a plain, stone hallway. Blast of cold air smacked me in the back, turning me around to two wide-open doors leading outside to town. I took off sprinting.

It was my sad tale that I was accustomed to violence, sickness, and death. I'd watched many a kind, older woman fall prey to the wasting sickness. I'd been attacked many times for the little I had, and survived. I'd also seen the remains of people who were attacked for what they had, and didn't survive.

I'd seen it all... but I'd never seen that.

I burst outside, and searing, mind-numbing pain exploded in my right leg.

"Ah!" I cried. Seizing up, it dropped me flat on my face, bouncing my skull off the icy stone. I slid across the ground—dazed and in pain.

"That was your worst escape attempt yet."

My insides curdled.

"How is it you're not learning from your previous?" Alisdair picked me up one-handed, and held me out dangling in front of him like a cat by the scruff. He was covered in blood. And me, upside down and eye level with my own knees, I realized I was too. "You cannot outrun me, little queen. Especially not when covered in sacred, magic runes promising that during the day, your place is beside me."

I glared, burning him where he stood. "That was awful. They came to you for help, and you killed them for no reason. You're a monster, and I hate you. Every day for as long as I live, I will *hate you*!"

"Aww," he mocked, setting my teeth on edge. "Do you promise?"

Alisdair waved his hand, and a glowing, beautiful starflower appeared between his fingers. He tucked it behind my ear. "And I promise you, my wife, my queen, to be worthy of it."

He carried me back into the throne room. Yes, carried.

Ignoring my kicking and shouting, he dragged me inside like a sack of oranges and deposited me back on my throne.

"As I was saying," Alisdair growled. Below us, servants scurried to clean the remains of the crocodile faeriken. "I will have no more of these territory disputes. No more killing and hoarding of food. If you are unable to live and work together civilly, then you will die brutally!

"Now who else wishes to test my patience?" he roared.

Half the people in line ran for the door, trampling each other in the melee. The brave few who remained moved up to receive their wisdom, but none from me.

I didn't speak for the rest of the morning, but inside, I thought of nothing but my mother. All these years, enduring a cruel, heartless, selfish man for our sakes.

I never understood her more.

***

"Away," Alisdair barked after what felt like hours.

There were still dozens more faeriken to be seen, but that didn't stop him snatching my hand and dragging me out the door.

Temper bursting in my chest, I lunged forward and sunk my teeth in his hand.

"Argh!" Roaring, he whirled on me, fangs growing in the blink of my eye.

I smashed my nose on his and growled right back. "I can do it too, Lord Shitsoul. That's the last time you drag or carry me anywhere. You wanted a pretend queen for your paper throne, so start treating me like one!"

His lips peeled back from his teeth. "Be very careful, pretend queen, or I just might bite back."

I pushed back harder. "I've seen your bite," I hissed. "It doesn't scare me."

We faced each other down, his rising growl sounding a warning that I should be heeding, but I knew a thing or two about bullies. Back down once, and you've lost the power forever.

"Ahem." Someone cleared their throat behind us. "The schedule has been written and delivered to the basks as requested. Lunch is also prepared and waiting for you both."

"Feed her." He pulled back so suddenly, I stumbled. "And make sure she eats."

Of course he knew.

"Bring mine to the tower."

"Oh, are you certain, my lord?" Aeris asked. "I thought you'd like to enjoy a meal with your new—"

He swept out the door, slamming it in both our faces.

Aeris smiled at my pinched, wane face. "No matter. Lunch is ready on the terrace, Lady Ana, and you'll find it a treat. We made all your favorites."

"How do you know my favorites?" I muttered distractedly. I rubbed my thigh, and the rune hiding beneath the cloth.

"Our spies."

How casually she spoke of the people who'd be executed the minute King Salman learned of their existence.

"Ooh, how pretty." Aeris drifted off my face, making me turn my head. "Did our lord give that to you? I worried you both weren't getting along. Happy I was wrong."

I didn't know what she was talking about, until I remembered the starflower. I snatched it, threw it on the floor, and ground it to paste.

"Or not," she mumbled. "This way, my—"

"What's the range on these runes?" I burst out. "How far from him can I be before it punishes me?"

"What? Oh, Meya, no." Taking my hand, she led me out much more gently than Shadowsoul. "It's not like that. You can't read runes, but I can. Yours are very clear in that you need to participate in the ruling of the kingdom. Lunch is hardly such.

"You're free to wander as far from our lord as you wish when—"

I broke free, racing to the doors that let the villagers in. Throwing myself against them, they pushed right back—zinging pain up my shoulder.

Locked.

"My lady? Queen Ana!"

I tore off back the way I came. Aeris made a grab for me, and I whipped off my shawl and tossed it over her head.

"*Awk!*" she squawked, flailing under the fabric.

Sorry, Aeris. You're nice, but I did learn from my previous escape attempts. If I can't climb higher or run faster, I have to be smarter.

I ran into the throne room and out through the other door, taking the steps two at a time. I came out into a gilded hallway. Two bird faeriken with bright blue plumage came down the hall in uniforms and swords on their hips.

Oh, no.

They lit on me.

"Good morning, Lady Ana," one said. "What are—?"

"Ahh!" I blared. Wildly waving my hands and head, I charged them—screeching my lungs out.

"What the fuck!?"

They sprung apart and out of the way, one of them colliding with the wall.

I hoofed it past them, gaining speed. It wasn't pretty, but one thing I learned after years of dodging torment was that people ran in the other direction of crazy.

Rounding a corner, I found myself in the grand hall, and oh, Meya, was it.

A grand staircase led to halls and rooms unknown. Torches burned in golden holders, chasing away chill and darkness. Over a dozen stands lined the walls, each weighted down with an expensive bust, painted vase, breathtaking jewelry, and riches I'd only dreamt of.

Directly beside me, smirking down at me even then, was a large, silver statue of Alisdair.

I looked at him, then kept looking—fixed on something just above his shoulder.

A window.

If I could climb up him and get to that window, I'd make it outside, then on to the village. I knew exactly what I needed, and who. I just had to get to them and set my plan into motion before I had six feet worth of fangs and evil chasing me down.

"Okay, okay," I breathed, rolling my neck.

This was a soft, dewy body that didn't do much—any—climbing. I was already wheezing harder than I should've been after my sprint through the halls. This wouldn't be as easy as if I was my true self.

If I was my true self, I'd be home with Mama and my faywens. Home, I thought as the pain of missing them settled into my bones. *I'm going home.*

Backing up, I sent a prayer to Meya, then jumped.

The ever-present sword on his hip was a fixture of his statue too. I grabbed hold of the sheath, vaulted up, slipped, and—

"Ugh." I crashed flat on my back. "Don't give up," I rasped. "You can't give up."

I repeated that over and over, eventually getting back on my feet. I jumped and grabbed the scabbard again.

Left, right, left, right. I monkey-climbed up the weapon to his elbow. Reaching for it, my fingers closed on—

"Ahh!" Down I went, landing hard on my ankle. Pain lanced through my leg, ripping a hiss through my teeth.

I forced it down and tried again.

Each try taught me the limits of my new, unwanted body. Scampering up the formed folds in his robe, I slapped my arms around Shadowsoul's neck, heaving myself up.

My legs took my arms' place. Hanging on tight, that smart, smirking mouth pressed against my rib cage while I considered my new problem.

I'm sure I can get onto that ledge from his shoulder, but how will I open the window once I do. I chewed my lip, craning to see a latch. *Maybe if I—*

"Far be it for me to question how my lady and my lord get off—"

I jerked, nearly falling off Shadowsoul to my death.

"—but isn't it more satisfying when that's done by the real version?" Bradach blinked at me, his head cocked at an unnatural angle.

"Shh." I flapped a hand. "Keep your voice down. Someone will hear you."

"I understand. You want privacy." He clapped his hands over his face. "I'll close my eyes."

"Don't do that," I whisper-screamed. "There's nothing to close your eyes to. What are you even doing here?"

"Many, many people told me our new queen has gone mad." He arched a brow. "They were right."

Why in the hell did I ever think I liked this guy?

"I've not gone mad. I just—" A thought occurred to me. "Bradach, you and Aeris, has that happened yet?"

His wings flashed out. I couldn't be sure, but I guessed that was a sign of agitation. "I'm sure I don't know what you mean, my lady."

"So that's a no," I replied. "How about this? If you can sneak me out of the castle and stall Alisdair to give me an hour, maybe two hours in the village, I'll name you my personal bodyguard. Aeris seems to be by my side always, which means if you're always by my side, you'll have many chances to sweet-talk her into fertilizing her eggs." I smiled down at him. "What do you say?"

"Hmm. You'll do this, and in return you ask that I help you go into the village?" He blew out a breath. "I don't know, Lady Ana. You don't know what you ask of me."

"I know it's a huge request. This castle is locked down tighter than the Crystal Palace, but I have to get out." Pleading bled into my voice. "Help me. I'll be forever in your debt."

He tossed his head, his wings doing that nervous flutter even faster and harder. "All right, all right," he burst out. "I will do this for you, but only because desperation is going to make you break your neck." Bradach reached for me. "Come down. Carefully."

"Thank you," I cried, hope filling my chest to bursting. "Catch me."

"What?"

I jumped off.

"Wait— No!"

Bradach shot back, leaving nothing between me and the stone.

"Ahhh—!" I hit the floor and bounced, flopping up and down like I was on a gray mattress.

I goggled at him as he closed his lapel, flashing a glance of the coudarian crystal inside. "What was that!"

"Forgive me," he said, sounding genuinely sorry. "But I can't touch you, my queen. It's not worth my life."

"What the fuck are you talking about!" Fear had a grip on my tongue, and my throat. My breaths tried and failed to leave a constricted airway.

"Surely you've noticed the smell."

"Smell?" I got to my feet. "So it's true, I do smell. Smell so badly you think you'll die from getting near me. How is that possible?" I asked myself. "I don't smell anything. Is it your faeriken senses? Do you smell things others can't?"

"In this case, yes, if it's true you can't smell it too," he admitted. "But it's not about being faeriken. It's because our lord marked you. Very heavily."

"Excuse me? Marked?"

He pointed. I followed his finger down to my dress, and saw nothing.

"The small cuts on your chest." Those sly lips found another smirk. "That's how beings like him inject their pheromones into their mates' bloodstream, marking them as theirs. Instead of walking around with the scent that is uniquely you, you now smell uniquely *him*. Even more him than he does."

My jaw fell further with every word.

"A smell that transfers to anyone you touch, or who touches you," Bradach went on. "Not an issue for the women, but if our lord discovers your touch on another man, he'll kill them." Bradach stated this with no inflection, irony, or grin. He was deadly serious. "Shall we?"

He set off, expecting me to follow. I chased after him, spitting mad.

"That cheating bastard. I can't believe he'd do something like this without my permission." I scoffed. "I bet it didn't occur to him to ask permission. The man truly thinks he was paid for a pet and not a person."

Bradach turned left, taking me down a hallway that was vaguely familiar.

"Being able to follow my scent everywhere and on everyone is a violation of his promise. I knew I couldn't trust him," I whispered. "But it doesn't matter. If he can lie, deceive, and jump through every loophole, so can I."

Bradach suddenly pulled up short. Tapping his lips with one finger, he pointed around the corner.

I looked to see and landed on four guards manning the main entrance. Quickly, I ducked back, shaking my head at him hard. We couldn't do it. It wasn't possible we'd get past all four of them without Alisdair finding out, and coming after me.

"Trust me," he whispered. "Watch how I do this."

"But—but wait," I cried, reaching to grab him, then remembering and snapping my hand back.

That split-second hesitation and he stepped into their view, ending my chance to stop him.

Bradach was going to hurt them. All to help me, and help himself get closer to Aeris. Not even Meya herself could be more shocked that I cared about the well-being of a couple faeriken, but I did.

Less than a week ago, I was certain being in a faeriken's presence resulted in death. Well, I'd been in the presence of many faeriken, and they'd been nothing but kind or deferential to me. Except for Bradach, but even he dropped everything to help me. He was even willing to go so far as to knock out his own countrymen.

Why didn't I tell him I didn't want any violence? I was expecting him to show me the door to an old servants' entrance. Not go after—

"Good morning, gentlemen. Lady," Bradach announced. He pointed straight at me. "The queen would like a stroll through the village. Send for her carriage."

"Of course, my queen." They snapped to attention, then bowed to the dumbfounded shadow behind the wall. "We'll have it brought out to you at once. Please, stay in the warmth until it arrives."

"I, uh— Yes," I croaked, stepping into the open. "Thank you."

Bradach brushed past me, shaking his head. I heard the word *keva* loud and clear.

Embarrassment flipped my stomach. I couldn't be faulted. I'd been a princess for a short while, and a queen for less time than that. I wasn't used to living in a world where I gave commands and they were followed without question. It never occurred to me that I wasn't a prisoner in the castle I ruled.

I groaned, memory assaulting me. "I owe Aeris a big apology."

***

An hour later, the carriage dropped me off at the drawbridge.

Aeris, Eadaoin, and Foalan waited for me outside in the cold.

"What are you all doing out here?" I asked. "Is everything okay?"

"It is not," Foalan said. "Lady Ana, it is not wise to travel without guards." He gestured to Eadaoin. "Your companion is trained in combat. Trained by *me*. I ask that in the future, you travel with her by your side at the very least."

"All right. I will, thank you." There was no reason to argue with him. I'd already done what I needed to do. I wasn't going to be around long enough to worry about who was with me when I went out.

I turned to Aeris. "Aeris, I want to apologize for throwing my shawl over your head to make my escape. I saw this for you in the market and... I hope you like it."

Wide, glistening eyes beheld the small, silver bracelet, graced by the tiniest snowflake charm.

"Oh, my lady..." She trailed off, smiling at me. "Thank you."

"My lady?" Eadaoin gestured behind her. "If you'll follow me, our lord requests your presence in the war room."

I opened my mouth to tell her where he could shove his request, and a spike of pain assaulted my ankle.

Gritting my teeth, I just nodded. "Lead the way."

I followed Eadaoin inside. Aeris and Foalan broke off when we entered the castle, heading down the hallway leading to the throne room. Aeris's laugh echoed behind her.

Our trek took us up three flights of stairs and down two twisting hallways. I lost my bearings immediately. I envied the queen consort who had to learn how to navigate these strange, winding halls. Thankfully, after the next morning, that would not be an issue.

Eadaoin stopped in front of a huge, red door and knocked.

"Come."

Sweeping it open, she moved for me to step inside.

I did. My jaw dropped before I stepped over the threshold.

Maps.

Everywhere. Of everything. For everyone. Plastered all over the walls, and spilling off the desks, detailed maps of Lyrica, Sarabai, Rajadom, Quatassa, and the human lands dominated the space. There were even maps of places I didn't recognize, with names impossible for me to pronounce.

Alisdair leaned over a slanted desk, speaking in low tones to Bradach.

My lips pressed into a thin line seeing Bradach's hand on his shoulder.

"See to it," Alisdair said.

"My lord." Bradach bowed, then left as quickly as I came in.

Alisdair hadn't raised his head from the map. I took that chance to study him.

The large, heavy black coat he always wore was nowhere to be seen. Lunch must've given him the magical energy he needed, because he never looked more fae. No lethal points tipped his nails. No fangs poked his deceptively soft lips. Even his horns were the smallest I'd ever seen them, giving the briefest hello from their nest of dark, pine-scented curls.

Outside the cloak, everything was on display. Of course, he'd already given me a rough and vigorous tour of his body, but without that, I still could've traced the outline of his shoulders and hard, stony muscles through his white linen tunic—buttoned barely above the belly button.

His pants were loose too, and that meant nothing to the large bulge between his legs. If I wanted to know why I still had a slight limp, it reminded me.

Alisdair lifted his head and I was already flicking away, narrowing in on a map of Lyrica before our eyes could meet.

"What is all of this?" A smile rose unbidden to my lips. "Seems you lied to me once again. Lyrica and its silly, old fool of a king are more of a threat to you than you let on." I motioned to the walls. "Why else do you and your spies keep such a close eye on all of Elva and beyond?"

"Don't be ridiculous, woman." The same cold dismissal. "This room isn't for defense. It's for planning. The time draws near for the first strike that begins our conquering of Elva. We, and therefore you, must be ready."

"Don't be ridiculous, beast," I breezed just as cooly. "We, and therefore *you*, will be doing no such thing."

I couldn't be certain, but I thought I saw the barest quirk of his lips. Ah, so the king found his pet amusing. He wouldn't be laughing for long.

"Besides, you won't get far until you hire a new mapmaker." I pointed to a map of the Stella Darna Sea. "There's no island there."

"There is, but it moves. That's where it was as of a month ago," he replied, as if he wasn't speaking total nonsense. "I sent my flying infantry to stake our claim, but it moved again."

"Oookkkkaaaay," I drew out. *It's so sad when a mind starts to go.* "So why am I here? And don't say it's for an invasion that will never happen."

He crooked a finger. "Come."

I planted my feet. "Why don't you try that again with a please, then—"

Alisdair snapped his fingers and I flew to his side, yelping as I collided with a wall of muscle. He put his arm around me instinctively, stopping me from falling. I swatted him for the magic-handling, but it was like hitting an actual wall. He didn't give my hit a lick of attention.

"This is why you're here."

I glanced down at the map before us. This one, I'd never seen before. Or more to say, I have, but all the times I did, it was nothing but a black, blighted spot on our great nation.

"The kingdom of Wind and Wild," he confirmed. "Its capital, its villages, its outer-lying territories. Familiarize yourself with it all."

"Why must I?" I asked, though I brought the map closer.

I couldn't help myself. I loved learning new things. If university wasn't wholly off-limits to the likes of me, it's where I'd be right then.

"Why are you teaching me any of this? You're using me for my position and power." I was nothing if not blunt. "Surely a *little bird* doesn't need to be taught to run a kingdom."

"You're correct, you don't," he bit back, glaring.

I rose a little higher, glaring right back. It was then I noticed his arm was still around me, and my chest still pressed to his.

We broke apart in a blink, staring down each other from opposite ends of the table.

"All things being what they should've been, you wouldn't need to know these things," he repeated. "Because you'd be dead. But since our plans have changed—"

I hated that he kept saying *our*—casually including me in his treason.

"—someone will have to remain here in Lumenfell, ruling our people and raising our children while I lead the conquer."

A roaring sounded in my ears. What did he say? "Excuse me? Children? Whose children?"

"Our children."

He repeated it, and it still didn't make sense.

"We are not having children."

"We will have so many children, they will outnumber all the basks in all the seas in all the world."

I choked, flinging away. "What!"

Face changing, Alisdair laughed. "You're so amusing when you squawk, little bird. Calm yourself. Two or three will more than suffice. You will stay here to raise them, and teach our heirs all that I'm teaching you," he said. "So pay attention."

Shock fled, and rage flooded in fast. "I'm the one who must stay behind and raise the imaginary children? Is that what you think a woman's place is? Having your beast-babies, raising your beast-babies, then putting my head down and ass up, so you can impregnate me with some more?"

"No, dear," he ground out. "I would happily stay and rear our heirs, but then you'd have to lead our armies against Elva. You've made such a tantrum of being against it, I assumed that wasn't an option for you." Alisdair raised a brow. "Or would you prefer we wage war together, side by side, and abandon our children here with nursemaids and servants?" He tsked, looking genuinely disgusted. "Very cold, my queen. You hate our *beast-babies* that much, and they're not even born."

My jaw worked, outrage stealing every word before it could leave my tongue. How had he turned this around on me? In one conversation, I became a bad mother to children that didn't exist, and a war-monger when there was no war!

"You enjoy this, don't you?" My eyes narrowed to slits. "Twisting words? Keeping everyone around you a little off-balance, a little distrusting, and a lot scared. Your mind games do not work on me," I said softly, drawing near. "But consider this while you play them. You might just be teaching me to rule the kingdom... that I'll steal from you."

I smiled brightly. "Begin with your lesson, husband. I'm listening."

"Yes," he replied, reaching for the map. "Finally, you begin to accept your fate."

He said that, but I saw it. For the barest second... Shadowsoul hesitated.

***

"Last is wolf territory," he said, drawing a circle around a stretch of land behind Castle Riagin. "As they change, they're becoming more possessive of it, leading to bloody conflicts around their borders. As a result, we've declared this area off-limits to all but Foalan.

"This means if such a conflict arises, you must punish both the wolf and the other party involved," Alisdair said. "Punishment for the violence. Punishment for provoking the violence by entering a forbidden area."

I swallowed hard, identifying that area all too quickly. *That dark, ominous pit. It was the home of bloodthirsty wolf faeriken that would've killed me on sight. The very pit Meallan tried talking me into entering. Instead, he helped me and let me go.*

Why did he let me go? And what would've happened if I'd taken his hand?

"What if—" I cleared my dry throat. "What if you wander into that area by accident? Surely no one should be punished for an accident?"

"You are queen. You do not know the meaning of accident." He rolled the map closed with a *snap* that echoed in my chest. "And you do not forgive them."

"I don't foresee me being the kind of queen you want, or expect."

"You don't foresee being my queen at all," he lofted, crossing the room. "Isn't your grand plan to escape through the dark, ice, and cold to the important *things* waiting for you in the kingdom of women-haters?"

I flushed. Again, every word out of his mouth was a dagger to my soft parts.

"Why should it make a difference to you what kind of queen I hope you to be?"

"It doesn't," I replied. "Because you'll be dead by then."

Slitted eyes tracked him to a darkened corner of the war room. He placed the map on the bottom of an overstuffed shelf, then waved his hand. Before my eyes, the bookshelf melted into the wall, leaving nothing but bare stone.

"How do you do that?" I blurted. "You're not wearing any crystals. Unless, they're... um..." I tried to stop myself, but I flicked down.

"You more than anyone know what's in my pants, and it's not coudarian crystals."

Regret is swift.

A long, golden rope hung from the ceiling. Alisdair pulled on it sharply.

"Men do not have Mother Meya's favor," he said, surprising me again.

Anyone else would've called me impertinent, tried to slap me, or barked at me to shut up and waste someone else's time with my questions. It was strange comparing everyone I was raised to trust against the man I was raised to hate. What does it mean when a good person treats you worse than a monster?

"We fight, struggle, and beg her for every drop of magic. Or, I should say, other men do. I brought Meya to heel a long time ago. Now, magic obeys my will. As all men do." He looked me straight in the eyes. "As you will soon."

Nothing. The answer is it means nothing when a monster pretends to be kind. He's still a monster.

"I don't know what disgusts me more," I said, "your blasphemy, or your delusional fantasy that I will ever obey you."

"Neither should disgust you. It is mere fact." He stalked toward me, tipping my head back, back, back to hold my glare. "I am now the god you worship. From the moment you stepped into that cauldron, you forsook all others and pledged your life, your hopes, your wants, and your body to me." Holding my gaze, he slowly brought my palm to his lips.

I could've stopped him. Could've pulled away. But my body wouldn't respond to the command. He pressed a gentle kiss to the inside of my wrist, scampering goose bumps down my arm. The other hand suddenly grasped my hip, startling a gasp out of me.

The thin fabric of my dress did nothing to hold back the heat from his touch. Pulling me close, he drew soft, slow circles on my back while kissing a burning trail down my arm—all the while holding me captive in his mesmerizing gaze.

If I was ever asked of this, I'd say he performed terrible magics on me, rendering me unable to move. But I'd know it was a lie then as I knew it now.

I knew what magic felt like. I knew it like I knew the well of trapped power, desperately clawing the cage around my soul. This was not magic or trickery.

No, this was all Alisdair Shadowsoul.

He brushed a kiss on my chin, teasing a sigh from me. "Kiss me," he whispered. "My wife, my queen. Kiss me."

Rising on tiptoe, my eyes fluttered shut.

"*Kiss me.*"

I frowned, blinking open—and locked eye to eye with the hideous, horned beast.

"Ahh!" I flung back and on a box of scrolls, tipping them and me onto the floor.

Alisdair laughed uproariously. "Do you see, sweet Ana? To deny my power over you is pointless. No matter what, no matter how—you'll always end up on your back."

"Fuck you!" I kicked and floundered under the avalanche of scrolls.

"It is that time, yes."

I heard the creak and wheeze of the door opening.

"I'll give you an hour head start tonight," he said as I finally kicked free and got to my feet.

I huffed, boring a hole in his arrogant head.

He didn't notice in the slightest. One of the servants came in, cleared a small table, and set down a food tray. Alisdair made short work of the apple.

"One hour?" I glanced out the pane window. It looked no different outside than it did an hour ago, or the hour before that, or five hours before that. "Why so generous?" I spat.

"It's only sporting, considering you'll need time to eat."

I quieted, looking from him to the tray, then the door. There was no chance of me running past him. I considered trying anyway.

Relaxing, I shrugged. "Thank you, but no. I'm not hungry."

My rotten stomach growled, betraying me instantly. Fruits, spiced vegetables, roasted lamb—their heavenly scent enveloped me. I wasn't a stranger to missing meals.

Emiana was. Her body wanted food.

Now.

"I'm not h-hungry," I repeated, voice cracking.

"Yes, you are."

"I'm not." I casually inched toward the door. "I ate a big lunch."

"Cease your lies," he growled. "Your stomach has been trumpeting for days. Why are you refusing—? Ah, wait. I see. You have no hope of outrunning me, so you're taking the coward's way out by starving yourself." Alisdair scoffed. "Pathetic."

"You are so—!" I cut myself off, taking a deep breath. Why did a man I'd soon be free of irritate me so greatly? "No," I forced out. "That's not the reason. I just don't... have a taste for Lumenfellen food is all."

"You have yet to eat Lumenfellen food, so you know nothing of its taste. Again you lie, and again you do it badly. What is the real reason?"

I didn't speak. My lips tightly pressed together. If I opened them again, I would shove that food in.

He hummed. "No, it's not cowardice. It's ignorance. You think if you eat our food, it will trigger the change."

Shadowsoul read the answer on my face. Sighing, he rubbed the bridge of his nose like I was tiresome. "Princess, it doesn't work that way. I cannot tell you what triggers the curse, but I can assure you it isn't food. The actual trigger has already begun its work."

"What," I cried, whipping around.

"Whether or not you eat will not change the result, or accelerate it. You starve yourself for nothing." He shoved the tray across the desk. "Eat."

I stared at the food for a long time, internal battle raging. Incredibly, I didn't think he was lying. Everything around me was cursed from the plants, to the mountains, to the air. The mountains were hardly eating roasted lamb, so it was never going to be as simple as refusing the food. I only wanted to believe it could be that simple, because if I faced the fact that the curse was in the air I breathed, the water that bathed me, or the stone beneath my feet, I had to accept that another curse was taking everything from me... and there was nothing I could do to stop it.

"Very well," I whispered, claiming the tray. "I will eat, but not here. You've given me an hour and I'm not wasting it." I abandoned the vegetables and snatched up the rack of lamb and the mug of ale. "I'll see you in the morning, husband..." I headed out the door, the lamb already half devoured.

"...as you're weeping and waving goodbye to the back of my carriage."

His laughter echoed through the hall.

***

I settled into my hiding spot, checking and rechecking that everything was as it should be.

This is it. Finally the nightmare will end.

The doors banged open, blasting a whoosh of air that blew out half the candles, plunging the room in dancing shadows and smoke. Alisdair stalked inside, fangs bared. He didn't look like a husband preparing for a night of making love to his new bride. He looked like a predator who finally caught his prey.

"Very clever," he growled. "It took me an entire five extra minutes to find you."

I dipped down in the bath, letting the water rise to the top of my mouth. Was it five minutes? It both felt like seconds and an eternity that I waited in my steamy, overly luxurious bath.

"Not clever enough," I said, rising back up. "I thought filling the water with every scented oil, and the room with every scented candle would be enough to block your cheat— Oh pardon me, I meant you're marking."

Alisdair grinned at my scolding. "It was enough, little bird, hence you earning my compliment. I couldn't smell my mark at all—"

"But then how—?"

"What I did smell was the thick, cloying scent of a bath that was all scented oil." He tapped his nose, tsking my shame. "Let that be your third lesson of the day. You cannot hide what belongs to me behind what doesn't belong."

"Hmm," I raised my chin, rising fully in the water. "A good lesson, but not one I'll need to know past tonight."

Alisdair ripped off his robe and threw the tatters into a corner. Sweet talk was over. "Come to me, Princess," he said, palming his smooth, already-erect cock. "I regret that there is no hairy cat mole—"

My face caught fire.

"—but it will fuck you all the same." He pointed down. "On your knees. Head down. Ass up."

Oh, yes, the sweet talk is very much over.

"Hold that thought, and look." I raised my hands, gesturing to the newest addition to the baths. "I got something in the village today. Something that's going to make things much clearer."

Scowling, he trained his gaze up. "A painting of you? Are you giving it to me as a... present?" The word sounded foreign on his tongue. "I don't want it. Get out."

Kakka. I strained to keep my tone neutral. "It's not a present. Just look at it, then look at me."

I pointed to the lovely, radiant picture of Princess Emiana of Lyrica, then pointed to myself, shook my head hard, then repeat.

The curse wouldn't let me speak my true name. It wouldn't let me write it down. It wouldn't let me give clues to my identity. I couldn't even describe my true face to the artist I met in the market square. But a painting of Emiana... that was easily done.

I thought of a million ways to get through to him that I'm not the princess, and he was teaching a poor peasant to rule his kingdom. In the end, simple was best.

His eyes narrowed to slits, the line down his brow growing more pronounced.

"Yes, yes," I cried. *He's getting it. He understands!* "Take me home. I have to go back—"

"Argh!" He jumped in the water, splashing half the bath in my shrieking mouth. "Enough of your presents and pantomime games. My *tiny little fella* failed to satisfy you last night."

The face of evil. It was before me.

"Seven orgasms weren't enough. Fucking you until you blacked out—twice." He tangled in my hair, ever so slowly drawing my head back. Alisdair was daring me to stop him, and loving that I wasn't. "Not enough.

"Clearly I have to redouble my efforts." He licked a stripe up my chin. "I'm going to fuck you until all the water's left this bath."

"What does that mean?" I cried. "The bath doesn't drain!"

But I knew what he meant. I knew all too well.

Our promise was that if he caught me, he was free to ravage me within an inch of my life, and I was the silly mare who didn't even run. Despite my ravings that morning, last night was the best sex anyone ever had, and I didn't need the samplings of other men to know it. Alisdair found every one of my body's treasure troves and plundered it for gold.

I rocked back against the rim, brought my feet up, and kicked in his chest.

That doesn't mean I'm making it easy for him.

He stumbled back and I shot past him—kicking and slapping at the water. I never did learn how to swim.

Claws clamped around my ankle and dragged me under.

The world disappeared in a soundless kaleidoscope of color. Hands grabbed mine. Threading our fingers together, he pinned my palms to the bottom of the water basin. No hesitation. No preparation. Alisdair buried inside me with one hard thrust.

My cry was bubbles in the water, floating to the surface to escape. I would not be joining them.

Alisdair started pumping, setting a furious, out-of-control, animal pace. Every breath I tried to hold exploded out of me in an ecstatic scream. Drowning has never been so pleasurable.

Alisdair was a monster. An evil, arrogant, impatient monster who used people as pawns, and crushed them when they ceased being useful. So why, in Meya's wisdom, did he not fuck like one?

If there was any justice in this world, his true face would be as hideous as his cursed one. His overconfidence would mask his insecurity over having a minuscule penis besieged by a hairy mole twice its size. He'd be selfish in bed, hoarding his own pleasure and leaving his partner bored, unsatisfied, and cold.

Something that was *not* his hand slipped between my legs, found my clit, and rubbed it so vigorously, my back snapped in half arching off the floor.

If he was the monster at night that he was during the day... I could hate him so much less.

I hated that my body responded to him. Hated that I was choking on moans more than water. Hated that my mouth snarled at him while my pussy begged for him.

He was making a fool of me...

Alisdair's lips pressed to my neck. The pinprick of pain smothered under my exploding orgasm, chasing away my rage at being marked again. Chasing away all thought entirely. The only thing that anchored me to reality was the shape of his smirk against my skin.

Yes, he was making a fool of me, and he knew it.

***

I woke up on the bottom of the dry bath basin. An unnaturally hairy arm slung a possessive grip over my waist.

Carefully, I wiggled free—stifling a groan over all the aches and sores that woke with me. Alisdair taught me my fourth lesson of the day. Never taunt him about sex... because he'll prove me wrong.

Sighing, I glanced up at the painting. A simple plan, but I had faith it would work. At least it would get him to question. Wonder why I was acting so strangely, and from there he'd begin to wonder other things.

"It was never going to be that easy," I said softly, getting to my feet. "Oh well." I walked—*limped*—away. "Time for plan B."

Chapter Seven

I entered the throne room later that morning, and my brows climbed for another reason.

"What's this?" I swept the bare, quiet, near-empty room. "Is the heat cycle over?"

"No, Lady Ana." She tipped her head to Alisdair, secretly smiling. "He saw that they bothered you, and ordered all but the guards on duty away."

"Oh," I said simply.

Such a thoughtful thing to do, I thought, gazing upon the whole and handsome Shadowsoul once again. *Must mean he's about to do something I'll hate even more.*

The guards clapped their hands over their noses, pressing their backs harder against the walls. I had a feeling they'd run out of the room if they were able. The night before, Alisdair covered me with so many mating marks, I had breaks all over my skin like the brush marks of the painting.

"What do I smell like?" I asked. "Is it a bad scent?"

"Just the opposite." Aeris brushed an ant-sized speck of fluff from my shoulder. Meya forbid I look less than perfect on her watch. "You smell like rain, pine, and almond pastries baked with honey."

Like Alisdair.

The man was a filthy, rabid beast who belonged on a leash... but he didn't smell like one. He smelled like every free, good, and delicious thing in this world.

Just another quality I hated about him.

It was the trick of the predator. The wolf with the soft, inviting fur. The lion with the cute wet nose and majestic mane. The fierce beauty of the leopard. All of it designed to lure you in, getting you close enough until there's no chance to scream because they've already ripped out your throat.

"It's having a much different effect on you than it is me." Bradach marched on my other side—stiff-backed and jaw clenched. "Although it might not be bad, every sense is screaming at me to get as far away from you as possible," he gritted.

"So listen to them," Aeris snapped, dropping her sweet tone immediately.

Bradach's grin couldn't be killed, not even among his obvious discomfort. "And deprive you ladies the gift of my presence? I wouldn't dare."

"I assure you, we'll survive."

I smothered a giggle.

Bradach held up his end of the bargain, despite humiliating me in the process, so as promised, I announced that he was to be my personal guard.

Well, to be accurate, *he* announced it when he blew into my dressing room in the middle of me changing. He and Aeris had been bickering ever since.

I studied them both out of the corner of my eye. It was hard to figure their relationship. Bradach flirted and threw himself at her every chance he got. Aeris rebuffed him every time—*hard*. But in the short time I'd known her, I got the sense that if she really wanted something to stop, it stopped.

Did she enjoy his attention and making him work for it? Or had I sold my soul to another smirking devil for nothing?

As I climbed the dais, Alisdair's tail grew from his body, wrapped around my throne, and drew it closer to him. I took one look at the thing and blushed. He took one look at me, and smirked.

Kakka, I mentally spat, though I was too busy staring at the floor to speak it. I did not want to think about the part that tail played in last night's activities.

Foalan was already posted at his side. Bradach claimed a spot next to me, standing even further away than the day before.

"Let them in."

Aeris heeded Alisdair's command, opening the doors to a new wave of villagers. They poured in—a familiar face among them.

I sat up a little straighter, fighting to keep the smile off my lips. *Plan B.*

I'm coming home, faywens. This promise I will keep.

He maneuvered his way to the front of the line and bowed to Alisdair. "Riordan, my lord. I've come to accept the job of royal traveling merchant," he said, "and thank you for the opportunity."

"I don't recall bestowing such a title on you." Alisdair slid a look to me. "Care to explain, my queen?"

I smiled wide. "We spoke of this yesterday, Alisdair, don't you remember? Someone who can pass as Lyrican will pose as a merchant, and open trade between our kingdoms." I produced a scroll from the folds of my skirt. "I have the merchant license right here. He can leave immediately."

"Can he?" Alisdair gave me a long, measuring look. "Why did you choose him? Do you know him?"

"No," I said simply. It was the only thing Emiana's mouth would allow me to say. "I never saw him before the day we rolled past him in the square, but I chose him because he's unchanged. What other reason would there be?" I asked. "Is there a problem? We did discuss this."

"So we did." Amusement laced his tone—both confusing and worrying me.

Why did it always feel like he was seeing right through me?

"Very well." Alisdair snapped his fingers and the merchant license flew out of my hands and into Riordan's. "Your cart and horses will be prepared for you to leave tomorrow. Go."

Riordan claimed the scroll and scurried out, sparing me a single glance on his way out. I kept the grin off my face.

Alisdair was watching me.

"Let go! Let me go!"

A man with a gorilla's face appeared in the entrance, and disappeared just as quickly. Grunting, he came back dragging an elbow, then the furry-faced boy that came with it.

Furry ears on top of his head; burnished-red fur starting on his forehead, continuing up his head, then down his back; an unnatural lengthening of his nose and mouth. He was obviously a fox faeriken, and even more obviously, he couldn't be more than ten years of age.

"Get off me!" He launched at the man and sunk his teeth in his arm.

"Argh!" Pain wracked his face, but the man did not let go. "My lord," he gritted. "I am Jotham. I request... to be seen f-first."

Alisdair flapped a hand at him. "Proceed."

Jotham hauled the boy in front of us and kicked the back of his legs, dropping him to his knees.

"Easy," I cried. "You don't need to be so rough."

"There is every need, my queen." Jotham was a portly man with the face, legs, and feet of a gorilla, but the rest of him was fae. It made him an even odder sight than the rest. "This little demon stole my entire basket of strawberry jam, then in his escape, slipped on the ice and broke them all."

"Geroff!" The boy pummeled his fist, straining to bite Jotham again.

"I used the last of my strawberries to make that jam," he continued. "They're my best sellers. The food and coin he's cost me— My family was relying on it! Because of him, we'll starve until the next harvest."

Jotham shook him. "I demand he be punished in the strictest sense. These thieves don't care who they hurt, who they ruin. I have a hungry boy too. Why should he starve because this brat refuses to work for a meal?"

Alisdair's expression hadn't changed throughout his entire speech. I doubted mine was as cool. I darted between the three of them, nearly tipping off the edge of my seat from wanting to grab that poor boy away from him.

I was once a hungry child who grabbed food off the back of a cart and didn't pay for it. Someone grabbed my wrist just like that, and hauled me before a man as terrifying as Alisdair. That was the worst day of my life, and I've had many.

"Let him go," Alisdair said. "He won't run."

Jotham obeyed, and the first thing the boy did was run.

He didn't make it a step.

Shouting, he dropped flat on his face—his left foot glued to the floor. His furious glare hit Alisdair right in the face.

"Where are your parents, boy?" Alisdair asked.

For a spell, I thought he wouldn't answer. "Dead," he finally snapped. "Brother, too. It's just me now."

"I see." He looked to Foalan. "Cut off his hands."

"What!"

The boy burst into tears as Foalan stepped off the dais.

"Foalan, don't move," I barked, shooting up. "You're not cutting off anything. You're not putting hand or magic on that boy!" I whirled on Alisdair. "What is wrong with you! Are you insane?"

Alisdair picked at something under his claw. "Being an orphan doesn't excuse thievery, little bird. Destroying a man's livelihood must be punished. The law is unforgiving, but it is the law."

"What law!"

He looked me straight in the eyes. "Me."

I clamped down hard on my jaw, penning in a string of obscenities that would've made half the room faint.

"No," I forced out, "being orphaned doesn't excuse thievery, but it does explain it. He's alone in the world and he needs our help. We'll help you," I said, turning on the little boy. "And, Sir Jotham, we'll pay you what you would've made for the jam."

I clapped. "Bradach, Aeris, will you see to it that Jotham gets his payment, and that this boy—"

"Sentence denied," Alisdair sliced in. "Foalan, continue."

Foalan converged on him, ratcheting the boy's screams louder.

"I told you not to fucking move!" I jumped between them, and tore Foalan's sword from its sheath. I leveled it directly against his heart. "Why would you reject my solution?" I demanded of Alisdair, but stayed fixed on Foalan. Commander of Lumenfell's army, I knew I only disarmed him because he let me. When he made a move to get his sword back, I had to be ready.

"There's no reason for you to say no."

"There's every reason. This isn't an orphanage or a charity. Once word gets out that you're throwing coin at every merchant with a down-on-their-luck story, and taking in every weepy beggar child, we'll be inundated with pleas—and then despised by everyone rejected."

My eyes narrowed to slits. "Don't give me that horseshit. When the bird faeriken were stealing, coin and housing are exactly what you gave them!"

"In exchange for work," he bellowed back, slamming his fist on the chair arm. "They couldn't fight their instincts. This boy has no such excuse. Foalan!"

I growled at Foalan when he dared to twitch. "I'll shove this sword so far through your heart, it'll come out your ass!" Little arms threw around my waist, hugging me in a death grip. "You're not hurting this child, Alisdair. You think it's some kind of problem if other orphans find out I helped him, and come with their hands out?

"I say nothing would make me happier, not even if Meya parted the clouds and struck you down dead. Me and all the forgotten children of Lumenfell will toast your death with the golden goblets collecting dust in your front hall, while wearing the diamonds, necklaces, and crowns rusting in the hall above that one!"

"Diamonds don't rust!"

"Argh!" Swinging my arms up, I lobbed the sword across the dais—flinging it directly at his head.

"Tiresome woman!" Magic stopped the tip an inch from his nose, and sent it soaring away.

Bradach cawed, jumping out of the way. The sword stuck in the wall, pinning his feather to the stone.

"Fine!" Alisdair broke the chair arm slamming his fist. It was made of pure bronze. "Since you're so attached to the thieving little beggar, he shall receive your sentence.

"Aeris, send him to the slave marts!"

I backed away, keeping both Foalan and Aeris in my sights. The boy stumbled back with me. "That is not what I said."

Alisdair's grin was nasty. "You said he should be treated like the bird faeriken."

"Oh my Meya, you enslaved them?" I rasped. "You— You— Monster!"

"Aeris, you were given an order."

I held him tighter. "If you dare try to sell him, I'll buy him myself. Then I'll set him free with a sack full of your riches, and your worthless severed head!"

A loud, dangerous snarl ripped from his throat—tumbling out with his lengthening fangs.

My grin was even nastier. "Those don't scare me, *husband,* they'll be between my legs soon enough."

Alisdair threw up his hands, making me lurch back. Something flew through the palace entrance and slammed into his palm. He threw it at Jotham. "Very well, the blessed queen of Lumenfell has spoken. We have bought your problem off your hands, and he now lives and works here—or he dies."

Jotham fumbled catching one of the very golden goblets I spoke of.

"Aeris, take him to the kitchens."

"Wait—"

Alisdair snapped his fingers and both Aeris and the boy were gone.

We glared each other down for a long, tense silence.

"I will find him," I hissed. "I'll set him free."

"A hollow threat. You can't even free yourself."

Deep, seething, corrosive hatred burned my soul to cinders. I ached to get away from him, or grab another sword and keep throwing until I hit something that hurt.

Lifting my chin, I climbed the dais and gingerly reclaimed my throne.

"Uh, my lord?" Jotham held up the goblet. "I don't know what to do with—"

"Get out," Shadowsoul roared, the beast ripping through his handsome visage in an instant.

Jotham stumbled over his feet running away.

In a way I could claim victory. I finally tore his calm, cool mask to shreds. We both flung back in our seats, throwing glowers and bared teeth across the divide.

Jotham blew out the door, nearly colliding with a newcomer. He sidestepped the fleeing man and entered the room, blowing through my rage.

"Seems I missed something interesting." He smiled at me. "Hopefully not so interesting it's put you in a bad mood, Queen Ana. I've come to request your favor."

"Brother." Foalan advanced on him. "What do you think you're doing here?"

Meallan pulled a face. "Brother? Who are—? Oh, Meya. Foalan, is that you? I didn't recognize you without the leash."

Growls erupted from Foalan, which set the naked Meallan off too. They appeared on the edge of ripping each other's limbs off.

Definitely not close siblings.

"You don't belong here, Meallan. Leave!"

"No, you don't belong here!" Meallan jabbed his chest. "You're a wolf. One of us! Yet you run around here playing lapdog to a king, when you should be king. You should be alpha!"

Foalan's eyes flashed. "We are not wolves, Meallan. We're men!"

"We are gods," he growled. "Stronger, faster, better than man and wolf. We are—"

Alisdair flicked his finger. That was it. A single flick, and Meallan and Foalan blew apart, crashing into opposite walls.

"T-too right, my lord." Foalan staggered to his feet, his forehead openly bleeding. "Thank you for punishing us for our disrespect."

The only response from the pile that was Meallan was angry growls, snaps, and roars.

I winced looking at him. He was unfortunate enough to fall ass over his head. His cock and balls flapped around like two rotund people straining to stick a pole on top of an ass crack.

"You test my already strained patience." Alisdair struck a glare through me to belie the words. "You will tell me why you're breaking the truce by crossing territories, or I'll move straight to killing you for it."

Meallan righted himself, mouth practically foaming with rage. He was nothing like the odd, smirking, calm stranger I met in the winter woods.

"You wouldn't dare," he barked, blowing my brows high.

With what kind of confidence, strength, or secret magic weapon did he speak to Alisdair that way? And where did I get it too?

"I am not here for you, toy king. I'm here for her."

I looked from Meallan, my surroundings, then back to him. The fact remained he was looking at me. "Excuse me? Here for me?"

"That's right, Queen Emiana, ruler of nothing and owned by no one." His brows smoothed out as his grin returned. "Surely you remember me? Why, wasn't it just the other night we had a delightful, naked interlude in the woods?"

A low, hair-raising, blood-chilling sound filled the room, tightening my grip on the chair arms. I'd heard Alisdair growl many times, but this was worse. Much, much... worse.

"Watch yourself." Bradach stepped forward. His grin was nowhere to be seen.

I blinked at him. I'd never seen such a murderous expression on his face before. Its closest match was Foalan's as they both converged on Meallan.

"Disrespect my queen again, and I'll introduce Foalan to his new *sister*." A blade appeared in Bradach's hand. He swiped his tongue across the tip, driving his point brutally home. "Go on. I dare you."

"Absolutely not, Bradach," Foalan said smoothly. "If anyone is going to turn this cur into a pup"—two swords were in his hands in a blink—"it'll be me."

Meallan laughed, further shocking me with his confidence. I didn't say how I knew, but Bradach and Foalan weren't joking.

"Settle down, pets. As I said, this is between me and Lady Ana." His gaze trapped mine over their shoulders. "You swore if we met again, you'd honor your debt and gift me a favor. That night has come."

Alisdair half rose from his seat. "Favor?"

"Correct." He shoved past Bradach and Foalan. "Your queen broke the truce and entered our territory. Not only did I spare you the death I was owed by rights, but I offered her shelter, and then aided her on her way when it was denied."

"What? That's nonsense. Lies," he barked. "You wouldn't do any one of those things. You'd skin your own mother and wear her for a coat if the breeze shifted. Not for a moment would I believe you spared and *offered her sanctuary*." Alisdair laughed nastily. "Get out, or I'll castrate you my—"

"But it's true."

All eyes flew to me. Alisdair's, Bradach's, Foalan's, and the watching villagers. Shock twisted their faces.

"What? What's wrong?" I asked, skin prickling. "He did offer to shelter me among his people the night I tried to outrun you and the runes. I said no, so he taught me how to mask my scent." The conversation came back to me. "I also said that I would help him like he helped me if I ran into him again, but, no offense, Meallan, I was hoping we would not see each other again." I turned a burning sneer on Alisdair. "Because it meant I didn't escape *him*."

"My deepest apologies, Lady Ana. Believe it or not, even though I'm here today, I did ask Meya to bless your feet, and curse his."

A large, dark figure was suddenly between us, overwhelming my nose with pine, rain, and nutty shaela bread drizzled with orange jam.

Yes, I thought, inhaling deep before I knew what I was doing. *That's Alisdair's scent. Empty, deceptive, a lie.*

"You come here today for your death. She was not my mate when she entered your territory, or when she granted you favor."

Meallan tsked. "Come now. You know as well as I those distinctions only would've mattered if she succeeded in escaping the mating bond. Now you are one. Your soul, your power, your promises are bound by magics we cannot comprehend... or defy.

"I will ask my favor, and it will be granted, or by rights I will claim the life I spared."

The sentence penetrated, clenching my jaw tight. Did Meallan just say he'd kill me if he didn't get what he wanted?

"There's no need for this. Enough with the shouting and threats." I pushed up and stepped out from behind Alisdair. "I swear, I've been in rowdy taverns filled with pissing, puking drunks that behave with more decorum.

"What is your favor, Meallan? Ask it already."

He bowed low. "Of course, Lady Ana. It is a simple request. One that in time we'll find is best for our people. Will you—?"

"No," Alisdair sliced in. "Now get out."

I shoved around him. "Will I what?"

"Will you dissolve the invisible border and allow the wolf faeriken to rejoin Lumenfell, its people, and your rule?"

Foalan dropped his swords. I thought I knew what shock looked like on his face. That expression blew it out of the water. "Dissolve the— You jest," he cried. "This is a trick!"

"It is no trick, it's sire's wish," Meallan replied to him, but looked at me. "Too long we've been separated, and we're both suffering for it. The successful union of your king and one of the stunted's princesses showed us we were wrong."

Stunted? They call normal faeriken stunted!?

"We can exist as one people," Meallan continued. "No matter which animal calls to us. So, what say you, my queen?"

My queen. Not Lady Ana.

"Will you end the conflict and unite our people?"

"No!"

I blinked and Alisdair was in front of me. Towering over me. Growling at me. Beseeching me. *Begging* me.

Imperceptibly, he shook his head. "Princess," he whispered. "Don't."

War raged in my head. Something was going on here that I didn't know or understand. Why was it a bad thing to end the conflict between them, and bring all the faeriken together? It was only the day before that Alisdair ripped the throats of two crocodile faeriken for committing the very sin of not working together. It wasn't a bad thing, except—

Alisdair's eyes said in every way that it was. At least with this fae-wolf and this conflict, the answer had to be no.

"Yes," I said, confident and clear. "I end the conflict, dissolve the borders, and unite our people." I smiled into his darkening eyes. "Meallan, your favor is granted."

Meallan said something. Foalan said something. Everyone in the room sounded, yelling and shouting on top of each other. All of it faded around us.

Alisdair closed the distance, bumping my chin against his chest. He spoke one word.

"Why?"

I balled my fists. Rising on tiptoe, I brought the venom etched in my face as close to him as it would go without seeping into his body. "I wanted you to free that boy and save him. Seems that neither one of us is granting each other favor today, *husband*.

"Huzzah, huzzah, my people, shout huzzah," I rang out, my voice echoing through the cavernous room. "For Princess Emiana has achieved the purpose for which she was solely born. To be the bargaining token for the end of war."

Alisdair's anger was a palpable, oppressive atmosphere—more oppressive than the marking pheromones that choked half the guards. Slowly, he turned his back on me and reclaimed his throne.

"My queen has spoken," he announced in the throne room, surprising me. "The wolf territory is dissolved and reclaimed for the wealth and prosper of Lumenfell. We are one people once more."

If I expected cheers and huzzahs, I did not get it.

No one moved. No one spoke. After a beat, Meallan dipped his head in a semblance of a bow. Turning away, he left without another word.

Alisdair was similarly silent watching him go. When the door slammed shut, he flicked to Foalan.

"You know what to do."

Foalan deferred him a proper bow, and strode out of the throne room.

I glanced at Alisdair but he didn't glance back. I sensed I had gone too far.

The boy's cries rang in my ear. *So did he.*

"A tip, my husband," I said lightly. "You can easily be rid of me and these innocent mistakes, if you run slower."

He didn't reply. I wasn't sure he heard me.

A mousy woman approached the dais. Yes, mouse. Twitching nose and whiskers drew my eyes, though I tried not to stare.

"Ethna, my lord." She bowed low, then didn't make it all the way up—hanging her head. "We have but one request."

"We?" I asked. No one else stood at her side, or looked in her direction.

"We ask that you allow us to kill the stunted queen."

I froze, eyes blinking rapidly. I couldn't have heard what I thought I did.

"What did you say?" Alisdair hissed, obviously suffering from the same roaring that sounded in my ears.

"When we heard that she broke the treaty and destroyed our chance for peace, we knew she was dangerous to you and Lumenfell, my lord. Now after what we've just witnessed? Her dissolving the borders so that the wolves can descend and devour us all..." She shook her head. "It's clear her only goal is to ruin us. The stunted have taken so much from us"—she raised her head, revealing an expression that wasn't nervousness, but hate—"they will not take anymore."

"Guards," Bradach roared, but it was already too late.

The entire line of villagers burst into action. Half split in every direction, running to meet the guards. The remaining, including Mousy, ran straight at me.

Scales, fangs, claws, feathers, fur, and cursed hybrids I couldn't begin to name rushed me in a horrifying parade. Clapping their hands together, they ripped them apart. Stone broke off from the wall dozens of places, shaking the throne room on its foundation.

The stone collided together, then flew at me.

"Aahhh!"

"Ana!"

A flash of feathers, then a hard force smacked into me and threw me out of the chair. I screamed as I was lifted into the air. This was the end. After everything I'd done. One day away from escape and freedom, I would die.

I kept going up, and up, and up. *Why aren't I falling?*

Prying my eyes open, I came face-to-red-face with Bradach. He held me tight, forehead dripping sweat, and soared away from the madness below. "H-hold on—"

"Are you okay? Why are you—? Ahh!"

Claws sunk into his back, hooking into muscle, bone, and sinew. The cat faeriken grinned at me with sharpened teeth. "Release your prize, little bird."

I shuddered. I didn't think anyone else could make that awful pet name sound worse.

The stones pummeled my throne, burying it under a brutal grave that was meant for me. One by one they fell off the pile, took to the air, and narrowed on me.

"Bradach, look out!" I screamed, but as the cry left my lips, I knew it was too late.

He was slowing down—wings beating furiously to carry me, and our hanger-on.

Stones converged on us from all sides, flying together to crush us into nothing. Fur flew at my face, making me shoot back screaming as she sunk her teeth into Bradach's neck.

Bellowing, his wings crumpled.

We fell.

Bradach released me. Hand slicing through the air, a wave of magic blasted my body—plunging me cold. My descent slowed. The rocks slowed.

Bradach didn't.

"*Ferramenta!*"

The dais rushed to meet him. Out of nowhere, a large mass erupted beneath Bradach and the platform, catching, then bouncing him groaning to the floor.

A sofa? Where did that—?

His hold on his magic broke, and I plummeted. A rain of stone fell to meet me.

"Ana!"

Arms caught and held me to a hard chest. We collapsed on the dais, and the rocks fell—pummeling his body too hard and brutally, I felt every strike resound through his body into me.

Alisdair pulled me in tighter, shielding me so completely with his arms and body, he had no protection for himself.

The last stone struck... and silence fell.

My chest heaved—eyes rolling in my head. *I almost died. They tried to kill me! If it wasn't for Bradach. If it wasn't for... Alisdair.*

He saved my life. Protected me. When only minutes before, he glared at me like he hated me, and wanted nothing more than to go back and plunge the sword through me at the altar.

"A... na?"

My breath caught. I didn't dare to move. To think.

Alisdair lifted his head as far as he could, resting his forehead on mine. A true grimace of pain ravaged his features. "Are you... okay?"

"Yes," I whispered.

I tried to stop myself. With every ounce of will and hatred in my soul, I rebelled against my body, but I couldn't stop the hand cupping his cheek. I couldn't stop the words leaving my lips.

"Thank you."

Yes, he was a terrible, brutal monster who killed innocents and chopped off children's hands, but I couldn't get back to my family if I was dead. He saved me. He saved them from believing for the rest of their lives that I ran away and abandoned them. How could I not say—

"Thank you, Alisdair."

He tensed.

"Alisdair?"

Head snapping up, he inhaled deeply—growls leaking through his growing fangs.

"Shit!" Bradach shouted.

Alisdair leaped off me. I flipped over as he launched at Bradach, claws lengthening to tear him limb from limb. Bradach took to the air and flew out the village entrance—Alisdair hot on his tail.

I pushed up on shaky knees. A guard—a female guard—came quickly to help me on my feet.

Leaning on her, my eyes took in the sight before me. "Furniture," I blurted. Nothing smarter came to my lips, but it didn't have to. Furniture summed it up.

All of a sudden, the throne room was filled with chairs, tables, chaises, and lounges. I blinked to see those were the large pieces. A broom and mop leaned against the wall where there previously were none. Two new rugs fell across the dais. Resting on the remains of my throne was, of all things, a teapot. Sprinkled around the pot were the smashed remains of a few teacups.

The strange new additions scattered about the throne room, and everywhere they were, a purple bud grew out of fiber or stone, flowering in the most impossible place.

"Is this—?" I croaked. "Are these the...?"

"Villagers," the guard said, leading me out of the room. "Yes."

"But..." My throat was dry. "Magic to transform one living being into an inanimate object would take so much out of you, it'd kill you. To do all of these people at once... I don't..." I trailed off, words failing me.

"Your husband, our lord, is a great and powerful man," she said, pride leaking out of her. "Nothing can stop him. No one can stand in his way."

"Yes," I rasped as the doors closed behind him. "I'm beginning to see that now."

***

"Are you sure he's okay?"

Aeris scoffed. "That fool is fine. Do not trouble yourself over Bradach, my lady."

Sitting me down at the vanity, Aeris began the process of unloosing my braids, and combing my hair until it shone.

"But it's my fault he's now banned from the castle until the marking scent fades," I argued. "I should've chosen a personal guard who could touch me without getting killed by my husband."

"You have such a guard." She nodded to Eadaoin in the mirror, who waved back. "That idiot knew he wasn't your guard. He was hanging around you for no reason, just seeking out trouble where he can find it."

I bit my lip, guilt burning my gut. *Bradach was hanging around me, because he wanted to be closer to you.* "Aeris, the only trouble he got into today was risking his life to save mine."

"I—" Hesitating, her frown softened. "I know, I know. Forgive me. Bradach did well today. He showed bravery I didn't know he had in him, and put your safety ahead of his own. He just... scared me," she said under her breath. "And surprised me. I don't like it when he does either."

It was funny, but I knew exactly what she meant. Alisdair both scared and surprised me that day too, and hours later, I couldn't sort through my jumbled feelings to understand why it unsettled me so much.

After Alisdair chased Bradach out into the village and sent him flying for the mountains, court was closed. I spent some time catching my breath in our freezing bedchamber, before changing and heading down to the war room. Part of me thought that Alisdair would breeze in while I studied the maps of all the places I dreamed of going.

It was Aeris who finally stuck her head in. She summoned me for a bath and dinner in my dressing room—alone.

Alisdair and I left things in such an odd place. He went from furious at me, to saving my life, then trying to kill an innocent man for touching me. What was I supposed to make of all that? What would I say to him that night when he came for me?

"Aeris, can I ask you something? What is this?" I produced the purple flower I tucked into my pocket that morning. It was so pretty, I couldn't resist. Part of me hoped to bring it home to Mama and my fay-wens, and plant a whole bush of them on our patch. "I've never seen a flower like this."

She glanced up, eyes bugging.

"It's obviously a magical flower but—"

"My lady!" Her shout made me jump. A quick wave of her hand, and the flower crumbled to dust.

"Aeris," I cried. "What was that for?"

"I'm sorry, Lady Ana. I didn't mean to startle you. It's just that by law, we have to destroy those flowers on sight."

"Wait, what?" I slapped at my hand. "Is it poisonous?"

"Not to us," she muttered.

Aeris tipped my head down, going for the braids along my neck. I wanted to ask her why she went through the trouble of doing my hair into intricate braids in the morning, only to undo her work that night. I wanted to ask, but I sensed I already knew.

The life of a paper princess is as tedious as a paper queen. We did all these pointless, time-wasting tasks to distract me from the fact that this kingdom survived without me for a century, it continued on during my presence, and would carry along just fine long after I left.

"That flower is poisonous to our Lord Shadowsoul."

My body went rigid. "Excuse me? What did you say?"

"The All Mother demands a balanced world. All things are born. All things die. She will not stand for an immortal being—although many have used magic and curses to achieve that very end."

I stared at my lap, listening close.

"Lord Lumenfell may very well be the most powerful being in this land or any other, but Meya always has the last word. Whenever he uses great amounts of magic—those flowers spring up. As I said, they're poisonous to him."

My mind spun. "Are you allowed to tell me this?"

"If you were anyone else, no. But you are his queen," Aeris replied. "You have to know so that you can protect him in battle as he will protect you. Husband and wife. Mate and eternal mate. Your weaknesses end where the other's strength begin."

"Too right you are," I murmured, gazing at the ash. "Thank you for telling me, Aeris. Thank you very much."

Soon Aeris finished combing my hair, then braided it into a single braid for bed. Meya knew the mattress called to me louder than it ever did before. How could it not when I spent the last two nights beneath Alisdair, instead of beneath the sheets.

I wanted sleep, but that would have to wait.

I paused at the threshold. "Eadaoin, are you coming with me?"

"I am, my queen, but if I smell him coming, I will have to leave. I may be your guard, but you made promises to your mate before Meya. No one is allowed to come between that."

It'd be a long time before I got used to the word mate. These were such old words, for old traditions, borne in an ancient world we left behind when we left the forests and decided we wanted to live like the humans.

"I understand. This is between me and Alisdair." Bradach flashed through my mind. "I don't want anyone else hurt for standing between us."

I set off, knowing Eadaoin would follow.

"Will you be running through the village?" Eadaoin asked. "I'm sure all the plotters were taken out in the attack, but in case there are more lurking in the village, a disguise wouldn't go amiss."

I shook my head. "I'm not going into the village. I'm not running at all tonight."

Her white whiskers twitched. "You're not?"

"No need. I'll be on my way tomorrow night. I've waited this long, I can hold out for one more night."

"Then where are we going?"

"I was hoping for a tour of the castle. More specifically, the servants' quarters."

She gave me a funny look, but shrugged. "As you wish, my queen."

***

Eadaoin led me through winding halls, reaching staircases, and grand rooms.

I asked to see the servants' quarters, but she took her time, leading me on a tour of the castle. With every minute that passed, I relaxed... because Alisdair wasn't coming.

There was no way he couldn't find me. I wasn't hiding or masking my scent. He was free to pounce and straddle me any time. Either he wasn't because arguing with him about the fox boy and granting Meallan his favor pissed him off so much he wanted rid of me. Or, he was seriously injured when he shielded my body from an avalanche of falling stone, and he was holed up somewhere recovering.

I wasn't sure which truth I wanted it to be.

"—and this, my queen, is the servants' hall." She threw open double doors. "This is where we take our meals and our breaks. Although, we don't have to break in here. Our lord gives us freedom to roam the castle. I myself prefer to lunch in the gardens."

"Uh-huh," I croaked, eyes darted around. "It's nicer here than I expected. The servants' quarters in the castle Lyrica is— It's— It's—"

I tried to speak of the plain, undecorated, utilitarian space I was forced in that fateful night in the castle, but the words wouldn't come out. That's when I realized Emiana had no idea what the servants' quarters were like in her own home. She never bothered to look.

"I don't know what it's like," I finished. "But I'm going to guess it's nothing like this."

"Hmm. Because the bookshelves, couches, and art?" Eadaoin asked. She gasped. "Or are their quarters even grander? All of Elva knows nothing can rival the beauty of the Crystal Palace."

"Uhh, no." I flushed hard. "That wasn't the difference I was thinking of."

The faeriken man finally lost—or won?—the tug-of-war with his cock, and threw his head back, glutes tightening. He perched on the dining tabletop, roughly ejaculating on the face of a pretty young woman with brilliant white feathers where hair should be. Said woman bent over the table, balancing on tiptoe, while another guy pounded her ass from the back.

It had been like this in nearly every room we walked into, and more than a few of the open hallways. Faeriken in heat going at each other like the continuation of the species depended on them.

Continuation of the species? a voice scoffed. *Unless these three need a conversation from their mamas on where babies come from, they know full well none of the things they were doing would result in a baby.*

This wasn't out-of-control heat cycles driving them to reproduce. This was sex. Pure and simple.

The man behind spread her legs apart even farther, and started pumping like a madman—ratcheting her moans to deafening.

I tried to look past them, and the couple on the couch in the corner, and commit this room and its place on my mental map to memory. It was quite nice with its long, communal table, overflowing bookshelves lining the far wall, comfy couches to recline, and paintings of rolling green hills and verdant forests.

"It's a good thing that I haven't seen any children yet," I remarked, "but where are they? Do you have your own rooms? Would a child servant have his own room? Or do you share living quarters?"

"We have our own rooms," Eadaoin replied.

Begs the question of why these sexual proceedings aren't taking place in their rooms.

"But the children don't, nor do they share a living quarter."

"Then where are they?"

She gave me a knowing look—decipherable even under her orange fur. "I know who you're looking for, Lady Ana, but I don't know where he is. Sometimes my lord employs children to work in the castle, but they never do."

"Never do?" I stopped dead. "Never do what?"

"Work." She looked away. "I've never seen them making beds, sweeping floors, or bringing down food trays. They're never running through the gardens, or clearing snow off the paths. Children come to Castle Riagin, and then they just... disappear."

I stared at her, trembling. "Disappear? How can they disappear?"

"I don't know, my queen. This castle has many secrets. That is one of them." She turned around and continued on.

I glared at her back. "What does he do to them! What does he do while you all hide your heads and sing false praises!"

She whirled around, glaring right back. But on her, with her two-inch fangs, it was more effective. "I don't know that he does anything to them," she snapped, "and neither do you, so I'd refrain from impugning my honor and the honor of our lord."

I clenched my teeth, throat burning. It wasn't the first time it struck me that the servants in Castle Riagin were much more comfortable speaking to their royals as equals. Kaelan was Emiana's lover, and he still snapped his jaw shut on a single look from her. Faeriken were not so cowed.

Of course they weren't. Dozens of them just tried to assassinate me in front of Alisdair.

Swallowing my anger, I spoke in a more even tone. "Where could they be if they're not in the castle? How do I find him?"

"I think you know there's only one person who can answer that."

I balled and unballed my fist, bursting with the urge to hunt *him* down and get that answer. Tomorrow was my last day in Lumenfell. I either found him before I left, or I came back for him after rescuing my family. Either way, this was another promise this liar had no intention of breaking.

"Let's go," I finally said, brushing past her. "You may not know where he is, doesn't mean no one else does. Shadowsoul ordered Aeris to bring him to the kitchens. We'll start there."

Eadaoin didn't fight me. Our tour continued on to the kitchens, which was filled with more rutting couples, threesomes, foursomes, and fivesomes. I tried asking a few of them questions about the boy, but got the hint and scurried away when a woman with a lot of teeth, a lot of claws, and a lot of fur snapped at me.

Eadaoin clapped me on the shoulder. "Are you sure you aren't in need of my sexual services, Lady Ana? It seems our lord has left you to your own pleasures tonight, and you are very tense." She held out her arms. "This is why I'm here. To make sure your every need is catered to always."

I studied her, cutting the instant rejection off on my tongue. "Eadaoin, what do you think of fae?"

"Pardon?"

"Fae like me," I said. "Unchanged fae. Do you think me stunted? Different? Wrong?"

Discomfort etched into her face. "Well... yes," she replied, surprising me. "How can you not be, my queen? Your magic was bound and stolen from you, and there's a slow and torturous death awaiting you because of it. Of course you're wrong." She gently touched my elbow. "Don't you think so as well?"

My lips parted, but nothing came out. Of all the reasons why I thought they called us stunted, that wasn't on the list. It wasn't all of us they were speaking of. It was just the faewomen. It was just me.

"Why aren't women bound here?" I heard myself ask. "Not that you should be. I guess I don't understand how Shadowsoul can bestow kindness with one hand, and pain with the other. Which man is the true one?"

"I don't know," she confessed, voice soft. "Is it kindness, or is it the nature of what we are now? In nature, the males attract the females. They dance, flaunt, gift, and woo them for the mere chance of mating, and when they do mate, they don't betray their partner for petty jealousies and insecure needs for control.

"Any man who stole my magic from me would lose out on every potential mate, seconds before he lost his throat."

The corner of my mouth curved up in a smile. I already pitied the man who tried to take a single thing from Eadaoin. Even if it was just the bread roll off her plate.

"It is a long, lonely, bitter life to be cut off from love, sex, friends, companionship, family. All those things would be lost if we became a society like yours." She squeezed my arm. "All those things are lost in your society."

I was quiet for a spell. "I agree with you completely, Eadaoin. It just amazes me... that Alisdair does too."

Thump.

I spun around, brows crumpling.

Thump.

"What was that?"

"What?" Eadaoin asked.

"Didn't you hear that?" I took a step. "It sounded like a thump or a thud or something."

"I've been hearing lots of thumps and thuds on the other side of these doors."

I tipped my head. "Very true." Crossing to a window, I gazed out over the ice and snow. "Anyway, back to what you were saying. Does that mean you don't want the curse on Lumenfell to be broken?" I said it out loud, and was thankful I did. As long as I could speak of the beast curse, it hadn't taken me. "You don't want to rejoin the Elvan nation, and be a summer fae again?"

She blew out a breath. "If it means having my magic bound, my title stripped, and my future ripped away so that I can become a *forced* sexual companion—fuck no."

I snorted a laugh.

"But."

"But?" I asked.

"But... if we could keep our land and our freedom, then I think I would like"—she touched her face—"to be beautiful again."

"Oh, Eadaoin, you are beautiful."

She flushed red under her fur. "Thank you, Lady Ana."

A wandering hand grasped my backside.

"Not that beautiful!" I swatted her away. "Behave yourself, you saucy minx."

She burst out giggling, which set me off too.

We continued our walk, lapsing into conversation like old friends. Eadaoin told me of her childhood growing up in Lumenfell. Or I should say, what became of her childhood after the village that used to exist a few miles away was consumed by the curse.

I told her of the childhood that wasn't mine—the words falling easily without me having to strain to recall. It was getting easier and easier for me to access Emiana's memories. What did that mean for me? When would it get harder for me to access my own? And would I even realize when it did?

"Oh," Eadaoin cried out, running ahead in the sandstone hallway. "I can't forget. This is the commander's barracks. If you're ever searching for Foalan, you'll find him here or in the training yard." She tapped her ear. "Although, he is a wolf, so yell loud enough, and he'll find you."

"Good to know, thank you."

Eadaoin tipped her head. "He's in right now. Let's say hello."

"Oh, no, we can do that some other—"

She threw open the door, revealing the activities on the other side before I had a chance to close my eyes. I guessed the activities on the other side, and I still wasn't prepared.

Foalan was lashed to the bed with so many ropes, I didn't know where he ended and the hemp began. Two naked bird faeriken stood over his ass, whipping it with riding crops.

Foalan saw me and smiled through the gag. "Hmm. Hmh phff nnm—"

"Lovely to see you too, Foalan," I squeaked, slamming the door shut.

The noise brought a head out of his room, surveying the hall for the source. I recognized him only a second after Eadaoin.

She pushed out her chest, whiskers twitching and a low, soft purr rumbling out of her throat. The guard who had his way with her in the hall the other day gave her the same look back.

I knew where this was going.

"Eadaoin, I can take it from here. Consider yourself off duty," I said. "Go enjoy the rest of your night."

She bit her lip, winking at guard man. "Are you sure, my queen?"

"Yes, I'm—"

She took off running, leaving me and my goodbye in the dust.

Leaving everyone to their night, I crossed to a window, gazing out over a snow-covered courtyard. Frozen raindrops fell from the sky, casting a hazy curtain over the rolling black mountains. There was a peace and quiet in Lumenfell that could never be achieved in Lyrica. Something about this place—this land the stars forgot—made me feel that if I stopped and listened closely, I could hear Meya whisper her secrets on the wind.

I breathed deeply, inhaling the staunch, unforgiving chill into my lungs. Even the air fought back in Lumenfell. A kingdom where every creature demands to be free, even if it means growing wings and soaring through the trees.

Lumenfell was beautiful. I'd never utter such a truth outside of my mind, but it was truth all the same. It was wild and free and ruthless. It was the jungles and forests our race was born in. The life we abandoned for riches and society. Yes, it's beautiful—

"But it's not home," I whispered. "I am going home tomorrow night, but not to the same life. And not alone. Where are you, little boy? This is one carriage ride we can't afford to miss."

I lit on something through the curtain of white. "Is that...?"

A glass dome stuck to the end of the east wing. I assumed it was the east wing because Eadaoin started our tour in the west wing, and we didn't happen upon any room that doubled as a conservatory, sunroom, or greenhouse.

If the little fox boy was still in the castle, then searching the east wing until it turned me out into the conservatory was my only chance of finding him.

I continued on by myself, making my way out of the soldiers' barracks. On my way, I lifted diamond necklaces off their displays, gold rings out of their cases, and a silver dagger with a pearl inlay hilt off its pedestal, and tucked it away inside my bottomless pockets.

Now I understand why princesses wore all those heavy skirts and cumbersome gowns. To hide all the weapons.

"Not just the bleeding kind." I grinned, twirling an emerald-and-gold tiara around my fingertip.

I was going back, packing up my family, and we were leaving. Leaving poverty, leaving Gutter Galley, leaving Kirwan, and leaving Lyrica. Maps upon maps collected dust in that war room, charting out the many lands where we'd be free to live in peace, or with plenty of coin to buy peace, if we were so inclined.

Leave it to the real Princess Emiana to determine if there was goodness beneath Alisdair's brutality. Let her repair the cease fire she destroyed. Lumenfell was an interesting place with many mysteries, but only one was mine to solve. The rest was her fucking problem.

I wandered the halls, sticking my head in doors, calling for little fox boys, and stealing everything that fit in my pockets. The little boy couldn't come with me to a land where he'd be jailed on sight as a faeriken spy, but half of these jewels would give him a new life in one of the outer-lying towns of Wind and Wild. I was suddenly thankful Alisdair saw fit to show me where they all were.

If there's time, I'll drop him off on my way out of this frozen enigma. If there isn't time, it will take longer, but I will see to it that he gets somewhere safe.

I paused beneath a ceiling-high window, and looked upon the soldiers' barracks—stark and staring across the way. I was heading in the right direction and searching every room along the way. No sign of him. Did this castle have a dungeon? Entirely possible considering the man I was dealing with.

Thump-thump. Thump-thump.

I spun around, my head whipping this way and that. It was that sound again. Despite what Eadaoin insinuated, it didn't sound like lustful noises. The noise was both close and far away. Like the whisper shared across the room that's trapped in a dome and escapes to you.

It sounds like...

I pressed the heel of my palm to my racing heart. "Heartbeat."

Thump-thump.

My feet moved on their own power, carrying me to the end of the hall. I touched the cool stone blocking my way, announcing a dead end, and slid to the right. Stepping lightly, my slippered feet told no tales.

My hand reached the end of the wall where stone was supposed to meet stone... and slipped through.

I couldn't stop a smile. It was clever. So very clever. At first glance, all you saw was three, bare stone walls—nothing special. Only by getting close did you see that two corners didn't quite meet, leaving space for a secret.

I pulled back and darted into an empty storeroom. Moving quickly, I upended my pockets, removed all the stolen trinkets, and hid them away behind an old, battered tin bucket. That done, I returned to the secret entrance.

Wedging my shoulder through, I squeezed in—coming out into darkness.

I felt around blindly. *Stone. Stone. Stone. Air.*

My hand fell through the air, finding a break in the wall. Shuffling forward, my foot hit the bottom step. Maybe this was it? This was where Alisdair hid the boy.

Thump-thump.

Or something else.

A heady mix of nerves, surprise, and excitement sped my pulse and quickened my breath. I didn't dare to believe I'd ever find Shadowsoul's cursed heart. Such a thing never entered a mind consumed with finding a way home. But what if I had stumbled upon it?

Our lands have been at war for over a century. My father died on a battlefield fighting to see the heart found and destroyed before it wiped out our home. Now the army had its sight set on my sweet, dreamy little brother, Jaclan. Tomorrow I would run away and leave this land of winter and ice behind, and with the heart in my pocket, tomorrow could also be the day the war between Elva and the kingdom of Wind and Wild ended.

I pressed tight to the wall, climbing higher—climbing faster.

Thump-thump. Thump-thump.

A faint glow filtered down the winding passage—signaling a torch ahead, and something that needed lighting.

I was running then. Bursting to the top of the stairs, I came to challenge with a large, oak door with brass panels, a brass knob, and a small keyhole.

Thump-thump! Thump-thump!

The beating heart was deafening. It called to me. Demanded me. Needed me.

I reached for the knob. "Dare I hope..." I grasped and turned.

The door swung open to my cry of delight.

Pushing it open, I took a step.

THUMP-THUMP.

The world spun on its head.

I barely got a scream before I was shoved against the wall, and the door slammed shut—snuffing out my glee like the light blown out behind Alisdair's eyes.

"Tsk, tsk. Naughty, naughty." Alisdair molded to my body, slipping his legs between mine. He snapped his apart which tore my feet off the floor and pressed both my thighs to the barrier blocking my escape. "A lost little bird will find the most interesting places to land, but I confess, I don't much care for where your curiosity has taken you tonight." His eyes flashed. "How did you get in here?"

"I walked," I lofted, smirking despite the fact I had not a single advantage over him. "Now it's my turn to ask a question. What's in that room?"

"None of your concern."

"I've made it my concern." I shoved against his chest. "Get off! I'm going in."

"I think not." Alisdair waved a hand, and the door dissolved.

"No!" I cried, but it was already too late. It melted into stone, leaving no entrance, no room, no mark. "Argh! Tell me the truth, Alisdair. Is he in there!"

"He?" His brows smoothed out. "Aww. I see. This is about your pointless, irritating quest to be that fox boy's champion and borrowed mother. How very stupid."

My face heated. Kicking and wiggling, I strained to get my feet between me and his body so I could *kick the bastard through the wall!* "It isn't stupid to fight for the protection and safety of those with none! A kingdom isn't measured by how it caters to its strong, wealthy, and privileged. It's measured by how it gives voice to the voiceless, stands up for the vulnerable, and does what's right for all people, instead of what's convenient for some."

I scoffed. "But I wouldn't expect you, Lord Beast, King of Blood and Torn Throats, to grasp such a simple concept. You're too stupid."

A beastly growl ripped from his throat, chasing a shiver up my spine. "You are a special breed of hypocrite, Princess. You dare to lecture me on the measure of a kingdom and its king?!"

"What's that supposed to mean!?"

"Your kingdom is barbaric!"

I don't know when we started shouting, but we were each doing it as well and better than the other.

"Mine? Ha!" My insane shriek of a laugh blew his brow up. "You slaughter people as soon as you look at them, and treat my body as your personal buffet. What right have you to speak ill of my people?"

"I have the right to speak ill of anyone who looks upon you and sees anything less than absolute magnificence," he threw back. "They stole your magic because you're a woman, but you are magic itself. Your body will carry our children. Your wisdom will lead our people. Your nights in my bed will soothe me at my most savage.

"Your people are worse than barbaric for underestimating you. They're plain fools."

My heart pounded my rib cage, banging its reply against his chest. My jaw worked trying to form a response, but he did it. He struck me silent.

Did Alisdair truly see me that way? Magnificence? Magic itself? Did he hate the summer fae all the more for what they did to me?

A million blushing thoughts raced through my head, then... he smirked.

Red descended on my vision.

"Enough," I bellowed. "I am sick of your games. Your manipulations. You don't believe a single word of the nonsense you're spouting. Not a minute ago, you were calling me the fool!"

Alisdair barked a laugh. "Both and all of those things can be true."

A snarl peeled from my lips. The beast curse was changing me, because my growl was positively feral. "I said enough. No more games. Tell me where the boy is now."

"How about this—?" Alisdair snapped his fingers, and I fell.

"Ahhh— Uh!" I bounced off silk and cotton, shocked to find myself in our bedroom.

On our bed.

Alisdair bore down on me, planting his hands on either side of my head and grinding his middle between my legs. A moan fell unbidden from my lips.

"—I'll tell you where the boy is if you ask nicely." His cock found its home, pressing against my entrance. "Very nice."

Grinding my teeth, I fought my body's reaction to him. I inhaled a deep breath and let it out slow. When done, my smile returned.

"All right. I'll be nice." My hand snaked between our bodies. "Downright sweet and pleasant." I reached between our middles, and squeezed.

Shadowsoul stilled.

"Easy now, husband." I pressed the knife tip to the back of his neck. "I've got you by both ends."

"A dagger?" His voice was calm. "Here I was believing we hadn't yet come to the point of needing props in the bedroom."

My lips curled in a semblance of a grin. "We need this one. I helped myself to Eadaoin's while she was busy feeling my backside. You see, I realized my mistake was stabbing you through the empty, rotted cavity where your heart used to be. I should've stabbed you where it hurts, and now that I know you do hurt..."

My grip tightened on his testicles, ripping a groan from his chest. "I will stab this through your neck, and rip out any chance of you spreading your demon seed, unless you tell me where the boy is"—the words pulled out of me—"and what's in that room at the top of the tower?"

"Little bird—"

I dug the knife in, feeling it pierce the skin. "Now."

"No."

My grin melted away. "Excuse me?"

"I said no." He sighed. "Oh, my queen. When will you learn to stop bargaining when you have nothing to offer?"

"Nothing to— I will do it!"

"Go ahead."

"This isn't a bluff," I cried, shaking. "I've stabbed you once before. A second time won't weigh heavily on my conscience."

"Undoubtedly."

"Tell me where the boy is," I burst out. "Tell me or you won't be having any sons of your own!"

He blinked lazily. "A lesson, Princess, once you start shouting your threats instead of delivering them, you lose all sense of authority."

Snarling, I crunched his soft, fleshy bits to burst—

Or at least, I tried to.

My hand wouldn't move. Neither hand would move. I lay stiff and frozen, mentally shouting commands at my nonresponsive body.

"Oh, little bird." Alisdair slid free and unharmed. "You are a unique and marvelous specimen. You make it so hard to resist you, but tonight, I must. You caused me no end of aggravation today, and I'm hardly going to reward that with multiple orgasms."

Reward?! Did this man think he was punishing me by denying me sex? As if I was the wanton minx chasing after him every night!

"You're done exploring for the night." He turned his back and walked off. "Take the time to think about what you've learned."

A blanket whipped out of the wardrobe and fell over me. Alisdair slammed the door on my internal shouts.

Chapter Eight

The next morning, Aeris led me out to the courtyard. Court wasn't being held that day while they did repairs.

Alisdair stood in the middle of the courtyard, basking under the shadow of a statue. I only saw its silhouette the night before. Morning didn't bring the sun, but it did bring the lighting of a dozen orblights scattered along the twisting paths—all casting their glow upon a beautiful stone woman with long hair, bare feet, and an expression of everlasting mourning.

I fell in beside him. "The true reward was a night free of you."

Alisdair flicked down to me, amusement tugging the corner of his mouth. "How many hours last night did you spend crafting that rejoinder?"

I warmed under my collar. "Shut up."

Naturally, he laughed at me. Alisdair was particularly handsome that morning, and that was saying something. It wasn't that his horns were diminished, because they weren't. Or that his claws retracted, because they hadn't. He was very much the beast bursting out of a summer fae's skin. No, he looked handsomer that morning, because he looked free.

Gone was the heavy black cloak. In its place were simple breeches, boots, and a tunic opened at the chest in defiance of the cold. His hair hung loose and free—a rushing raven waterfall drawing my gaze to him again and again. Every time I saw him, his face was a mask of boredom, rage, or irritation. But not this time. Alisdair looked like he had decided the day was going to be a great one, and it had barely started.

"What has you in a good mood?" I snapped.

"Likely whatever has you in a bad one."

I flashed him an obscene gesture, which only made him chuckle.

"The disappearing island that we spoke about. We found it," Alisdair said, again surprising me with a straightforward answer. "Our men were able to retrieve something that's going to make all the difference in the coming war. It's on its way now. Our victory is absolute."

I clenched my jaw hard. He was right. This news had the opposite effect on my mood. "Stop saying *we* and *our*. What you do, you do for yourself and your revenge. No one wants war. No one ever wants war."

"What we want are things only war will achieve. It is the same thing, little bird. If Elvans truly desired a simple, peaceful life, they'd return to the trees."

I scoffed. "Just because you say it in a slow, calm voice doesn't make it wisdom."

His laugh was light and free. Oh, yes, he was very pleased with the destruction he was about to cause. "Do you not want the laws in Lyrica to change, and for women to be allowed to keep their magic?"

"Of course I want that."

Alisdair looked me in the eye. "Then, how do you intend to wrest power away from the cruel, uncaring hands of your fathers, sons, husbands, and brothers, if not through war?"

I met his gaze unflinchingly. "The same way I'll wrest it from you, but don't worry, husband. That's the gift of mothers, daughters, wives, and sisters. We don't need war to bring a man to his knees."

"Is that so?"

The grins reflected in each other's eyes were absolutely feral.

I blinked and Alisdair was behind me. A warm hand snaked around my waist, pulling me close—drawing me into his heat—and every muscle in my body went rigid... because of what was in his other hand.

"Do demonstrate that for me, Princess." He pressed the tip of my stolen dagger to my heart. "Bring me to my knees. Make me surrender." Alisdair licked the shell of my ear, then bit down, making me moan. A moan I'd swear on my life was no more than a gasp. "Keep in mind that my strike will hit true if you succeed. Or if you fail," he mused. "I haven't decided which I desire more."

I grasped his wrist and pushed it away. He let me. "The true fun is in not knowing when it's coming, husband dear. Although, I can promise you that the day is coming soon when I make you the fool. You'll be the one watching everything and everyone you love ripped away, and all your plans for the future crumble to dust. On that day, you'll wish you hadn't underestimated the power of a quick and clever little bird."

"You misunderstand me greatly, my queen." Alisdair's nose traced a design on my cheek, sending my head spinning. I couldn't breathe without drowning in his spicy, sweet scent. I couldn't move captured in his hold. "It is not you I underestimate."

Alisdair waved his hand and a tiny, cheeping golden bird appeared on his palm. Sunlight glinted through feathers so lovely I could weep.

"But the question is this: how grand and mighty can any creature be—" Golden rods burst out of his palm and clamped around the bird—weaving, locking, and interlocking as it screeched. "—when its weakness is a small cage."

I tore away from him, a million heated replies launching to my lips, but nothing coming out.

"Your obedience is taken, but your fire is surrendered."

Mama's words echoed in my head, along with my usual replies. They were eerily similar to Alisdair's. What did fire matter if someone can put you in a cage?

I forced myself to turn back to the statue. Anything other than falling deeper into his glittering, dark orbs. "So what imaginary thing have the soldiers in your dreams retrieved from the island of make-believe?"

Chuckle. "I will tell you when I'm in a mood as poor as yours, so that you cannot bring me lower."

He received another foul gesture for that. "Is this her?" I asked, studying the woman's stone face. "Raelina?"

"No."

I waited for more, but none came. Alisdair's candor had limits. I didn't push.

"When do our lessons start?" I asked.

"Why?"

"I need to go out into the village today," I heard myself say. "See the people. Meet them. Give them a chance to get to know me. I can hardly fulfill my promise to reign as a true queen if I'm hiding in the bowels of the castle, terrified assassins are around every corner. If you give me a couple hours, I—"

"Cease your blathering, woman, and do what you wish. What interest is it of mine?" He strode off.

"Ass," I hissed, stomping off the other way.

Aeris stood five feet away, talking in low tones to one of my attendants.

"Aeris, send for my carriage!" Pulling up short, I tossed my head—eyes wide. That wasn't me. That was how Emiana addressed her household staff. It was not how I addressed a single soul.

The barrier between me and her is already crumbling. I have to get out of here while I can still remember who Olene, Meliora, Jaclan, Gisela, and Savia are.

"Excuse me, Aeris," I said. "What I meant to say was can you have a message sent to Eadaoin, telling her to wait for me in the grand hall? We're going out into the village this morning."

"Right away, my lady."

Half an hour later, Eadaoin and I left through the palace gates for the village. There was a palpable change in the air since my last visit. The clouds were heavier and darker, pressing the orblights to work harder dispelling the doom. A stiff wind whipped through Lumenfell—slamming doors in the distance, smashing flowerpots, and beating against my overcoat. All of that chilled me, but none so much as the new inhabitants. Everywhere I looked, there were wolves.

Just like Meallan, they were naked and creeping—moving quietly at the edge of things as if not wanting to take part, but needing everyone to know they were there.

Eadaoin drew closer to me. "My lady, would you happen to have that dagger you took from me last night?"

"Yes, in my pocket." A direct question deserved a direct answer.

"No," she hissed under her breath.

I didn't know why she was whispering until I remembered her saying a shout from the other side of the castle would bring Foalan running.

"Do not put weapons in your pocket. You waste precious time fumbling for them. On your belt always."

"I don't have a belt or weapons holster."

"Then we change that today."

I nodded. "Eadaoin, why are they so... different?"

She didn't ask what I meant. "Wolves aren't like other animals, my lady. They don't live in peaceful coexistence with other species. They dominate whatever area they call their territory, and will go out of their way to hunt down and kill coyotes, bears, cougars—any creature that dares to live on their land and eat their food.

"As their instincts took over, the wolf faeriken became more and more dangerous to the rest of us. They began killing and terrorizing us indiscriminately—for no other reason than they've decided Lumenfell belongs to them."

Oh no. What have I done?

"But that's not what makes them different." Eadaoin nodded to one of the patrolling guards passing by. "They're different from us... because they like it," she rasped. "They like being wolves. They like being—" The curse made her skip over the word she couldn't say. "They like the strength, the power, and the bloodlust. They've fully embraced the change by shedding the clothes that separate us from the animals, because they like Lumenfell, Lady Ana, and they believe it should all be theirs, and we should all be dead."

I swallowed hard. "No wonder the villagers wanted to kill me."

She didn't argue.

"Why didn't Alisdair tell me this?" I cried. "He spent hours telling me about the outer-lying villages, but couldn't spare a moment to mention why the wolves had to *stay* in theirs?"

"I can't speak why our lord does or doesn't do anything. But why did you give in to Meallan's request?"

"There was the little matter of his threatening to kill me if I didn't."

"Ahhh." She nodded, patting my shoulder. "You promised him a favor, didn't you?"

"Not intentionally. He helped me, and I said I'd help him too if the opportunity arose. It's just what you say."

"It's not your fault," she said gently, picking up on my defensiveness. "You didn't know that Lumenfell is different. Here, all we have is what we can trade. We take promises and bargains very seriously. Reneging on them is most often than not a death sentence. Meallan, that bastard, took advantage of your ignorance." She cursed. "Many nights I've stayed up late wondering how such an evil shit came from the same litter as Foalan."

"What will happen now?" I asked, stepping off the bridge. "Are the villagers in danger?"

"Yes," she said bluntly. "But the guards will watch over them."

We dropped the subject as we joined the hustle and bustle of town, although our first stop was to the leatherworks to fit me with my new holsters. All three of them. One for my ankle, thigh, and underbust for the knife nestled between my bosom.

"Wow." I poked my chest. "So many creative places to hide these things. How many do you have on you?"

Eadaoin winked. "You'll never know."

"I love that reply. I'm stealing it."

She laughed.

Eadaoin and I weaved through the marketplace, picking up glances and stares as we went. There was something special on that day. Little tiger cubs, bear cubs, piglets, hatchlings, and other young faeriken raced around, eating sweet apples, waving spinning fans, and shrieking in unintelligible delight.

A platform surrounded the frozen fountain and glaring stone Shadowsoul, holding a jumpy, jaunty band—playing a tune that bobbed my head and tapped my feet. Despite the heavy air accompanied by the watching wolves, the people were determined to enjoy themselves, and enjoy themselves they were—dancing, eating, laughing, and flirting to their heart's content.

"What's the occasion?" I called over the noise.

"I don't know. I had no idea this was happening today." Eadaoin accepted a sweet apple from a giggling snake girl. "Thank you, sweetling." She passed it to me. "Shall we join?"

I hesitated. I couldn't get distracted. I was leaving Lumenfell for good that night, and there was still much to prepare before Shadowsoul summoned me back for my lessons. "There's something I have to do first."

Walking up to the stage, I signaled the fiddler once, twice, five times before he noticed me and stopped playing. Annoyance lit his feathery chicken face until he got a proper look at me. He grabbed the flute player's elbow—eeking out a harsh, discordant sound.

The music stopped. The dancing stopped. Everything stopped.

Steeling myself, I climbed onto the platform. The band shuffled to the side.

"Excuse me, everyone. I'm sorry to interrupt your celebrations, but there's something I need to say." All eyes were on me—as blank and void as the eyes on me when the villagers attacked. Every smile and laugh wiped away.

As much as it pained me, I understood why they hated me. Their king set off to throw over the foreign princess they tossed in his lap, believing her to be a spy. Instead, he brings her to Lumenfell, and the first thing she does is unleash the literal wolves on them.

The funny thing was I'd be a hero back home in Lyrica if they discovered what I've done. Setting off a civil war and making the enemy they can't defeat tear each other apart until they defeat themselves? To all of the summer fae, my blunder was a gift from Meya. But to me...

I was never supposed to be here. Presiding over life and death, setting off wars, playing the deadly game of politics. It wasn't my life or my responsibility, but if it was, this wasn't how I wanted to use my power. Maybe Kirwan, King Salman, or even Princess Emiana could crow and celebrate the slaughter of harmless villagers living out a simple life of farming, trading, and raising their children, but not me. I had done wrong.

"And I need to say so," I rang out. "I'm so sorry that I didn't take the time to learn about the customs and traditions of Lumenfell before I presumed to make decisions for it. I know you think me your enemy, but the truth is"—I hid a sad smile—"I have more in common with you than you might think.

"I don't wish a single one of you harm, and by my honor, I will see to it that you're protected." My eyes traveled back to the wolves standing at the fringes. "If even one innocent person is hurt or killed by a wolf faeriken, Meallan will be killed, and Foalan named alpha of their pack."

The blowback was immediate.

"*Argh!*" Snarls and growls turned the air as the wolves surged forward—coming for me fast.

"You do not name the alpha of our pack," one woman roared. "We do!"

"You have no right!"

I smirked. "I have every right. I am your queen. Unless..." My grin widened. "If you're claiming I'm not your queen and you're not under my authority, then Meallan lied about dissolving the borders and welcoming the wolves as equal members of *my* kingdom.

"If you're not members of my kingdom, the deal is forfeit and you're trespassing on my territory. In that case, you can form an orderly line back to your dark pit in the forest."

No one breathed. The only movement were the eyeballs rolling around in the villagers' heads, shooting back and forth between me and the wolves.

"What say you?" I snapped. "Am I your queen, or are you leaving?"

The wolves shared a look—their lips peeled back from their fangs. I sensed their desire to sink them in my throat.

"You are our queen."

I spun around.

Meallan leaned against the platform, munching on an apple. He winked at me. "And a formidable queen you are. Whatever ignorance you had of our customs, you've made a quick study." He flung the half-eaten core over his shoulder. "Never fear, my oh so favorite madwoman, we have no intention of harming the villagers or a single innocent person. So certain am I that this will not be an issue, that I will accept your terms.

"If anyone in Lumenfell is unjustly slain by wolf hands, I will be put to death and my loathsome brother named alpha." His smile was almost sweet. "Acceptable?"

I simply nodded.

"Then we'll be on our way, and leave you to your celebrations." Meallan jerked his chin and the wolves melted into the shadow—gone as eerily as they arrived.

Sighing, I turned back to my audience. "There. I hope that makes up for—"

"Huzzah! Huzzah! All hail Queen Emiana."

I blew back, choking on a cry of surprise.

"Huzzah! We knew you would save us."

"You are our savior."

"Our champion."

"Our queen!"

"Oh, ahh..." I was blushing worse than when Alisdair gave false, sweet compliments to torment me. These praises were actually real. "Th-thank you. My pleasure. Please enjoy your—" I scrambled down, helped off my Eadaoin.

"Wow, my lady. That was wonderful." She squeezed my shoulders, jumping up and down. "You're a genius. Of course if they're one of us, they're beholden to the queen. If there's anything Meallan would chew his leg off to prevent, it's Foalan being chosen as alpha in place of him."

"The solution just came to me," I confessed. "Although, when you live under a tyrant, you learn many awful ways to bring people to heel by force."

She laughed. "You shouldn't speak of your husband that way."

Crazily, it wasn't Alisdair I was thinking of. It was my fath— It was King Salman. Standing up on that stage, a memory assaulted me. A woman once came to the castle, crying because her entire harvest had been seized to feed the army. They hadn't paid her for what they took, or left her so much as an ear of corn.

Salman listened to her weep for her starving children, and said that her land was in Lyrica, and Lyrica belonged to him. Therefore, every scrap of land and the food growing on it belonged to him—free and clear. If her crop didn't belong to him, it meant she wasn't a citizen of Lyrica. She was a dissenter and a traitor, and should be put to death on the spot.

She ran out of the throne room crying. Emiana never found out what happened to her after that.

Alisdair's right. There is plenty of cruelty and barbarism on my side of the wasteland.

"Should we stay and enjoy the festivities?" Eadaoin asked.

"We shouldn't. We don't have much time before—"

"Mangoes! Get your sweet, juicy mangoes here!"

I took off through the cheering crowd, picking up pats on my head, shoulders, and back. Stumbling over a raised cobblestone, I fell on the mango cart—popping the merchant's brow up.

He was a tall, hefty man with grayish, leathery skin, ears twice as large as his head, and large ivory tusks growing from his jaw. I'd never seen an elephant outside of a storybook. The curse sought to change that.

"Mangoes?" I cried. "Truly? You've managed to grow mangoes in this climate? How? You must tell me."

"Not easily, is the answer, my queen." He tossed me one, stealing an embarrassing shriek of glee from me. "They love sun, heat, and humidity. All in short supply in Lumenfell."

"An understatement. They need eight hours a day of direct sunlight if they're to thrive," I said, holding my mango close. "And these are huge." My eyes were big and round, straining to take in the red, orange, green, and pink treat. I had a mango only once in my life. They were expensive and hard to come by even in Lyrica, but I treated us one year on the twins' birthday. One bite, and we devoured them so fast, the mango was gone in less than a minute. I promised the twins I'd learn to grow them, so we'd have them all the time.

Now I can go home with the news that I learned how to do it! I was so happy, I was bouncing up and down.

I got so deep in the conversation, listening to how he used magic to mimic the sun's rays, that I almost didn't hear someone calling me.

"—queen? Excuse me, Queen Emiana."

"Ana," I corrected automatically.

A cat woman stepped out from behind her cart, holding a basket. "If you like tropical fruit, you'll love these."

"Oooh," I breathed, gazing at the big, purple fruit. "What is it?"

"We call it pranganut. Tough outsides, but inside are a bunch of little seeds that burst with sweet, tarty juice with every bite."

"That sounds delicious. Would you tell me how you grow them?"

"Oh! How about I write down the instructions and put them in your basket?" she said, running back. "You have so many tributes to accept, I wouldn't want to slow you down."

"My basket? Tribute?"

"Yes," she said, gesturing behind me.

Turning around, I fell on the crowd of villagers—all smiling, watching me, holding baskets of some type or other, and waiting.

I blinked. "What's this? Is something wrong?"

Eadaoin stepped forward. "Nothing is wrong, my lady. They're honoring you by paying tribute."

"Me?" I squeaked. "Tribute to me? Because I dealt with the wolves?" I groaned under the heavy basket of pranganuts shoved into my hands. "Wow. You all forgive so easily."

"Easily?" repeated the mango man. "Do you mean because we intended to kill you?"

We?

Eadaoin shot between us, growls hazing the air.

The man looked at me over her shoulder. "That's in the past, my lady."

"It was yesterday!"

"Exactly, yesterday," he said, inclining his head. "Yesterday when our lord risked himself and sacrificed his people to protect you. We thought this marriage was forced on him by enemy kings seeking to destroy our home. Now we know we were wrong." A beaming smile split his face. "You will save us, Queen Emiana of Lumenfell. You were his choice, now you are ours. And if that wasn't so, why would we be celebrating you and your blessed marriage?"

I couldn't have been more confused if he slipped into another language. The festival celebration was in honor of me? An honor they were bestowing before I apologized for unleashing the wolves.

"What do you think, my lady?" Eadaoin whispered.

I blew out a breath. "I think if they're willing to forgive, so am I. Would you mind helping me get everyone into orderly lines?" I asked. "Also, I'll need my carriage if I'm to carry all these baskets back to the castle."

"Uhhh..." She looked from me, to Castle Riagin, to the line of people that was only growing longer. "Okay, but stay here," she ordered. "I won't be long."

"Of course."

As soon as Eadaoin ducked out of sight, I turned and left.

"I'll be back to accept your tributes in a few moments," I called back. "Keep those mangoes safe for me."

"Yes, ma'am," Mango Man replied.

Quickly, I hurried through the square, letting my mental map head me around carts and stalls to the quiet part of the village where they made their homes. I went farther still, lighting on the horse stall.

Riordan lifted his head from the horse's coat when I slipped inside. "My queen." He dropped his brush bowing to me.

I almost snapped at him to bow deeper, respecting my station. *You're not Emiana,* I snapped at myself. *Remember who you are.*

"Stand up, Riordan, and call me Ana." I reached to help him up, but he jumped back—nose wrinkling. I nearly forgot about Alisdair's wretched marking. "I only came to make sure everything is in order for tonight," I said, backing away until the tense line of his shoulders relaxed. "We have to leave at sundown. Exactly at sundown."

"Everything is ready, my queen. As you said, the villagers all accepted an upfront payment with the promise of even more when their crops are sold in Lyrica. We have more carrots, sprouts, broccoli, cabbage, spinach, and peas than we'll know what to do with." He beamed at me. "And may I say again, what an honor it is to have been personally chosen by you for this position."

"It had to be you," I said absentmindedly. I moved from stall to stall, inspecting the horses. They had to be quick and strong enough to evade a beast.

"Me? Why did it have to be me?"

"The change hasn't taken you yet."

He inclined his head, accepting that easily. Which was good because it was the only reason the curse would let me give him.

"And the other matter that we discussed?" A lovely white-and-brown horse with a brown mane pushed against the wood to lay its head over my shoulder. I couldn't fight a smile as I stroked her. "Olene, Meliora, Jaclan, Gisela, Savia."

"Yes, Lady Ana. I understand that you want me to find and take you to them, but I don't understand why." There was shuffling behind me as

Riordan resumed his task of preparing the horses for our trip. "You said you don't know them."

"I don't," I rasped, heart panging. "But it's important."

"I understand and I'll do as you ask. I'm sure they're still living in the same place. No one makes it out of the Galley."

I peered at him over the horse's muzzle. "May I ask you something? What are you doing here? You have a Lyrican accent, so your home wasn't overtaken by the curse. You chose to be here," I stated. "Why?"

He shrugged, smiling. "I never wanted to join the army, but my parents needed the money, so they sold me. Can you imagine? Selling your child to the battlefield to fill your own bellies." Riordan tossed his head. "Anyway, I woke up in a hot and stinking tent one day, surrounded by hot, tired, and hungry soldiers, and I decided it was enough.

"Enough of war, death, and pain. Right then, I packed up my stuff, walked out of the tent, and set off for the kingdom of Wind and Wild," he said. "I resolved to find the heart amid this frozen hell, stab it through, and end it once and for all."

"And then?" I breathed, rapt. "What happened?"

He sighed. "And then... I discovered this place. I realized Wind and Wild wasn't some frozen hell filled with filthy, bloodthirsty beasts. They're just people, my queen. People suffering under a terrible curse. A curse that they want to be freed from just as much as the rest of Elva. They just don't want to be slaughtered before they are.

"What happened is I saw the truth of what we—the summer fae—have done. It was us who started this war. Us who keep attacking and invading. Us who refuse to end the fighting. All the faeriken have done is defend themselves."

"We had to go to war," I blurted. "The curse is spreading. Eventually, all of Elva will be a land of winter and ice. A land forgotten by the sun and stars."

Riordan nodded. "It's true. Even if the faeriken aren't invading Rajadom, Quatassa, Sarabai, or Lyrica, the curse most certainly is. Obviously, we can't sit by while the curse kills the land and turns us all into mindless beasts. But that's reason for us to work *with* the faeriken to end the curse. It's not a reason to turn victims into enemies."

"You're right," I agreed. I found a brush and joined him, preening the coat of my new friend. "I see that now. The faeriken are no less fae than us. They're normal, regular people like us. They deserve help to break their curse, not a death sentence. But how will they ever get such help when the man who holds the cursed heart refuses to free them, or us, from its punishment?"

His smile remained. "Well, that's where you come in, isn't it?"

"Me?" I pulled a face. "Is that the answer? Is that why the villagers are so excited that Shadowsoul didn't let me be crushed to death? They think I'm getting close enough to him that he'll tell me where the cursed heart is, and let me destroy it?"

Riordan laughed. "That is always the answer, my queen. Beautiful women such as you are the weakness of every man's heart."

I'll tell Emiana you said so the next I see the rotted bitch.

"My lady?"

I whipped around, landing on a shifting shadow outside the stable door.

"My lady, what are you doing in there?" Eadaoin asked.

I swallowed a curse. Alisdair's marking would be the death of me. It was a beacon telling him, and everyone with a heightened sense of smell, where I was.

"Be ready for tonight," I told Riordan. Reaching into the folds of my gown, I handed him a small pouch. "No excuses. No delays."

"Yes, my queen."

Eadaoin burst in. "Lady Ana?" Her eyes narrowed on Riordan. "What's going on?"

"Nothing's going on. I simply wanted to see the horses." I brushed past her going outside. "Come now. Let's not keep the villagers waiting."

***

I stood on the training field, shivering in my calfskin boots.

I had the first enjoyable morning since entering Lumenfell. Villager after villager paid me tribute in fruits, vegetables, berries, and more. The best part, I got into long, fascinating conversations with nearly all of them about how to grow such in bitter, chilling weather. At some point, a group of us were gathered in the square—laughing, drinking ale, and trading tips.

It was truly fun... so, of course, my blessed husband would see to its end.

"You look ridiculous."

I threw a furious look at the kakka.

"Truly moronic."

Growling, I swung the bow and arrow on Alisdair.

Foalan waved his hand and the bow burst into feathers before it could make its flight. "My queen," Foalan said flatly. "Kindly cease trying to assassinate our king."

"No!"

Foalan sighed. "Lady Ana, you're doing well. You just need to maintain your stance, and then take a breath before you release. It will help steady your aim."

"Why must I learn to use a bow and arrow?" I asked. "I take no issue with weapons training, but why this weapon? Can't I begin with a sword or dagger?" I looked right at the smirking Alisdair when I said that.

The man had me plucked from the village, but not for more map-memorization. Aeris brought me straight to the snow-covered training yard, and Foalan.

Orblights did their best to light the field, but there wasn't much to illuminate. Snow six inches deep covered my boots. Three yards before me were the targets. On my left side, faeriken soldiers sparred and trained with each other. On my right, Alisdair leaned against the stone yard fence, testing how quickly Foalan could take away my arrows before they pierced his skull.

"The bow is the best weapon against the Taken," Foalan explained. "Taken are foul, unnatural creatures born from dark magics we can't comprehend. They have a strange, deadly effect on those they draw near—filling them with irrational terror."

I shivered, swallowing hard.

"It's hard to think, let alone fight close combat when your every instinct is screaming at you to run. That's why you'll fight with the bow, my queen," he said. "You'll kill them before they get close."

I just nodded. I wasn't expecting such a good reason, and that was the best. Killing those horrible things before they closed in on me was most certainly what I preferred to do.

"What are they?" I asked softly.

"I don't know. They aren't beget by"—he gestured to his wolf face—"or we wouldn't be able to speak of them. But they don't exist anywhere but this land, so we'd be a fool to believe they aren't related." He shook his head. "Maybe they're what's borne of a broken heart."

"Have you given up already?" Alisdair called, setting my teeth on edge. "Well, at least watching you flailing around, shooting arrows at the ground, was entertaining."

"Cease your blathering, beast," I barked, "or get over here and help me. You and I both know I can't learn properly when my instructor isn't allowed to touch me."

"Very well." Alisdair hopped over the fence. "Regard me."

"Wait, what?"

"Foalan, you're dismissed." Alisdair grasped my waist and I spun—gasping to find myself crushed to his chest and tucked under his chin. "I fear you'll regret this, little bird. I'm not nearly so forgiving an instructor as Foalan."

"You fear nothing," I said, hating the desperate look I threw at Foalan's back. "Least of all giving me regrets."

His chuckle rumbled against my back. "To begin, point your feet away from the target." We moved as one. Nudging his leg between mine, Alisdair moved my feet shoulder width apart. "Relax," he ordered. "You're tensing up before you've even touched the bow."

I sent the call for my muscles to relax, but they didn't obey. Alisdair had never been this close to me without fucking me senseless, or protecting me from getting pummeled. To have his body pressed to mine in a benign situation, wasn't one mine understood.

"You're both pulling back too far, and holding on to the bow too long," he said. "You're tiring yourself out before you've released, and then the force of it knocks you off-balance."

I found myself nodding along. What he was saying made sense. "What do I do, then?"

"Relax," he murmured. "Only pull back to the corner of your mouth, and then release. Don't hesitate. Don't overthink. Just let go."

Nodding, I lifted the bow and—

"Stop," Alisdair broke in. "You're overextending."

He reached out and laid his hand over mine—touch surprisingly cold. Surprisingly gentle. His other slid around my waist, moving me back into the proper position... pressed against his middle.

"You want your elbow slightly bent," he said, pulling my mind out of rushing thoughts. "Now draw back, anchor to your mouth, and—"

I let go, a small cry leaving me as the arrow sailed away.

Thwack!

The tip burrowed into the target off-center. Very off-center, but it hit the target.

"Ahh," I cried, jumping up and down. "Did you see that? I did it."

"Again."

His warmth left me so fast, I stumbled.

"You will continue until you either hit the bull's-eye, or your fingers bleed," he said, returning to his post against the fence. "I suggest you hit the bull's-eye."

"You can't be serious."

Alisdair was deadly serious.

He made me shoot again and again and again—going so far as to magically glue my feet to the snow-covered ground when I tried to leave.

Dry, cracked fingers pulled, yanked, and gripped the bow until my tears ran and my skin split open—slicking the wood with blood. I tried to draw it again and the string slipped, snapping me across the face. I dropped the bow, hands flying to my face, then crying harder for the pain of my touch.

A shadow fell over me.

"Go," I shrieked. "You've gotten your wish, seeing me bleeding and crying in the dirt, so just leave me!"

"Don't despair of blisters, little bird." Hands grasped mine, drawing them away from my face. My breath stopped as cool, tickling magic washed over my skin. "For they become calluses.

"Stronger than they ever were before."

The open, weeping seams on my fingers healed. Still pink and raw, but no longer bleeding and painful. I touched my cheek, finding its pain gone too. I looked up as Alisdair walked away. "Well done," floated over his shoulder.

***

That evening, I ate my dinner in our strange, three-walled bedroom. It was the perfect place to keep watch for the orblights to brighten to their maximum—the sole signal that the sun had gone down beyond the dark clouds.

I checked and re-checked my coat, boots, and supplies a dozen times. I mentally ran through my plan a dozen more times. This was it. I was finally going home.

The minute the lights blasted their radiance, I bolted out the door.

Foalan and Aeris were walking past the end of my hallway, deep in a conversation that had them both laughing. They caught sight of me.

"Good evening, Lady Ana," Foalan said brightly. "Is everything all right?"

"Run," I shouted, and then launched at him—throwing my arms around and rubbing my body against him in the most obscene hug I'd ever given. "Preferably in the opposite direction."

"My queen!" Foalan bellowed, throwing himself back much too late.

Aeris's face went deathly pale. "My lady, what have you done?"

A roar ripped through the castle, rattling it off its very foundation.

I ran.

Racing through the halls, I touched, grabbed, and threw myself at every man I came across, leaving shouts and panic in my wake. Alisdair thought his mark would keep me on a leash, but that's the thing about leashes. They can also be used to hang the bastard holding the other end.

I made it outside and kept running, holding back the laugh trapped in my throat. *Goodbye, Alisdair. All the best with the shortest, most ill-conceived invasion in history. It ends the minute I get home and tell the world about you.*

Riordan glanced up when I came sliding across the corner, feet scrambling on the ice-slicked cobblestone. His weighted-down carriage was waiting right beside the path out of Lumenfell, and filled to the brim with vegetables for market—with one other addition. Magic aided him in building a wooden roof and compartment for a small, nimble person to hide in, buried under mounds of goods.

"Arrggghh!" A roar resounded over the horizon, chasing birds, rabbits, and all manner of flying creatures out of the trees, and winging away as fast as their wings could carry them.

"That would be my blessed husband," I said, grinning wide. "Chasing my scent to every corner of the castle."

"We've no time for gloating. My lord will realize he's been tricked sooner rather than later. Hurry, Lady Ana," Riordan belted. He tossed me a dura dura. "Get on!"

Dura dura. The most foul-smelling fruit in these lands or any other. Working fast, I held my breath and rubbed the stinky thing over my face, hands, clothes, arms, and everywhere.

Screams went up in the village, telling me it was past time to leave.

Heart thundering out of my chest, I threw my stuff in the hidden compartment, then hopped on.

Riordan took off like the hounds of hell were snapping at his feet, waiting for one trip or stumble to claim their prize and drag him to damnation. The horses surged up the hill—jostling their burden over the uneven, rocky path. It was only magic that kept the vegetables from falling out.

Or maybe it was fear. They had no desire to roll down and face what was coming for me.

Come on, I thought as squawks, screeches, howls, and barks went up in the village. *Faster!*

We broke over the hill and took off, racing down the snow-covered path.

The first thing I'd do when I got home was hug Mama, Meli, the twins, and baby Savia for five minutes each. Then, I'd pack our meager belongings, move them into one of the grand mansions on the hill, and then take extra pleasure in watching Kirwan shouting himself purple outside the gates when he discovered that home was his.

My dear husband, Alisdair, made such a show of insisting everything that was or would be was *ours* absolutely. Binding us as surely as the runes bound our souls. There was nothing wrong in filling my pack with the riches collecting dust on display.

Everything was about to change for me and my family, and after it did, I'd hunt Emiana down in her hiding places, drag her back to Lyrica, force her to give my body back, then throw her to the country she betrayed.

Riordan and I sped away from Lumenfell, leaving it farther... farther... and farther behind.

"Yes!" I cried, brimming with joy. I did it. I couldn't believe I'd finally outsmarted the great and terrible Lord Alisdair Shadowsoul. This little bird had broken free of her cage.

A shadow appeared in the distance, moving fast across the horizon. I wasn't certain if it was Shadowsoul or one of the Taken, and I didn't plan to find out.

"Faster!"

"Ye-ah! Ye-ah!" Riordan bellowed, going harder on the reins. Glowing orblights swirled around the cart—lighting our way and shining a beacon in the darkness. No option of diminishing them. It was too dark, and the path too dangerous. Gnarled tree limbs stretched across the divide, desperately trying to tear him from his seat while dips and rocks sought to overturn the cart.

"Arggh," he roared, and I knew without a doubt. The shadow was Alisdair, not the Taken.

He tore fast for the cart and the prize hidden inside. Fully changed, I got a flash of the beast coming for me. Lethal fangs, unforgiving claws tearing up the ground, curved back covered in black fur, and a body honed with a weapon-defiant hide and thick, ropy muscle. This creature was an instrument of killing, and nothing could stop it.

Riordan whipped back and forth, the white of his eyes drowning his irises the closer Shadowsoul got. Riordan was shouting before he pounced—leaping on the back of the cart and tearing it apart. A shower of carrots, cabbage, and spinach rained from the sky. Alisdair found the secret compartment and ripped it off as Riordan hit the ground and started running—not so much as looking back.

Alisdair found his prize—a pile of clothes covered in my scent.

I almost laughed as his roar ripped through the forest, bouncing off the trees to resound through the mountaintops. I leaned forward in the saddle, silently urging my horse on, and leaving Alisdair and his rage behind.

Of course he'd chase after the big, hulking carriage of the man I'd suspiciously chosen to ride back to Lyrica. And while he was wasting his time chasing after all the wrong men and all the wrong scents, I'd ride off into the lands of summer and sun.

Soon, everything faded behind me—light, sound, Alisdair.

I slowed my horse, then slid off her back. The two of us moving quietly and carefully across the perilous, shadowed landscape. Another hour passed. Then two. Then three.

On we trod, escaping the land of Wind and Wild as assuredly as we were escaping the night. Oh so soon, the sun would rise beyond the clouds, and the runes would strike Alisdair down. I eluded him until daybreak. He had to let me go.

Let me go he will, to return to Lyrica and save my family from the grip of Kirwan, but the truth is I'm not done with Lumenfell yet.

I nodded to myself, letting that thought sink into my bones. I couldn't be done with Lumenfell until I found and saved the fox boy from Shadowsoul. Of course, I couldn't delay my plan to break free of the marriage and runes. I could hardly free the boy from the castle when I was trapped in the castle.

But once I no longer had the runes boiling my skin, I'd come back with something Alisdair wanted, and trade for his freedom. Although, what he wanted was the issue.

It was abundantly clear that Alisdair wouldn't settle for anything short of complete, total, soul-crushing revenge against King Salman for what he did to Raelina. He certainly wanted it more than he wanted a tiny, desperate thief. The question was how could I deliver that without committing treason?

I couldn't lie. I held no fondness, respect, or regard for my king. I didn't before I had Emiana's memories, and I had even less after. Emiana experienced nothing but neglect, and she witnessed nothing but cruelty. The few times Salman tore himself away from the arms of his harem to hold court and meet with his subjects, he did the Alisdair equivalent of tearing their throats out.

He stole their land and coin while claiming it property of the kingdom. He jailed anyone who complained of the rising taxes. He suggested to struggling women that he would happily ease their burden if they joined his harem, and after they refused and walked out, he ordered his advisors to lay even more bullshit taxes and repossessions on them—driving them to the brink to force their *no* into a *yes*.

Salman was swine. To know him was to hate him. Lyrica would never become a free and just country with that man on the throne, but the fact remained, treason carried too high a price. In Lyrica, when an individual is charged with treason, they and their entire family are put to death. Made for a very strong incentive to never think such a crime, let alone carry it out.

What if there is a way to get Alisdair his revenge without committing treason? My mind spun, carried off by thoughts and theories as we ventured deeper into the dark forest. *What if I went back to the beginning with Raelina?*

Murder is murder. Outlawed in every land. While King Salman may be untouchable, he wasn't king when he murdered his wife, Raelina. If I could find proof of what he did, I'd hand that proof to Shadowsoul and let him show the world who Salman really is.

I tossed my head, shaking that idea loose immediately. If there was proof of his crime, Alisdair would've found it already. One doesn't resort to murdering someone's daughter at the altar, or changing his mind and marrying his most hated enemy's heir to get his claws into her rightful throne... if he hadn't exhausted all other options.

Okay, I can't get him proof but what if I could... could... get him Emiana!

My head snapped up. That was it. Emiana broke the treaty and tricked both nations into an arranged marriage with an imposter. If anyone committed treason, it was her. She sabotaged the treaty that would've ended the war, and was indirectly responsible for Alisdair having to attack King Salman.

Salman tried to strike his *daughter* for defying him and fighting the marriage, because said daughter was a fucking stranger forced to take his real daughter's place. Treason against Lyrica, her interests, and the throne, and I had no doubt Alisdair could strongly make that case. And once Emiana was convicted, by law, everyone in her family had to be put to death.

Including her blessed father.

My mouth curled around the edges. Salman would hang himself on his own barbaric laws, and it would all be legal, undeniable, and unable to fall on me or my family. Alisdair would get everything he wanted, Raelina would receive justice, and with Salman and Emiana dead, Shadowsoul couldn't use her claim to the throne to take over Lyrica.

He couldn't use it anyway because he bound his soul to a poor peasant, not a princess. A fact I'd take great pleasure in telling him, while I impressed on him that he would be accepting my deal without argument or complaint.

I nodded to myself, grinning wide. I'd done it. I saved my family. I saved the boy. I saved Lyrica from a tyrant king and a terrible war. The only thing that could've possibly sweetened the moment is if I found the heart and destroyed it—saving all of Lyrica—but one mustn't get too full of themselves.

Savior of Lyrica will do just fine. I wonder what second name they'll bestow on me. I laughed. How delicious it would be to make Shadowsoul give me my second name. The woman who outran, outsmarted, and outmaneuvered him. When I returned, dragging the true Emiana behind, he wouldn't dare to call me an entertaining little bird then.

"How premature."

I snapped around, scream clogging in my throat.

"A mouse shouldn't smile before it's escaped the trap."

Snow and dirt crunched under Alisdair's paw— No, foot. He was rapidly changing, the beast clawing back under his skin for the smirking, handsome king to emerge. My horse took off so fast, she kicked up a wave of snow that smacked across my cheek.

My voice was a thin rasp. "How...?"

"Clever," he hissed. "Oh, so very clever. I confess, I underestimated you. Spreading my mark on every male and man in creation. Using a decoy to carry me in the wrong direction. Masking your scent with that"—his nose wrinkled—"unfortunate smell."

Alisdair started circling me, standing the hairs on the back of my neck on end. "Everything I was told about you was wrong. And to think, I was going to kill such a magnificent, intelligent creature." I cried out, flinching away when a clawed finger suddenly stroked my cheek in the dark. "I bow to you, my queen."

To my shock, he did it—bowing his head in deference to me.

"You are truly formidable. More than worthy of being my mate. My match. But..." He tore his clothes clean from his body. "This was always going to end one way. Come to me."

"W-wait," I cried, finding my voice. "Alisdair, please, you have to listen to me. I need to go back to Lyrica. I swear it's important! You said I didn't have anything to bargain, but I do— I will. Let me go and I'll return for the boy with everything you need to get revenge against the king without war and bloodshed."

He ate the distance between us.

"Or! Or," I rushed, backing away. "Come with me. After I've done what I must, I'll return and we can go together. There's a cottage in Sarabai. A treehome in Rajadom. A guest lodging in Quatassa. Any one of those places could hold what you seek—"

Alisdair sliced the buttons of my cloak, letting the wind whip it away.

"—to get your revenge against Salman."

The front of my bodice was next. Alisdair was a man possessed—slicing a thin, neat line through my clothes, unwrapping his mate.

"Alisdair, this is no trick. You have to trust me, if you do, everything will be put right." I surged forward, grasping his face in my hands. "It's not me you want!"

"I've told you, my queen..."

He waved his hand, and our surroundings melted away. The snow, the dark, the shifting shadows of the night—all faded.

"You're all I want."

I found myself in our bedroom. Seemed there would be no rough tree bark against my back, or snow melting under my feet. Alisdair meant to have me on a bed of silk and cotton.

My lips parted, telling him that I wasn't Emiana. That we'd both been played for a fool by a selfish and desperate princess, and I had to get back to my family before Emiana's desperation destroyed more than one life.

I opened my mouth to tell him if he let me, I'd bring him to his true mate—a woman just as ruthless, calculating, and treasonous as him. I opened my mouth, and nothing came out. Not because the curse held my tongue... but because Alisdair did.

He captured my lips in a rough and hungry kiss. Alisdair molded me to him—fitting our bodies together like puzzle pieces.

His hands were everywhere. Caressing my thighs. Tangling in my waves. Memorizing every dip and curve. Slicing up the remains of my clothes.

He nipped my lips, demanding entrance. The rough, forbidden ecstasy of our tongues tangling weakened my knees. I stayed upright only for Alisdair's grip on my ass—holding me firm to him, wrapping my legs around his waist, moving his hardness between my middle.

Alisdair broke free and threw me. I swallowed a cry, soaring across the sheets and landing on the pillows. Muscles rippled on his back as he stalked toward me—the predator and his prey.

He kissed the inside of my ankle, making me shiver. My skin was alive like it'd never been before. I was acutely aware of the silk tickling my back. The glow of the flickering orblights, casting our shadows over the fireplace. The press of all the things I needed to say, lodging in my throat.

No.

I could say no. I could end this. Deny him the pleasure of ravaging my body like he denied me my freedom. His caged bird didn't have to sing.

He skated up my thigh, his lips following in his hands' wake. Little whimpers escaped my mouth under rough, biting kisses.

More markings. More claims of absolute ownership... and only one word to remind him I belonged to no one.

"Say it." Alisdair shredded my undergarments—a flimsy barrier that was no match for him. "Go on, say it."

I swallowed hard. He couldn't know what I was thinking, and yet somehow, he always did.

"Say what?" I rasped.

"You look as though you have something to say, my queen. Do it," he hissed through gritted teeth, gaze pinning me through. "You have my ear, as you have my bed, as you have my soul. Tell me what troubles a little bird."

I held his gaze, body shaking. "I... I wish that you would trust me. There are things that you don't know. Forces that are playing us both for a fool. If you let me go, I can put all things right."

"Let you go?" He tsked, swirling a finger around my pussy, collecting the drops of wetness already coming. "I have let you go. Every night. You cannot fault me for your not being quite fast enough."

I tensed. "Why are we playing this game?"

"Again you ask me questions I've answered many times."

"Because your answers are lies!" I exploded. "You can hardly keep the mocking smirk off your mouth when you spout them! You don't want me, so let me go!"

Alisdair sighed as he slipped one finger past my folds, then another.

My breath caught on a moan. Never had I hated myself more than when I dropped my knees, opening myself wider to him.

"Very well," he said, his husky voice wrapping around my ears. "If everything I say is lies, then let me tell you something you'll know is true.

"I will never let you go."

My fingers stilled curling in the sheets.

"It is only the runes binding my soul that I allow you the illusion of running from me, and even then I gnaw at the leash—pouring everything I know of magic into burning them away during your precious head starts—just to catch you all the faster." He dove in to the knuckles and spread his fingers, stretching me wider than I was ever meant to go.

"It doesn't matter what you do, or what you say. You can shout to the heavens of small, mole-ridden cocks. You can bring Lumenfell to ruin. You can betray me and our conquer of Elva, but I will never run slower. As long as the moon and stars reign, I will chase you to the ends of the world and beyond.

"You are mine, little bird. My toy, my pet, my wife, my queen. So tell me—" His fingers jerked, striking that spot dead-on. My cry almost smothered him. "Do I lie?"

Body trembling, I gazed into his eyes... and shook my head. He wasn't lying.

"I ask you again," he continued. "Do you have something you wish to say to me?"

One word. That's all I had to say and he'd pull out, walk away, and leave me to the torment of my failure in peace. Alisdair did own me in nearly every way. He didn't have to have my body too.

"No," I hissed clearly. Firmly. I let the power of it sink into my bones, and then— "I have nothing to say."

"Good."

We leaped at the same time—mouths colliding in a chorus of moans and clashing tongues.

I reached for Alisdair's shaft but he was faster. He grabbed my hand and pinned it over my head. The other hand met the same fate.

His kiss was rough. The grip on my wrists iron-clad.

I bucked, trying to flip him. He snarled and pinned me down harder. Were we fighting or fucking? I wasn't sure. Maybe both. All I knew was my body thrummed with pure, naked excitement and all the wrongness that came with. More truths than one were revealed that night. I wanted this man, this body, this cock, and there was no point denying it anymore.

My whole life I've done what I'm supposed to do. Been the good and responsible girl, denying myself of all the pleasures that weren't already taken from me. For good and responsible girls, there was nothing more morally decayed on this earth than desiring Alisdair Shadowsoul.

He was a monster and a murderer. He courted death and war with a smile on his face, and tightened the screws of my cage while daring me to complain. There was a reason the curse was turning him into a beast. Not a bird, or a cheetah, or a wolf, or a mole rat. But a vicious, deadly beast only conjured in nightmares.

It was because that was the pure state of his soul, and knowing that I brought such a creature to heel between my legs, was hot, desperate need that burned my core to cinders.

Alisdair clamped my wrists with one hand, then shredded my bodice to ribbons. My breasts fell prey to his ministrations—his rough calluses gliding over my sensitive skin, leaving a trail of popping goose bumps leading the way to the innocent nub.

My moan poured from my lips.

Alisdair tweaked my nipple with abandon, making it ache with need. He descended like a swooping raven faeriken. Taking my nipple in his mouth, he scraped it mercilessly with his teeth.

"Fuck!" I cried out, pure heat shooting through my veins.

Alisdair was incredible like this. Rough, demanding, slavish to my pleasure, and *distracted*.

Bringing my knees between us, I kicked him off me.

"Argh!" he snarled, flying back on his back. I pounced on him, pinning his arms down. "You're going to regret that."

I smirked. "Promises, promises."

Straddling him, I feasted on his body—palms flat on his chest and beginning a slow journey down. My toy, my pet, my husband, my king.

My fingers skated over the jagged scar on his chest. Bending down, I kissed it.

Thump-thump.

I froze, lips puckered. *His heartbeat? Did Alisdair put his heart back in his chest? When? Why?*

"You are a strange one," he said softly, drawing me up. "Unpredictable. Unknowable."

My smirk returned. "I wouldn't say that." Rising up, I dropped my knees on his arms, and my pussy on his lips. "I'm sure you can predict what I want you to do next."

Alisdair's grin mirrored mine. "Oh, but you do make yourself so hard to resist."

The room spun. In a blink, I was looking up at the ceiling. I strained to get up and found I couldn't. My shoulders were magically glued to the bed. "Ugh! Why must you always be in control?"

"Why must you always be too weak to make me cede control?" His palms slowly rolled down my body, flattening me to the sheets, then spreading my legs wide. "Once again you blame me for your shortcomings."

I tried to kick him but he was already ducking down. Already taking control.

Riiippp.

Something soft and silky wrapped around one ankle, then the other. He bound them tight. I stared at him in confusion as he lifted my legs and stuck his head between them, dropping my ankles on his shoulders.

I made a shocked noise when he bent me in half, dropping his hard, muscled body on mine.

A swift, hard bite on my lower lip was all the warning I got before Alisdair pushed all the way inside, filling me to my limit.

"Uh," I moaned—anchored by the sudden sharp pains above and below.

Propping his arms on either side of my head, Alisdair drew all the way out to the tip, then thrust back in.

I screamed, eyes rolling up in my head. Every muscle in my body clenched.

"Hmm. Not quite loud enough. Let's see if I get it right the next time." He started pumping— No, bouncing. Alisdair found that spot and he pounded it through relentlessly, going faster and faster until I popped on and off the mattress with every thrust. I was getting hit in the face with my own knees.

If he was seeking louder screams, he achieved that on the second thrust. I grunted, moaned, and screamed so loudly, my cries echoed through the missing wall—sounding my ravaging to all of Lumenfell.

"Yes, yes, ah, fuck! More, Alisdair. Harder!"

Alisdair was a man possessed, growling as he pumped faster still. Shredding the sheets trying to hold on to something real as raw, dirty pleasure carried him away.

It was too much for me. Pressure built in my lower belly, rising to a fever pitch. I wouldn't last for one more second.

Alisdair struck that spot, and I screamed, back arching off the bed as explosions of light, heat, darkness, color, and pleasure ravaged my shuddering body. My cries scraped my throat raw, climbing higher and more unhinged when Alisdair stiffened.

He seized up—claws tearing straight through cotton and goose feathers as hot, sticky wetness exploded out of him and filled me to the brim.

He didn't bother to get free before collapsing on top of me. He flattened me in half—weakened by his desire for a tiresome little bird.

"Not... so..." My pants heaved my chest. "...in control now... are you?"

His chuckle was a warm tickle on my neck. "Don't be so certain. Tonight I will have you in every way a man can have a woman. You won't walk for days—let alone run."

He slid out from between my legs before I could respond. One snap, and my silk bindings were gone. Capturing my gaze, Alisdair dropped to his knees.

Is he—?

He buried his face between my legs without so much as a warning. I made a strangled noise as my legs snapped over his ears—back arching off the bed. Alisdair plundered my entrance—licking, nipping, and sucking on a particular bundle of heat and lightning that made stars burst behind my eyelids.

"Oh, yes, right there," I gasped. "Oh, Meya, that's amazing!"

I twisted and writhed on the sheets, yanking his head off his shoulders. What delicious irony it would be if after all my assassination attempts, it was my overzealousness in bed that finally ended the great and terrible Alisdair Shadowsoul.

I didn't want to think of what my second name would be then.

My fingers found my nipples, tweaking them as rough and commanding as he did. I couldn't believe it was only a short while ago that I ran from Shadi and the girls' description of sex. Was I ever so innocent?

Oh, if that innocent girl were to see me now—teasing myself while the most feared in Elva licked the filthy drippings of my arousal and his seed clean from my pussy... Well, if she saw that, she'd be just as wanton with need.

My orgasm was already returning fast, and I was so weak from the first one, all I could do was shudder and scream as it ripped through the last of my defenses—shattering the last illusion I had of ever again pretending bedding Shadowsoul wasn't the most thrilling, sexiest, and deliciously wrong thing I'd ever done.

All those other times, I could say I was helpless to his body and power, but this time, I knew what I was doing—and I knew I wanted more.

The top of his head disappeared. A warm, confident swipe across my puckered hole shot me upright.

"Oh! I didn't realize that's what more was!"

Alisdair trapped me with a hand flat between my breasts. Slowly, he drew me back.

"Easy, little bird," he said in that unhurried, mocking drawl. "I haven't begun to show you more."

Sweat beaded on my skin even as it tightened with excitement. Alisdair had his way with both holes—teasing one, tasting one, and then switching it up.

Moans pealed from my lips—loud and begging.

"A-Alisdair," I cried. Heat melted my core, contracting it almost painfully. "Alisdair!"

My husband bit that bundle of nerves, and I exploded.

"Uhhhh!" I moaned, feet drumming the side of the bed. Again and again pleasure bowled me over, blowing up my mind as one explosion ended and the other began. The chain reaction carried me all the way down, leaving me a flopping, sweaty mess on our sheets. "Oh, wow. People really undersold this whole orgasm thing."

"They didn't." Alisdair lazily licked me off his fingers. "They've just never been with me."

Cracking a smile, I put my feet on his shoulders, and kicked. Moving fast, I flipped over and scrambled away as fast as my jellied limbs would carry me.

"Argh! Damn you, woman! I will shackle those blasted feet to the bed!"

A shadow fell over me. The only warning given before Alisdair tackled me.

We flailed and rolled—swiping, shoving, straddling, and shoving each other again. I finally got him under me and sat on his face.

"All this time, I've been helpless to you. You *will* know what it is to be at my mercy!" Was that a lover's promise or a threat? I'd say it was both and neither.

Alisdair grasped my thighs and lifted me off him—easier than lifting a pillow. "Not before you."

He tossed me head over heels.

I flopped flat on my front with no chance of getting up. Alisdair jumped on me, lifted my hips, and thrust in to the hilt.

The sharp stab of pain rocked me, clenching the moan between my teeth.

"You wanted the beast," he growled. "Rejoice. You married him."

A long, filthy string of vile curses assaulted his ear while he pumped—pounding my aching hole senseless.

Alisdair stretched me to bursting, then stretched me some more. Sweat slicked our bodies, sounding a *slap-slap-slap* chorus that timed perfectly with my curses and cries.

"Fuck you, Alisdair! I hate you. I'll always hate you— Uh, yes, right there," I breathed. "Harder, you beast, obey your queen."

He laughed—an insane, terrifying sound. "As you command, my queen."

I knew my mistake immediately, but there was no taking it back.

Alisdair brought us both up to our knees, and impaled me on his cock.

I lost all capability of speech as he bounced me off his thighs, fucking me so hard, my head would've rattled off my shoulders and rolled away if it wasn't attached.

"Ahh," I screamed, walls tightening on him. "AHH!"

A variety of sounds, cries, and moans poured from my mouth while he rode me like an animal— pumping between my legs, bouncing me on the sheets, and filling my body with pleasure it had never known. I was trapped under his thrall. His little bird would not escape him.

"Oh, Alisdair, I can't—" The heat was blazing out of control. Sweat slicked our bodies. My fevered pants hazed the air. "Please, I can't— I can't—" I twisted around, my gaze pinning him through. "I can't believe this is how fast you can go."

Oh, yes. Insane and terrible. That was the right way to describe that laugh.

Alisdair angled me up, struck that spot that rolled my eyes up in my head, and drilled it with impossible speed.

"Yes, ahh!" The first wave crashed and dragged me under. Pleasure so intense and searing exploded every nerve ending in my body over, over, and over again. And then again.

I blacked out.

At some point my lids fluttered open to find Alisdair draped over me, winding my fiery strands around his finger. He didn't even seem winded.

"It's about time," he remarked, smooth and calm. "You'll have to be awake for this part, since you'll be upside down."

My voice was a thin croak. "Wait, what—?"

The room spun again.

Chapter Nine

The next morning, Alisdair declared we were going out to hold court among the people since they couldn't come to us. He also claimed it was a great opportunity to let every skeptical and secretly resentful villager see the others paying tribute to me, and know that any more attacks against me would summon the wrath of all of Lumenfell.

His suggestions sounded reasonable and wise, and it would've been, if my husband wasn't an evil bastard.

Alisdair strode alongside my litter proud and puffed up like a peacock faeriken. There were no two ways about it. He fucked me so hard the night before, I groaned myself to a shaky, standing position getting out of bed that morning, then promptly collapsed on my ass. I was sore all over, and I wasn't walking anywhere. Let alone traipsing from village to village.

Alisdair was only too pleased to present the litter, letting all and sundry witness the mess he made of me.

Despite the humiliation, the litter itself was a throne of beauty and comfort. My platform had small, raised sides to hold the bed of silks, blankets, and pillows. Starflowers and roses painted on the sides, and a small, carved headboard cradled my back. Six men held me up by the handles while Talulla walked on the other side with grapes, apple slices, and a bowl of pranganuts. I'd discovered a taste for the tart little fruits and I couldn't get enough of them.

Our party made our way out of Lumenfell to another, smaller village two miles away, Dervlen.

"Stop," Alisdair ordered, making the procession pause at the side of the path.

I peered over the side as he bent down, and gasped. The most beautiful flower peeked out of the snow—its petals light and lovely as angel wings. I thought no other flower could be as pretty as a starflower, but then I'd never seen this flower, a twin of the butterfly—speckled, delicate, and flying with the wind.

Alisdair picked it and presented it to me. "For you, little bird. Delight in how even this flower's beauty pales in comparison to yours."

I glared fit to burn him where he stood. "Your pretty words and false gifts do not fool me. You don't get to behave as a beast at night, and a gentleman in the light."

The corner of his mouth quirked up. "I resent the accusation that I was anything less than gentlemanly last night. Every time you said harder, faster, and deeper, didn't I obey?"

My face caught fire amid the guards' shifting glances and smothered chuckles. "I didn't know what I was saying," I cried. "The things you do to me... It's like I lose my mind."

"Then you're halfway to me, my queen." He tucked the flower behind my ear. "Because I lost my mind and all sense of control the moment I met you."

If there was something to say in response to that, I didn't know what it was. It was odd, but I was starting to get the feeling that somewhere along the way, Alisdair had stopped hating the pointless, decorative child of his most hated enemy... and had started respecting me.

That threw me even harder than his threats and cruelty.

Even so, that night, I covered myself in more dura dura fruit and jumped on the back of a shocked and squawking bird faeriken, warning him that if he didn't want my husband to tear his wings off, he'd better fly fast.

We made it five miles out before a dark, growling figure burst through the trees. The poor servant was so terrified, he dumped his load directly in Alisdair's hands and took off for the mountains.

Alisdair magicked us out of the Taken's territory and into the war room, where he proceeded to bend me over the table on a map of Lyrica, then pounded me from behind. He said he wanted me to enjoy a good long look at Lyrica how it was, because the next I returned, it'd be nothing but rubble.

I screamed curses at him even while I screamed for another reason.

The night after that, I ran through the woods behind the castle—covering myself in all the starflowers I came across. My failing was continuing to mask my scent with stronger scents. I needed to be invisible, not a walking stink beacon. I should no more stand out than a blade of grass.

Glowing like an orblight, I found a cave and tucked myself in there for the night—jumping and twitching at every snapped twig or shifting shadow in the distance. It wasn't Alisdair finding me that frightened me. It was the Taken finding me first.

I sat in the dark in the cave for hours and hours. So long, night began to fall away and I sensed the sunrise coming for me.

Alisdair laughed a second after I shouted with glee. He had found me an hour before, but decided to let me taste victory before he snatched it away.

On it went for a week, and then two. Every night, I stretched the limits of my cleverness to outsmart a beast, and every morning, I woke up sticky and sated beneath his arms.

On the fifteenth morning, I couldn't recall Savia's face.

I remembered her name. I remembered a sweet laugh, pudgy fingers, and the screams of kakkas who got a face full of her soiled wrappings, but try as I did, I couldn't remember what my youngest sister looked like.

I sat at the vanity, methodically combing through Emiana's long and lovely hair. Behind me, Alisdair lay on the bed—his true form unleashed. I gazed at him, then at the delicate, glass comb trapped between my fingertips. How easy it would be to break it, then plunge the jagged pieces in his throat.

And what a waste of time that would be. Precious, precious time that I was quickly running out of. There was no outrunning Alisdair Shadowsoul. No outsmarting him. No fooling him. And no killing him.

There was only one thing left for me to do. The one thing I swore I wouldn't do. The option that wasn't an option... because it was doomed to fail.

I glanced out at my unwanted kingdom—its people rising under the burden of a terrible curse. Just like me.

"Meya, never let it be said I don't know when it's time to stop fighting and accept your will," I whispered. "I'll do it, All Mother.

"I'll make the man with no heart fall in love with me."

***

I watched Alisdair out of the corner of my eye. We were in the training yard. After that first lesson, Alisdair declared that every morning I'd learn the running of the kingdom, and every afternoon, I'd be in the training yard, learning how to defend it.

Despite my resolution to break the curse by making him fall in love with me, I had no idea how. I'd never been in love. I'd never seen love. I knew not a single thing about love.

That's not entirely true, I thought. *Mama used to tell stories about the things Papa did that made her fall in love with him. Stories about how even when she rolled out of bed with ratty hair and stale breath, he'd kiss her and say she was the most beautiful creature he'd ever seen.*

Compliments. I stood up straight, nodding to myself. *That's as good a place as any to start.*

I cleared my throat. "Alisdair?"

He paused his explanation, lowering his bow. He'd been in the middle of telling me how to aim for the eye. "What?"

"You... You look..." Truthfully, it wasn't hard to think of a compliment for him. He'd let his hair down that day, allowing his ebony waves to whip and roll with the wind. At some point, he shed his cloak and shirt for training, and now all that stood before me was six feet of tall, hard, and handsome. "You look well—nice—*handsome,*" I finally got out. "You look very handsome today. Actually, not just today." My face warmed under his gaze. "You look handsome every day, but today you're particularly... handsome. A very handsome man."

He gave me a long, flat look—stretching out the silence until I could literally die from embarrassment. "All this I know," he said flatly. "Are you finished?"

Lifting my chin, I nodded.

"Good. Now, take a breath before you notch the bow," he said, returning to business. "That will steady your aim. After, you will..."

We continued on with the lesson. I wasn't sure whether to be annoyed that he ignored my compliment, or relieved that he didn't comment on my nervous rambling.

After the lesson, Alisdair strode off without a word or look back. Aeris ran over to take my bow and bundle me in a warm shawl.

"Where does he go in the evenings?" I asked her. "I mean, in the time after lessons and before he begins the chase. I am having my supper, but what is he doing?"

"Why, he's having his supper of course." She vigorously rubbed my arms, spreading warmth into my frozen limbs as we headed inside.

"So he does eat."

She laughed. "Of course he eats. You say the funniest things, my lady."

She may laugh, but I'd certainly never seen the man eat. Alisdair made sure I ate, by barking at the nearest servant to feed me, but he'd never sat down to eat a meal with me. I told Aeris as much.

"That's because my lord takes his meals in the dining hall with us while you dine in your chambers."

"What?" I halted, pulling her up short. "Why? Why am I eating alone? Did he decree that I had to?"

"No," she cried. "It wasn't my lord, it was..." Discomfort ruffled her feathers. "It was I who thought it best for you to dine in the peace and comfort of your chambers. I told our lord it was for the best."

"Why would you do that?"

"I'm truly sorry, Lady Ana." She grasped my hands. "We know what the other fae think of us. That we're beasts and savages and we can't control ourselves." She winced. "All of those rumors are confirmed when you watch us eat."

"Aeris." I looked her straight in the eyes. "I will be eating with my husband and our people tonight. End of discussion."

"Yes, ma'am. I will get you changed and ready right away."

Aeris and I went upstairs to my bath to wash off the tiring target practice. My attendants already had the water hot, steamy, and scented with oils, while Eadaoin and Talulla stood by with my dinner tray. Aeris sent the tray away while the attendants undressed me. I long since stopped arguing with them about dressing and undressing myself.

If compliments don't work on the empty-chested man, what will? What else did Papa do to woo Mama?

My mind went through the stories she told me as I stepped into my bath. The doors blew out, snapping me out of my memories. Bradach walked inside.

"Bradach," I cried, slapping my hands over my exposed bits. "You're back."

"That I am, my queen." He bowed low, wings crowning and spreading the calming scent of wind, rain, and pine. "As proud as I would be to die for you, I can happily report I did not."

"That's great, but"—I flapped a hand—"would you mind?"

"Mind what?"

"Leaving! I'm naked."

"Oh, right. If you insist."

"Thank you."

He then proceeded to strip off his clothes. "Now, where was I?"

I gave up.

"Aeris, my blossom," he said, kneeling beside her sitting on my chaise.

"What?" she snapped.

"I missed you most of all."

Her eye roll made me giggle.

"I can't apologize enough for scaring and being away from you for so long, but I hope this comes close." Bradach got something out of his pocket and covered it, holding up his closed palms to her.

Aeris tried to seem disinterested. "What is it?" she breezed, gaze fixed on a spot on the ceiling.

He opened his palms. "It's a snowflake from the highest mountain peak in all of Wind and Wild, where the stars still shine. I encased it in everlasting glass for you." He placed the beautiful silver necklace in her hand. "If the stars won't shine on you, my love, I will bring them to you. My wings will carry you until the day your heart flies side by side with mine."

"Wow," someone breathed.

It was me. Was that the kind of sweet, flowery stuff Papa said to Mama, because if it was, I understood why she said she'd never known a love like theirs.

Me, Eadaoin, and my attendants fixed on them—wide-eyed and waiting for Aeris's response. She reddened under our gaze.

"Will you wear it?" he asked.

"Well, I mean..." She roughly cleared her throat. "You— Nothing you said made any sense," she cried, "but if you went through all that trouble... I could... I could possibly wear it.

"Thank you," she mumbled so low, I almost didn't hear her.

Her tomato-red cheeks shone brighter than an orblight as he lifted her hair, and carefully placed the necklace on her feathered collarbone.

"You're beautiful." Bradach bent and pressed a featherlight kiss to her lips.

Aeris's eyes fluttered shut—the softest sigh escaping her.

Then her lids ripped open and she shot up, spinning her back to him. "Bradach, you forget yourself in the presence of our queen. Leave us, you're making her uncomfortable."

I blinked at them. I was feeling something, but discomfort wasn't it.

"Very well." Bradach rescued his clothes from the floor, and bowed his way to the door. "I'll save you a seat at dinner."

I was suddenly very glad to be attending that dinner. Why had I dismissed Bradach as the court's jester? Aeris did nothing but snap and bark at him, but given a few sweet words and ice off a mountain, and she was ready to have her way with the man right there on the chaise.

Mama's stories were of friends falling in love, but Alisdair was never going to make it easy. I wasn't wooing the banished heart of a man who was half in love with me already. I was trapping and capturing the heart of a beast who swore to give me anything but.

Besides, I mused, following Aeris and Eadaoin down to the dining hall. *Bradach is Alisdair's companion. Who better than his bedmate to teach me the ways of seducing him?*

A flash of anger roared in my chest at the thought that Bradach was *still* his bedmate. A thought I'd been trying hard to ignore. Alisdair marked me so that another man couldn't touch me. I had no such marking on him, and of all the promises he made me during the mating ceremony—fidelity wasn't one.

Together, we entered the dining hall, and my eyes blew wide. Beasts. Savages. Can't control themselves.

Aeris was being kind.

There wasn't a single utensil in sight. The faeriken tore at the meats, cheeses, bread, and vegetables with their bare hands, while snarls, snaps, and demands for more filled the air. A ring of masticated remains surrounded the long, oaken table and high-backed velvet-covered chairs. All the makings of a beautiful, formal dinner in a royal palace—if not for half the guests scrambling over the table to tear apart a turkey, and attacking each other for the bigger piece.

Alisdair sat at the head of it all with food that was only for him—easily seen from the fact that no one else dared look at his chicken, turkey, slab of beef, tray of bread rolls, four mugs of ale, and the fruits and vegetables from my tributes.

No. No one else dared lay a finger on his food... because they'd lose a finger bringing it that close to his mouth.

Alisdair was more the beast than the man. Long claws shredded the chicken and shoveled its tender meat into his mouth. He snatched up a mug and drained it, spilling ale all down the sides of his face and soaking his half-exposed chest.

"That is enough!" Aeris roared, making me jump. A dozen heads snapped up—growls, screeches, hisses, squawks, and barks peeling from their throats. Aeris screeched right back. "Get a hold of yourselves! Your queen is in your presence, and she is used to finer things and proper decorum. You will sit in your seats. You will chew and swallow your food before taking another bite, and you *will* use utensils!"

They all glared and groaned... at me. I truly was in another land because to look at my fath—King Salman with the fury they were throwing me was to be smote for treason. I knew because Emiana witnessed him do it when a peasant dared to look at him with the contempt he deserved.

Even the sweetest, gentlest dog will growl if you try to take their food while they're eating. Some instincts are too deeply ingrained, and protecting your meal is one of them.

Slowly, I rounded the table and made for the empty seat next to Alisdair. Had Aeris called down for them to leave a seat for me, or was it always sitting empty—the constant symbol that their queen was too high and refined to eat with lowly faeriken?

Quietly, I reached for my seat. Aeris was quicker and pulled it out for me to sit down.

Alisdair scoffed. "Lo and behold, our table manners have been found lacking. Get your bibs and forks, everyone."

Mocking laughter went up around the table.

"Will that satisfy you, little bird, or should I have a servant cut your food for you? Possibly chew it for you too? They can also—"

I pounced on the food, shoveling it into my mouth faster than I could chew. I'd never been at a table with this much food in my life. And meat! So much meat of all kinds and types. The rare times I had a full belly, it was full on the meager vegetables from our garden. It was then I realized Aeris had been instructing the cooks to feed me the dainty portions worthy of a princess. Why hadn't I demanded to eat with everyone weeks ago?

Blown brows and hanging jaws stared at me. I blew past them all and narrowed in on Alisdair's hand. "Are you going to eat that?" I snatched the turkey leg from his slackened grip and let out a belch that made Alisdair jerk in his seat.

I met the wide eyes with round eyes of my own. "What's everyone looking at me for? If you're not going to eat this, I will."

Alisdair let out a strange and terrible sound, making me slow my chewing to give an expression more shocked than Aeris's.

He laughed. Full-blown, raucous, pounding-the-table belly laughs. "You heard my queen." He gave me the first real smile I'd ever seen on his lips. Not a smirk. Not a mocking grin. But a smile. "Let's eat."

The faeriken descended on the food—eating almost as fast as me. The pretty silk sapphire gown Aeris chose for me was ruined by spilled ale and food stains in minutes. Everyone was too focused on unhinging their jaws and shoveling food inside to chatter, and wasn't that the way it should be?

Memories flashed through my mind of Emiana sitting at a mile-long table, picking at her apple-sized portion of a meal, and being forced to stop eating every time someone insisted on making meaningless small talk with her. Apparently, it was rude to eat while someone was speaking to you, or speak while you were eating. The result was Emiana always went to bed hungry.

"Fuck that," I belted, "and fuck table manners!"

"Yeahh!" bellowed my court—laughing and pounding the table with their mugs.

Bradach clapped Alisdair on the shoulder. "You did good with this one, my lord. Dare I say better than you deserve."

Alisdair tore off a bite of beef, grinning at me. "This I know."

***

I pushed away the remains of my meal, letting out another belch. I was stuffed to the gills. Couldn't eat another bite if I tried, and I'd never been able to say that in my life.

"Twenty minutes." Alisdair picked food out of his unnaturally long and jagged teeth with his claws. "I'm feeling generous tonight."

Nodding, I pushed away from the table. "Bradach, come with me, please. I need your help with something."

Bradach stiffened. "My lady, I live to serve you, but I humbly ask that you not mark me and use me for a decoy. I'd rather not spend another fortnight on a mountain."

Half the table jumped up from their seats, readying to run away from me.

"That's not— I wasn't going to!" I cried. "I just want to talk to you, I swear. I'll keep my hugs to myself."

Narrowed eyes held suspicion. Slowly he rose from the table and followed me out, keeping a healthy distance between us. When we were far enough away from Alisdair's earshot, I rounded on him.

"How do you do it?" I demanded. "One minute, Aeris can't stand the sight of you, and the next it's a good thing she's sitting because she's about to pass out from swooning. How do I do that? How do I get Alisdair to... do that?" I finished, flushing deep.

Bradach frowned at me, then his brows smoothed out. "Oh, I see. You're asking me how to make him fall in love with you."

I don't know why him stating it plainly made me want to run and hide, but I didn't. I simply nodded.

"And you've come to me because I'm his closest companion and most trusted advisor." He puffed out his chest, ever the vain, cocky raven. "I'm flattered, my queen, and more than happy to help, but we men are grossly simple creatures."

"What do you mean?"

"We all want what we can't have," he explained. "Our lord already has you, or so he thinks." Bradach smirked, winking. "Make him know he doesn't, and that he has to work, bleed, and sweat to have you. All the things he will discover through want of winning you will naturally lead to love, for how could any man who knows you, not love you?"

My face warmed, heart fluttering in my chest. Oh yes, I could definitely understand how Bradach was thawing the ice around Aeris's heart.

"Thank you," I said lightly. "That's... good advice."

Aeris and Eadaoin chose that moment to come around the corner, looking for me.

Bradach gave me one last bow and a wink, kissed Aeris's blushing cheek, and walked off.

My companions fell in step with me as I burped my way through the halls, pinching Aeris's lips tighter and tighter. Eadaoin couldn't hold back her giggles at the both of us.

"You continue to surprise me, Lady Ana," Eadaoin said. "But how will you tackle your daring escape in this state? I could practically roll you down the hall."

I laughed. "No running, no rolling, no daring escape. I have something else planned for Alisdair tonight."

Fifteen minutes later, a large hulking shadow crossed the threshold of our bedroom. He observed me reclined on the bed—relaxed.

"What manner of trick is this?" Alisdair breathed deep, scenting a trap. "Why are you lying there? Why aren't you running or hiding in a pile of manure?"

"That was an act of desperation that I'll never repeat again," I snapped. "Mostly because it didn't work."

He circled me, back gliding against the wall—keeping me in sight. "And what about this is supposed to work?" Alisdair chuckled. "Let me guess. You're going to suddenly leap off the bed and throw yourself off the cliff where Bradach will be waiting to fly you away?"

I smiled back. "Now that's good. I probably would've done just that if Bradach wasn't wary of me by now. But no, I have something else planned for tonight."

Alisdair tensed like I was going to attack him. His lips peeled back, growls leaking through his fangs as he readied for my strike.

"Woo me."

The growls stopped. "Excuse me?"

"Seduce me, husband." I peeled back my robe, letting it fall off my shoulder. I wore it and nothing else. "If you want to have me... you'll have to earn it."

The predator stalked closer. "Is that so?"

"You've gotten everything your way, but not me."

"Hmm." He moved around the headboard. His voice rolled over me, shivering my spine. "I seem to recall having you my way last night, and the night before that, and three times the night before that."

"Not anymore," I rushed. "You wanted a mate, Lumenfell. A queen to rule and wage war by your side. A partner to have and raise your babies. You burned your promises to me on your soul, and now it's time for you to deliver. By day I am your queen, but at night, you're my husband. Act like it. Seduce me, woo me, tempt me, flirt with me, compliment me."

"No."

"And if you do, I'll—" I blinked, the words halting on my lips. "What?"

"I said no. You're speaking utter nonsense, woman, as usual."

As usual?!

"What reason have you to say no to me? I bet you wouldn't say no to Bradach."

"You—" His face crumpled. "Bradach? What on earth are you talking about? What does he have to do with this?"

"Don't give me that. I know everything. I see the way you laugh, joke, and touch him. I see how he laughs, jokes, and touches *you*. I know he's your companion."

Alisdair's eyes blew wide, jaw slackening. I'd never seen that look on his face. I don't think anyone's had for a thousand years. "He's my— Don't be absurd!"

"You're absurd if you think you're going to lie to me now. Bradach told me himself. He's your right hand, your most trusted advisor, your sage counsel, your truest comrade, and your closest *companion*." I smiled at him in equal parts irritation and triumph. "Are you calling Bradach a liar?"

"Unreservedly and without hesitation," he dropped, tone flat. "That fool is none of those things to me. He's only bold enough to say otherwise because he's proven extraordinarily difficult to kill," he gritted. "Blast him and those fucking wings."

My jaw worked. "Oh."

While it made me feel marginally better to know he wasn't denying me because he preferred someone else's company, it was hard to swallow that the only reason Alisdair Shadowsoul had a friend... was because he hadn't figured out how to kill him yet.

I cleared my throat, shaking away the thought. "Well, then, if that's the case, you have no reason to say no. Woo me, husband."

He snorted. "I have no reason to say yes. I fulfill my husbandly duties to perfection nightly. I cater to your pleasure above my own—as is the Wind and Wild way. I do not let you sleep until you've completed at least four times. I ensure you can't walk in the morning for limping. Beyond that, I've bestowed my protection on you, making sure my enemies dare not lay a hand on you, and I waste considerable time teaching you to fight and rule my country.

"No other husbandly duties are required of me." Alisdair ripped off his clothes. "Now hands and knees. Head down. Ass up."

My jaw worked but nothing came out. I didn't know where to begin. Marking me was to protect me? It wasn't to cheat or make it harder for me to run? Was that true? Could I possibly believe it was? But more importantly, did he just say putting my pleasure above his own was no more than a faeriken custom? Did that mean he didn't enjoy his nights with me? Why did the thought of that cut as deep as him saying every minute he spent with me—teaching me to rule and fight—was a waste of his time?

Why would this man put any effort into winning me? He already had a pet. He didn't need a wife.

I turned away, my lips pressed tight to stop them trembling. "You're right," I rasped, drawing up my robe. "Just forget it."

"What's this?" he demanded. "What's happened?"

"Nothing happened." I blew out the candle on the nightstand. "You win, okay? I ran, you caught me. Let's just go to bed."

"No, you're crying. Why are you doing that?"

I hurriedly wiped my eyes. "I'm not crying, I'm tired. It's been a long day, and I wouldn't want you to *waste* any more time on me."

A heavy silence filled the room.

"I see," he said. "Very well. I will seduce you."

"What? What do you mean?"

"Prepare yourself, woman."

"I don't— Ah!" A hand grabbed my ankle and slid me across the bed, depositing me gaping beneath him.

Slowly, deliberately, Alisdair ran a finger down the length of my body—from my neck to the crown of my thighs, parting my robe.

The fabric fell to the sides, exposing me to his cold eyes—something that's happened every night since I met the man, but that night, I shivered under his gaze.

Dropping down, Alisdair pressed a light, tickling kiss to my ankle, then continued the trail—dropping soft pecks along my leg, knee, and up my thigh—coming to my slit where he passed over and went to the other thigh, and gifted it the same tender treatment.

I was wide-eyed and still, afraid to move and break whatever spell he was under. Where was the man who barked at me to put my ass up, then took me before I had the chance?

Alisdair rose over me, cupping the back of my head. I gasped as he kissed me—a slow, tender creation that parted my lips with the softest nip, and invited my tongue to dance—unhurried and teasing.

I didn't have to search my memory. This was the first Alisdair had ever kissed me in this way. He rarely kissed me at all, but when he did, he was rough, fierce, and passionate. I felt like I was in a hurricane, clinging to the ground by a blade of grass.

But this kiss... felt like we were both in that hurricane, but Alisdair was holding me. Protecting me. Anchoring me through the storm.

Eyes so cold. Words so harsh, but his lips were soft and warm. They banished my hate, anger, and fear, leaving nothing behind, except me and Alisdair.

He guided me onto the pillows, our bodies and mouths still connected. I'd never drunk to excess before, though I had to believe this is what it was like. My head spun. Pulse raced. Breaths quickened. I felt clear and silly at the same time. Like I was about to jump off a cliff without wings, but the joy of falling through the air was worth the end.

His tongue tangled with mine, inviting me to play. I moaned as he caressed me, his hands trailing up and down my body, and I was suddenly sure that this was nothing like being drunk. If wine gave this feeling, no one in the land would set down a bottle.

Fingers tickled me, skating higher along my thigh and slipping between. I dropped my knee, making clear what I wanted him to do.

Breaking from me, he brushed a kiss on the tip of my nose. "You are perfection, intelligence, and ferocity itself. To bask in your presence is to be humbled. To delight from your lips is to slip between the veil and walk through the meadows of Meya itself."

"Ug—" I got out, throat restricting. What did one say to words so beautiful? And what did they say when those words came from their terrible, beastly husband? Did he mean them?

Did I want him to?

Alisdair brushed over my lower lips, and kept going—chuckling at my grunt of irritation. He seemed to just want to touch me. Soak in every inch of my body.

Her body, a quiet voice broke in. *It's the famed beauty of the east who he admires. Not the little wretch from the Gutter.*

"Don't frown, my queen," he said, trapping my gaze. "When you do, I'm forced to remove that frown by any method necessary—usually sexual."

I giggled, making him laugh in return.

"That was easy." Alisdair lifted his hand and a starflower appeared on his fingers. He tucked it behind my ear, smiling at me. I couldn't say how I knew, but it was a true smile.

Alisdair bent and kissed the ghost of a laugh still on my lips, then he kissed my cheek, my nose, my lids, everywhere—dropping sweet gifts on my soft skin.

My skin started heating, beading sweat on my neck and stomach. My breaths came too fast, heaving my chest, and straining to contain my pounding heart. What was this? How was he doing this?

Alisdair captured my lips again and I moaned, limbs melting like ice in a land with sun.

Breaking away, Alisdair rose up on his knees and draped my legs over his thighs.

I pressed my palm to his heart, wondering if it beat as hard as mine. Wondering if it beat.

But there was nothing there. He hadn't returned his heart to his chest. He was still keeping it far away from me.

"Another frown?" Alisdair gently smoothed the line between my brow. "I will banish it for good."

He kissed me again—hard. The sudden fierce and fiery kiss sent my heart galloping away, chasing a moan from my lips. I broke from him gasping. My vision spun as his mouth moved lower, leaving nipping, teasing kisses down the valley of my breasts to my tender stomach. Alisdair flipped me over, continuing his path one by one, kiss by kiss down the ridges of my spine. I arched like a cat—pleasure rippling goose bumps over my skin.

My excitement built as he moved lower, lower, low—

Growling, Alisdair buried between my legs—tasting me with abandon. I gasped on a cry, eyes rolling up in my head.

Alisdair both took his time and chased me to a high. His tongue probed, and rolled, and flicked my tortured nub, waiting until my cries grew hoarse to stop and start all over again. I was a sweaty, limp mess in no time at all.

"By the A-All Mother," I stuttered, feeling the fire burning through my veins. One more and I'd—

Alisdair flicked the nub and I exploded—spasming on the bed, coming so hard white spots danced on the wall.

He draped himself over me, humming as he bit the shell of my ear. "I will fashion a paradise for you, my queen. I'll burn all of Elva down, and remake it in your image."

My pants tickled the back of my hand, but I couldn't move it. Alisdair laced his fingers through mine.

"You will want for nothing for the rest of your days, and not as a discarded decoration," he whispered, nipping my ear. "You will have books, and tutors, and university."

My eyes popped open—shock parting my jaw. *How did he know that's what I wanted more than anything?*

"You will be all of the incredible, enigmatic, troublesome things you are meant to be," he said, making my eyes fill.

Alisdair dropped a kiss on my shoulder. "Although, I confess, it escapes me how you plan to improve upon perfection."

My heart thundered so hard, it thrummed louder than the howling wind. Cold ripped through our exposed bedchamber, but I was warm. Warm from his body heat. Warm from the lingering aftershocks of my orgasm. And warm... from him.

Alisdair had never spoken to me this way without a mocking tone and a smirk thrown in for good measure. To hear him say all the things I never dreamed a man would say to me, but deep down, wished he would...

It undid every lock, chain, and trap around my heart.

"Alisdair," I whispered, stroking the fingers holding mine. "I—"

Alisdair tipped my chin. We kissed slow, sweet, and mind-scrambling.

How had he done this to me? I melted into the kiss. *I think I'm falling—*

"No!" I ripped away. "No, no, no!"

"Princess?"

"No." I scrambled out from under him and snatched up my robe. "Absolutely not. We are done. *You* are done! This— Whatever this is," I cried, waving my hands between us. "It's over."

He gave me a crazy look. "What the— You demanded I do this! You bawled like an infant when I refused!"

I flung a pillow at his face. "Well, lucky for you, the bawling infant is leaving!" I stormed off—my anger burning away whatever delusion-induced feelings I thought I was having.

"Fuck's sake!" Alisdair's roar rattled the door on its hinges. "You're impossible!"

I slammed the door, then immediately dropped against it, sliding down to the floor.

I wasn't versed in the ways of sex, attraction, marriage, mates, or soul-bindings. I never felt the emotions that others labeled, so how could I know which label fit?

All I did know was whatever Alisdair made me feel in there, it could never happen again.

***

The next day, I followed Eadaoin down the many staircases to a part of the castle I'd never been before. It amazed me that there were still new depths to plumb in Castle Riagin.

Memories of last night flashed through my mind on a loop, warming my face and tightening my lower belly every night.

That could not happen again. Leave it to Alisdair to turn the tables, and make seducing me a bid for power that he won. Won absolutely.

The plan was for him to develop feelings or me, it wasn't for me to form feelings for him. It made no sense that his initial rejection hurt me.

I hated the man. What did it matter that he slept with and spent time with me out of duty? It shouldn't matter at all... but it did.

I didn't want it to be true, but it felt good when he praised me. Felt even better when he was impressed with me. And it thrilled my heart when he respected me and my opinion. No one, ever, in my whole life had done or felt any of those things toward me. No one except my family.

To have Alisdair turn around and say all of that was a waste of time cut me to the bone. And then to have him kiss and have me tender and sweet, healed all the broken parts of me right back again.

That wouldn't do. I could *not* get overly invested in a man who planned to wage war on my home, my family, and my life. He was a monster and the only way this marriage ended was by me breaking my curse and leaving him—whether he loved the real and true me or not.

"Eadaoin," I spoke up. "How did you and your soldier man fall in love?"

"Love?" She laughed. "I wouldn't say we're in love. More like having a bit of fun."

"Really? Well, you two seem to have *fun* every free minute of every day. It's a wonder to me that you don't walk with a limp."

She nudged my shoulder, laughing. "What can I say? When you're having that much fun, you don't want it to stop."

"But the way he looks at you." We stepped into a darkened hallway—heavy with a damp, musty smell. "With such need and lust like he can't get enough of you. How do you... uh... invoke that in a man?" I forced out. "How do I make *him* need *me*?"

"Ahhhh." She gave me a knowing look. "My lord's giving you trouble, is he?"

I prayed Meya would open the floor and swallow me.

"Don't worry, my queen. I know many a trick to bring a stubborn man to heel." She threw her arm around me. "And may I say, I'm so happy you're finally partaking in my sexual experience."

"Or you could just kill me," I mumbled. "End my humiliation now."

Naturally, she laughed at me. "All right, first thing you want to do is make him jealous. That's what I did with Keefe. I started bedding his friend Oisin. After weeks of watching how much fun we were having in the bed next to him, he finally leaped across the room, tackled me off Oisin, and had me right there on the floor." She shivered. "Mother Meya, it was *good*."

I gaped at her in horror. "That's what you suggest I do! Bed another man in front of Alisdair? He tried to kill Bradach for saving my life. He'd tear that poor soul to shreds."

She winced. "Excellent point. Definitely do not do that. It'd be a violation of your marriage runes anyway." Eadaoin pointed to one on my elbow. "It'd be enough to give another man your attention. All your attention. Trust me, when you do, our lord will be driven mad with the need to have that attention back for himself."

I bobbed my head, considering. It wasn't the worst idea, and besides, Eadaoin was skilled in seduction. If anyone would know how to twist a man around her finger, it would be her.

"In here," she said, stopping short beside a small, dirt-covered door. "This is where our lord said to bring you."

One step inside and I saw why.

"Whoa, whoa!" Foalan shouted. "Careful on that side!"

My happiness at seeing Foalan had returned to Castle Riagin in one piece was overshadowed by the spectacle that had the attention of everyone in the dungeon.

A spherical glass tank wobbled and rolled on the dirty stone floor, bouncing off a wall of magic shot by each soldier it tried to flatten. The women, and Foalan, formed a ring around it, sweating hard for the effort of keeping it in— No, of keeping her in.

My feet moved on their own power, bringing me closer to her. Brilliant, iridescent scales caught the orblight and reflected it into a million billion rainbows dancing through the water. Dark ebony hair like silk ribbons swayed with the water, forming a halo around the loveliest face I'd ever seen. Far more lovely than the one I saw in the mirror.

Shimmering, aquamarine eyes beheld me—twisting me in their pools. Dusky, desert-sand skin was smooth and unbroken—never knowing a scar, pimple, or blemish. Full, pouty lips twisted with her pert, wrinkled nose, and she looked at me like I was the source of her displeasure—or her salvation.

Emiana wasn't the beauty of the east. This creature was. She was the beauty of this land and every other.

"But she—she's a—a—"

"Mermaid." Alisdair stepped out of the darkness. "Otherwise known as…"

My gaze trailed her long, dazzling fish tail.

"A siren."

"What is she doing here?" I whispered, drawing closer. *Her eyes… Such beautiful eyes…*

"At the present, she's attempting to kill you."

The dry reply only just began to penetrate when that beautiful face morphed. Hard, ridged, scaly lines erupted on her nose and forehead, appearing as fast as the second, jagged row of teeth that descended from her jaw. A fierce, watery screech turned to bubbles in the water as she came straight for me—teeth heading for my throat.

Screaming, I lurched back and she struck the glass head-on—turning purple in her foiled rage.

"Careful, Princess." A firm grip on my elbow guided me back. "Just because her voice doesn't work on women, doesn't mean she's any less lethal to them. Too long staring into her eyes and it'll be the last thing you ever do."

"I—I don't understand," I cried. "A mermaid? A real mermaid? How can she be here? Mermaids went extinct centuries ago. Long before dragons did. She can't be here!"

"And yet, she is." Alisdair encircled her—his smile terrible to behold. "I told you, my queen. We found the vanishing island. A land where many an impossible thing exists," he said. "It took some effort, and a few lives, but our soldiers brought her here—for us."

"Us?" I repeated. "What are you talking about?"

Alisdair paused, pressing his hand to the glass. "She is all we need to win the war. Once I figure out how to harness her voice and use it at will—without killing myself—we will unleash it on the armies of Elva.

"They say a siren's song is so beautiful. So enchanting. Its majesty consumes you." He shook his head. "The second it ends, you realize you'll never again hear anything so wondrous in your life, and that's not a life worth living. A single verse of her song, little bird, and the men will turn their swords on themselves—wiping themselves up without a single drop of spilled blood on our side. My queen," he breathed. "Our victory is assured."

My eyes bugged, horror leadening my bones. "Stop saying our! That's horrible, Alisdair. Worse than horrible! How can you even think such a thing!"

He turned a cool gaze on me. "How can I think to end the war quickly without sacrificing our people? What a ridiculous question. I could think of nothing else." I blinked and he was in front of me—towering over me. "This is mercy, little bird. It's what you once wanted of me."

"This isn't mercy, it's insanity!" I shoved him back. He didn't move an inch. "You can't wipe out every man in Elva! Do you have any idea what that'll do to the kingdoms?"

"Yes," he said, smirking. "They'll become matriarchies once again."

"You—" I choked. "Wait, what?"

"Every vile person that fights to keep your women stunted and oppressed will find themselves on the other side of the veil, facing Meya's judgment. Once they are, the kingdoms can start over. The forced magic bindings will stop, and the young, adolescent boys will be raised properly—without their fathers' hatred and prejudices teaching them to look down on their own mothers and sisters.

"Elva will be cleansed, my queen, and yes"—he inclined his head—"there will be grief and tears and wailing, but you and I will lead our people out of the dark into the new age. All of Elva will be like Lumenfell," he said, throwing out his arms. "Harsh, cold, brutal... but equal and free."

I stared at him amid the shouts and barked orders from Foalan and the soldiers. "A return to the matriarchies," I said slowly. "That is something you want?"

"Why would it not be? I was born in the old age, Princess. In the times of peace and equality. I can assure you," he said, "it was a much better age than this one."

"But, Alisdair—"

"You said you wanted the bindings, the oppression, and the wasting sickness to end."

My throat tightened thinking of Mama slowly starving to death in a small, desolate room.

"That doesn't happen without war. Without sacrifice," he hissed. "So now is the moment you decide."

I snapped up, eyes wide.

"Will you fight for your freedom, or die on your knees?"

I didn't speak for so long, he turned away. "Can you undo the binding spell? Can you free my—?" The curse stole *mom* off my tongue. "Can you free the women of Elva?"

"I can't," he said honestly. "I've tried to unbind you every night since you got here."

I started. I wasn't expecting that.

"It's a simple spell, but a powerful one. The magic it'd take to free you would kill me, but this"—he raised his clawed hand—"has no such limitation."

It took me a second to understand what he meant. "The beast curse?" I whispered. "It undoes the binding spell? That's why all the women in Lumenfell are free?"

He nodded. "The binding is put on the person you are. But when you change, you become someone else. When that happens, the chains that were once on your soul simply... fall away."

I looked into his eyes. "Elva would be a better place if the curse consumed the land."

I said it. I hated myself the moment it fell from my lips, but... I wouldn't take it back.

"Until, of course," I continued, "we all turned into mindless beasts—swinging from trees and flinging our feces."

"One thing at a time," he breezed. "First we conquer all in our path, then we save it."

"Meaning only once everything and everyone is under your power, will you finally destroy the heart?" My blunt words went straight to the point. "At least it makes sense now. Why you've let this go on for centuries. It's a ransom, and all of Elva are your hostages."

"My queen, how many times must I tell you?" A slow, wicked grin twisted his lips. "All of Elva are *our* hostages."

My fist balled, aching to punch that smile in. I hated what it revealed in myself. I hated even more that I couldn't voice the denials screaming in my head.

"Unless, of course," Alisdair continued, stepping back. "You've decided to die on your knees." He gestured to the siren. "If that's the case, say the word, and our only hope of complete victory will be returned to the swamp we fished her out of."

"Send her back," I said without a second's hesitation. "I want Elva to return to the days of equality and freedom, but not this way. What you mean to do is slaughter, not mercy."

"Hmm. No."

"What?" Disbelief colored my tone. "You just told me to say the word."

He shrugged. "Because I assumed you would choose correctly. You're still not ready to do what needs to be done. That's fine. When the change has taken you and all that simpering civility is smothered by the true beast within—you'll see things my way. Even more, you'll know what it is to be free again, and you'll be willing to give that gift to all the people—no matter what it takes."

"Oh, save your manipulative speeches!" I spat. "You're not doing this to free Elva. You're doing it to get revenge against my father!"

His grin went nowhere. "Why can't it be both?"

"No," I ground out. "You're not torturing that creature in the name of wiping out half the population of Elva. I do want to fight for the end of the bindings and the freedom of the women of Elva, even if it means going to war, but you said this is *our* fight. If you mean it, you'll stop making decisions without me.

"We rule together. We fight together. We decide together. Equals. Anything less and you're no different than the shitty, evil bastards who held me down when I was ten years of age, and ripped my magic away from me while I screamed."

His smile melted away. Slowly, he ate the distance between us. "If you're saying this—if you mean this, you're telling me our nightly runs are at an end. You're forsaking Lyrica and allying yourself with me as my queen. My wife."

I didn't look away. "That's exactly what I'm telling you."

Alisdair gave me a long look. "Well, then, there's only one thing to say to that." Stepping back, he bowed. "As you wish, my queen."

My eyes narrowed to slits. The mocking in his tone rang loud and clear.

"My wife has spoken," Alisdair called, rising up. "The mermaid will be kept here—safe, unharmed, and untouched—until we decide the best way to wage and win this war. Together."

All the words were right, but I didn't trust a single one of them. "You promise me?"

"I promise," he replied—light. Easy.

"Will you ink that promise on your skin with runic magic?"

The corners of his mouth quirked down. "I'd say yes, but you can't read runes, so you still wouldn't trust me."

"Very true," I said, smiling. "That's why you're going to teach me to read runes. Add that to our many lessons."

"As you wish, my queen."

Once again the urge to punch him overwhelmed. Only Alisdair could mock me while giving me exactly what I want.

I cast one last look at the siren, then flicked away when our gaze connected. "Foalan, will you heed *our* orders?"

"Yes, my queen."

Now him, I believe.

"Very well." I sniffed in Alisdair's direction—a habit of Emiana, though warranted in his case. "I have business in the village. I won't be long. When I return, we'll begin our rune lessons."

"Your wish is my command."

I left before I made another failed attempt to attack him. I was trying to make the man fall in love with me, giving in to my disdain for him wouldn't achieve that goal.

On the way out, I picked up Eadaoin on my tail. We passed through the market, picking up cheery hellos and polite conversation as we went. Lumenfell truly was a nice, peaceful village, and despite the harsh everlasting winter and the animals consuming their bodies and soul, the people seemed happy.

Seeing them, I knew Alisdair was right. A woman in my position would have to make a choice. They'd have to draw their allegiances in the ever-shifting sands of morality, and say *this is where I stand. I will free my people and my kind, and I'll cut down anyone who stands in my way.*

But the woman in that position—the one as his wife and queen—could not be me. Of course, I'd take up arms and life for my freedom, Meli's freedom, Gisela's freedom, Savia's freedom, and Mama's life. But I'd do it as the true me, and I'd do it for all the forgotten in Gutter Galley.

I would not do it for Alisdair's revenge, or his thirst for power. I'd also never be in the position of having to since I would leave the moment I was free of the curse. Let his true betrothed make that choice. Knowing Emiana as I was beginning to, she'd jump at the chance to dig her slippered heel into the throat of the nation that spurned her.

"Queen Ana, hello."

I shook myself, pulling out of my musings. Riordan waved from his market stand. His table was loaded down with three times as many goods as people dropped off their produce for coin.

"Riordan." I ran over, a true smile breaking out on my face. "I'm so happy you're okay. The last thing I saw was you being thrown from the carriage."

He winced. "Ah, yes. Our lord wasn't kind in his ripping apart the cart to find you. I understand now why you told me to have a replacement waiting. All the same, once I made it back to the replacement cart, I left without a problem."

"And you did well in Lyrica?" I asked, sweeping over his fresh and vibrant haul.

"Very well, my lady. They paid even more than you said they would. I sold everything I brought to market down to the last carrot."

I looked around. Eadaoin was across the way, speaking to a woman who sold jarred fruit jellies. "What about the other thing I asked you to do?"

"As ordered, I delivered two sack-fulls of jewels and gold to Aya Olene and her children. She was so shocked, she fainted."

Was she okay? How did she look? The questions refused to leave my mind. "Is that all?" I asked instead.

"What do you mean?"

I strained to find words the curse would let me say. "Just—! Did anything else happen?" I burst out.

He hummed, pushing his lips out. "Not really. They didn't want to take them at first. Meliora kept asking who they were from, but I wouldn't say—like you told me. She didn't like that," he muttered. "Said I either told her, or I could walk out the damn door with my stolen loot right then."

I cracked a smile. That sounded like Meli.

"I didn't want them getting rid of it because they thought it was stolen, so I just said someone important wanted them to have it," he said. "Wanted to make sure they were taken care of. They seemed to accept that because when I left, they were jumping up and down—crying and laughing about how everything was going to change."

It was me who was crying and smiling. I nearly jumped over the table and hugged him, if not for remembering at the last second that Alisdair wouldn't take too kindly to that. "Thank you, Riordan. You have no idea how much I... Just, thank you." I held my hand out to him, resting it an inch above his heart. "If there's anything I can do for you, name it."

He smiled. "My queen, you've already done everything for me. I've got this great position and... uh..." Riordan glanced past my shoulder. I followed his gaze to a tall, dark-haired bat faeriken. I only knew she was a bat from the spindly wings fluttering on her back. The curse had yet to touch her face, and what a pretty face it was.

I flicked away from her charming smile to her round, pregnant belly. It suddenly made perfect sense why Riordan abandoned Lyrica and took up the charge of uniting the fae and faeriken.

"It's really going to help our family," he finished. "We're even moving into the castle tomorrow. Everyone employed by the royal family has the right."

"That's great, Riordan," I said, and meant it. "I'm really happy for you."

He beamed at his love.

"I have another sack for you." Urgency made me return to the point. I had to get back to Alisdair before the runes demanded it. "Would you mind delivering it to Aya Olene again?"

"Not a problem, my lady." He took the sack of diamonds and tucked it under the table. "Maybe this time I'll get to see her."

My ears quirked up. "Who?"

"Just an old friend of mine." He softened, surprising me. "She was the best. Tough, fierce, but kind too. She saved me from some bullies, and this was after her magic was bound. Imagine the guts that takes. Standing between a scrawny kid and three guys twice your size, with no magic to help you.

"But that's Volka," he said, laughing. "Fearless."

I found myself laughing too. *Volka.* I hadn't heard that nickname in a long time. It meant wolf.

His smile dimmed. "I asked Aya Olene about her, and their dancing and laughing stopped. They wouldn't say what happened, but I know. The Gutter took her," he rasped. "Like it takes us all in the end. It's terrible because out of everybody, I always thought she'd be the one to make it out."

I did, Riordan! I made it out. If only I could tell you. My hand fell to my side. *If only I could tell Mama and my siblings they don't have to stop smiling. Everything's going to be all right.*

"My lady."

I turned to Eadaoin, who pointed at the flickering orblight. It was only recently I was informed they flickered every hour, on the hour, to help the Lumenfellians track the time in this land of dark and ice.

"Goodbye, Riordan," I said, "and thank you."

***

I let myself into the war room, causing Alisdair to raise his head. He glanced at me, then to the man behind me.

"What do you want?"

The leopard faeriken bowed. "I am here at my lady's request."

"This is Fintan," I broke in, saving him. "I remembered you saying how busy you are, dear husband, and what a waste it is having to teach me. It was unfair of me to demand you teach me to read runes too when you already have so much on your plate." I gestured to him. "Hence, Fintan. He will take over my runic lessons."

"No," Alisdair replied. "Get out."

I laughed. "You're so silly, my lord. Come, come, Fintan, it's all right." The guy was already halfway out the door. "My lord makes these jokes all the time.

"You just continue working," I told Alisdair, "and we'll be over here."

I herded Fintan to a small table in the corner. Under Alisdair's watchful, narrowed eyes, I gathered parchment, inks, and quills, and brought it back for us to begin.

"Okay, uh..." Fintan tried not to look at his glaring king. "How much do you know, my lady?"

"Nothing. You'll have to start at the beginning, and teach me absolutely everything you know." I winked at him. "But a smart, clever guy like you? You're just the man for the job."

He started. "Oh. Th-thank you, Lady Ana."

"You are most welcome," I said, brushing back my hair to reveal Emiana's pale throat and ample cleavage.

Aeris didn't know when she chose my blue silk gown with the plunging neckline, she was helping me and Eadaoin complete the next step in my plan to make Alisdair fall in love with me.

I couldn't tumble the man in front of Alisdair—and I also didn't want to—but I could give him my full and adoring attention.

"Let's begin." Fintan grabbed a quill and parchment and began writing out the runes. "There are six thousand five hundred and seventy-eight runes in total, but you only need to know four thousand for fluency."

I nodded. That much I knew.

"Let's begin with the twenty most common ones. This is the rune for water and—"

"Actually," I broke in. "I was hoping we could begin by learning my marriage runes. They're bound to my soul. I should know what they say."

"Very sensible, my queen. Which one would—?"

I slipped my sleeve off my shoulder. A deep, furious growl smothered the room.

"Princess." The warning in his voice was loud and clear.

I ignored him. "This one." I pointed. "What does this mean?"

"It— Uh— It means—" Fintan flicked back and forth between me and Alisdair. "It means fidelity."

Of course it did. "Would you show me how to write it?"

He did—tracing a loopy, entangled design that reminded me of a mangled heart.

I shrieked laughing. "Wow, Fintan, you have such lovely handwriting. I do love a man that's good with his hands."

Alisdair growled louder.

"What about this?" I covered my shoulder back up and picked a rune on a less scandalous spot. I tapped the tiny one on my wrist. "What does it mean?"

"It means run."

"Run," I repeated, committing it to memory. I truly did want to learn. "Hey! You never got to finish that funny story you were telling me on the way up." Alisdair's growl was a steady thrum in the background. "Please, go on."

"Um, well." Fintan was quite cute for a leopard man. He had intense, round yellow eyes and whiskers, but they did nothing to impede his shy, nervous smile, or the way his dreadlocks perfectly framed his heart-shaped face. "All I said was that I tripped on my sword getting out of bed this morning."

I howled, slapping the table. "That's hilarious. Tell me more."

"That's not hilarious," Alisdair barked. "He's clumsier than a one-footed fool. Fitting that the first thing you do in the morning is humiliate yourself."

Fintan flinched. "Yes, my lord."

I flapped a hand over my shoulder. "Don't mind him. I want to learn everything about you. Tell me about your family. How did you come to live in Lumenfell?"

"I thought this was a runes lesson," Alisdair said. "Not mindless chatter time."

"Oh," I cried, covering my mouth. "You're right, husband. We wouldn't want to disturb you. We'll be quieter." I leaned over the table, putting my mouth close to his ear.

Alisdair's snarls ratcheted up so high, my natural survival instincts flooded my pumping heart with adrenaline. All my senses were telling me to run.

"So," I whispered. "What were we talking about? Oh, right! You were going to tell me how you became so smart and sweet."

Crash!

"That's enough." Alisdair sprung to his feet, toppling his chair. "This lesson is over. Back to your post."

"It's not done." My hand flashed and grabbed the head of Fintan's chair—trapping him between me and the wall. "I've only learned two runes. Fintan, sweetie, be a dear, and teach me what the ones on my arm mean."

"Uh... uh..." Poor guy looked like he wanted to be anywhere but here.

I felt bad for using him, but Eadaoin was a genius. Most of the time when Alisdair and I were in the same room, he was ignoring me, barking instructions at me, mocking me, or drilling me from behind. This was the first he ever fought for my attention.

It was the first time he'd gotten jealous.

"This is... nightfall," Fintan croaked. "That means—"

I leaned in closer. "Do you have a lover, Fintan? Handsome man like you, someone must have snapped—"

A blur roared up out of the corner of my eye.

Alisdair ripped Fintan out of the chair, and threw him headfirst out the window. My screams echoed over the shattered glass and fading shouts.

"Mother Fucking Meya!" I shrieked, eyes popping. "What did you do!?"

"What I did was tell him to return to his post." Alisdair sniffed, dusting himself off. "Next time he'll listen."

"Next time?!" My voice was hitting undiscovered octaves. "There won't be a next time! You killed him!"

I rushed to the window. Fintan was a black, unmoving mass in the snow. A dark, reddish pool grew around him, staining the white red. "Oh no," I breathed. "I have to go see if he's ok—"

A fist punched the wall—scattering flecks of stone that hit my neck. Now, I was the one trapped.

He leaned in—closer, closer, closer—until there was an eyelash's-length distance between our bodies. "You will never speak to that insubordinate worm again, or next time, I won't be so forgiving. Am I making myself clear?"

I swallowed hard. Why didn't I learn from our first meeting? I plunged a sword in his chest, and the man married me. Alisdair never does what I expect.

Chest heaving, I lifted my chin. "Maybe I want to speak to that insubordinate worm again?"

His fiery displeasure vibrated from his chest to mine.

"I'll have to," I plowed on. "He's my runic magic teacher."

"*I* am your runic magic teacher!"

"You're too busy to teach me!"

"I'm never too busy for you," he roared, blowing me back. "Never, little bird. You always have my time and attention. Always."

My lips parted, but nothing came out. There wasn't a chance to speak. Alisdair was already slamming out the door.

I slid down the wall, sitting down hard. Closing my eyes, I pressed the heel of my palm to my fluttering heart. "Don't do that," I whispered. "You can't fall for your own game. I can't cut you out too."

***

That night, I skipped dinner in the dining hall, and asked for a tray on the terrace.

The Riagin Gardens were beautiful at night. There were no starflowers, but magic I'd never heard of bathed the flowers in steady warmth. It melted the snow around the flowerbeds, allowing the ice water to flow into little contraptions rigged up to spray a steady mist over the begonias and orchids.

I was so enamored with it all, my pheasant chilled on my plate while I crouched in the snow—studying how it was all done.

"Mimicking the humidity," I muttered. "Giving them hot and wet in a land that's cold and dry. Genius."

I didn't grow flowers back at home. Flowers didn't fill a hungry belly, but if I had the chance, I would've loved to fill our tiny, cramped space with beauty. There was just something about taking a tiny, helpless seed and nurturing it to its full and natural potential.

I couldn't control anything in my life. I couldn't stop them binding my magic. I couldn't keep Kirwan out of our lives. I couldn't prevent Mama's illness. But what I could do was take a seed and grow a cucumber. A small and unimpressive power, but it was mine.

"I'm never too busy for you."

I tossed my head, groaning. I was doing well. I'd gone a whole hour without thinking of Alisdair and what happened in the war room. The flowers couldn't distract me for long.

Let it go, my mind ordered. *You know he didn't mean it. He says things like that to mess with your head. Don't allow it to work. You're here to make him fall in love with you. Not the other way around.*

I repeated that to myself over and over until I believed it. I made Alisdair jealous, so he reasserted his ownership of me by his usual methods of violence and head-scrambling compliments. What mattered is that I did what I had to do. I made Alisdair break down and prove I was something he wanted. Not tolerated, endured, or despised.

Wanted.

That's what Eadaoin was trying to tell me. Her soldier didn't know what he wanted until she was right there, bouncing on another man's lap. The first step was getting him to stop masking his feelings behind sarcasm and disdain. What I needed to do next was improve upon my progress and... and...

"And what?" I sighed. "I have no idea what to do now. I can't even face him."

I needed another distraction—quickly.

Rocking back on my heels, I tried to recall the nursery rhymes I sang to Savia. Those were my favorite memories with her—crooning softly to my baby sister while she slept peacefully in the sling. Maybe, just maybe, the right verse would bring her sweet face back to me.

A song floated to the surface—alive in my memory and Emiana's. Seemed her mother used to sing to her too. Before the sickness took her.

Leaning back over the flowers, I sang—crooning for my dew-kissed begonias.

I don't know how long I knelt there, singing to the garden, but Savia's face never came to me. Though tears did.

Crunch.

I stopped and quickly wiped my face. "Aeris, there you are. Did you check on Fintan? Is he—?" I twisted, and landed on Alisdair in the doorway.

He watched me—expression unreadable.

I froze as if not moving would stop him seeing me. What was he thinking? Was he mad he caught me asking after Fintan's welfare? If he was, too bad. I got the poor man thrown out of a window. The least I could do was apologize.

"We don't need that siren," he said. "The beauty of your voice would bring any man to his knees."

He walked away, leaving me blinking and shaking in the snow.

Alisdair was right. This was the deadliest game I've ever played, and I couldn't tell whether I was happy or sad... that I was losing.

Chapter Ten

"Forgive me for giving you such terrible advice, my lady."

Eadaoin accompanied me on another stroll through the village. One of the traders in the market said they'd show me the inside of their greenhouse. It wasn't an exaggeration to say I'd never been more excited.

"Terrible advice? What do you mean?"

Her shoulders slumped. Eadaoin was a mask of misery. "I told you to make our lord jealous. If it wasn't for me, you wouldn't have embarrassed yourself by clumsily flirting with Fintan, then getting him thrown out of a window."

"Clumsily? I wouldn't say that—"

"He told me everything, my lady. I almost hid my face out of shame for you."

And to think, I was having such a pleasant morning. "Is he going to be okay?"

"He'll recover... in several months."

"Full recovery?" my guilt asked hopefully.

"I didn't say that."

I sighed, rubbing the bridge of my nose. "I can't apologize enough. I should've known Alisdair would not take kindly to my giving attention to another man—whether I touched him or not."

"No, it's my fault. I didn't realize you were completely new to the ways of love, sex, and seduction. I mean..." She waved a hand over me. "Look at you. How could so beautiful a woman be so naïve."

"You're cramming a lot of insults into this apology," I gritted, then sighed. "But it's true. I don't know what I'm doing. I actually already planned to use this walk to ask you for help. How do I do this, Eadaoin? How do I get him to open up and allow himself to feel for me, while keeping my own heart out of it?"

"Is your heart in it?"

"No." I didn't hesitate. "It can't be."

"All right, I understand," she said easily, surprising me. "I do have another idea for you. One that will not get anyone else thrown out of a window. Today, you'll finish lunch early and then I'm taking you somewhere. Somewhere you'll learn all about the ways of seduction."

Several hours later, I was standing in an impossible place.

"It's... It's hot..." I got out, then my voice failed me.

"Mhh hhh." Eadaoin peeled off her shawl and coat. "It's the only room in the castle that is, because it's right on top of an underground hot spring."

"Hot spring." Palm fronds tickled my cheek, the first to welcome me when I stepped through the door. My gaze darted everywhere at once, trying to take it all in. Palms, lilies, violets, orchids, birds of paradise, and the stunning, painted faeriken stretched out among them—basking in an eden of summer and flowers. "That explains it."

I stepped down into a sunken living room and all eyes turned to me. The room wasn't unlike my bathroom with its chaises and marble. The only thing it was missing was the bathing pool. My bathing chamber also didn't have a dozen faeriken women who were so gorgeous, their duck, fox, leopard, and bird faces did nothing to diminish it.

"Welcome, my queen." Eadaoin swept out her hand, beaming. "It is my pleasure to introduce you to the royal companions."

"Royal companions?" I repeated. "Royal as in—"

"Our lord's companions," finished a white fox faeriken. She was draped across a chaise and basking under the shade of a potted palm tree. She laughed. "You needn't make that face. He hasn't laid a finger on us since he brought you to the castle. We're all quite bored as a result." She shuddered. "The orgies used to go on for days."

I hadn't realized I made a face until I relaxed at her assurance Alisdair wasn't cheating on me, then scowled again full force at *orgies.*

"Why have you brought me here?" I snapped at Eadaoin. Emiana's lips parted, and her true voice came out. "Explain yourself."

She patted my hand. My lip curled at the servant for daring to touch me. "You said you wanted to learn how to tempt our lord without falling in love with him." She flicked from companion to companion. "Who else to ask but the experts?"

Understanding dawned, and chased away the ghost of Emiana. "Eadaoin, you're a genius."

She grinned, whiskers twitching. "Ladies," she called, clapping. "Work your magic."

Eadaoin trumpeted the horn for war, and they descended on me. Six pair of hands led me around the indoor garden to a standing mirror.

"First, we have to get rid of these clothes." She tore my dress off faster than Alisdair did. "Honestly, Lady Ana, Aeris terrifies me too, but you are allowed to choose your own wardrobe."

I would've responded if my jaw wasn't firmly clamped in the hand of the fox girl. She wiped off my subtle lip stain, and replaced it with a deep, plumish purple that I never would've had the bravery to try even if I was born a princess.

My elegant gown was torn to shreds. In its place, they covered my body with a forest-green gown that was tighter and thinner with a neckline plunging to my belly button. My nails were painted. My braids were unwound, leaving my hair falling in soft waves around my shoulders, and then, the lesson started.

"No, no, no," cried Honora, the fox woman. "You have to drop your hip, then roll. Drop, then roll, and twist." She demonstrated—wining her body in a slow, sultry dance that made me blush to see.

"Um, I don't think my body was meant to move that way." No, I knew I wasn't. Both my and Emiana's memories confirmed, neither of us knew how to dance. "Is there possibly a beginner's seduction dance?"

Honora laughed. "You are adorable, Lady Ana. I'm so glad nothing they said about you is true."

I was afraid to ask what they said.

"Now, don't overthink." She grasped my hips. "Loosen up. Move with me." Honora worked my hips like a puppet while the others conjured instruments and played a tune.

"Alisdair likes this?" I asked, finding my rhythm. I twisted, wined, and twirled, beginning to join in on the laughs and smiles.

"Oh, yes." Honora shared a grin with the other companions. "He *loves* it."

I nodded, steeling myself. "Well then, teach me everything you know."

***

That night, I wasted another head start and waited for Alisdair in our bedroom.

He stalked inside slow and cautiously as usual, searching for a trap, and found me perched on the end of the mattress—draped in a thin, silk robe.

I strained to keep the sultry smile on my face while my teeth chattered. "Good evening, husband. Make yourself comfortable." I patted the sheets. "Tonight, seduction is—"

"No," he sliced in. "I'm not enduring another one of your mad episodes. Get on your knees."

I clenched my teeth tight, penning in a vicious reply. Insults were hardly in line with the romantic atmosphere I was attempting to create. "If you had let me finish, you would've heard me say that seduction is my honor tonight. Just sit back and relax, Alisdair, while I tempt you."

"Is that so?" His brow climbed higher than the corner of his mouth. "You mean to seduce me? Before or after you run screeching from the room?"

You can't kill him. You can't kill him. You literally can't kill him. "Before," I returned, holding on to my smile. "Now, are you going to lie down, or would you prefer to talk yourself out of a treat?"

"I'll never deny a treat from you, little bird." Slowly, he peeled off his clothes and climbed into bed.

My heart thundered as he reclined against the headboard, draping his arm over the pillows. He gestured for me to proceed, and my lips tightened. Only Shadowsoul could make a finger flick sarcastic.

Shaking my head, I refocused on my goal. *The only way home is to make this beast give his love and heart to me. I do this for my freedom, so I cannot fail.*

I cleared my throat. "Tonight, I tempt and seduce you, my husband, with..." I let my robe fall to the floor. "...a dance."

The tight, see-through, lace shift dress revealed itself in all its glory, so did a bulge rising from the middle of the bed, and his legs.

I hid a grin. I'd never tell a soul, let alone myself, how much it thrilled me that I had such an effect on a cold and terrible man.

Slowly, I lifted my arms—holding them out to my sides as if ready to receive my lover—and began to dance.

Drop, turn, twist. I wined and gyrated my hips, dancing like a snake under a charm. Slowly I spun, gifting him a view of every naked inch of me. If only I had skipped getting men thrown out of windows, and went straight to the companions. No one could stand strong against this dance. I fell half in lust with Honora while she taught me.

Eat your shriveled, removed heart out, Alisdair. I bent at the waist, shaking my ass for his benefit. *Two can play at the game of love and lust. You're mine. Your love will be mine—*

A noise sounded behind me, snapping me up and twisting me around.

Alisdair clamped hard on his mouth, but he couldn't keep it in. Dam breaking, Shadowsoul burst out laughing.

Loud, bed-shaking, eye-watering, chest-wracking guffaws split his sides and threw his head back. He howled so hard and loud, he couldn't breathe.

Humiliation flooded my body and cheeks, lighting my face on fire. "You bastard!" Whipping around, I lit on the nearest weapon, and flung it at his head.

***

Soft, tsking, growly chuckles sounded a continuous chorus—as did my grinding teeth.

Alisdair and I found ourselves in the newly remolded throne room the next morning. I wore a fixed glare, and he sported a large, purpling bruise on his forehead, courtesy of the candelabra.

A line of peasants beheld their cold, evil king with wide eyes. The man before them was bruised, relaxed, and laughing his ass off.

"My lord?" Aeris stood two paces back, as if wary of getting too close. "You're in a good mood today."

"I am indeed," he crowed, shooting me a grin. My balled fist ached to punch it in. "I was treated to a show last night—best I've seen in ages. Would you all like to see it too?"

I stiffened as murmurs and yeses went around the room.

Alisdair turned that blinding smile on me. "My queen, would you do us the honor of treating us all to a dance? It'll surely brighten the day ahead."

I glared at him through the narrowed slits that were my eyes. "No, thank you," I gritted. "I'd much rather show them my candelabra-throwing skills. I've gotten quite good at it. I beat the target to death every time."

Alisdair laughed out loud, as always, unconcerned by my threats.

Thump-thump. Thump-thump.

Frowning, I twisted in my seat. *What is that?* It sounded like a heartbeat, but how could it be? How could it be Shadowsoul's? I'd believe he'd hide his heart behind a magical wall in his castle, but he wouldn't put it back in his rotted chest, or cart it around the throne room. Was I imagining things, or...?

I pressed the heel of my palm to my thrumming heart. Was this about my curse, and not his?

"You seek permission to divorce?" Alisdair repeated, breaking me out of my thoughts. "Must it come to that? Why not tempt your wife with a dance of seduction? Works every time."

I hated him.

By some Meya-blessed miracle, I made it through court without killing him. The minute I was released, I took off in the opposite direction of the war room, gritting my teeth against the searing pain lancing my ankle off at the bone.

"Fox Boy? Fox Boy?" I limped through the dungeons of the east wing, knowing behind one of the doors was a siren. Who knew what other secrets these doors concealed? "Is there a little fox boy down here? Come out or call to me. I won't hurt you. I want to get you out of here."

I screamed up and down the dungeon, then hobbled upstairs to scream through the servants' quarters. Yes, screamed. The growing pain in my leg wouldn't let me do anything else, but I didn't care. I was finding the boy and we were getting the fuck out of this place. Alisdair would never love me. The beast was incapable of love! Let him rot in this frozen wasteland, cursing the little bird who flew away.

"Fox B—"

"Lady Ana?" Aeris appeared at the end of the hallway. "What are you doing? You must be in agony! You need to return to my lord's side at once."

"Fuck him!"

She tutted, giving me a knowing look. "Here, let me help you."

I was in too much pain to stop her putting my arm around her shoulder and leading me off.

"What's happened, Lady Ana? Have you given up making our lord fall in love with you already?"

I'd have thrown her a shocked look if I was capable of doing anything but grimace in agony. "How... did you know?"

"I know everything," she replied without irony. "What I don't know is why you went to Eadaoin or that fool Bradach for advice before you came to me?"

"Because Eadaoin is trained in seduction and Bradach is successfully seducing you." Pain addled my mind too much for subtlety.

Shockingly, Aeris laughed. "It does look that way, doesn't it? Like the closed and hard-hearted Aeris is being swept along by the roguish flying man." She laughed harder, popping my brow. "What you couldn't have known, my queen, is that Bradach is an incorrigible bed-hopper. He's had his way with every woman in the castle, and only set his eyes on me because I was last on the list.

"Bradach is..." Her expression softened. "Smart, sweet, brave, and funny. But I did not know any of these things until I forced him to see that none of his tricks would work on me. If he wanted sex, he could get that anywhere. But if he wants something real, he has to open up, show me the true him, be vulnerable.

"Ana." She wiped a stray tear from my cheek. "Dances, face paints, and insincere puffery was never going to work. To love is to be vulnerable. It's to give your soul to someone knowing you'll never get it back, and that's okay, because your soul will live happier entwined with theirs than it ever did alone and yearning within you."

"But... how do I do that?" I croaked. "How do I get Alisdair to open up to me?"

"That is not for me to say, my lady, but I wonder, do you know anything about the real Alisdair Lumenfell? Where he's from? How he began? What he likes? What he curses? What he wishes for? Do you know any of these things?" Aeris deposited me in front of the war room. "Have you even asked?"

I stared down the hallway she disappeared around long after she left.

***

I studied Alisdair out of the corner of my eye. He said nothing of my late arrival when I walked into the war room. He merely dismissed Foalan, then pointed to the table next to him.

I went over and found a list of runes, their translations, and tracing paper for me to write them. I got on with the work without a word.

"What?" Alisdair asked, making me jump. "If you have a question, ask it."

I have a great many questions, but is it truly as simple as asking them? Is that all I have to do to get you to open yourself to me?

"How do you do it?" I asked instead. "Hold back the curse. None of the other faeriken do."

"Because they can't. It takes more strength, magic, and concentration than even the strongest among my people possess."

"Why do you do it? Surely you don't have to. None of your people would judge you," I said. "Or is it vanity?"

"Do you think me handsome enough for vanity?"

The question quickened my pulse, because the immediate and only answer was yes.

"And that is why," he continued, looking up to meet my eye. "I do it for you."

I blinked, mind slowing down trying to process that. "Me? You use all your magic and strength to appear fae for me? Why?"

"Because I promised you that first day in the carriage that I would have you every night, four times a night," he replied, tone matter-of-fact. "The least I could do was not put you through the indignity of being mounted by a hideous beast."

My lips parted but nothing came out. Of all the reasons I considered for why Alisdair had to remain his coldly handsome self, that he was being considerate of me never made the list.

I asked something true about him, and this is what he tells me. He had to prove there was decency somewhere in his empty chest. Decency to make my own chest thump harder and faster.

"What are you working on?" I sharply changed the subject. "Your plans for the conquer of Elva?"

"I could be working on nothing else," he replied, without looking up from the map. "There's nothing more pressing."

I sat up straighter. "We said we'd make a plan of attack together."

"I welcome your opinion at any time, my queen."

My brows furrowed, but I didn't sense any mocking or sarcasm. "Well, if that's true, I do have an idea, but there's something I need to know first."

"Such as?"

"You have spies in Lyrica, yes? And the other kingdoms too?"

"Yes," he replied easily.

"For them to be effective spies, they can't have undergone the change. How did you recruit them if they're not from Wind and Wild? I've seen the babies and children here. The curse takes them young."

"Most are enemies of your kings." Alisdair crossed something out on his parchment. "They offer their services to the enemy of their enemy in exchange for equal compensation."

"Paid informants." I nodded, turning that over in my head. "But are any of them Lumenfellians? As in loyal to you and the kingdom?"

"Some."

"Among those some, are any of them women? Unbound women," I clarified.

"Fewer still." Alisdair gave me his back, crossing to the bookshelf. "Even if their magic isn't bound, they have to spend every day pretending it is. If they're discovered, they're forcibly bound, then imprisoned. It's the choice between living free as a beast, or a secret in the shadows."

Sighing, I deflated—flopping back in my chair. "Yeah, you're right. It wasn't a very good idea. I was thinking why go through the horror of slaughtering every man in Elva, when we could simply embed unchanged Lumenfell women in key places in the kingdoms, waiting for the perfect time to strike. But if—"

"Stop," he sliced, making me jump. Alisdair spun and advanced on me so fast, I backed up against the wall. "Say that again."

I blinked owlishly at him. "I... I said there's no need for mass slaughter if we could surround our enemies with silent, innocent-looking assassins. No one would ever suspect a woman." I scoffed. "Especially not a woman who still wields magic. They believe they ended that threat hundreds of years ago."

I shrunk under his intense stare. "What? Why are you looking at me like that? If you think it's a bad idea, just say so. I've had enough of your teasing for one day—"

"That's brilliant," he breathed. "Genius."

What did he say?

"Fuck's sake, why didn't I think of that?" Alisdair crossed to the door and stuck his head out. "Foalan, get in here!

"Continue, Princess," he said, turning back to me.

"You're serious? You really think it's a good idea?"

"I think words that I once said sarcastically were in actuality the truest thing I've ever said, or has ever been said," Alisdair replied, tone serious. "Everyone in your life who dared underestimate you is a damn fool. Including me."

Alisdair took my hand, drawing me away from my rune practice to the maps he was poring over. "Where?" He pierced the parchment tapping the map with his claws. "Where would you embed our assassins?"

I heard him say *our*, but the issue was, I heard myself say *our* too. I didn't want war. I was sick to death of the pain and sorrow war had brought to Elva for longer than anyone's living memory could recall. But what I did want... was to keep my promise to my faywens.

I told Meliora and Gisela they would grow to be anything they wanted to be. I swore to Mama I wouldn't stop searching for a cure to ease her suffering, and give our mother back to us. I told my sweet, dreamy Jaclan that no one would ever steal his fanciful dreams, and shove a soldier's armor in their place.

Maybe it was the curse secretly working on me, turning me into the most animalistic version of myself. Maybe it was merely Alisdair's bad influence. But he was right. One could shout all the live long day that they don't want war, but if they want things that only war will achieve, what's the fucking difference?

If asking nicely could've ended the forced bindings and death sentences placed on women, we wouldn't still be here centuries later with pleas on our lips.

Power isn't given. It's wrested away from cold, dead fingers, and when again in my life would I have a great and terrible man willing to wrest away said power... and give it to me.

"The Crystal Palace," I said, signing the seal of treason. "My father has an army of female servants, because of course changing sheets and scrubbing toilets is *lowly* work only fit for women. He even has two perch over his bed at night, fanning and keeping him cool while he snores away," I said. "They wouldn't need magic to slit his sleeping throat, but magic would certainly help them slip away without a trace."

Alisdair leaned over me, enveloping me in that heady scent of jasmine and pine. "And you would be okay with this? Ordering the death of your father?"

"I hate that man." Emiana's truth fell from her lips, fired by the hatred etched into her bones. "Why shouldn't I order his death? He ordered mine when he had me bound. He ordered it again when he sold me to a man who had every intention of killing me." I gave him a wry grin. Alisdair grinned back. "That man never showed an ounce of loyalty or care for me. Even less for the women of Lyrica. They suffer while he grows fat and rich, gorging himself on sex and looted coin."

I scoffed, lips curling. "Let him die. I'll stand on his corpse to sit upon a throne that was never his and always mine, and rise higher than a son of his ever could. He'll burn for the rest of eternity, wishing he hadn't underestimated the princess of Lyrica— No..." I smirked. "The queen of Wind and Wild."

"You are magnificent," Alisdair gruffed, heat pouring off him and setting my skin ablaze. "I would have you right here."

I laughed. "Huh, so that's all it takes to seduce you."

I don't know who moved first—him or me—but in a flash, we were tearing at each other, ripping off any piece of clothing we got our hands on.

Alisdair threw everything off the table and tossed me on, pouncing on me before I caught my breath. We mauled each other for hours—interrupted only by Foalan walking in, taking one look, and walking back out.

As Alisdair pressed my head to the table, pumping my ravaged hole from behind, I accepted that Aeris was right about everything.

I kept trying to make Alisdair fall in love with me through sex and lust, but that was never where he held back. His desire for me was obvious from that very first day in the carriage, and if that was enough to make him give his heart, I would already have it.

No. Somehow, I had to get through to the man who had told me nothing real or true about him since we met. I had to get him to open up to me. I had to make Alisdair Shadowsoul, the most feared man in Evla, vulnerable.

***

"What about Rajadom's councilor?"

I reclined on my litter, snuggled under blankets and a raised roof on the snowy, bleak day. I demanded they added the roof when Alisdair announced we had to make a trip to a neighboring village, to speak to the person who'd help us find the right assassins for our plan.

"Why they can't come to us, I have no idea," I snapped at Alisdair. "We are their sovereigns. It's offensive that I should be out in this cold, trekking miles to meet with a peasant." I flicked the head of the servant carrying me. "Drink!"

Obediently they raised the tray holding my warm, spiced cider. I took a sip and hummed, getting comfortable against my pillows. I'd say something for the beasts, they knew how to treat their betters—

Stop it! my true voice blared. *Get out of my head, you monster!*

I tossed my head, coming out of the fog. It was getting harder and harder to know what was her and what was me, but those horrid thoughts—that could only be her.

"Excuse me," I rasped, clutching my head. "That was rude. Thank you for the cider, Mavendale, and thank you all for carrying me. You can put me down now. My feet work just fine."

"Are you sure, Lady Ana?" Eadaoin asked. "We don't mind."

"I'm sure." My voice was firm. "I'll walk."

Even though nothing but Alisdair declaring his love for the true me could break the curse, it was clear that indulging the things Emiana would do made it harder for me to remember where she ended and I began. I had to cling to me. Behave as I would behave. Do what only I would do.

Remember the ones I love.

"Sorry, Foalan. What were you saying?"

"Rajadom," he prompted, falling in step with me and Alisdair.

Obviously, we weren't announcing our military strategy out in the open, but there was no harm in discussing what I knew about the other kingdoms and their rulers. And Emiana knew quite a lot.

More proof Salman was a fool to dismiss the silent, watching listener sitting in the background during all of their royal summits and discussions. He handed her everything she needed to bring about his downfall, and it was clear from her memories, King Salman's downfall was what she wanted most. She probably would've summoned the courage to assassinate him herself one day, if he hadn't sold her off to the kingdom of Wind and Wild.

"Chancellor Mahoun is difficult," I said. "Paranoid. Untrusting. The times he visited my father in Lyrica, he'd only eat food prepared by his own servants, and would let no one but them wait on him. He also prefers men. Male lovers. Male servants. Male advisors. And only the comeliest. He has a wife, but after securing the line with four sons, she took up residence in the winter palace and they live separate lives."

I didn't say more, since Foalan was wise enough to draw his own conclusions on how difficult that would make it to get a woman close to him.

"Is there a way?" Foalan asked simply.

I opened my mouth to say I didn't know, then the answer came to me—easily supplied by Emiana's memories. "Guilt," I blurted. "He is a staunch and devoted worshipper of Mother Meya, and deep down, he believes the All Mother will punish all of Elva for what we've done to her daughters.

"That hasn't stopped him," I spat, "or prompted him to repeal a single unfair law, but he does visit the temple morning and night, praying for forgiveness."

"The high priestesses," Alisdair and Foalan said at once.

I nodded. The temple priestesses were bound like every woman in Elva, but the one advantage they had was that they still commanded respect. Everyone bowed in their presence and heeded their word. They lived safe and pampered lives in the temples of Meya scattered about the nation.

The only time Emiana had ever seen Salman give a woman respect was when he bowed, waited his turn to speak, and kissed the feet of a temple priestess.

"Sarabai?" Foalan asked.

Again I opened my mouth to say I wasn't sure. Again, Emiana's memories interrupted to give me the answer. What irony that, in a real way, she was bringing about the downfall of her hated father.

I replied to Foalan, then cut a look to Alisdair striding on my other side. "So, Alisdair," I began. "What was your mother like? Tell me about her."

"No."

The reply was so swift and curt, I tripped over my feet. The bastard didn't even take a moment to think about it.

"Why not?" I barked, a little of Emiana's patented pampered outrage bleeding in. "I'm your wife. You're my husband. We should get to know each other."

He said nothing. Didn't so much as tip his head to look at me.

Irritation swelled up in my chest.

"Alright," I forced through clenched teeth. "What about fair play? Every question you answer, I'll answer too. Tell me about your mother and I'll tell you about mine."

"You are near perfection, my queen," he said, surprising me with the compliment. "Your only flaw is you continue to bargain with worthless coin. It isn't possible for me to care less about your mother."

My fist went flying, heading straight for that bastard's hard jaw.

Alisdair ducked me, laughing cruelly. I blinked and he was on Foalan's other side.

"Beast," I bellowed. "You make everything difficult!"

Eadaoin shook her head out of the corner of my eye. I knew what she was thinking because I was too. Making this dead-inside monster fall in love with me was not going well.

Eventually, we arrived in Bevin—another small township of Lumenfell proper. Bevin was similar to Lumenfell's main village in that the warm, deep-brown cottage homes and attached greenhouses were shared by both, but that's where the similarities ended.

No one passed us on the street, and while Bevin also had orblights, theirs were smaller. Dimmer. Casting barely a glow to beat back the shadows. I squinted, gazing around—searching for the whiskered couples walking hand in hand, the bustling square, or giggling children skating around the fountain.

Nothing.

The only signs of life were the lights trickling through the breaks in drawn curtains.

Alisdair took me on a tour of a few of the surrounding villages. I was beginning to see why he left this one out.

"Is everything okay?" I whispered to Alisdair. "Why is it so dark and quiet? We're not in wolf territory again, are we?"

"Opossum faeriken." Alisdair always answered my questions, unless they were about him. "A mix of solitary and nocturnal results in this. Everyone keeps to themselves."

I swallowed the rest of my questions, although I was dying to ask how a solitary fae-beast living in a dark corner of Wind and Wild was supposed to help us.

Twenty minutes later, I was sitting at a kitchen table, clamping my mouth shut to keep in ever more questions.

A woman with round, beady eyes; a long, furry nose; and thin, spindly, almost-rat-like hands bustled about the small cottage, but it wasn't her appearance that drew my wide eyes. Well, in a way it was, since her accessories were a sight I'd never seen before.

No less than six infants hung in slings on her person. Four sleeping on her back, and two babies in front freely nursing. It suddenly made sense why Alisdair had us go to her. Not even he was cruel enough to make a mother trek miles through a dark, frozen forest with six babies hanging off her shoulders.

Despite the dark and gloomy outside, inside the cottage was warm and inviting. A crackling fireplace dispelled the chill from my bones—prompting me to shed my coat. Paintings of rolling meadows, sunny skies, and crashing waves covered every wall, showing her babies the world beyond Wind and Wild.

"Well, don't stand on ceremony," she said, beaming brightly. Treasa was tall, thin, and flitted around on the balls of her toes as if she was a dancer in another life. "No need for formality here. Get comfortable, my lord, my lady. I'll start the tea."

"Please, ma'am, let me." Foalan guided her to a seat by the fireplace and took charge of the tea.

Alisdair and I joined her at a slower pace. It was only the four of us—actually, ten of us in the cottage. Obviously, we didn't need everyone knowing our plans.

"There are no cribs," I murmured quietly. "Opossums carry their babies everywhere. Don't tell me the call of the animal is so strong, she can't even allow herself the rest of putting them down."

"This community was among the first to change." He spoke under his breath like me. "By now, the instincts are so ingrained, the entire town is made of only women and their children." He noticed my confused look.

"Opossum fathers don't stick around after mating. The mothers are on their own."

My brows blew. I couldn't imagine that. Yes, I looked after Mama and my siblings, but the only baby in our cottage was Savia. Six infants at the same time was a humbling that would bring me to my knees.

My eyes suddenly narrowed to slits. "And what about the kind of beast you are?" I hissed. "Instincts or no, you better not have it in your head that you won't stick around after *mating*."

Alisdair chuckled. "If such a thought were in my head, the immediate thought following it would be that my fierce and brutal queen would hunt me down, and bash such a foolish notion out of my skull."

"Too right she would."

"Is everything okay?" Treasa asked, catching the end of my reply.

"Everything's fine." I kept my voice low out of respect for the sleeping babies.

Long, furry noses and bony, clawed hands poked out of their slings. If the curse took this community first, it explained why there was no preamble with the next generations. They were all born cursed.

"We've come to ask for your help," I continued, dropping down in the armchair across from her. "Although, I admit I don't know how you're meant to help us."

Alisdair took over. "Treasa is the only one to help us. She is the spymaster of Lumenfell."

I gaped at the beaming, barefoot woman covered in babies. "I beg your pardon?"

She laughed. "My lord flatters me with such an important title. I am merely a go-between for him and his loyal servants within the other kingdoms. You see, Mother Meya saw fit to bless me with a gift." Treasa pressed her finger to her temple and turned to the side.

"What am I—?" I lurched back, clutching the chair arms.

A mirror appeared before Treasa's face, and the reflection in it... was mine.

My round eyes, hanging jaw, and whipping head as I tried to see how she was doing that.

"I pierce through the veil of distance and space," Treasa said, "allowing me to keep a concerned eye on the nations. I can also do—" Treasa picked up a pillow and tossed it through the mirror. It appeared out of the air and plopped on my lap. "This."

"Amazing," I breathed. "I've never heard of such an incredible power."

She smiled serenely. "It is my honor to be blessed by Meya. It is incredible the gifts that can develop when our magic is allowed to grow and change freely."

Foalan took that opportunity to bring out the tea. I sat back and sipped while the three of them made idle conversation.

For centuries, Elvans have cursed their inability to defeat Shadowsoul, and for centuries, they didn't know it was because they continued to underestimate him. The wealth and power he hoarded in his small, barren, freezing corner of the world was staggering. A spymaster that could freely and discreetly watch King Salman while he plotted, planned, and took a shit? Elva had already lost the war, they just hadn't accepted it yet.

But what about my war? I paused bringing the cup to my lips. *Isn't Treasa the key to everything? She could look in on my family. She could pass them a message. She could help me break this curse.*

"Aya Treasa," I blurted, breaking into the conversation. "Can you check on some people for me? Olene, Meliora, Gisela, Jaclan, and Savia. I—" I tossed my head. "Actually, forget Jaclan. I don't know why I said that name. I don't know who that is, but the other four," I pressed, leaning in. "Can you look in on the other four? Just to—" *make sure they're okay,* was stolen off my tongue.

Of course, Emiana wouldn't care in the slightest about the well-being of a few peasants. "Just to check," I said instead.

Treasa shook her head. "I'm sorry, Lady Ana." It stood my hairs on end that she already knew I preferred to be called Ana. "I can't look in on people I've never met, but I can tell you which of your loyal servants would do well inserting themselves into key positions and places around Elva. That I can do easily."

"One would need to pose as a temple priestess in Rajadom," Foalan added.

She whistled. "You do bring me the most interesting challenges, Foalan. As you know, priestesses are chosen from birth. One doesn't simply walk in and request the job."

"Is my spymaster telling me she means to fail me?" Alisdair's voice dropped the freezing temperature another twenty degrees.

One of the babies stopped nursing and stared at him, as if sensing danger, and knowing exactly where to look.

Treasa's smile went nowhere. "I have never failed you, my lord. I have no intention of doing so now. Give me two days. Assignments will be handed out and assets moved into position by then."

"Very well." Alisdair stood to leave.

"What about the siren?" I asked. "We have another strategy. A better one. Send her back to her home."

"She goes nowhere until after we've won. A general goes to war with a thousand strategies, not just one. Should our plan fail, we will need her and her power."

"But, Alisdair—"

"I would worry less about a fish woman, and more about yourself."

My expression told him I didn't know what he meant.

He smirked. "You're about to earn your second name, little bird. They call me Shadowsoul. What will they call you? Kinslayer? Slaughterer? The One Who Ended the War Shadowsoul Began?" Alisdair laughed. "Queen Ana, Destroyer of Elva."

He backed out of the door, the shadows claiming him and his open delight. "I do so look forward to finding out."

I sat there for so long—silent and shaking—that Treasa came over, squeezed my shoulder, and handed me a baby. Even as the sweet little furry face nuzzled against me, drifting off to sleep, I couldn't shake away the vision that my hands were staining her with blood.

***

Eventually, I drank my cold tea, gave Treasa her sleeping babe, thanked her, and went out to meet the silent party waiting for me. It was just Alisdair, Foalan, Eadaoin, and three guards.

"We sent the litter and the bearers on," Eadaoin explained. "Hope that was okay."

"Of course, it's okay. No reason for them to stand around in the cold." I pulled my coat tighter, shivering in the strange, silent village. "Can we not do something for the women here?" I asked. "I know they can't control their instincts, but it's not right that all of the mothers have been abandoned to raise a litter of children, just because it's what a skulking rodent would do."

Alisdair hummed. "It is already law that I'll rip out the throat of every faeriken that uses instinct as excuse for running out on their responsibilities. Served as a deterrent for a while, but then they learned to run faster and hide better." He bowed over my hand, dropping a kiss on my frozen knuckles. "But Foalan is ready and willing to organize a squad to hunt them down. Per my queen's wishes."

My fist clenched within the folds of my sleeve. I knew Alisdair enjoyed this. Horrifying me with his cruelty, and then delighting when I threw it back. He said on the very day of our true mating that his deepest wish was to corrupt the crown jewel and hope of Lyrica, but—

Is it me he's corrupting? I thought, gazing into his eyes. *Or is he merely drawing out the cold and cruel nature of his true soulmate—Emiana.*

The day before, that rant about hating Salman and rising higher than a son of his ever could, was all her. It was my plan to use silent assassins instead of genocide, if it meant innocent people wouldn't die to give Alisdair an easy victory. But the delight in what that victory would bring... that wasn't mine.

But Alisdair loved it.

I was trying to make the man fall in love with the true me, and all I was achieving was his infatuation with the bitch who destroyed my life.

"No, Foalan. You needn't send out any death squads. There's no point," I said, pulling away from Alisdair. "It won't deter anything or help anyone.

"You can't make someone love you. You can't make them stay." I looked upon Alisdair as his grin faded. "In the end, instinct always leads you to the place you're meant to be... and the person you're meant to be with."

Giving him my back, I walked off alone into the dark.

After a beat they all caught up to me, and then pulled ahead, leaving Alisdair and me trailing behind.

I felt him watching me out of the corner of my eye.

"Something has happened," he said. It was a statement, not a question.

"No."

"Yes. You're making that face again. You're seconds away from bawling to put Treasa's younglings to shame, so out with it. What's wrong with you?"

I faced away, expression blank. "There's nothing wrong with me, Alisdair. I don't know what's led you to believe otherwise, but everything's the same as it was yesterday. And the day before that. And the day before that one. I suspect it will be the same tomorrow and the next too."

We left Bevin behind, setting off down the frosted path.

"You should be happy, husband." I pulled my hood up against the falling snow, further concealing my face. "Your little bird has finally accepted her fate."

He grasped my shoulder. "Ana— Foalan, on your left!"

Figures exploded out of the trees, trapping my scream in my throat, then ripping it back out.

Horrible, mangled accidents of Meya poured out of the shadows, pouncing on Foalan, Eadaoin, and the guards. Yellowed fangs, foot-long claws, tangled patches of fur stretched over leathery, black skin.

Taken.

"Ana, get down!"

Movement flickered out of the corner of my eye. Even as I spun and was blasted in the face with foul, rank breath, I knew it was too late. Claws fell from above, eager for the spray of blood my severed head would bring.

"Ugh!" A force slammed me from behind, burying me under body and snow. Alisdair's roar shredded my eardrum, letting me know he took the hit that was meant for me.

"Stay here," Alisdair bit out.

"What? What are you—? Alisdair!"

He climbed off me, heading straight for the mass of claws and fangs that claimed our friends. Leaving me behind.

"Alisdair?" I flipped on my back, terror flooded my senses and whiting out my mind as more, more, and more Taken burst out of the trees—descending on me. "Alisdair!"

"Argh!" They pounced on me, drooling jaws glistening, and smacked hard—cracking their noses and spurting oozing, black blood on the barrier.

Heart yammering, I reached out, my fingers tracing the cool glass. *He protected me. Alisdair saved me.*

The creature leaned over me, looking straight into my eyes as its lips peeled back. The first time I saw the Taken, I saw madness in their orbs. This time... I saw intelligence.

Fear flooded me deeper and more chilling than the cold. I wasn't safe. We weren't safe. No one in Elva or beyond was safe as long as these beings roamed the world. Trapping my gaze, the monster looked directly at me as it raised its fists, and smashed it on the glass.

The first strike sounded the call. The Taken went wild—pounding, kicking, scratching, punching, and attacking the thin barrier protecting my life.

"Alisdair!" I strained to find him through the chaos. It was so dark—Why was it so fucking dark in this cursed hell forsaken by the sun! I couldn't see where Alisdair was, or if he'd gotten to Foalan, Eadaoin, or the others in time.

Bang! Bang! Craackkk!

I snapped up, alighting on the long crack spiderwebbing over my head.

Their leader shoved one away from the pack. I thought it was to stop anyone else from getting to me first, until the creature came back with a branch.

Yes, very intelligent.

The branch fell in an arc, pounding the crack wider, wider, wider.

"Alisdair!" One final scream, and the glass shattered.

"Ana!" His voice found me as claws encircled my throat, hauling me off my feet. "Shut your eyes!"

I snapped my lids shut, screams leaking through my teeth.

"Anchana!"

The sun exploded.

Light burst before my lids, assaulting the thin, sensitive barrier and flooding my irises. Bright spots stunned me, throwing my head back—and finding myself falling.

I crashed to the snow, the claws around my neck gone. I peeled my lids open and white-hot light blazed my eyes to dust.

No. That was the sight of the horrid, unnatural creatures before me—exposed and laid bare.

I took one look at them and screamed. Almost as loud as they did.

Dropping on all fours, the Taken fled before the light, the fight, and all—racing into the thick and twisting trees.

My chest heaved, rocked by ragged, rapid breaths that wouldn't come in fast enough, and left too quickly. I dropped to my knees, my hand falling beside a pretty, purple flower—sprouting rapidly, as if wanting to gift me beauty after witnessing hideousness.

"I—I—" I willed moisture into my dry mouth. "Is everyone okay?" I croaked.

"We're alive." I turned to see Foalan staggering to his feet—a sword clutched in one hand, and his bleeding arm clutched by the other. "That'll do for now."

"What was that!" Eadaoin had to be helped up. A long, vicious gash split her cheek. "The Taken have never attacked in such large numbers before. We've only ever dealt with stragglers and opportunists. That was an ambush!"

"Not... only." I made to stand and promptly tipped over. Alisdair was there in a blink. Catching me under the arms, he held me up and steady. "They ambushed our carriage when I first arrived in Lumenfell. I'm starting to think they've taken a particular dislike to me." I forced a laugh, no one joined in.

Foalan shared a grim look with Alisdair. "They didn't chase after you, my lord. They stayed behind, tearing and fighting to get Lady Ana."

Alisdair nodded—curt. "I assumed they would follow me. I was attempting to draw them off, but as you said, they were fixed on another prize."

"Me?" My voice was barely higher than a squeak. "Why would they want me?"

"I couldn't begin to guess. They do have some sense of intelligence," Alisdair admitted. "They always go for the strongest in a group, killing them first and then taking out the rest. But this time, they separated you from help, and focused their bloodthirst. Why not give their attention to the strongest?" He eyed me. "Unless they believe the strongest in our party is you."

I looked around as though he was talking about someone else. "Me? Obviously not. They must've thought I was an easy meal, and then rage took them when that meal was put under glass."

"Hmm." Alisdair did not look convinced. "Further your mystery deepens, little bird."

"There is no mystery. Nothing is— Look out!"

The lone Taken surged out of the dark, proving he hadn't forgotten his ways after all. He lunged straight at Alisdair's back.

I didn't think, I moved. Snatching up the fallen branch, I shot around Alisdair and struck—plunging the jagged wood into his chest. The creature clutched his downfall, and laughed.

Fear flooded me, weakening my knees. It wasn't their presence that struck fear into the souls of faemen, it was that awful, high-pitched laugh.

"Agh!" Alisdair clamped his face, claws piercing his skull. Fire poured out his palm and into the Taken's open mouth—burning it from the inside out.

Its charred, mangled corpse fell to the ground—the smile etched on his face.

"Ana." Alisdair spun me around and kissed me so hard, my toes curled. I broke away flushed and panting. "Your boundless mystery is only outpaced by your bravery."

"I—uh—"

Alisdair walked off, my time of praise over. "The flowers," he barked. "Destroy them. Every one."

I kept a look out as little fires erupted all over the path, turning his one weakness into ash.

"Let's go," Alisdair said when they were done. "We've been here too long. And from now on, Lady Ana travels with a full guard."

"I'll protect her." Eadaoin moved to my side and took my hand, staining it with blood. "I'll never leave her side again."

"Thank you," I said simply, seeing no need for argument.

I glanced down as we walked off, my fingers curling around the delicate, purple flower.

Go ahead and fall for the woman who jammed her soul down my throat, you obstinate bastard. Nothing will stop me from getting home to my mother and sisters.

I tried every method there was, now it was time for the one that works. As Alisdair said, a general doesn't go to war without a plan B.

Chapter Eleven

That evening, the palace court gathered around the dining table—devouring everything in sight.

"What about siblings?" I threw in Alisdair's direction. "Did you have any? Do you have any?"

He responded by snatching the turkey leg off my plate and tearing off a bite. I used the distraction to drop my addition in his ale.

I peered around, but no one was sounding the alarm. No one even looked in my direction. So in the end, that's how easy it was to fell the great Alisdair Shadowsoul. All it took was a little flower—

Alisdair downed the ale in one messy gulp.

—and a little bird.

An hour later, I entered our bedchamber. Alisdair lay stretched on the mattress—pale, sweating, and still. I don't know what I expected the poison flower to do to him. Possibly hurt him? Ravage his insides or make him sick? But it didn't seem to be doing any of that.

Alisdair didn't look to be sick or eaten from the insides. He looked like he'd run around the entire world, and collapsed right on that mattress—too weak and jelly-kneed to carry on.

Yes, that was it. For the first time since I met the impossible man, Alisdair was weak.

He caught sight of me, and not quickly. It was a slow, agonizing turn of the head that narrowed his gaze in my direction. "My queen..." he drew out, sounding like he was choosing every word carefully, for each cost him dearly. "Something... is wrong. Fetch... Aeris. Now."

"Aeris?" Slowly, I closed the distance, my prize clutched behind my back. "Why would you need Aeris? Your wife is here. I will help you." I lofted the knife high, enjoying the slow widening of his eyes. "I'll make everything better."

"Princess—!"

My knife fell, slicing the rope in two. Moving fast, I pounced on him, caught his wrist, and roped it to the headboard. The other one received the same treatment. Alisdair truly was weak magically and physically. He barely put up a fight.

"What are you doing, woman! Untie me!" His bark had much less of a bite when he was leashed to a headboard. "Untie me this instant!"

"Nope," I sang. "I don't believe I will." I wriggled down his chest, dropping comfortably on his middle. Cheerily, I peeled off my robe. "I told you, husband. Warned you even. I said that one day soon, I would have you at my mercy."

"You?" he hissed. "You did this to me? Did you—you—*poison* me?!"

I laughed. "It was just half a petal in your ale." I clicked my tongue. "You really should be careful with those. Could do a lot of damage in the wrong hands."

Roaring, he reared up—growing fangs splitting his lip. Alisdair made it halfway, and flopped back down, panting hard.

I patted his chest. "Nice try, dear. When you speak of this in the future, you'll be able to tell everyone you gave it your all. But now it's my turn."

Alisdair growled, latching on to the knife I still held in my hand. "What are you going to do?"

"Oh, well, that's simple. It was recently pointed out that you can't fall in love with someone without being vulnerable, and you, Alisdair, are never vulnerable. You hold all the power in our marriage. You inked those very words of power on my skin in a language I can't even read." I pressed the knife tip to his collarbone, and slid down—slicing his tunic in half.

"You even hold all the power in the bedroom. Eadaoin says it's the Wind and Wild way for men to put a woman's pleasure first. Much in the way male animals attract and tempt a female, but even though it would bring me pleasure to be on top every other night, you've allowed no such thing to happen. I must always be at your mercy. I must always beg and plead beneath you—not the goddess receiving pleasure, but your puppet to it."

"And so you will be tonight." His eyes flashed. "And every night thereafter. My wife. My puppet. Mine."

"I dispute none of that." I flicked his nose, earning a snarl. "I'm merely opening your mind to the Lyrican way. The women of my kingdom know a few tricks to please a man too." My hand traveled down, slipping past his waistband, and gripping the length that had been tearing me in two every night. I paused. "Ah, but there are rules."

"The rule being that you're never to do anything like this again!"

I giggled again. "No, definitely not that. I've actually hidden away a few petals in case you don't learn your lesson tonight." I swore the glare he gave me was murderous. "No, the rules are that you must share an intimate detail about yourself. Something you've never told anyone."

"And that will make you cease?" he snapped.

"No." My grin widened. "That's what you must do... if you want me to keep going." With that, I freed his cock from its confines, dropped my head, and swallowed him to the hilt.

Alisdair howled. Yes, howled like a wounded animal. The howl was smothered by a choked groan when I sucked hard, caving in my cheeks. Even though Eadaoin said it, I didn't truly believe it. Alisdair had his own harem basking in a sauna oasis. I'd met them myself.

I didn't believe he hadn't done all the things there were to do in the bedroom, and more. But then I underestimated the man who shocked his staff by announcing his hunger. To not be in control at every moment? To allow his pleasure to be at someone's discretion, and their power? That was not the Alisdair way, and the customs of Wind and Wild had nothing to do with it. This was the first time a woman pleasured him with her mouth, and I was going to make it count.

I sucked, bobbed, and stroked—my fingers tight around the base of his cock, but my tongue a dancer's minx—light and playful teasing his member. I only had the little I remembered of Shadi's advice to aid me, but confidence was my guide.

She did tell me that his groaning, moaning, and carrying-on would be all the encouragement I needed to know I was doing it right. If that was the case, I was doing it very, *very* wrong.

Alisdair growled, thrashed, and kicked—snapping and clawing at the ropes. Fighting to get free like an animal caught in a trap. The last time someone sounded this furious with me... they attacked.

The poison flower was still doing its work. His claws weren't as long as they could be. His fangs not as lethal. His thrashing only served to drive his length deeper, making me moan to rumble the vibrations down his pole, and hitch his breath every time.

I withdrew and sucked on the tip, scraping my teeth across his hole.

"Agh!" he grunted, yanking harder on his restraints. The man was going to wrench his arms out of the socket.

"Sorry, husband. You're not getting out of those." I leaned forward, capturing his cock between my breasts, and sliding them up and down—gifting the glory of the valley of my breasts.

Alisdair was so incensed, his eyes glittered like the insane rage of the Taken.

"I understand," I breezed. "Believe me, I do. You haven't surrendered to another soul in a thousand years, but if you wanted to retain tight control of everything and everyone, you shouldn't have married me."

He started thrashing back and forth, trying to pry the very headboard off. His roars echoed over the horizon.

"I will get you to open up to me, and doing so before and after I sit on your face, will be the cherry on top of a perfect—"

His claws broke through and shredded the ropes.

I ran.

Scrambling off him, I leaped—

A hard body tackled me, crashing us both foot over limb across the sheets. Alisdair grabbed and pinned me down, turning the tables on me so fast, I couldn't recall how it happened.

I swallowed hard, losing my grin fast. "Are... Are you going to kill me?" It was a fair question. The last time Alisdair looked this enraged, he ripped out someone's throat with his teeth.

"Kill you?" He pressed his forehead to mine. "My queen, I'm going to throw a parade in your name and the women of your land. Today will mark the grandest celebration in the entire kingdom." He growled, "Now do that again."

I was so shocked, I lay there gaping and blinking at him for a full minute.

"But, you— Don't forget our deal," I blurted. "You have to tell me something about yourself. Or am I still bartering with worthless coin?"

Alisdair gritted his teeth—his warring emotions splashed across his face. "Damn you," he belted—the war won. "I do have a sibling, all right. Pleased with yourself?"

"Immensely." I kissed his wrinkled nose. "But I'll need more detail than that." I laughed at his rising growl. "Come on, you wouldn't want me if I made this easy for you. You said have, not had. Who is this sibling? What's their name?"

"You know well who the fool is and their name. The flying bastard makes himself known."

My jaw slackened. Flying bastard? I didn't need more detail than that. "Bradach?" I cried. "He's your brother? But you two look nothing alike."

"Borrowed brother." Alisdair looked pained, like the explanation was being yanked out of him. "The little beggar wandered into our home one day to steal food, and my mother kept him. She made me swear to look out for him. Mother Meya has kept me honest to this promise by giving him wings."

I clapped my hand over my mouth, smothering a giggle. I couldn't help it. Suddenly it made so much sense why Alisdair had both an abundance of patience and an abundance of irritation toward Bradach. Siblings demanded both in equal measure.

"But when—"

"Again!" he demanded, flipping me squealing over the pillows.

I squirmed free and shoved him back down, pouncing on his hard, weeping ridge with the same enthusiasm. Groans and moans filled the room—the right ones. Alisdair was definitely enjoying himself, and I was definitely doing it right.

But in typical Alisdair fashion, he dominated me within an hour of being introduced to our new activity. He propped me against the headboard, holding my head back by the hair while he pumped my mouth—straining to keep hold on his thin tether on control.

I was far from stopping him. I gripped tight to his thighs, urging him on with every squeeze and moan.

Alisdair suddenly stiffened—limbs going rigid. I relaxed as he came, his seed spilling down my throat, and me accepting all of him.

Shadowsoul collapsed on the sheets, chest heaving. The effects of the petal must've still lingered, because it was the first I'd ever seen him out of breath. "So what would you like your day of celebration called, my queen?"

I laughed. "Nothing too scandalous, I hope."

He gave me his suggestion, and it was so scandalous it burned my ears. I picked up a pillow to whack him. Alisdair caught it in time and tugged, dropping me laughing across his chest.

"Although..." His eyes sharpened. "I will see every one of those petals destroyed. In front of me. Now."

I hummed. "No, I believe I'll hang on to them. Just in case your stubbornness gets in the way of my will again."

"Either you destroy those petals, or you'll wake up one night roped to the bed."

"Oooh." I winked. "I might like that."

Alisdair snorted. One look at each other, and we burst out laughing—a loud, cleansing, raucous laugh that let me know... I wouldn't need those petals again.

***

"I'm partial to toffee."

I bit my lip hard, holding back a grin by the actual skin of my teeth.

"I've read all the early works of Garban Wordweaver."

Picking up my rune instruction book, I crossed the length of the library, returning it to its proper place.

I didn't spend much time in the library, and whenever I crossed its threshold, I regretted that. It was such a calm, quiet place. Cold, yes, but filled with warm, squashy armchairs and sweeping ceiling-high stacks that encouraged me to stay. Simply shut myself inside and keep out the world.

Alisdair followed, trailing me across the shining, marble floors. "I was born with a full set of teeth."

I broke, a giggle bursting free. "I'm almost certain you're making all of these up."

He shrugged, leaning against the stacks. "You'd have to prove that, my queen, but in the meantime, I expect you to keep with the terms of our deal."

"A deal you've taken to with vigor," I replied, brow high.

"Is that a complaint? I could always be less... vigorous."

I shivered. *Mother Meya strike you down if you dare.*

Aeris was right. There was no moving forward with Alisdair while he treated me like a toy, a duty, or a bunch of fuckable holes. He had to be vulnerable, and she was correct to put that obvious notion in my head.

But I was right too.

If he was going to fall in love with me, then I had to be me. I didn't dance, or flirt, or hand out clumsy compliments. I gave one warning, then I acted.

Like the single warning I gave to recruiters, telling them to keep their notices off our door or receive a face full of soiled cloths. Like the single warning I gave to the bullies chasing Riordan, telling them to back off, or I'd do to them everything they did to him. They walked off laughing, but then came and beat him the next day—breaking his nose, wrist, giving him a concussion, and bruising him all over.

Kahir I kicked down the stairs. For Brenden I lay in wait outside his favorite war wife's house, hit him with a brick when he rounded the corner, then stomped him until he cried and wailed for me to stop. Conri got his hands on a coudarian crystal and taunted me with all the ways he'd tear me inside out if I tried attacking him. I took the crystal off him while he was passed out drunk at his usual table at his usual pub, then broke the whole arm and smashed his face on the bar table for my trouble. I broke his nose and three teeth.

I may not have been so brutal if not for the reason they chased and beat up Riordan. It was because my friend intervened and chased them off when the three filthy kakkas cornered Meliora in an alley and tried to rape her.

And then there was Kirwan, and the second and last time he struck my mother. The second because I warned him after the first that if he ever hit her again, I'd kill him.

He laughed at me, naturally. A thin waif of a thirteen-year-old girl against the king's advisor, the hero of the battlefield, and the heir to House Dawnbreaker? I wasn't a threat.

And then, months later, he hit her again. That evening, I walked into the deepest part of the woods where the plants not meant for the sun and light grew. I picked something my mama warned me never to eat, snuck into his grand manor through an open servant's window, and slipped it in his midnight cordial while he slept next to his unsuspecting wife.

He was on death's door for weeks. It wasn't thought he would make it. After he recovered, he returned to my mother's house with a look in his eyes like he knew what I'd done. But he never accused me, and he never hit her again.

The truth of me was very simple. I never let anything—size, power, position, magic, or threat—get in the way of protecting the people I loved. Alisdair and his stubbornness was in the way, so I felled him like an oak tree—

—and what an amazing decision that was.

Alisdair took to blowjobs with the expected gusto, and he wanted more. All the more.

As good as the sex was before when he catered to my pleasure, it somehow became three times more incredible. I ran out of my second-hand sexual knowledge pretty quickly, but that didn't stop us from getting creative.

There was no other word for it but that we were having *fun* now. Our bedchamber was filled with teasing, laughter, fevered moans, and conversation. Alisdair told me of his favorite books and music. We talked of the beautiful, kind woman who raised him and took in his brother, Bradach.

He told me the myriad of ridiculous, troublemaking scrapes Bradach got into that Alisdair always had to save him from. He told me about his first horse, and what life was like before forced bindings, hatred, and war.

Alisdair also told me how he liked his eggs, that he was nine pounds at birth, and that he once saw an eagle snatch a rabbit off the ground and carry it off. He truly scraped the bottom of the mundane barrel for the sake of holding up his end of the deal, and getting me on my knees—wherever and whenever the mood struck us.

I once ran away from all the amorous couples partaking in their naked activities outside of their rooms. Who knew it would only take me a few short weeks until Alisdair and I were one of them.

It wasn't an exaggeration that we couldn't get enough of each other. And it wasn't a lie for me to say that somewhere along the way, I thought less of tricking him into falling in love with me, and more about how I'd stop myself falling in love with him.

"I once caught a bee with my bare hand."

I spun on him, hands on my hips. "Now why would you do a fool thing like that?"

The wicked smirk danced on his lips, heating my core though he had yet to put his hands on me. The effect Alisdair had on me—had always had on me—neared forbidden. "To impress a girl, of course."

"It didn't sting you?"

"It not only stung me. It made my face swell to grotesque proportions. Said girl ran away screaming."

I snorted obscenely, shaming my etiquette instructor. I couldn't help it. Alisdair Shadowsoul was funny. Of all things, I never expected him to be funny.

He heaved a sigh. "You think my face grotesque too."

"I do not," I cried, and blushed doing so.

"You do"—he spun me squealing off my feet—"that's why you're going to sit on it."

Alisdair dropped us both down on an armchair, him draping my legs over the arms and disappearing under my voluminous skirts. I'd have switched to breeches long ago, but all the layers did the best job of keeping me warm. That is, of course, when Alisdair wasn't undressing me.

His claws neatly shredded everything in his way. It was a good thing this cold, filthy place was wealthier than anyone knew or believed. I was spending a fortune from our coffers getting new clothes made.

"Cover every part of me that displeases you," he said, ridding me of my undergarments. A swift swat on the backside made me yelp and swat him back—laughing. "I deserve no less."

"Hmm." I dipped low, then drew back up, dangling his prize out of reach. "You do have rather a filthy mouth. Should I smother it into obedience?"

"How else will it learn?"

I dropped down—keeping to my word and smothering those lips with my own. I was too eager for him to delay with flirting.

I rocked my wet, hungry pussy on his tongue—moans peeling from my lips. I laced our fingers together, making him the firm, steady anchor as I bounced on his face, impaling myself on that impossibly long, thick tongue.

"Agh, Alisdair," I breathed, throwing my head back. "I take it back. I love your filthy mouth."

Alisdair caught hold of my thighs, latched on to that small, sensitive nub, and *suuuucccked harrddd.* My cries bounced up the stacks and danced among the rafters. Alisdair may have given in to the fun of letting me be on top, but I had no illusions. Alisdair dominated me mind, body, and soul. My pleasure was always his to tempt, twist, and tease. Riding him was like being thrown about on a bucking bronco. Yes, I was on top. Yes, I was holding on. But to think that meant I had control over the raging, deadly beast was a fool's dream.

Alisdair was handsome, smart, fierce, strong, and deadly. Since the day I met him, he kept me under a spell of pretty words, praise, and cold indifference—addicting me to him. Making me crave the barest drop of kindness or attention, just for how rare it was.

It was a game of seduction that had no doubt crushed many a heart beneath his boot. A game he surely believed I'd fail too, but they didn't call me Volka for nothing. I would addict him to me. I'd make him fall in love with the girl who loved to read, learn, sing, and get grubby on my hands and knees—growing precious gifts from the earth.

I'd make him toss and turn every night from the dreams of our passionate tumblings. I'd have him begging and trading every secret in the darkest corner of his mind, all for my lips around his cock, and my body within his arms.

I'd have him level every enemy in my path, and delight in finally finding someone as wickedly harsh as him—doling out death to everyone who made this world dangerous and unbearable for me, my mother, and my sisters. Like I once did to Kirwan. I'd make Alisdair Lumenfell fall in love with me—

—and then I'd leave him and never look back.

"Ah, yes!" I bounced on his face, out of control. My lower belly was so tight it bent me in half, and still I rocked faster—fucking the shit out of myself on his tongue.

Alisdair grabbed my collar and tore my front clean off, freeing my breasts from their cage. He kneaded it under his strong, calloused hands—tugging roughly on my sensitive nipple. My eyes rolled up in my head—pleasure flooding every nerve ending and drowning them.

"Yes, right there, right there, right—"

The door banged open and Aeris walked in. I tipped over the side, scrambling to cover myself, and landed hard on my face.

"Ow!"

"Ooh, oh dear." Aeris rushed over to help. "I'm so sorry, my lady. I didn't mean to—"

"To what? Knock!" I slapped her hand away. "How dare you go barging around my castle without so much as a by your leave! Servants have sense and respect where I come from." I shoved up to my feet, glaring at a calm and smirking Alisdair as he slid up and lazily licked my juices from his lips. "This is your fault," I snapped at him. "You let them get away with this nonsense."

Aeris backed away, eyes huge—feathers ruffled. "I truly am so sorry, Lady Ana—"

"That is Royal Highness Emiana to you."

Lips pressed tight, she bowed deeply. "Your Royal Highness, I apologize. I was told you were having a rune lesson in here. If I'd known you were up to more amorous pursuits, I would've knocked."

My amorous pursuits were hanging free in the open air and running down my leg. "Are you going to do something about this?" I demanded of Alisdair, gesturing to my nakedness.

"As you wish, my queen."

I bristled. I hated how he did that—mockingly used my title as if my Meya-given power was no more than a joke. The beast didn't know how lucky he was to be married to me. To share my bed, to breathe my air, to live another day now that I had the purple petals in my possession.

Alisdair snapped his fingers and my clothes magically reknit themselves.

"What was so urgent, Aeris?" he asked.

"It's Foalan. Terrible news, I'm afraid, my lord. The Rajadom chancellor went to temple today and prayed for Meya's mercy," she said, "because he's dying."

"He's what? Fuck!" Alisdair blared, punching the chair.

I was having the same reaction, but decorum wouldn't let me show it. It may have seemed strange to be angry that a man we wanted dead was dying, but it was the second-worst possible news we could've received. The worst being that our assassins were discovered. Still, finding out that Rajadom was about to initiate succession protocols was pretty bad.

"All of the heirs are about to scatter to the far corners of Elva and go into hiding, waiting until he's passed and his chosen is safely coronated," Alisdair gritted. "Killing the heirs was supposed to be the simple part. Only the chancellor was the challenge. If it's a slow disease, they'll stay in their holes for months."

"Which means our plans are delayed for months," I cut in. "Unacceptable. Give the word to kill the chancellor and his heirs now."

Aeris's face was grim. "That's why the news is terrible, my lady. The heirs have already left. The chancellor didn't share his news with the priestesses until after he sent his sons off to the summer palace. Treasa checked with your servant in the summer palace. It's empty, dusty, and everything is covered in white sheets. No word was sent to open it," she said. "They're not going there. We don't know where they are."

"Fuck," I shrieked, decorum be damned. "I will not have this. Not now when everything was finally in place. There has to be something else we can do."

"Treasa is looking for them, of course," Aeris said. "As soon as she does—"

"No." My hand sliced the air. "My father will not live a second past his due. What about the siren? Have we figured out how to harness her song?"

"You forbade it," Alisdair reminded. "Ordered me on multiple occasions to return her to her home."

I planted my hands on my hips. "Well, thank Meya you didn't listen to me. We tried the method of least resistance, it didn't work, and now we move on to our next plan." I met his eyes. "As a general should."

He flashed me an unreadable smile. "Well said. And it no longer bothers you that it will kill every man—heir and innocent—who hears it?"

"Should it?" I turned back to Aeris. "As for that rat woman, bring her here. It's unacceptable that we're receiving vital information after it's passed through half a dozen ears."

"But, my lady, it's difficult for Treasa to travel with the babies."

"Then send the litter for her," I snapped. "Must I think of everything?"

"No, Your Highness." She backed further away. She bowed deeper. "It will be done."

"Good. Now leave us."

Aeris didn't move. "There was one more thing. Eadaoin has asked to see you. She's in the garden."

"Excuse me?" I scoffed. "The servant *asked to see me*? Who is she to send for me like a kitchen maid?"

Aeris's blandly polite expression didn't change. "She said it was a topic you preferred to speak about in private. She merely thought the garden best for such privacy. Of course I can send for her if you wish."

I pursed my lips, but didn't give the order. Something we needed to speak about privately? I confessed, the tiger-beast piqued my interest.

"It's fine. I'll go down to the gardens. In exactly ten minutes, send one of my attendants out with my hot cider."

I left without listening to her agreement. She'd do what I ordered. Why wait around for her to confirm it?

Heading out to the garden, I spotted Eadaoin sitting on a bench under the rose bushes, waving me over. I barely kept control of my curling lip. It was simply disgusting how familiar these peasants were with their betters.

"There you are, my lady. Come, come." She took my hand and tugged me down, letting me go before I slapped her off. "I have good news—Well, I hope it's good news. I think I know where the boy is."

I stared at her, patience running out fast. "Boy? What boy?"

"The fox boy," she said. "Honora was in the east wing earlier today when she overheard a child's voice coming through the wall. There wasn't a door to the room in that hallway, so there has to be another, possibly concealed, way in." Eadaoin looked at me expectantly. "Well, isn't that good news? That child must be the fox boy, and he has to be on the other side of that wall. All you have to do is find the way in."

Snowflakes dusted my hair, hands, and shoulders—spreading their cold gift and chasing away the lingering warmth of my almost-orgasm. Along with my razor-thin patience.

"Why in the name of Elva would I do that? I don't have time to go chasing around after little peasant beasts," I snapped. "If you haven't noticed, we're at war!"

Eadaoin flinched, her smile melting away.

"Meya knows why I was so obsessed with that brat." I tossed my head. "I had obviously taken leave of my senses, and how dare you make fun of me by rubbing it in."

"But I wasn't," she cried. "I was only trying to help, my lady. Honest."

"I don't need help from the likes of you."

Eadaoin's eyes blew wide. Pathetically, her eyes filled.

Egh. Don't tell me she deluded herself into thinking she was my friend. As if I'd ever lower myself that low for company.

"I'm certain whatever Lord Lumenfell did with the boy was for the best," I continued, "and don't ever question him or his will again."

"Yes, my lady." Fixing her face, she straightened. "It won't happen again."

A fluttering noise turned my head up to the falling snow. I saw nothing but white, black, and gray. "See that it doesn't," I said, rising to my feet.

"Do you still wish me to escort you?"

I halted. "Escort me where?"

"To Riordan. It's at this time that you usually bring him a sack of jewels." She noted my surprise. "Yes, I know, my queen, but it's not my business to question. They are your jewels after all."

"Yes, they are, but all of that is done with." I tossed my head, feeling a memory coming and throwing it back. "We're about to go to war. We need all the coin in our coffers. Now is that all?" My voice said that it had better be.

"Yes, my lady." She rose to her feet. "I'll escort you to your archery lesson now."

I held up a hand. "My archery lessons are over. To imply that I need to learn to defend myself is to say that my guard intends to fail in her single, most important task—which is protecting and defending me with her life. Is that the case, Eadaoin?" I stuck my face in hers. "Are you such a pathetic excuse for a companion, guard, and soldier that I'd better learn to rescue myself, because you're no better than a furry-faced ornament?"

"No! Of course I'll protect you. I will not fail you."

I sniffed. "Good. Now if you ever mention archery to me again, I'll have you flogged for—"

"Excuse me, Lady Ana."

I spun around. "What!"

Cold, freezing water splashed in my face. My scream echoed over the mountaintops.

"What the fuck is wrong with you, keva?" Bradach demanded. "First I heard you dressing down Aeris for doing nothing wrong, and now you're berating Eadaoin for helping you and keeping to *your* schedule?"

I breathed hard, gaping at the birdman as snow and ice swarmed my wet face and clothes, eagerly making more of itself.

"Is this your stunted sickness?" he asked, voice softening. "Wasting, I believe you call it. We've heard that it sometimes takes the mind. Is that why you're not yourself?"

"*Not yourself.*"

The question hit me like a brick, scraping the claws of Emiana's ghost out of my head. With it gone, everything I'd said and done came tumbling in.

"Oh, Meya," I breathed, clapping my hand over my mouth. "Oh, no, I'm sorry. I'm so sorry!" Twisting around, I grabbed Eadaoin in a fierce hug. "I didn't mean any of those awful things I said, Eadaoin. I can't believe any of that came out of my mouth."

She hesitated. "Is... is it true, then? Is the sickness taking you, my lady?"

"It's definitely a sickness," I said firmly. "Terrible, evil one that spreads misery without remorse. I didn't think it would take me this quickly." By it, I meant Emiana's soul. I'd only been in Lumenfell for less than two moons, and in that time, she was wiping more and more of the true me away.

At this rate, I wouldn't have long before I forgot why I had to get home. Actually, when she took me over completely, I wouldn't want to go home at all. Not until our war plans were a success, and Alisdair reduced all of Elva to rubble and crowned her the empress of a broken, desolate kingdom. When that happened, I'd walk up to my family, assuming they survived the war, and kick the dirty peasants out of my way.

"I'm sorry," I whispered, tears staining my cheek.

"My lady, it's okay." Eadaoin hugged me, rubbing my back. "You don't have to apologize that much. I know the true you. You're sweet and kind and only yell at our lord."

"He deserves it," I rebounded, then we laughed.

The tension broke.

"It's me that's sorry." Eadaoin drew back, squeezing my arms. "What they've done to you is unforgivable. I wish I could've protected you then, Ana. I truly do."

I smiled sadly. "Me too," I whispered.

Shaking myself, I cleared my throat. "Okay, forget all that nonsense I said before. I do have another delivery for Riordan. I stashed it behind a statue in the west hall. I'll go get it, then I'll take another poke around in the east wing. I'm not surprised someone else noticed that wing is hiding secrets. It's about time I uncovered them. When I'm done, I'll meet Alisdair for my archery lesson."

"What if you can't get the east wing to reveal its secrets?" she asked. "Wouldn't the simplest solution be to ask our lord where he is? You two are on better terms now—fucking anywhere, everywhere, and all hours of the day."

It'd be a long time before me and my overheated cheeks got used to how open and casual faeriken were about sex.

"Won't he tell you now?"

I sighed. "I did ask him again, and he said the answer would forever change the way I see him"—I swallowed hard—"and there'd be no going back after that. I haven't asked since."

Eadaoin blinked at me, jaw slack. She didn't have a response for that either.

I turned to Bradach, who wore a trickster's smirk on his lips as usual. "Thank you, Bradach. You have my permission to throw freezing water in my face whenever and wherever you need to."

"Thank you, my queen. I will abuse the privilege shamelessly."

I snorted, smothering a laugh. Alisdair found him ceaselessly tiresome, but I couldn't help but like Bradach.

"Shall we?" I asked Eadaoin.

She followed me indoors to my hiding place for the jewels, pearl necklaces, and two gold chalices. I placed them in her safe hands. "Would you mind taking these to him? I don't have much time before the runes demand my presence on the training yard. I want to check the east wing while I've got the time."

"I overheard Riordan say last time the family you're blessing are becoming more insistent about knowing who is giving them these treasures." She cocked her head. "Why don't you want them to know?"

I want them to know more than anything. "Because the answer would only lead to more questions," I replied. "It's easier this way."

"Are you sure you want to keep looking for the boy?"

Eadaoin's whispered question stopped me mid-turn.

"What if you can't handle the truth of why every child who comes to Castle Riagin disappears?" Her eyes were low and hooded. "We fae live long lives, my lady, and yours is now forever tied to Lord Lumenfell. If you discover he's a monster the likes of which would shame and horrify other monsters, it'll be a long life of misery."

I was quiet for a long spell. "I had all of those thoughts, Eadaoin, but for better or worse, I made a promise to that boy. We're only as good as the promises we keep, and if I break this one, I'll be the monster that shames and horrifies other monsters."

She smiled at me—soft, fleeting, and a little sad. "This is the true you, Lady Ana. Even if this is impertinent to say, I hope the change takes you... so that you don't."

I thought about what she said while I made my silent trek to the east wing. Eadaoin and Bradach saw the real me, but did Alisdair? Bradach gave me a freezing bath for dressing down Aeris, but Alisdair just looked on in amusement while licking me off his lips. I was being an interesting little bird once again.

As much fun as we were having together in the bedroom and out, how was I supposed to know if he was falling in love with me? Alisdair had certainly never said he loved me or anything approaching the feeling.

I was quick, clever, magnificent, the owner of a sweet and tasty pussy and toffee nipples, but his love? He never suggested such a thing. Not even sarcastically.

How was I supposed to know if I was doing it right? What was the proper way to make someone fall in love with your true self other than being your true self? One fucking thing this curse won't let me do! And that wasn't even approaching the problem of how I would get him to learn my true name.

I groaned, clutching my head as I rounded the corner and headed downstairs. What was I meant to do? Emiana got harder and harder to push out every day. If he couldn't see the real me by now, he never would. And I'd be lost forever.

"Maybe I should ask Aeris for advice again. Assuming she ever speaks to me again." I groaned again thinking of the huge apology I owed her. "A thousand sorrys won't be enough—"

A hard force struck my ankle and ripped it out from under me. My leg went flying and took me with it—all the way down the stairs.

"Ahhh!"

Feet over head I tumbled, smacking my shoulder hard on the stone step. Vicious pain clamped my jaw down on my tongue. Blood filled my mouth—smothering my final cries.

"My lady!"

The spinning, falling, tumbling, everything stopped, except my screams. Chest heaving, my shrieks bled through my blood-stained teeth.

"My lady, are you okay?" Foalan's magic buoyed me on a soft pillow of air. Gently he floated me down to him. "Thank Meya I was nearby. Are you hurt?

"You," he shouted back at someone I couldn't see. "Fetch the healer now."

"S-s-s-someone tried to kill me! They grabbed my ankle! I've been attacked!" Emiana's voice bled through my fear and panic, shoving me away. "Someone dared to attack me!"

"Attack you?" Foalan looked up—his fur-covered face crumpled in a frown. "There's no one there."

"You dare question me?" I tried to slap the beast, but it easily dodged the blow. "A disgusting, filthy, no doubt *clawed* hand grabbed me!"

"I do not doubt you," he said kindly. "What I meant to say is that if this wasn't a physical attack, it was a magical one. You have an enemy outside of these walls, my queen. A serious one."

"Outside of these walls?" I clutched my shoulder, tears leaking down my cheek. "Who says so? You?" My derision told him exactly what I thought of that. Of course High Commander Masochist refused to suspect his people. It would mean he failed in his basic task of protecting his sovereigns.

I'll have his head for this. Alisdair won't dare fight me. Commander Foalan has howled at his last moon—

"I do not say so," Foalan continued, rising up and carrying me floating next to him. "Sense does. If you had an enemy within these walls who sought your death, they wouldn't need to lay a trap on a staircase and hope you spring it. It is not as though you prepare your own food or bath. And you frequently traverse the castle without protection or weapon. You also have no magic to defend yourself. You're the easiest target there could be within these walls."

My mind quieted under howling pain.

"Whoever did this sought a small window of opportunity and thankfully failed in its execution."

Emiana faded back into the depths from whence she came. This one was for me. "The boy," I whispered. "Someone randomly approached Eadaoin... and told her she thought the boy was in the east wing." I gritted against the pain. The shoulder was dislocated. No question. "Those are the only stairs leading to this wing. It's the only way I would've gone."

Even through the agony, I shared a grim look with Foalan.

"I will guard you myself from now on," he said firmly. "This will never happen again."

"Of course it won't happen again," Emiana shrieked. "From this day forward, if even another scratch is laid on me, it'll be your head!"

Chapter Twelve

The outrage over the assassination attempt kept Emiana's hooks on my mind and mouth for hours. I harangued and accused everyone—screeching and making a nuisance of myself for so long after my shoulder and mouth were healed that Bradach threw another bucket of ice water in my face.

I came back to myself sputtering and gasping. Alisdair observed the exchange with a raised brow, but didn't question his brother. He was likely as relieved as I was that Emiana had finally shut the hell up.

"Whoever did this will be found and slowly killed," Alisdair dropped without irony or inflection. "That I promise you."

I just nodded, sinking back against the wet sheets. Alisdair snapped his fingers and the sheets and I were dried. I was lying down in our bed, though I didn't need to be. The healers did their job well.

"Who was it who told Eadaoin they heard a child's voice in the east wing?" Bradach asked. "Surely that's our culprit."

"Eadaoin said it was Honora," I replied to him but looked at Alisdair. "The same person who taught me that stupid dance, claiming you'd love it."

Alisdair inclined his head. "Luring you into a death trap isn't the natural leap from tricking you into humiliating yourself."

"I didn't humiliate myself, *you* humiliated me," I snapped.

"I did no such thing. I was merely a captive to the comedy play."

"You know what, have you considered that Honora told me to do that dance so I'd kill *you*! My only regret is that a dented skull wasn't enough!"

Alisdair laughed heartily. I looked around for another candelabra to finish the job.

"As amusing as this is, are we truly considering Honora?" Bradach broke in. "Why would she wish Lady Ana harm? She wants this as much as we all do."

"Wants what?" I asked, flicking between them and their locked stares. "Guys? Hello? What does she want?"

"She wants you to be happy," Bradach said, finally turning to me. "As we all do. Like my lord said, a silly little trick is nowhere near trying to kill you. I don't believe this of her."

I gave him a grave look. "Then, do you believe Eadaoin is lying, and that she's the one who—"

"No."

"Exactly," I said. "Neither do I. Eadaoin wouldn't hurt me. And even if she wanted to, she wouldn't need to lure me into a trap. I'm alone with her more than anyone else in Lumenfell. Meya knows she's had plenty of easy opportunities."

"Both Eadaoin and Honora are innocent of this," Alisdair stated, crossing to the bed. His touch was light stroking my shoulder. "Whoever did this hoped we would come to the simplest conclusion that whoever passed the message of the voice in the empty hall, was the culprit.

"But the fact is this, there was no child's voice coming through the wall because there was no child in that hallway. So who was it really?"

I stared at him. "Oh," I whispered.

He nodded. "No magic is strong enough to turn Honora into a traitor. But voice-mimicking magic couldn't be simpler. By now, everyone knows you're looking for that fox boy. All one has to do is make a passerby believe the child you're looking for is in the east wing, they pass the message on to you, and off you go. Simple, yes, but clever," he growled, eyes glittering with rage even as gentle fingers stroked my cheek. "Clever little bastard, I will enjoy ripping him apart and spitting out his bones.

"I'll enjoy it very much."

My heart fluttered, toes curling. His protectiveness over me was a good thing. It was a sign of the love I needed to bloom in his empty chest. But my reaction to him whenever he was... that was not a good sign.

"What do we do now?" I asked. "Foalan is commander of the army and we're in the middle of planning a war. He doesn't have time to follow me around all day."

"Why in the name of Meya would he? You're my wife," he said. "I will protect you—watch over you day and night. Should a single person even glare in your direction, I will pluck their eyes out. No one and nothing will ever hurt you again."

Thump-thump. Thump-thump. THUMP-THUMP!

I didn't need to know whose heart that was or where it was coming from.

It was mine, and I was in trouble. In more danger than I'd ever been in my life, but not because of any assassin.

My breath hitched when Alisdair laced his fingers through mine.

Fall in love with me quickly, beast... before I fall in love with you.

***

Alisdair kept to his word over the next fortnight.

He went where I went. Or more accurately, I went where he went. Trailing him throughout the day and glimpsing what he did outside the times we planned in the war room, or practiced archery on the field. I was treated to what Alisdair Shadowsoul did when I wasn't looking—

—and it was horrible.

A coyote faeriken knelt in the snow, still under the shadow of two swords, but not silent. He growled a steady, ferocious snarl—his expression showing nothing resembling remorse.

"You don't have to do this!" I jumped off the litter and threw myself at Alisdair—holding him back with my body alone.

Emiana enjoyed watching this, but she never got to the end. My horror always brought me back to consciousness.

"We can put him in jail," I cried. "Life sentence. He deserves nothing less."

"We do not have jails, Princess." He kept walking, easily dragging me behind him. "Children are put into corners to think about what they've done after misbehaving. But adults know what they've done, and *this* adult knows the cost. He chose this."

"That's bullshit!"

Alisdair raised his arm—claws growing to their lethal, impossible length. I dangled off his elbow trying to bring his hand back down.

"You'll keep an innocent siren imprisoned in a dungeon, but your criminal subjects are too good for the same treatment!"

"Because they get worse," he roared, flinging me about trying to shake me off. "You're still not ready, little bird. You're soft!"

"And you're still a bastard!" Heaving up, I sank my teeth in his forearm.

His bellow echoed through the endless night. "Damn you, nightmare woman!" Alisdair tore me off and tossed me over his shoulder, ignoring my kicking and pummeling. "Fine!" he barked. "Since you've declared me unfit to be judge, jury, and executioner, I will pass the task to another."

"Good. I sentence him to the dungeon—"

"Not you," Alisdair sliced in. He turned on a twitching, trembling figure in the snow. "You. What say you, Oona. What will his sentence be?"

Oona looked from Alisdair to the kneeling coyote man—shaking harder. Oona was older than me, but not by much. Brown and gray fur covered her head to toe, and flicking over her shoulder, was a large, bushy tail.

She was the first squirrel faeriken I met in Lumenfell, and she seemed just as skittish and nervous as the animal who possessed her, but it wasn't hard to see why. Oona clutched her arm to her chest. It was bandaged with thick, heavy wrappings soaked in healing ointments. A smell so strong it turned the nose of every faeriken with heightened scent.

The care was necessary considering that the same coyote man kneeling in the snow bit through fur, skin, and muscle when he tried to eat her.

"Oona," I called, straining to see around Alisdair's back upside down. "You don't have to do this. I will—"

"Kill him." Oona shook and twitched, but her voice didn't. "My lord, do it. Slit the worthless son of a whore's throat."

Alisdair didn't even put me down. He ripped the head off the coyote's shoulders, spraying warm, thick blood on the back of my boots and legs.

My scream disturbed no other ears than mine.

***

We were a silent party trekking back to Castle Riagin. Alisdair left three guards behind to clean up the mess and escort Oona back to her home. The rest protected me, including Alisdair.

"I can't believe you bit me," he gritted. "I should've traded an actual fucking bird off Salman. At least that creature wouldn't be so ill-mannered!"

I bared my teeth. "I'm ill-mannered? You do these horrible fucking things for no reason, and you dare to say that I'm the problem? My only regret is not tearing a chunk out of you like he did to Oona— Oh," I cried, slapping a hand over my mouth. "Of course I can't. If I did, you'd rip off my head!"

"Don't be ridiculous!"

"Ridiculous? You mean to say your terrible, barbaric laws don't apply to me?" I scoffed. "If only you could spare such mercy for your people."

"Barbaric, you say?" True anger burned in his eyes. "You are a wonder, Princess. You've ruled in my kingdom for an entire two moons, and you believe you know better what my kingdom and my people need?

"Bradach." Alisdair spoke to him, but glared at me. "Who's next?"

"Emer. She says Sheena stole her baby out of the cot, put her own child there in his place, and then she put Emer's child out in the cold to die," Bradach replied, dropping my jaw. "They were able to save the baby in time, but Emer's calling for blood."

"Oh, Meya." My stomach churned thinking of that poor child stolen and left to die. "Why would this Sheena do such a thing?"

"Cuckoo birds," Bradach replied. "It's what they do. Throw all the other eggs out of a nest, lay their own, and leave the borrowed mother to raise their offspring. Sheena wasn't in her right mind when she did it." He shook his head. "But that's little comfort to Emer."

"The change has taken her." Alisdair's deep baritone floated to my ears. "Her faemanity has so eroded, she abandoned one child and tried to kill another. As my people become more and more animal-like, the laws of fae are discarded for the law of beasts, and in the wild, the only thing an animal fears is a predator."

The litter stopped. I peered from the blankets into Alisdair's shadowed eyes.

"I am the law, Ana, because *they fear me*. They don't want to be an animal. They don't want to give in to their instincts, because then they become my prey. As long as that is true, there is peace in Lumenfell, and when it isn't true... there is death."

I slowly sat up, holding his gaze. "Alisdair, I'm not saying this woman doesn't deserve punishment. I say she doesn't deserve death. Bradach said himself that she wasn't in her right mind. She didn't know what she was doing."

"But that's the point, my lady." Bradach moved to Alisdair's side. "She will never be in her right mind again. This isn't like your sickness. I can't shock her system and bring her back. Once the change takes you completely, your true self is gone. From this point on, every time she gives birth, she will abandon that child and kill another in the process. You have to know that can't be allowed to happen."

My throat was so tight, I choked swallowing. "Y-yes. Of course I know that, but it doesn't have to be done this way. We could take them somewhere. Away. Where they can't hurt each other or anyone else."

"Prison," Alisdair dropped bluntly. "Sheena was once a singer. Had the most beautiful voice in the five kingdoms, and dreamed of proving it—singing far and wide through Elva and beyond. Now she's a feathery madwoman who shits herself and tries to kill infants."

I flinched.

"So you tell me what she would want— No," Alisdair said, bearing down on me. "Tell me what you'd want. To die as your true self, or to live out the rest of your days as an animal trapped in a cage?"

I dropped my gaze, fists shaking. Alisdair didn't know the true question he was asking me. What would I want if it was me, because it was me. Would I rather live the rest of my life an angry, bitter, cruel, resentful princess with no love, no family, and no hope? This body was my own prison, and would someone not be doing me a kindness if they sent me to the Meadows of Meya while I was still me, instead of letting Emiana kill me all on her own?

"Okay," I said softly—evenly. "I understand why you do this. I even see why you believe it a kindness. The person Sheena was is gone. You want to protect the memory of the beautiful singer, instead of the infamy of the baby-killing fae-beast."

My eyes narrowed. "But you need to hear this, Alisdair, and heed me well. You didn't trade a bird off Salman. You married me. A woman with her own mind and opinions. I will challenge you, argue with you, and bite you when necessary. If you have a problem with that, too bad. I'm not going to change, so take me as I am, or leave me."

Hear that, Emiana. You will not take me.

Alisdair rocked back, observing me. What he was thinking, I couldn't begin to guess. His expression gave nothing away.

"Hmm. Very well," he replied. "I'll take you." Alisdair shrugged, a smirk overtaking him. "And, to be fair, I did bite you first. But you liked it when I did that."

My skin flushed hot and sudden as the tightening in my lower belly. *Of course he would bring that up in the middle of an argument while we have an audience!*

"Would you like me to carry you the rest of the way?" he asked, shocking me. "I've found I like having your rump on my shoulder and within easy smacking distance."

"Away with you, you beast!" I shrieked, lobbing a pillow at him.

Alisdair snagged my wrist and spun me, tossing me over his shoulder laughing.

If I laughed too, it was smothered by his cloak, so he couldn't prove it.

That night, I lay next to him in bed, watching him sleep.

The beast couldn't be held back in a dream. Every terrifying inch of him towered beside me. The claws, the fangs, the fur, the muzzle, and mishmash of every predator in creation thrown into one. All of the others were turning into animals while Alisdair turned into a monster.

"But you're not one..."

All those weeks ago, Aeris shamed me for thinking I could get a man I didn't even know to fall in love with me. Now I saw how right she was.

All the world saw of the man they dubbed Shadowsoul, was a fearsome, unrepentant king sitting back on his throne while the curse he created ripped through all of Elva—destroying our land and the fae living on it.

I'd never know the truth of how the curse began, and he'd never be able to tell me, but I understood now, that Alisdair wasn't uncaring of the devastation he caused. He ruled a kingdom of beasts with a clawed iron fist to maintain order in chaos. He put down anyone who became a threat to the peaceful, happy people dancing in the square while their children giggled and skated on the frozen fountain.

And then, after he was done being an incorrigible ass, he sat down with me in private and listened to my ideas for how we could care for the people who were taken by the madness of the curse. He didn't agree with me, and we argued *loudly*, but he did listen, and by the end, he agreed to let me decide which cases were hopeless, and which we would relocate to somewhere private, enclosed, and safe where they couldn't harm any else.

The man I was raised to hate wasn't supposed to be this way. He wasn't supposed to value my opinion, teach me to rule a kingdom as his equal, protect me from all threats, and care enough about my comfort, he held back his beast for me.

He also wasn't supposed to have a wicked sense of humor, a love of reading, a brother he swore to his mother he'd protect, and the respect and love of his people. Not cursed captives who slaved and were pining for freedom—but happy, equal people who pitied everyone outside of Wind and Wild, because we were many things, but happy and equal weren't it.

He wasn't a monster. The curse and his reputation tried to paint him as one, but he was just a man. A powerful, wicked, harsh, funny, sex-obsessed man, but still a man. A man that can know love.

A man that can be loved.

My heart thrummed a beat as I stroked the rough, hairy folds of his face. I played the game and I lost. I see now that I was always meant to lose. Even when Emiana took me over—the heartless, arrogant, nightmare of a woman—she fell prey to his charms. She giggled under his attention and heated at his touch. She turned her nose at everyone and everything... except him.

Alisdair was always going to claim my heart. It's why he laughed at me while I stood at the altar, swearing my eternal hatred and devotion to destroying his life. He knew even then, that we'd end up here.

I smiled tracing the shell of his foot-long ear. Alisdair grunted in his sleep, his ear twitching and swatting me away.

I giggled. "You may have known I'd fall eventually, but what you didn't know is you will too." Leaning in, I pressed the softest kiss on his snout.

Thump-thump. Thump-thump.

Pushing up, I looked around the three-walled room until I landed on the door. I was up and out of bed before the thought fully crossed my mind. Quickly I dressed in the dark and slipped out.

I'd been hearing that heartbeat everywhere, and more and more every day. Was it madness? Was it Emiana? Or was it Alisdair? Was it his heart?

Slippered feet padded through the opulent castle, carrying me far away from our chambers, into the east wing.

I stepped lightly on the steps, clinging tight to the wall, but I didn't spring any traps.

Thump-thump. Thump-thump.

Dropping down, I hurried down the hall, carried along by a tug on my chest—driving me forward, pulling me faster, refusing to let go.

I found myself in that same hallway I found all those weeks ago, staring at a familiar wall. Moving forward, I placed my palms against the cool stone, following the lines and cracks down until—

My hand slipped through that break in the wall, and the rest of me followed.

Thump-thump. Thump-thump. Thump-thump.

The heart beat in time with my footsteps, carrying me up the stairs. What was this place? I once mentioned it to Eadaoin, but she had no idea what I was talking about. She had lived in this castle for fifty years; it was hard to believe she didn't know every inch of it. Was this place one of the secrets of the east wing? And did it hold the one secret coveted by all of Elva?

I topped the final step, coming face-to-face with the simple oak door. I approached it like it could hurt me—the very doorknob coming to life and biting off my fingers for daring to touch it. But dare I did.

Closing on the knob, it turned and swung open, revealing the dark space beyond. The heartbeat was almost deafening in my ear—urging me on. Demanding it.

I stepped inside and hissed, clutching my robe tighter. It was worse than freezing. It was so cold, the air was living, physical knives stabbing my skin, chilling my lungs, and petrifying my bones. I nearly turned and left on the spot.

THUMP-THUMP!

"Where are you?" I blinked against the gloom, eyes adjusting. "Where is this?"

Fuzzy, undefined shapes rose in my vision. The tower wasn't necessarily big or wide, but it appeared to be long. One long room with narrow walls and nary any furniture.

"What I wouldn't give for my own magic," I mumbled, inching farther inside. "A torch wouldn't be unwelcome right now. Or the heat."

I was a talent with fire magic when I was little. It occurred to me then that when the curse took me, I would be again.

Do I want the curse to take me? I made out strange, white rectangular shapes leaning against the wall. Reaching out, my fingers brushed cotton. *Would getting my magic back be worth the cost of turning into a howler monkey?*

Is that really the question haunting you right now? another voice asked. *Isn't the true one, what would you do if you find the heart?*

I lit on something toward the back of the room. Padding closer, the temperature dropped another five degrees, then another five, then another ten.

My teeth chattered—breaths turning to ice for every exhale. Stumbling forward, a faint, pinkish glow began to take form—drawing me in.

A rose?

I questioned but there was nothing else it could be. Resting on an ivory pedestal was a beautiful, brilliant red rose protected under glass.

Sweetly delicate petals burst from the stem, defying nature and refusing to wilt, brown, or die.

It defied nature in every way. It had no roots, no water, and no foundation. The impossible rose floated above the pedestal, glowing with the magic that made it be, and as I took it in, the thrumming heartbeat stopped instantly—leaving only its faint echo in my ears.

Beautiful. So very beautiful... and I wanted to throw up at the sight of it.

The flower was *wrong*. So terrifyingly wrong, I wanted to rip off the glass and smash it—crush it under my heel and wipe the horrid thing from the world. I might've done so if I could bring myself to get closer to it. I didn't even want to be as close as I was.

Clapping my hand over my mouth, I fought the bile rising in my throat. *The cold and dark.* This thing was the reason. I didn't know how I knew, but it was sucking the heat from the air, the light from the world, and the joy in my heart.

Revulsion and hate burned in my chest gazing at the thing. Bitterness and regret drowned me. The voices in my head screamed for me to run!

This was not Alisdair's heart. This was no one's heart. Nothing and no one could've ever survived with that thing in their chest. This was some kind of dreadful magic—earthed from the deepest, darkest depths of forbidden spells.

This thing... was a curse.

I flung myself away, gagging. My feet tangled and I fell, my hand flying out grabbing for something to break my fall. I closed on something and it gave way—dropping me flat on the freezing floor.

Groaning, I pushed up and locked on to furious, rage-filled eyes.

"Ahh," I cried, scrambling back. But she didn't follow.

The glow from the appalling rose cast long shadows over the portrait, revealing her face bit by bit.

Hard, unsmiling mouth. Dark eyes. Severe cleft chin. Sharp cheekbones casting their own shadow over gaunt cheeks, and raven hair falling in wisps and tangles around her shoulder. At first glance, it was a portrait of a woman during tragedy, but flicking back to her eyes I knew... she was the tragedy.

Hurriedly I grabbed the sheet and threw it back over her. I suddenly didn't know why I was here. Alisdair wouldn't hide his heart in this cold, dark, frightening place. I wouldn't even tie Kirwan up and lock him in this room. This wasn't for things you cared about. It wasn't even for things you hated. It was just a room you didn't go near like an abandoned cellar that had been flooded over and was now riddled with mold and decay. There was nothing for you down there. There was nothing for me here.

Moving away, I turned my back on that rose and was glad to do so. I would return to my bed and my husband, letting his warmth and nearness banish the chill from my bones, and the sludge that ghastly thing leeched on my soul.

Passing the floating rectangles, curiosity tickled me. Were they all portraits of that strange woman? If so, who painted them? Was it Alisdair?

Alisdair never told me he could paint, and he told me a great many things in exchange for my knees on the floor and my lips around his cock.

I slowed, lingering on a sheet-covered canvas looming on my right. My fingers curled around the linen before I could stop it, pulling it off.

"Wow," I breathed, coming to a standstill.

No. Every portrait was not of that woman. She was night and day the woman smiling back at me, and I meant that almost literally.

Where there was anger and distaste bleeding out of the brushwork of the first portrait, the one before me was bursting with life, joy, and color. A beautiful woman with sun-burnished auburn hair beamed the widest, brightest smile—teasing the dimples from her cheeks and the light in her hazel eyes.

I didn't have to ask if this was Raelina. Her name was scrawled across the bottom of the canvas. Seeing her, it was easy to understand how two men could fall hopelessly in love with her. And it was simple to see why one man would hate the other for the rest of his life for destroying this woman and her smile.

I swept the gloom, taking in the many covered paintings. Crossing to the other side of the room, I reached for another sheet.

"What are you doing?!" A hand snatched mine back, hauling me across. I screamed as I was shoved back and pushed against the wall. "How did you get in here!"

Alisdair's red, bulging eyes threw me into a sea of rage. I'd never seen him so angry.

"I was— I was just—"

"You were what!"

"I was just leaving," I cried, yanking at my captured wrist. "I'm sorry, I didn't mean—"

"What? What didn't you mean, Emiana? To barge in here after you were told to stay away?" he roared. "To assume that just because I like fucking you, my people and my castle are yours to dictate and trample on!" His lips twisted. "Or did you not mean to delude yourself into believing I'd actually fall for you?"

My heart stopped hearing the sweet words I whispered to him thrown back at me.

"Get this into your fucking head," he hissed. "Nothing in my kingdom is yours to do as you see fit. Not my people. Not my castle. And not my heart!"

Tears blinded me. "But, Alisdair—"

"GET OUT!"

He released me and I ran. Bursting out the door, I crashed into the wall, cracking my head, but still I kept going—tripping down the steps, shoving through the crack in the walls, and bolting through the castle, my sobs bouncing through the halls.

I ran and didn't stop running until I threw myself outside and was smacked by the cold, bracing air. Picking up my skirts, I raced through the snow and flowers—disappearing past the tree line into the dark.

***

The next day, I stayed far away from Alisdair—gritting my teeth against the blinding agony tearing apart my leg. I didn't care. The pain was nothing compared to what I felt every time Alisdair's words roared through my head.

It was as though he shoved his fist down inside of me and tore everything out. I was an empty shell of a stupid girl who deluded herself into thinking she was falling in love.

The proof of that was knowing that Alisdair could smell me hiding out in Riordan's horse stall, surrounded by the gentle, curious creatures, but he didn't come. He didn't come to speak to me, apologize, or relieve the pain he knew I was feeling—in my leg or in my heart.

Because he didn't say a word he didn't mean, a small voice whispered. *You don't apologize for the truth.*

It was my fault for believing anything had changed between us. He liked fucking me—that didn't and never had amounted to love.

Kirwan loved bedding Mama. He didn't love *her.* Salman loved nothing more than romping with his harem at the end of the day, but would as soon slit their throats if a single one of them looked at him wrong.

Sex wasn't love. I knew it. It was drilled into my head before I could walk. And still I let myself believe a heartless man would be an exception to the rule.

I choked on a sob, curling tighter on the hay bale. "He's never g-going to love me," I whispered to my silent audience. "He'll never free me. I will live the rest of my days as a cold and hateful queen married to a colder and more hateful king, and everything I was..." I thought of Sheena. Of the sweet, talented, beautiful singer. "Gone."

I raised my head, receiving a compassionate headbutt from the mare sharing her stall with me. Back I tipped my head, gazing through the roof slats to the heavens.

"Yes, yes," I said softly. "I understand, Mother Meya. Never let it be said you had to tell me your will twice."

It was a long time before I dragged myself to the castle. Yes, dragged. My leg was a useless stump trailing behind me, screaming to be cut off.

Eventually I staggered through the castle doors and crawled up the steps to our bedroom. Alisdair reclined in an armchair, sipping a mug of ale, and gazing out at a hidden sunset like nothing ever happened. He cast me a cursory glance when I fell through the doors, near in tears when the pain finally eased.

"Princess," he drawled. "Nice of you to return. Did you enjoy your time in the stables?"

I shoved up and locked on to the mess in the mirror. Hay stuck to every inch of her, as clingy as the stink of manure and the redness of my eyes and cheeks. "I did, as it happens." My voice was a thin rasp. "It was very illuminating. Gave me a chance to clear my head."

He studied me, face unreadable. "I assume we understand each other now."

"We do."

"And me," he repeated, force bleeding into the word. "Do you understand *me*?"

I raised my chin. "More than ever, Alisdair. Shall we?"

"Shall we what?"

A smile broke out on my lips. Closing the distance, I peeled off my clothes—raising his brows higher. "Shall we make up?"

Alisdair didn't move. "What is this?"

"What do you mean? I had time to think and you were right. I shouldn't have been snooping," I said. "Honestly, I didn't mean to go up there again in the first place. It was strange. It was like something..." I tossed my head. "Anyway, it's not a reason for us to fall out. I'll respect your privacy from now on, and you'll continue to worship at the altar of my pleasure." I flicked his nose, giggling. "Everyone wins."

"You're certain," he replied slowly. "There's nothing more we need to discuss? You're not going to yell, rant, or bite me like a rabid animal?"

I laughed louder. "Don't be silly. The only rabid animal in this room will be you, my husband." I stood up and pulled him with me, skipping over to the bed. "Now are you going to remind me why I put up with you, or not?"

He hesitated, but only for a second longer. A smirk stretched his lips. "If you need a reminder..." His clothes were torn off in a blink. "I'm more than happy to oblige."

Alisdair pounced on me. Snaking around my body, he held me close to him and dropped kisses on my shoulder. The burning trail continued along my neck, behind my ear, and to a soft, sensitive lobe that received a playful nip.

Turning my head, I captured his lips—kissing him deeply, passionately, thoroughly—pouring everything I felt for him.

Alisdair tangled in my hair, drawing me closer still. Our tongues tangled—caught in our never-ending battle for dominance. I surrendered easily—letting him plunder my mouth like he plundered every part of me—taking everything, leaving no survivors behind.

He broke away, coughing.

"Are you all right?" I asked.

Growling, he snatched me back, smashing our lips together.

Just as quickly as the kiss started, it was over again. Alisdair doubled over, besieged by another coughing fit. Clutching his chest, he dropped—tumbling off the bed wheezing and hacking.

Slowly I rose up, my sweet, seductive smile bleeding away. "You really should've insisted that I give you the rest of those petals, dear husband." My voice was flat. Dead.

"Wha— What did... you do?"

I gazed down at him, burning with rage even while another emotion toyed with my heart—*still*! Even now, after all he'd done and said, it hurt to see him this way.

"My mistake was trying to be clever. Use my mind to outwit you." I stepped over to him and grabbed my clothes. "It was only ever my body you cared about. My body was always meant to be the trap."

"Ana!" he shouted and paid for it immediately—hacking as the scant amount of air in his lungs fled.

"I crushed the petals, smeared it on my lips, and coated my mouth in the rest." Before my eyes, he changed. Clutching his throat, his fangs receded, his horns shrunk, and his claws began to shrink. The larger-than-life, all-powerful beast of Lumenfell... was nothing but a man.

"You're never going to love me," I said softly, "and that's okay. But you don't get to keep me either. I'm going home, and you're not going to stop me."

"A-A-A... na—"

I seized his wrists, and pulled. "Goodbye, Alisdair. I wish it didn't have to come to this, but you can take one thing for comfort during your trip." I dragged him to the edge of the room with three walls. "Even after everything you've done to me, I'll still spend the rest of my life regretting that this will be our last and final kiss."

"Wait!"

I kicked him off the cliff.

"Ahhhhhh!"

His shouts faded down the canyon.

I didn't waste another second. There were too many faeriken in and out of the castle with superior hearing. One or more of them would've heard the scream and would be along to check on their beloved king. I needed to be gone before then. Racing to my wardrobe, I grabbed the warmest coat I could find, then bolted out the door.

Riordan was long gone. He left for Lumenfell with a cart full of vegetables, and a sack full of jewels. He wouldn't be able to carry me home.

There was only one way, and one person I could go to. I just had to get there quickly.

Escaping the castle, I crashed through the snow blanketing the garden—running a path so familiar to the one I ran that fateful night when Alisdair made me his true mate in every way.

Darkness claimed me. Bare branches ripped, tore, and appeared out of the gloom to meet me head-on. Was I running because I feared Alisdair was dead, and my own friends would hunt me down and kill me? Or was I running because I was afraid... he wasn't?

I didn't know, and I didn't slow down.

Bursting through the shadows, I ran full speed, and my foot came down on nothing.

"Ahh!" I tumbled off the edge.

"Whoa." A hand snatched and pulled me back. "Not again. You really must watch where you're going, my queen." Meallan spun me around, grinning into my eyes. "It's dangerous in these woods."

"I've done it," I blurted. "Alisdair's done, but maybe not for good. And now that you have your scent on me." I flicked to the grip on my wrist. "He'll be after you too. We need to leave now."

Meallan's smile morphed in an instant. "Not for good? What are you talking about? We talked about this last night when you blundered into my territory, weeping and wailing for your doomed love. You were supposed to kill him," he gritted. "Only then would I help you get back to your kingdom."

"I poisoned him and threw him off a cliff," I snapped. "That's enough killing for anyone else, but I can't be sure with him. He only got traces of the poison in his system. I don't know if it was enough to—"

"ARGGGH!"

The roar ripped through Lumenfell and punched me in the gut, cannoning bile into my throat. There was only one person that could be.

Meallan swore foully. "This is the path we walk now. The good news is any amount of that flower within him will dampen his strength, senses, and magic. We can still get you away, but we have to go now."

"Let's go."

"This way."

We hurried through the brush—not pausing to cover our scent or worry about noise. We had one focus and one focus only—getting away.

I scurried behind him in silence, staying close enough that I could follow his tall, fur-covered outline in the dark. Meya help me, it was so dark. This never-ending night was a scourge on this beautiful land, and the kind, caring people living within it.

No one but me would ever know how much I came to love Lumenfell, or its people. Walking the square with Eadaoin. Chatting with villagers about their plants, flowers, and crops. Being fussed over by Aeris. Watching Bradach woo Aeris, and watching Aeris pretend she didn't love it. Studying runes with Alisdair. Holding court with Alisdair. Practicing archery with Alisdair. Tumbling Alisdair. Alisdair, Alisdair, Alisdair.

Wind and Wild had taken a piece of my heart while I was looking. Alisdair had taken a piece of my heart while I wasn't, but he didn't want it. He didn't want a queen, he wanted a war, a coup, and a throne. All things that Emiana gave him, but me... I had nothing for him, and he wanted exactly that.

Nothing.

"What has happened?"

I jumped at the sudden voice penetrating my thoughts. "What? What do you mean?"

"You're crying," Meallan stated.

My hand flew to my cheek, confirming the truth.

"Why? Have you lost your nerve?"

"That's a pointless question," I replied, voice dull. "Nerve or no, I have to do this. I have to leave."

"You fell in love with him, didn't you." It sounded like a question, but it wasn't.

"I didn't, but—" A twig snapped, drawing my eye to the right. I swept the gloom but saw nothing. "But I could've," I continued. "If I'd been given the chance."

"Hmm."

We lapsed into silence, traveling deeper into the dark wood. I knew Meallan was right in front of me. I reached out every other minute and touched his back to be sure of it, but I could barely see him and he was directly in front of me.

"Maybe we should stop and look for some starflowers. Something to light our way."

"We do not need them. I am a wolf. My vision is excellent," he replied. "My people were made for this land."

We lapsed into another silence. I didn't know the conversations Meallan was having in his head to fill the quiet, but the conversations in mine were loud and circular—bringing me further down the moral spiral of what I'd done— No.

What Emiana had done.

It was me who ran crying from the tower, but her who carried our feet to the starflower meadow where we hid the rest of the stolen purple flower. It was her who made a deal with Meallan to get us out of here, in exchange for killing Alisdair, and settling whatever long-standing feud existed between them.

It was her who did it all, and then she disappeared from my head as I entered the stables, leaving me to decide whether to go on as I was, or go through with her ghastly plan and finally return to my family.

In the end, there wasn't really a choice to be made. I had to keep my promise and return home to my faywens, and Alisdair would have to keep his, by letting me go once daybreak crested the horizon.

"What do you know of the Taken?"

Meallan surprised me again with the sudden question.

"The Taken?" I shivered thinking of them and drew my coat tighter. "I don't know anything about them. Seems that no one does."

"That is true and untrue. There is something about the creatures that we can't know, can't understand, and can't talk about. They don't seem to be born, and they cannot die."

Another sound turned my head. I frowned, squinting through the dark but seeing nothing. Not even shadows.

"Of course they can be killed," Meallan amended. "But they don't die. Not of natural causes or old age. Not by sickness or disease. They just are until they aren't anymore."

"Fascinating," I replied, not the least bit interested. "Why are we talking about them? I'd rather not. Something about those creatures..." I shuddered. "They frighten me."

"They frighten everyone. It's what they were made to do." Meallan stopped. Hands grabbed and lifted me around the waist, helping me over an obstruction I couldn't see. "Beings of pure fear. The wolves have always been curious about them. Where they came from, why they haunt this land."

"Because of the curse," I said.

"That's the obvious conclusion, but I don't believe so." I felt his eyes on me in the dark. "The change is good and right. It brings the fae to the pinnacle of their speed, intelligence, strength, and power. Nothing as foul as the Taken could come from the change."

I eyed the faint impression of him. "Good and right? Do you really feel that way?"

"I do."

"Even though the last stage of the curse is losing your speed, intelligence, strength, and power, and becoming a mindless beast that tries to eat people and live in a tree?"

He laughed. "My queen, that is the last stage of everyone's life. Fae live for hundreds of years, but in the end, sickness, old age, and disease take our bodies and minds. At least faeriken get to live life at the top of the food chain before that happens."

"I guess." Although I didn't sound too sure. "Why are you telling me this?"

"I simply want you to understand us. The wolves," he explained. "My pack. My people. I know you must've heard a number of unflattering things about us, but it's not true. We're treated as evil outcasts because we dare to like who we are. We embrace it instead of cloaking ourselves in self-loathing, and pretending we're still fae."

Thud.

I whipped around. I was certain that time. Someone was out there—close by.

Alisdair?

"All we desire is to stay as we are, and live the life that Meya intends for us."

"Meya didn't intend for you to be cursed," I responded immediately. "That was fae treachery, not her divine hand."

"Meya created magic, magic birthed curses. Everything is traced back to her divine hand."

I shook my head, pressing my lips together tight. Every fae worshipped Meya, but some of them worshipped her a little too hard, and a little too fervently. I learned a long time ago that there was no point arguing with a zealot. But still, it steamed me to even think someone would suggest that it was Meya's plan for Emiana to destroy my life, steal my body, break my mind, and endanger my mom and two sisters in the process.

She could never be so cruel.

"Even the Taken," Meallan continued. "There's a reason they were placed here with us. They're the key."

"The key? The key to what?"

He laughed. "I told you. The key to living forever. If we could understand them—understand how and why they never get sick, old, or diseased, we could harness that ability for ourselves. Even more if we could understand how they strike terror with their mere nearness. We'd have eternal lives, and every day of those lives, no one would dare approach us to end them.

"The powers of the Taken combined with the strength and power of the faeriken would create a new, stronger, and the best race of fae."

My stomach heaved. "You would actually want to look and be like those vile things?"

He blew out a breath. "We've certainly tried. For years, my pack has captured and experimented on Taken, attempting to unlock their secrets. We've learned much, but ultimately not what we're looking for. For example, we learned that certain scents attract them like moths to flame.

"A mixture of linseed, rosehip, and suet drives them mad. They come running far and wide," he said. "I arranged for that mixture to be put in your bath that day you and your king traveled to Bevin—"

I stopped dead on the frozen path.

"—but, of course, you survived."

Meallan's outline disappeared into the shadows. I panted hard, spinning this way and that for any sign of him—any sign of where he'd strike from next. "What are you saying?" I croaked. "You're the reason the Taken attacked us that day?"

A laugh echoed out of the dark. "I'm the reason for a lot of things, *my lady*. I'm the reason poisoned food was placed on your gilded tray and carried up to your royal bedchamber. Sadly, you weren't in said bedchamber"—anger bled into his voice—"because you chose that night of all nights to dine with the court.

"Aeris, in her wisdom, had your meals prepared separately, so that you always dined on your favorites. The meal for the main table is not so pompously handled. You've taken every meal with the court since that night, and we lost our chance." He swore. "The last attempt, tripping you coming down the stairs, was desperate. I admit that."

Horror filled me.

"You kept slinking away from death like a scampering rat. So what else do you do with rats but lead them into a trap?"

"How could you!" I spun, trying to find him. "Why would you do this!"

"It was nothing personal." I didn't have to see him to know he was shrugging—the unrepentant kakka. "Believe it or not, I like you. If this were different, I'd want you as my own mate, but alas, it wasn't meant to be."

My lips twisted. "That's disgusting. I wouldn't *mate* with you if it'd unbind my magic!"

"I couldn't give a shit about your bindings," he growled. "This is about my own."

"What are you talking about!"

"I'm talking about you! Every day, the change spreads deeper and wider—turning this land and the fae into what we're meant to be. But then you chits show up, seduce Alisdair, fill his head with stupid love nonsense, and risk the chance that he'll throw it all away to destroy his heart, and love you back. If that happens, it all goes away," he roared. "We return to being nothing!"

"Being a summer fae isn't being nothing, you lunatic! Rolling around naked in a dirty pit with fangs and claws isn't a better life!"

"You like this life just fine, or you wouldn't be crying for leaving it."

I clamped my mouth shut, breathing hard. As I just said, there was no point in arguing with a zealot. The only thing I needed to do was get away from him.

Slowly, I backed up—desperate not to let the words "*I have excellent vision*" deter me.

"Alisdair has no right to rid our land of the change, nor does he have a right to rule it. Wind and Wild is wolf territory. We are its natural-born and rightful leaders. When Raelina threatened that..." His voice whispered through the dark. "When she got too close to him and began addling his mind, my father turned around and addled hers.

"He cursed her with a love curse that made her hopelessly obsessed with that bastard Salman. She practically chased after his carriage out of town." He barked a laugh. "Curse or not, it was pathetic."

"You monster."

"I'm the monster?" He sounded right next to me.

I spun to the left, fist flying, but struck nothing.

"Your husband is the monster. He's a violent, uncaring beast, and we were certain you were no threat, because there was no way a pampered princess such as yourself would ever fall for him, or make him fall for you."

Thud. Snap.

"Seems we were wrong, so you had to go. Three times we tried, and then you did something wonderful." Another harsh, chilling laugh. "You walked straight into the wolf's den."

"But you don't have to do this," I snapped. "I walked into the wolf's den because I want to leave him and this cursed place. Holding up your side of the bargain would achieve the same end!"

"I can't take the chance. What happens when Shadowsoul showers you with enough gifts and praises that you forget this temper tantrum and come running back to him? The only way to end your threat is to get rid of you for good."

I swallowed hard—feet coming to a stop. "We're not alone," I said—voice flat. "Are we?"

"Afraid not," said a female voice.

"Nope," sang another.

"This is where it ends," said someone else.

I nodded slowly, mind churning. My own mind. Emiana had gotten me into this mess, and it appeared she had no intention of rising up to get me out. "All of this because you're all too chickenshit to kill Alisdair yourselves, or indeed, even face him yourselves. You'd rather skulk around in the shadows, arranging the deaths of innocent women." I scoffed. "Pathetic."

A hand roared out of the dark and slapped me across the face. I bit my lip against the pain, not allowing a single sound out while my ears rang.

"Watch your mouth, slut!" How quickly Meallan did away with *my lady* and *my queen*. "We've tried every means of killing him, but he's too smart. His cult of loyal followers trail him everywhere, destroying the poison flowers the instant they appear, and throwing their lives before the blade to protect him.

"And unlike us, Alisdair has unlocked the secret of the Taken. Or he's harnessed enough power and magic that the result is the same. He doesn't age, wither, get sick, or die. He just keeps going, he just keeps ruling the kingdom that belongs to me.

"All we need is for him to die as the empty shell he is, and then the heart will remain where it is. Safe, hidden, forever cursed. Until that glorious day, we cannot allow whores like you to give him or the faeriken hope. We can't risk him breaking the curse," he whispered in my ear, "for something as worthless as you."

Shaking my head, I laughed. "So that's it? That was the grand plan for why you wanted to reenter Lumenfell society? So you could sneak around, plotting poisonings, and getting close enough to sense if I'm getting too close to Alisdair, therefore threatening your *rightful* rule?" I laughed louder.

"What is funny?" Meallan barked. "The only joke here is you!"

My laughter ceased abruptly, strangled by my disgust. "No, you whining, mewling pup. You're the joke. A stupid, pathetic, delusional joke if you truly believe you're meant to rule Wind and Wild, or that if you even tried, the people wouldn't rip you off the throne and tear your ass limb from limb."

I sensed the other hit coming and jerked back, catching the tips of his claws across my cheek. Vicious pain sliced my face open, but I didn't stop.

"You'll never have Wind and Wild, and you'll never defeat Alisdair. You can't even open your eyes wide enough to see I was never a threat to you. Alisdair doesn't l-love me." My voice cracked. "He never has, he never will, and he'd never wanted to. You underestimate your enemy, and that's why you always lose, Meallan.

"It's why you can't rise higher than a dirty, dark pit."

"Argh!"

The shadows lunged and I jumped—hands reaching blindly, and smashing against their salvation. Seizing a limb, I heaved myself onto the branch and climbed as fast as my adjusting vision would let me.

It was so dark. I couldn't see past what was directly in front of me, but I was a child of the forest. The trees were my natural home, and the beasts below were the bastards of curses, mud, and dark holes. All I had to do was keep moving, keep climbing, keep jumping. They would never catch—

A hand grabbed my ankle and yanked me down.

"Ahhh!" I screamed, falling hard on the snow and dirt.

A chuckle sounded over the wind. "I may underestimate Shadow-soul"—a kick landed square on my middle, sending me flying into a tree—"but I overestimated you, War Wife Emiana, Queen of Nothing, wanted by no one."

Their laughter echoed through the forest as I lay wheezing—pain wracking me with every shuddered breath.

"Kill her," Meallan announced. "Slowly."

Furry bodies pounced on me, their claws penetrating my arms, legs, stomach, and neck.

"Alisdair!"

"Scream for him all you want, whore." Meallan laughed. "You'll nev-er—"

"Argh!"

Meallan *oomphf*ed as a large, quick-moving shadow slammed into him.

I couldn't see where he fell. I couldn't see anything but the knife-tipped canines closing on my throat.

My captor was ripped off me so violently, I went flying along with her—torn out of the grasp of the others. Their claws raked gashes across my arms and legs, leaking excruciating tears from my eyes.

I crashed on a bed of snow—smothered by the freezing cold. All around me, all I heard were snarls, barks, roars, and the grim squish and snap of torn flesh and crushed bones.

Heat and light ripped through the dark, assaulting my eyes. Meallan staggered to his feet, bleeding heavily from a cut on his forehead. Fire magic consumed his hands—twin deadly torches aching to return the favor. But it wasn't that bastard I cared about.

"Alisdair!"

My husband swayed on his feet, panting like he felt every mile of his run from the castle. And I had no doubt that he did. Never had Alisdair looked more... human. Not fae. Not faeriken.

Standing there wheezing in the snow, covered in blood and bruises, but not horns, claws, or fangs. He seemed smaller. Weaker. *Harmless.* As harmless as the clunky, awkward humans with their blunt ears and magicless bodies. He didn't look like he could win this fight even if he had iron weapons.

The wolves picked themselves up, laughing as they circled him as if they were thinking the same thing.

"You fool." Meallan's laugh was nasty. "You came running to the rescue of a traitorous whore who poisoned you? She threw you off a cliff, then came to me to help her get away from *you.* That was our plan the whole time," he taunted. "From the very beginning, she poured nothing but lies in your ears, all so you and I could end up here on your last day."

"Liar!" I screamed.

"Every word is true!" Meallan crouched, preparing to strike. "She stole the flower. She gave you a deadly kiss. Last night, she laughed about how easy it would be to tempt you into your own downfall—"

"So?" Alisdair sliced in—voice steady even as he swayed on his feet.

Meallan stiffened. "Excuse me? Did the poison stuff your ears? She planned this! Luring you to your death. Throwing you off the throne, and then running back to Lyrica and her stunted little life. She doesn't love you."

"Shut up!" I cried.

"She never loved you," Meallan hissed, "and she never will."

A strange, husky growl dropped from Alisdair's lips. "And again," he said, laughing, "So? What does any of that matter? She is my wife. She can murder me a thousand times, but no matter what, it is my honor to die for her... and my pleasure to kill for her.

"No one who wishes to keep their hand lays it upon my queen." Alisdair began circling him, keeping in pace with a growling Meallan, but with his stumbling, it was more accurate to say my husband was tripping in a circle. "But since it's you, I'm going to rip off that filthy paw and feed it back to you.

"Come now, boy," he barked, making Meallan jerk. "You lied, cheated, and manipulated from the shadows to get me this far, all because you were too much of a cowering little bitch to face me beast to beast.

"Now that you have made me as weak and helpless as you—attack. Claim the hollow victory handed to you by a little bird who's smarter than you'll ever be—"

"Kill him!"

The wolves charged, leaping on my husband four-on-one. Alisdair disappeared under a torrent of fangs, claws, fur, and blood. My scream shredded my throat.

For all his bluster, the poison had done its work. Alisdair should've transformed into his unstoppable beast form and ripped out their throats without blinking. He should've summoned fire from the pits of hell itself and burned their eyes out of their skulls. He should've been sauntering over a pile of corpses, smirk riding his lips, and claiming his prize—me.

But none of those things were happening.

Alisdair covered his head and face with his arms, his only protection against the onslaught. Meallan raked his fire-tipped claws across his stomach, spilling hot, steaming blood on the pure snow, sizzling his skin, and bellowing a roar out of Alisdair that made me sob. The woman was right next to him, sinking her teeth in his leg and tearing free a chunk of flesh and muscle.

Alisdair couldn't stop them biting and tearing him apart, while the two focused on his head—pummeling, stomping, kicking on his arms to get through and bash his skull in, ending the fight before it started. Their laughter howled above the whipping wind.

"Stop it!" I shrieked. "Get off him. Leave him alone!"

I may as well have been an ant before a thunderstorm. They didn't hear my screams. They didn't care for such a lowly creature when there was devastation to wage. I was nothing. Queen of Nothing and feared by no one.

I twisted this way and that, looking for a weapon—something. Anything!

Nothing met my eye except for more snow and dead trees. *If that's all I have, at least I have something!*

Meallan snarled when I jumped on his back and smashed a handful of snow in his face. He tossed me off and spun around, eyes widening in the bare second before I smashed the branch into his face.

His head snapped around, but didn't bring his body with him. Meallan weathered the blow without rocking an inch off his feet. His growls ratcheted up tenfold as he slowly turned on me—eyes red and fangs glistening with his blood. It was impossible to me that this monster had anything to do with the sweet, kind, patient Foalan.

"I've had enough of you, bitch!" He raised a backhand, fire dancing on his knuckles. "Shadowsoul, I hope you're watching this!"

"Don't you fucking dare!"

His hand fell.

A hard force tackled me, blowing me off my feet. Meallan's claws raked the air my neck no longer occupied.

Alisdair and I tumbled through the snow, his body shielding me as the wolves chased us—raining blows on his back.

"R-run," Alisdair rasped. "Get far away from here. Leave me—"

They tore him off me. Throwing him on the ground, they descended on him—united in one goal: killing Alisdair Shadowsoul.

"Stop it!" I screamed, and screamed, and screamed.

Every ounce of Meallan's hatred, brutality, and obsession with ruling fed his blows and the heat of his fire. They kicked, beat, bit, and clawed him again and again, my screams the backdrop of their fun.

Alisdair wasn't going to survive. No one could.

Rage, fear, and desperation swelled in me, igniting the deep and pulsing well of magic resting within my soul. It bashed against its bindings—surging, swarming, swelling to reach the far corners of my being, and then burst beyond—eager to do my bidding.

It smashed against the barrier, and stopped.

"No!" I pulled harder—demanded *more*! "You're my magic! You cannot be kept from me. You cannot be taken!

"Eldur," I bellowed—unearthing a spell from another time and another life. "Eldur!"

My magic thrashed against the barrier, pummeling and beating it harder than the wolves beat me. It felt like I was being savaged from the inside out—taken apart by the seams. Any more and I'd explode.

I pushed harder.

My screams pierced my eardrums. My nails bent painfully back digging in the ice and dirt. *Agony! Heart-wrenching agony!*

And still I kept pulling, drawing, *forcing* my magic free of its chains.

Alisdair would not die like this—murdered by a pack of dim-witted wolves, led by a cowardly fuck who was too afraid to face him at full strength. If anyone was going to kill my frustrating, harsh, smirking husband, it was going to be me.

And I will fucking kill him if he dares to die and leave me forever cursed, forever lonely. Forever without him. "Eldur," I screamed. "ELDUR!"

I broke.

Glowing, white light erupted from my skin and escaped the tree line, reaching for the heavens. Dark, swirling clouds heavy with ice cracked down the middle—peeling before the light beam. Our moon, our mother, our Meya of the moon, earth, sea, and stars rose from behind her own barrier and shone down on me.

Long, white locks swirled around me—alive with the same energy bursting beneath my skin. I knew as my lips parted that it was over. Meallan would wake up minutes from then in the pits of hell, cursing his failed coup to the far corners of his fire pit and back.

"El—"

Pain exploded in my temple. I went flying, thrown off my hands and knees—tumbling through the snow. The glow left me, racing away with my magic behind the barrier as if it was never there. Never anything but a fool's desperate dream.

Meallan stood over me, holding the branch in his grip. Behind him, Alisdair lay broken, bleeding, and still.

"What was that?" the woman whispered. "How did she do that? I thought her magic was bound."

"I don't care why or what the fuck she is. Kill her and be thorough," he said. "I'll take care of Shadowsoul's body."

I lay in the cold, my spinning vision making my stomach twist.

Meallan snarled when no one responded to him. "Tullia! Kuan! I told you to—" He spun around on their bleeding corpses. Three bodies littered the snow, and my husband wasn't one.

"Wha—? Where is he!"

"I believe I promised—"

Meallan twisted, raising his meager wooden weapon high.

Alisdair severed his hand at the wrist.

"Ahhhhh!"

"—to feed this to you," Alisdair finished. Snatching up his hand, he shoved it in Meallan's bellowing mouth—choking him on his own fingers.

Bronze flashed in the moonlight. Alisdair buried the sword in his abdomen, cutting his muffled cries short. Meallan thudded to the ground—the shortest coup in Lumenfell history over in a blink.

My husband dropped down beside me. "Princess." He touched the side of my head, his fingers coming away tacky with blood. A furious growl rumbled his chest. "I'm sorry," he said, apologizing to me for the first time ever. "I should've... been f-faster."

Somehow, I smiled. "You were fast enough. Let's get you—"

He collapsed.

"Alisdair!" Scrambling up, I fell next to him—a cry trapping behind my teeth.

He looked terrible. A frightening mass of blood, torn skin, and gore. I didn't know how he'd found the strength or magic to summon a sword, let alone use it. He looked like it was long past the time he should've entered the Meadows of Meya.

Alisdair coughed and blood spurted from his lips. "I always knew... you'd be the death of me, woman." He chuckled a laugh that was more a gasping wheeze. "Leave it to you to... do it cleverly."

"Stop your nonsense," I sobbed. I gently cradled his head, placing him on my lap. My tears dripped down his cheeks—shedding the tears he couldn't. "You're not going to die. You can't because..." I moved down, laying my palm over his scar. "Because I love you."

"C— C—" He reached for me, straining to speak.

His hand flopped down at his side. Alisdair's final words to me disappeared with the light behind his eyes.

Chapter Thirteen

It took half the night—screaming and pulling Alisdair behind me—before Foalan heard me over the howling wind. He, Eadaoin, Aeris, Bradach, and a contingent of guards rushed out to meet us. Aeris screamed at the sight of him. Eadaoin threw up.

Bradach grabbed his brother and took to the skies, flying him straight to the healers.

I raced all the way up to our bedchamber, and was thrown out the door by the head healer.

"We need space, time, and everyone," she barked at me. "Get all the healers. Now!"

For hours I hovered out in the hall—pacing, crying, and shaking off everyone who tried to help or comfort me.

It made no sense. I began the night with every intention of killing him and running back home to Lyrica. Nothing had changed with that plan until he said—

"So? What does any of that matter? She is my wife. She can murder me a thousand times, but no matter what she does, it is my honor to die for her, and my pleasure to kill for her."

"How could he say that, the frustrating, changeable beast!" I pounded my head, wishing I could bang his words out of my skull. Of course he had to go and say something so confusing, so ridiculous, so stupid, and so wonderful. He had to hopelessly jumble my mind until I said something equally stupid and told him I loved him.

I groaned, sinking down to the floor. I loved him. I loved Alisdair Shadowsoul, and I realized it in time to betray him in the worst possible way, and then get him savagely maimed.

What if he doesn't make it through the night? What if this is how it ends? Me left alone to rule a cursed kingdom and wage a borrowed war. What if I never get the chance to make that irritating fool realize that he loves me too?

"My lady?"

I shot up, hurriedly wiping my face. Healer Soulstitcher stepped out of our bedchamber.

"Is he okay?" I asked. "Is he... Is he still—?"

"He's alive," she broke in. "But barely. We closed his wounds, and stopped the bleeding, but he lost a lot of blood. My lord has never carried coudarian crystals on him. Honestly, it's always been a mystery to us from where he draws his power." She shook her head. "Whatever that source was, he's not drawing from it now. He may as well be a human."

"What does that mean?"

"It means he's not helping us help him. He's not using his magic to heal himself, and there's only so far our healing magic can take him." She stepped to the side. "The rest is up to you."

"Me?" I squeaked.

She gave me a wan smile. "You must remind him of his reason to keep fighting. Of why he's not ready to run through the Meadows of Meya. It's because he has to run back to you."

I blushed stupidly, not knowing what to say. Not having the courage to say it even if I did. "Oh... Okay."

Slowly, I stepped inside. The parade of healers vacated at the sight of me, tromping out one by one while I bit my tongue—stopping myself from asking them to stay.

My eyes didn't know where to go. To the bandaged, silent figure on our bed, or the fourth wall looming behind him.

"I did that."

I didn't turn at Foalan's voice. Part of me already knew he was there. Where else would he be?

"It seemed best not to tempt you a second time, my queen."

I turned then, gazing upon him coolly. "You know."

Foalan emerged out of the shadows, tapping his ears. "I know all that goes on within these walls."

"Do you also know the identity of the traitor who helped your brother poison my food, bait me for the Taken, and toss me down the stairs?" My eyes narrowed. "Or am I in their presence now?"

"I am no traitor, my lady." His voice was just as cool. "I did not try to kill you. Your death would achieve no useful purpose."

"My death would achieve the purpose of keeping this land dark, cold, and cursed. That's what your brother said anyway. Something about the risk of loving Alisdair is the risk he'll destroy the cursed heart so he can love me back. I didn't know that was possible. All my life I've been told the heart cursed the land, not that it cursed him not to love."

"And that very well may be true," he said almost conversationally. I say almost because he was circling me like... like a wolf. "We are no more privy to understanding the cursed heart than anyone else. All we know is that during the years Raelina walked the halls, Lumenfell changed. The kingdom and the man.

"The snow began to melt. Buds bloomed. Children were born with hands and feet instead of claws and fangs. And the sun..." He tipped his head. "One morning, the sun rose. As if it always had.

"My father and brother were terrified of what this meant. They saw their destiny slipping through their fingers, so they ruined Raelina... and sent me to kill Lord Lumenfell."

My eyes widened slightly, my only reaction.

"I failed, of course." He chuckled. "And my lord thrashed me soundly. I thought for sure that was the end. He was going to kill me. He *should* have killed me. But he just... stopped. My lord held up a fist and an open hand, asking me if I was ready to live on as my own man, or die as my father's bitch. I'm certain you can guess what I chose."

I studied him, tracking his slow pace around me. "Why are you telling me this?"

"Why else? It's so you stop running from him, my queen."

I froze.

"You're not the only one in this room to try and kill him. We're not even the only ones in this castle to do so. If he can forgive all of us and give us another chance, he'll most certainly do so for you."

My eyes stung, warping Alisdair in a sea of tears. "I made a terrible mistake, Foalan," I rasped. "I wish I could blame someone else." I thought of Emiana and her deal with Meallan. "But it was me. I told myself I was doing it to get home, but deep down, I just wanted to punish him for breaking my heart."

He whistled. "You punish a heartbreaker by poisoning and throwing him off a cliff? Remind me never to cross you."

A startled laugh burst out of me. "Come now, Commander. We both know it's your deepest, fervent wish for me to punish you."

He smirked—so darkly and wicked, I suddenly understood why women wanted to pick up a crop and spank the bad wolf out of him. "My lady, if I dared answer that, our lord would rise from his bed and finish the job." Foalan backed out of the room. "Go to him, Ana. You're what he needs. I'm sure of it."

I stood there long after he left, feet glued to the floor. Foalan said I was what Alisdair needed, but in the same conversation, he proved I wasn't. When Alisdair was with Raelina, their love was so strong, it brought back the sun.

Alisdair had been laughing, teasing, and tumbling me for two moons, and nothing had changed. If anything, I swore Lumenfell was darker and colder than when I first arrived.

Even if Alisdair could forgive me, he didn't love me. He'd never break my curse, and we'd spend our days slowly wasting away—losing ourselves bit by bit. Him as a beast, and me as Emiana, and then as whatever animal Emiana turned into.

There was no happy ending for us, so why make him endure the presence of the woman who betrayed him and nearly got him killed? We would surely live and exist apart from now on—going through the motions as king and queen during the day, then acting as strangers at night.

Whatever I thought we were building between us was over. Better I stay out of his way until he got back on his feet to send me away for good.

Turning my back on him, I walked out the door. "Aeris? Eadaoin?"

The two stuck their heads around the corner immediately. I knew they hadn't left after I ordered them away. I could hear their poor attempts to whisper quietly and breathe softer.

"Yes, my lady?" Eadaoin asked.

"Eadaoin, fetch cold water and cloth," I ordered. "The last thing we need is fever to set in. Also, send for a servant to light the fires. Send another down to the kitchen and tell the cook to prepare chicken broth.

I doubt he'll be able to keep down much, but I have to try. You need strength to recover, and you don't get stronger on an empty stomach.

"Aeris, get ointment and bandages from the healers. There's no sense in them running back and forth when his dressings need changing. If there are any other medicines he needs, bring those up too with instructions."

"Yes, my lady."

They hopped to—taking off in different directions. That done, I returned inside, grabbed the chair from my vanity, and placed it and myself right next to my sleeping husband. His handsome face was hidden under a mask of ointment-soaked bandages, but all I saw was him.

"If you need a reason to hang on, you listen well, Alisdair Lumenfell. If you leave me, your fierce and brutal queen will rip open the veil, chase you through the Meadows, and bash the notion that we were ever meant to be apart out of your head.

"You didn't marry a bird, you married me," I whispered. "And you are just as much mine as I am yours."

I couldn't tell if he heard me, but it didn't matter. I'd hold him to the promise all the same.

***

The next few days passed in a blur of changing bandages, slathering ointment, spooning broth past unresponsive lips, and murmuring sweet, pointless chatter at his still form.

"You should rest, Lady Ana." Aeris fluttered behind me, chasing me around with a bath robe and jeweled comb. "Your bath is ready and waiting. Please, bathe, eat, and then sleep for a few hours. Eadaoin and the healers will watch over our lord while you do."

"No," I replied—as I did when she asked an hour before, five hours before that, and a day before that. "I'm not going anywhere until he wakes up. Alisdair needs me. For once, I'm not running from him."

"My lady, you're dead on your feet. You haven't slept in days. You think you're speaking to me right now, but I'm over here!"

Blinking, I twisted around, landing on the Aeris standing in the doorway—not following behind me as I thought. My eyes crossed trying to focus on the real her.

"If you continue on like this, you'll find yourself sharing the sickbed with our lord. Take a rest."

I sighed. "Do the healers have something that can keep me alert and awake?"

She pressed her lips together tight.

"You don't want to say, but the rule-follower in you won't let you lie to your queen," I said, smiling. "Go on. You can tell me."

"Fine." She sniffed. "They do have such an aid, but do you know what would be even better? Proper rest, food, and sleep."

"No." I was beginning to understand Alisdair and his abruptness. Why waste time with pleas, excuses, and explanations when an entire sentence was already contained in one word? "Fetch the aid for me, please, Aeris. Thank you so much."

Aeris stormed out, mumbling something about obstinate, pain-in-the-ass queens, and it was all I could do not to giggle. The stress of Alisdair's situation was getting to everyone if the prim-and-proper Aeris was finally breaking decorum.

I glanced at Alisdair, and the urge to laugh vanished immediately. It had been days, and there'd been no noticeable improvement. Healer Soulstitcher said at some point, Alisdair needed to find the will to summon the magic needed to heal him the rest of the way. If that was true, he hadn't found that will. He wasn't summoning that magic.

"She calls me the pain in the ass, but you're the pain in the ass." I bent over and dropped a kiss on his nose, the only part of his face free of the bandages. "All you have to do is wake up, but you're stubbornly refusing because you can never give me what I want without torturing me a little first." My smile was soft as I slipped my hand under his. "The joke is on you, because I'll wait as long as it takes."

I'd be waiting a long time was Alisdair's silent reply.

A week passed, and then two. My husband didn't open his eyes.

"Conn obviously didn't learn from his predecessor Lorcan. The basks only have the right of the territory I give them," I said. "Tell him he and his people return to the northern marsh, or I'll have his throat ripped out and replace him with a leader who listens."

"Yes, ma'am," the soldier replied, bowing out of the room.

I was already done with her and fixing on Foalan. "I want you to increase the guard presence in the village, Bevin, and the other outlying towns. Reassign the palace guards if necessary. Attackers can't invade the palace if they never get past the village."

"Yes, my lady."

"Aeris," I continued. "Round up the palace staff and begin clearing out and preparing all the empty rooms. Evacuate the families in the villages beyond Hathal and bring them here to shelter until the threat has passed."

"If they leave their homes, their plants and crops will wither and die," Aeris replied. "They'll return home to no food."

"Precisely why I hired five more traveling merchants this morning. Riordan will have company when he sets out within the next few days. Two of them are traveling to Quatassa—much closer than Lyrica." I shook my head. "It has to be this way, Aeris. We'll spread our forces too thin if we try to cover every single village. When the threat has passed, we'll provide food assistance until they are able to revive their resources."

"Yes, Lady Ana." She set out without another word, ready and able to carry out my will.

Holding court in my bedchamber wasn't ideal, but I wasn't leaving Alisdair's side and there was a kingdom to rule. Especially because the morning after the wolves attacked, Foalan returned to the scene and found four corpses—the three wolves who aided Meallan, and the lone guard who went back alone after I dragged Alisdair away. The only trace left of Meallan was his severed hand.

Somehow the loathsome rat survived and scuttled off. Foalan had enough time to order the wolves living in Lumenfell out before the rest attacked Bevin, Gibarden, Lutran, and a bunch of innocent people—heeding the orders of their vengeful, humiliated alpha.

The attacks continued for days until they were driven out to the darkest, coldest part of the forest where only the best trackers with senses better or equal to the wolves could follow.

What Meallan hoped to achieve with these attacks, I had no idea. If his plan was to piss off and enrage the citizens so much they overthrow me and Alisdair, and hand him the throne, it wasn't working.

"What about the other war we're waging?" I asked when it was only the three of us in the room.

I eyed the babies sleeping, cooing, nursing, and slung on her back. Actually, the nine of us. "Were you able to find Mahoun's heirs?"

Treasa walked past the baby cots I had brought up for her as if they were cacti, and not comfort for her and her babies. "So far we've found one," she replied. "As you know, there's no point killing one if we can't find the rest."

I sighed, gazing at Alisdair. He was impatient for this war. Emiana was impatient for this war. I was impatient for a better life for my mother and my sisters, so impatient, I gave them both the key to bringing about their blood-soaked victories.

But is this truly the only way? Just because Alisdair believes change can't come without blood and slaughter, doesn't mean I can't prove him wrong.

"There's nothing that can be done," I finally said. "When Mahoun dies, they'll swear in the new king, everyone will come out of hiding, and our spies can kill them then. That will give us a few months to think of something better."

"Better?" Treasa bounced up and down, burping two fussy babies and rocking the other four. "My lady, the plan you chose is as wise as it is creative as it is merciful. You found the path of minimal and only necessary bloodshed. No messy war. No collateral damage," she said kindly. "I don't believe there is another way. Certainly not a better one."

"But that's just it, Treasa." I talked while I picked up Alisdair's broth and began the slow, gentle process of feeding him. "To assume there will be no messy war or unnecessary bloodshed is to assume we can create a power vacuum, appoint ourselves the rulers to fill it, and everyone in Elva will simply fall in line.

"Of course they're going to fight back," I cried. "They've been raised their whole lives to believe faeriken are evil, bloodthirsty beasts. They will not take kindly to one slaughtering their kings and forcing them under his rule."

She inclined her head. "There will be rebellion, yes, but those would be easily quashed if you proceeded with developing a weapon with the siren's voice."

"Excuse me? You can't possibly be suggesting I torture an innocent, beautiful creature to create a weapon of genocide!"

She appraised me calmly. "It is not for me to suggest, my queen. Merely to inform you of the resources at your disposal, and how they can be used. The decision is only yours."

"No one touches the siren." A thought occurred to me. "And if I ever say otherwise. If I rant and scream and order you to hurt that poor creature, ignore me. Matter of fact, tell me to shut my horrible fucking mouth up."

She laughed. "What an odd request. But your point is made. You will not step on the throat of the innocent to ascend the ladder of power. It's what makes you a good queen, my lady," Treasa said, surprising me. "Maybe even a great one."

The barest smile tugged my lips, and I deflated—slumping next to Alisdair. "A great queen would have another solution except the obvious one. One Alisdair said himself all those days ago."

She gave me a look like she already knew, but needed me to say it out loud.

"The curse has to take Elva," I rasped. "All of it. Everyone."

"Why?"

Again I had the sense she knew the answer, but wanted to hear me say it.

"There will be rebellion. There will be attacks and war from those who want Elva to stay exactly how it is, but those of us who have been stepped on so others could ascend the ladder of power... they'll fight beside us because our kingdom is the only kingdom that wants them to be free."

"Free and changed?" she reminded. "Living in a land without sun or warmth. Forever cut off from the forests. Some things are worse than that to a summer fae, but not much."

"The worst is having your magic bound," I flung back. "It's screaming and crying and begging with the trapped power inside of you to save the people you love. But you can't. Because it's just as trapped and useless as you are."

I tossed my head. "The women of Elva have to be free, and the curse is the only way to free them. Even if there is rebellion. Even if there is war, it'll be put down and stamped down quickly, because thirteen million faewomen are not going back to the way things are now."

"Is it your wish, then, to wait until after the change takes Elva to enact our plan?"

"No." There was no hesitation. "That would take centuries. We must claim the seats of power now. Start the process of change now. If only to get monsters like Salman off the throne. The things that he's done. Atrocities that he planned, carried out, and then blamed on faeriken—knowing that no one would question him, and executing anyone who dared to anyway." I shook my head. "He's a monster the likes of which would sicken a worthless piece of shit like Meallan.

"The throne of Lyrica never belonged to him. He's not going to sit on it for another day past his due."

"What is your decision, then, my queen?"

I opened my mouth, and asked the question that sealed my fate. "Is there a way to spread the curse faster and wider? As in within the next few months while we wait for Mahoun to pass?"

"There is," she replied, smiling enigmatically. "But of course I cannot tell you. The cursed can't speak of their affliction."

"You don't have to speak it if you can do it. Can you do this, Treasa? And can you do it quickly?"

"I can do both. But I need you to say it plainly, my lady. Say that this is your decree and you will accept the consequences on both your behalf."

I paused. "Will anyone be hurt?"

"I believe many people will get hurt when they wake up one day with unbound magic and pig snouts where their nose used to be."

That reply earned her a hard look. "I know you knew what I meant. Will whatever you have to do to trigger the fast spread of the curse risk innocent lives?"

"No," she replied easily. "No one innocent will be hurt."

"Then yes. I decree that you spread the beast curse far and wide to every corner of Elva. Whatever the consequences may be, we both accept them."

Bowing slightly, she turned to leave.

"Treasa?"

"Yes, milady?"

"If you'd like to take a break, rest, or get something to eat, you can leave the babies with me for a few hours." I spooned a little more broth past Alisdair's cracked lips. "You already know they love their Ana Hae-owen."

She looked at me in surprise. "You're dead on your feet, haven't slept in days, and of all things, you volunteer to watch six infants just to give me a break?"

"Oh. If you rather I call Aeris or—"

"No, no," she rushed. "That's not it, I just— No matter what circumstances brought you here, you were the queen Lumenfell was meant to have. Not a good queen, but a great one." She continued on, carrying her brood with her. "Never believe otherwise."

I wasn't sure what to make of that, but I let her go—returning my focus to Alisdair. "I made the decision," I whispered. "The decision I know you would've made and... the one I think is right. One day history will tell us if we were wrong."

"You are the clever one."

I lurched back, the bowl crashing to the floor and showering me with broth and broken pottery.

"Something tells me history will bow to your will," he rasped, "as all men do."

Alisdair blinked up at the ceiling as if he'd never seen it before. It was impossible to see his face, covered as it was, but an air of bemusement collected around him. I had a feeling it'd been a long time since he'd gotten seriously hurt. Maybe a thousand years.

"You were attacked," I said slowly, while approaching even slower. "By Meallan and three other wolves. That was a fortnight ago. We didn't think you'd make it because—"

"My queen poisoned me."

His throat was ragged from disuse. It made the sentence sound ever more sinister.

"Yes," I whispered. "I did."

"At least we've continued the tradition of me waking up bound and dying after."

Silence hung thick and heavy—smothering me. A thousand apologies sprung to my lips, but none of them were adequate. What was I supposed to say? *I'm sorry. I did it because I realized too late that I love you, and realized even later that you'll never love me back.*

"Alisdair, you have every right to be angry with me. If you let—"

He sliced in, "You say it's been two weeks?"

"I— Uh— Yes," I got out. "The attack was two weeks ago, and much has happened since then. Including me realizing that I—"

"Then, you can go."

I stilled. "Excuse me?"

"You can go, Princess. Send for Aeris and I'll have her pack up your belongings and prepare the carriage myself."

My lips trembled. I tried to stop my voice from doing the same. "Alisdair, please."

"Two weeks I've lain here, little bird. Two weeks I haven't chased, caught, and claimed you. Fourteen nights and fourteen times I've broken our marriage vow."

"I don't care about that!"

"You care. All you've done since you stood up on that altar is fight to be free of me, and now you finally are. Look for yourself," he said. "The rune that kept you bound to me and Lumenfell is gone."

I twisted, staring down at my ankle. Alisdair was right. He was right and I hadn't even noticed. The rune that mangled my leg whenever I left his side was no more—merely a forgotten blemish on a pale, untouched ankle.

"So go," he hissed, striking my heart through. "It's what you always wanted. Congratulations, little bird. The cage is open. You've finally gotten your wish."

I swallowed through needles, my whole body shaking. Despite my deep-seated survival sense telling me to stay away, I moved closer to him.

I took his hand.

"Alisdair, I'm sorry for what I've done. I made a terrible mistake—first by hurting you, and then again when my lies and bluster actually convinced you I wanted to be anywhere but by your side. But after what I've done, I know what I want doesn't matter much anymore.

"What is your wish, my husband? Do you want me to leave?" I kissed his bandaged fingertips. "Are you telling me to?"

"I am telling you to leave."

Nodding, I set down his hand and scurried away—racing before to door before he sensed my tears.

"But my wish..."

I halted, hand closed on the knob.

"...is that you never leave me, nightmare woman. Because if I knew how to be without you, I would've run slower."

I dropped my forehead against the wood—smiling so hard and wide I thought my face would break. Only when I trusted myself not to do something embarrassing like burst into tears, or tackle a sick man and have my way with him, did I turn and face him.

"Well, if you insist," I teased, returning to his side. "I'll stay."

***

I climbed the stairs the next day, loaded down with fresh bandages and healing ointment. With Alisdair awake and fighting back with magic, he was healing twice as fast, but Soulstitcher insisted we keep it up until he was out of the woods.

Turning the corner, we locked eyes.

The fox boy blinked at me. Clutched in his grip was a jeweled cane that belonged in a display case in the grand hall.

"You!"

Spinning around, the boy took off running.

I didn't think. The bandages slipped out of my hands as I chased after him, heart pounding out of my chest. "Wait," I cried. "I'm not going to hurt you. I don't care if you stole that cane, I just want to talk to you! Make sure you're okay!"

The boy ran faster. I lost sight of him whipping around the corner and picked up my feet, spurring my soft, princess body on. *He's here. I can't believe after everything, I've found him safe, and just as eager to escape.*

"Please, slow down," I called. "I just want to help you. I—"

I turned the corner and met with nothing.

Skidding to a stop, I spun this way and that—disbelief throwing me for a loop. He was gone. Just like that, the child disappeared in an empty hallway as if he was never there.

"How?" I took a step, then another—slowly peering around.

There were no doors. No way in or out, barring the windows. Said windows were still intact, so the boy hadn't done anything unbelievable like throwing himself through glass to fall three floors.

The only thing the hall had to say for itself was an unadorned, depressed wall, boasting two empty plinths. I flicked down to the base of the support, spotting a single brown shoe.

The boy's shoe. What is it doing there?

I walked over, bending down to pick it up, and then I saw it.

A crack in the wall, imperceptible to someone looking at it straight on, with no reason to give a blank wall further examination.

Wedging myself through, I stepped into a curtain of ivy and blinked up through their twisting, tangled vines—basking under the orblights.

"Here you go, Alisdair!"

Alisdair?

I reached out, carefully parting the curtain. A courtyard opened before me—laying the path of auburn cobblestones and rose bushes pampered in their own heated oasis. Actually—

"Hot." I peeled off my shawl and coat. The courtyard was as hot as the companions' room. What was this place?

I peeked around a chin-high rose bush, alighting on Alisdair.

He gripped the jeweled cane and reclined on a stone throne, no doubt of his own conjuring since it was wholly out of place in the middle of the garden courtyard. His court didn't seem to mind because all around him, children of different ages, heights, and animals ran playing and shrieking around him.

Off to the side, chatting quietly, were a group of four women—an elephant faeriken, two lioness faeriken, and a faeriken possessed by an animal I'd never seen before in my nineteen years of life.

Looking properly, the courtyard was actually more of an oversized balcony, rimmed by a large, stone railing that overlooked the snow and trees below. As dark as it was down there, it was well-lit above with orb-lights and torches.

"Are you going to come out or hide behind that bush all day?" Alisdair called.

Lifting my chin, I walked out—disapproval etched into my pores. "What are you doing out of bed? You woke up less than twelve hours ago, you're in no condition to be moving around."

"I'm much improved than I was twelve hours ago." He lazily waved and a throne for me appeared by his side. Alisdair had freed his face from the bandages. Healing cuts and pinkish scars raked across his features, but did not diminish his handsomeness in any way. "My magic is slowly aiding the healing ointments and potions. Lying around like an invalid won't speed up or slow down that process."

"That's not the point, and I'm fairly sure it's not true. Running about the place will certainly slow down your healing. You're going straight back to bed," I ordered, claiming my seat. "After you tell me what's going on here. What is this place?" I counted fifteen children, maybe sixteen. They were running around so fast it was hard to be sure. "Why are all of these children here?"

"This place is where you live, my queen. We're still in the north wing. Just in the part of it that's hidden."

"Why would any part of it be hidden?"

"For the children," he replied.

I gave him a hard look. "I require more explanation."

"The children who come to Castle Riagin. This is where they live, and no," he said, meeting my eyes, "not as slaves. They are free and safe here. They have three full meals a day, their lessons in the morning, and then they run around like hellions in the afternoon."

I sat back, taking it in. "Are you telling me that you care for these children? And the fox boy?" I cried. "After all that bullpie about our castle not being an orphanage? Why would you lie to me?"

"I did what I must. That morning in the throne room, I was testing you."

"Testing me?!"

Alisdair gave me the same hard look. "Yes. I told you I had spy reports on you. They all said you were harsh, prejudiced, and unforgiving. You cared not for anyone below your station. Worse, you treat them like *bullpie* stuck to your slippers.

"I won't entrust my people to someone who sees a hungry, desperate child, and pulls out a sword to chop off their hand."

I sputtered. "But that was your idea! I chose mercy from the start. You were the one spouting mad, crazed nonsense."

"And you didn't back down," he shot back. "You physically stood between me and Foalan to protect a boy you didn't know. You even kept searching for him to make certain he was safe.

"I won't lie, you quite endeared yourself to me through those actions. I bedded you twice as hard that night in reward."

I fell back, shaking my head. "You're unbelievable. Only you could lie and manipulate me, and then act as though it was a reasonable thing to do."

"It was reasonable. Talk is pointless. Action is all," he said. "To know the true you, I had to see what you do, not bother about what you or others *say*."

Rubbing my temples, I let it go. Arguing with Alisdair on if he was right or wrong would go nowhere, especially since I understood his reasoning. The true Emiana would've been a terrible ruler of faeriken. If she'd been put through that test, she'd have sharpened the sword herself. She cared not a whit about the troubles of a hungry little orphaned child.

"Why do this, though? Why keep them hidden away and separate?"

"It's for their sake," he said, gesturing with his chin. "You know how our people behave when the day's work is done. That's not for a child's eyes."

I did think of the many orgies taking place everywhere and every night. "That cannot be argued with," I muttered. Finally, I relaxed—gazing upon the happy children with a smile. "How did they come to be here?"

Alisdair relaxed too. The smile he gave me did funny things to my stomach. "The usual unfortunate ways. Either their parents passed away or abandoned them. But they aren't commonly dragged in by irate jam-sellers. My soldiers know to bring every lost child they come across here." He nodded firmly. "Where they can be safe and cared for."

"But, Alisdair, I don't understand. Why in the name of Meya did you tell me I should stop looking for the boy, because if I discovered what you did to him, it would forever change my opinion of you?"

He trapped my gaze, a smirk stretching his lips. "Well... hasn't it?"

I swallowed hard, pulse picking up. By the All Mother, yes. My opinion had changed. That morning, when Alisdair sentenced that boy to slavery, I thought him the lowest form of slithering worm. Even as we got to know each other, and our nighttime activities became more fun and frequent, what he'd done to that fox boy was always at the back of my mind—reminding me that I couldn't fall in love with him.

Because Shadowsoul was a monster.

But looking at him then, I was thinking other things. About how sweet he would have been to Meli when she was little. About how sweet he would be to our children from the moment they were born.

Alisdair wasn't the kind of beast who abandons. He was the one who stayed, who protected, who cared when everyone else forgot to.

He was the beast I loved.

I stood up. "Well, well, well," I sang. "This looks like a fun game, but it's missing something."

The fox boy skidded to a stop. "What?"

"A tickle monster!" Roaring, I chased the kids shrieking around the courtyard—tickling breathless whoever I caught.

Everyone laughed, but no one as loud as Alisdair.

***

That night, we were back in our bedroom, and I was finally tending to his bandages.

"Although, it doesn't look like I need to," I said, examining the closed and healing scars. "You're healing better without my fussing."

"Don't say that." Alisdair sat up in bed, reclining against the pillows while I unwrapped each bandage; checked his healing, pink scars; and rewrapped the wounds that needed more time. "Your fussing brought me back. I heard you when I was in the Meadows. Something or someone wanted me to stay, but you wanted me here.

"So I came back."

I ducked my head, cheeks flaming. I never knew what to say when he spoke to me this way. Nothing had changed on that score.

I cleared my throat. "The Meadow, huh? I'm surprised Meya let you anywhere near the place." Smiling, I poked his side to let him know I was kidding. "Figured it would've been the Burning Plains for you."

Alisdair chuckled. "I'm not a monster, little bird. I only look like one. Meya knows that better than anyone."

I know it too, Alisdair.

"Her name was Constance." Alisdair gazed at the horizon that was no longer there—because of the walls and the darkness. "It's rare for humans to be born with magic. Exceedingly rare, but not impossible. When they are, the women always discover their power. It's in them. A part of them. It can't be denied.

"Whereas for the human men, when they're born with the power to draw magic out of their environment, they more often than not never know. Why would they? They don't have crystals, runic knowledge, or any of the tools needed to access their power. They don't even know they should.

"That's why when magic was discovered, and the humans did what humans have always done to the different, they only came for the women."

My quick, working fingers slowed. "Came for them? Do you mean they...?"

"They hunted them down and killed them."

I hissed. Mama said our land was protected by magic—concealing us from human eyes, weapons, technology, and any method they might use to find Elva. But she always said that if these protections somehow failed and I ever crossed paths with one, I had to run. Run so hard and fast, I didn't stop until there was half a world between us.

"Among the different, Constance was even rarer than rare," Alisdair said. "She was born with incredible power. More than anyone I've ever known. More than Gisela Raekin. More than me."

My brows blew. Someone more powerful than the most powerful man walking the earth? I couldn't conceive of that.

"She was blessed, if not for the fact she was born in the wrong time and the wrong place."

"They tried to kill her."

"They did kill her," he dropped. "They burned her at the stake. Her flesh bubbled off her bones while they laughed, cheered, and toasted their good works."

"Meya, take it! That's barbaric." I shook my head. "That poor woman."

"Don't feel sympathy for her just yet," he gritted, wiping away my mask of sorrow. "You see, people don't understand curses. Not even the fae. We study them, we use them, we live under them, but we don't know how they're born, or why. And fewer know that a curse doesn't need incantations, potions, or even intent to be born. All it needs is the hatred in one's heart to take root."

Understanding dawned. "When they burned her. She cursed them."

"She didn't know that was what she was doing when she screamed and raged at them, swearing revenge. But with all of that raw, bottomless power swirling within her, it responded," he said. "When the dawn broke and the fire was nothing but smoking cinders, Constance stepped off her funeral pyre, and left behind a sea of corpses."

"Her murderers? They died and she lived? How?"

"Not even I fully understand her curse. Near as I could figure, whatever someone tries to do to her, it's turned around and done to them. Stab her and your chest splits open instead. Burn her and your skin chars and bubbles. Slap her and the pain explodes in your cheek. Kill her... and you die. Die in the same method and manner you chose for her. And it didn't end there."

"It didn't? But what more could the curse do?"

"After her murderers died, they weren't allowed the peace of waking up in the Meadow. It's how she healed and survived their attacks. In that moment, she'd steal and eat their souls. The soul became pure, raw, magical power for her—making her stronger. While the would-be assassin became nothing more than an empty husk."

I whistled. "Wow. That's awful—for her attackers. It doesn't sound like a curse for her."

"It was, Ana. As you know, Meya demands balance. She will settle for nothing less than order and harmony in nature, and because of what Constance made of herself—an immortal, all-powerful, souleater—Meya birthed the means to destroy her."

"What was it?"

"Fire." Our own fire seemed to crackle louder, dancing in his eyes. "Has to be fire from a burning oak, the same wood her stake was made from, but oak is easy enough to acquire. Everywhere she went, she was hunted down, chased, and besieged by torch-carrying mobs. She could stop the people, but Meya wouldn't let her magic put out the fire when it started."

I thought of Alisdair ordering his servants to destroy the purple flowers instead of doing it himself. The All Mother was exacting in her rules.

"That's why the night she and her lover woke to a room on fire, she couldn't save him. She couldn't stop it."

"But she was so powerful," I cried. "Her pursuers were only human. Couldn't she hide?"

He shook his head. "The All Mother wouldn't let her. Meya made sure her location was discovered every time." He laughed—a short, harsh sound. "I tried to hide too, my queen, and then a cold and barren wasteland sprung up around me. The All Mother won't stand for an immortal being any more than she'll stand for not being obeyed. Magic was a gift she gave us. It's not our tool for disobedience."

I nodded slowly. "Alisdair, why are you telling me this now?"

"Because there is only this," he rasped—eyes unfocused staring off in the distance. "There was always only this."

I wasn't sure what he meant, but I didn't ask. "So what happened to her?" I said instead.

He didn't reply. For a minute I thought he didn't hear me. "She fled. She had no other choice but to flee. Constance stole a boat and sailed out into a storm, looking for a safe haven.

"She found Elva instead."

"Elva? Our Elva?" A stupid response, because of course our Elva, but my surprise was warranted. "How could a human stumble upon our land?"

"She was so strong by that point—bloated on the power of thousands of souls. She saw right through the protections around our land, and from the minute she arrived, she was determined never to leave."

"Why?" I asked, although I had a strong guess.

"Think of the world she left behind, Ana. A twisted, ignorant, misogynistic hellscape where men and women have magic, but only the women die for it. But then she arrives here, and not only is magic free and abound, but women are respected and revered. They're the leaders and rulers of matriarchies.

"Constance had discovered her destiny. She was meant to be here, live here, rule here... as high empress of Elva."

It was my turn to bark a sharp, incredulous laugh. "Excuse me? She, a human, thought she was destined to be ruler of our home?"

"By that point she was completely warped by bitterness and hatred. Much had been stolen from her, so she decided even more was owed to her in return." He shook his head. "We were still simple people then. Farmers and traders. Half of us hadn't left the forest yet. We had our own way, and it was right for us.

"But Constance only saw ignorant, long-eared simpletons. We *needed* her to educate us and lead us into modernity. That's why she determined she was to be our empress. She was the only one with the knowledge and power to lead us into the future, and she would make that happen by any means necessary. Elva was her prize after a lifetime of suffering."

My lip curled, mirroring the same scorn on Alisdair's scarred face. What disgusting arrogance. To see a group of peaceful people living a different way from you, and take it upon yourself to decide their way was wrong.

"I take it all didn't go to plan." I scoffed. "Or at least, I pray it didn't."

He laughed. "Oh yes, little bird. We long-eared simpletons put up quite a fight. Much more than she bargained for. Every attempted coup was foiled and put down. She was thrashed within an inch of her life by Gisela Raekin herself. And when we discovered her fear of a simple little thing like fire..." He hissed. "She was chased right back into hiding."

I didn't fight off my grin. "They discovered a way to hurt her even though she was cursed to transfer pain?"

"Ash from an oak tree. They coated themselves, their fists, and their weapons with it. Constance wasn't so arrogant then." He grinned back. "I myself don't know how they figured out that trick, but they did. You are descended from the brightest and strongest women of an age, and you prove yourself brighter and stronger every day. Never forget that, my queen. Never forget how proud you make them."

My insides warmed. Not because he said something wonderful. He'd been saying wonderful things about me since we met. I warmed because this time, I knew he meant them.

"Were they able to drive her out?" I asked. "Kill her for good?"

His grin faded away. "How I wish they were. But she was too strong, Ana, and stupid is a word she'd never been called. Our queens proved to be too fierce to defeat... so she created the binding spell."

I shot up, eyes blown. "The bind— The binding spell?! *She* created it?!" My mind spun—thrown in the whirlwind of everything I thought I knew flushing down the gutter. "But how? Why! How could she do that to faewomen after what was done to her?"

"To Constance, the bonds of sisterhood only extended as far as unquestionable loyalty to her ended. They became a threat to her, so she ended the threat with a single spell—binding their magic forever." He sighed, dropping his head. "As you know, knowledge of the spell traveled far and wide, and Elva was forever changed."

"Because of her," I croaked. "Some random evil human bitch that never belonged here in the first place."

He just nodded.

I sat down hard, staring in disbelief at the same spot Alisdair chose in the wall. "Why didn't I know this?" I whispered. "Why haven't I ever heard of Constance or what she did?"

"Because all knowledge of her and what she did was erased," he replied. "By me."

My lips parted, but nothing came out.

"When she went into hiding, of all the villages she could've chosen, she wandered into mine." He turned to me, smiling mirthlessly. "If you think me handsome now, you should've seen me when I was young and in my prime. I couldn't walk in a straight line for all the women throwing themselves at my feet. The men too."

I snorted, though my mind summoned the image all the same. Alisdair even handsomer than he was now? If such a thing were possible, I would've surely been one of the women shackling myself to his ankle, unwilling to let his beauty out of my sight.

"Constance coveted me from the moment she saw me. She cared not that I was already mated and had three children."

The truth would've shocked me if I had any left to give. I just took his hand, lacing my fingers through his. "You had children."

"Three beautiful daughters. Just as quick, mischievous, and perfect as their mother, Raelina."

I squeezed my eyes shut—an emotion I couldn't name rising up and strangling my tears before they fell. I wasn't sure at first, but right then I knew. This wasn't simply any historical tale. This was a story of tragedy and woe, and I'd be forever changed after it was told.

"*The* Raelina?" I whispered. "The Raelina that Salman...?"

There was pause, then he nodded. "Constance pursued me relentlessly, growing more and more enraged with every rejection. Meya owed her, you see. Not one but three of her lovers were murdered by mobs and witch hunters. Now that she had found *love* again, she refused to let a little thing like my free will stand in her way."

I was already so sick, I nearly threw up. "What did she do to you?"

"It wasn't what she did to me. It was what she did to Raelina," he said. "One day, I came home, Raelina was gone, and *that woman* was sitting on my couch—cool, calm, and braiding my daughter's hair as if she was exactly where she belonged.

"She told me she'd locked Raelina away somewhere. Trapped her in an inescapable prison, and if I wanted her to ever emerge alive, I'd leave with her right then and never look back.

"With her hands that close to my child's throat, I agreed. I didn't have a choice," he growled, anger bleeding into his voice. "I left with her, hoping that if I did, she'd free Raelina, and my loves would be together and safe."

"But she never did."

He shook his head. "She held Raelina's imprisonment over me like a puppet master tugs the strings. I tried to free her. I tried to kill Constance and free us all, but she never let me anywhere near a thing resembling a crystal. Even when I summoned the power, I couldn't store it, so I had one shot and one shot only.

"I missed."

"Oh, Alisdair, I'm sorry." I rubbed his hand, trying to spread my love and comfort into him, but I knew it was as useless as my sorry. Nothing anyone said or did could make what she'd done to him better.

"She was never going to let us go," he continued like I hadn't spoken. "And all the while, my girls were alone. So, I escaped her and ran back to them again and again—each time finding a new hiding place and a new hope that she'd finally give up and wouldn't find us. But every time she did."

"What was wrong with her? How could she be so sick and obsessed?"

"I don't know, but sick and obsessed she was. She got it into her head that I kept running back to my children because we didn't have a few of our own."

"Oh no," I breathed, clapping my hand over my mouth.

Alisdair fixed back on that spot on the wall. "She violated me over and over again—shoving so many love and lust potions down my throat it's a wonder I didn't drown from the inside out. But for all her magic, there was one single truth she couldn't defeat, and it drove her deeper into madness and obsession."

My voice was soft. "What was the truth?"

"We're not the same species. We cannot reproduce."

My head slowly bobbed. Of course it was as simple as that. Meya was exacting in her rules. "But again, she didn't give up, did she?"

"No. The opposite. She got it into her head that her becoming a summer fae was the key to everything. She'd belong in Elva if she was fae. We'd accept her as empress if she was fae. I would love her and she'd give me a *better* family... if only she were fae.

"She put herself and innocents through indescribable, torturous experiments all for the sake of trampling the laws of nature, and the result was just as hideous as the acts."

"She didn't become fae?"

"She became something resembling fae. The right appearance, the right mannerism, the same affinity with nature, but if you got close enough to her. Truly saw into her heart, you'd *feel it*," he hissed. "That she was *wrong*."

He growled, lips twisted. "Even though she thought she succeeded, she still wasn't able to get pregnant. I broke from her and ran a final time, and she snapped. If my children were the string that led my heart away, she'd sever that string. Permanently."

"Alisdair, please." Tears spilled down my cheek. "No."

"She slaughtered my daughters. All three of them," he croaked. "And not quickly."

I dropped my head on his chest, crying for the pain he suffered—and all the while I never knew. No one knew.

"How could she do that? What kind of wretched monster was she!"

"A monster." A warm hand cupped the back of my head. "That's what I became when she killed my children. Something different. Something broken. Something new."

"You're not," I said firmly. "I see the good in you. Your people see it too. That's why for all Meallan's whining and feet-stamping, the only ruler your people would ever choose is you. At the end of the day, we know the difference between those who would kill us, and those who kill for us. It's the difference between a monster... and a protector."

"My protection hasn't amounted to much, Ana. It wasn't even the goal I carried in my heart when I"—the words stole off his tongue, taken by an unforgiving curse—"and met her on the battlefield that final day.

"I wasn't avenging the pain she caused Elva. I only cared about the pain she caused my children. I struck her down on the altar of my hatred and revenge," he said, "and I was stupid enough to believe that was the end."

"The beast curse."

"Yes." Alisdair gently stroke my hair, soothing me though it was me who should've been comforting him. "For centuries, I wasted away here, trapped in the ice with my regrets until—"

"Raelina came."

I didn't have to see him nod to know he did. "One day she was just there. I couldn't believe it. It was impossible but... she was there."

"Constance's death freed her from the prison."

"She wandered for years," he went on. "Lost, confused, and unaware of the past until she came to Lumenfell and the change took her—freeing her soul and mind from Constance's bindings. From then on, it was like we were given a second chance. We were together and we were happy, until she left with Salman."

"She didn't want to," I cried, snapping up. "Meallan told me. He and his father addled her mind and made her believe she was in love with that snake. It was because of them that she left you."

"I know," he said, stroking my cheek. "Foalan told me everything the night of his failed assassination attempt. It was because of the shame and disgust written on his face that I spared him. He hated his father and brother as much as I."

"What happened?" I asked. "Did you go after her?"

"You know our story, Ana. When she came to me singing his praises and speaking of love, I sensed something was wrong and forbade her from leaving with him, so she escaped with him in the middle of the night. She knew me," he said. "She knew how to evade my nose and my magic. By the time I tracked her down, she was dead and Salman was marrying his new wife."

I shook my head, my saliva turning to poison on my tongue. "No wonder you hated him."

"There isn't a soul alive that knows King Salman and doesn't hate him. He inspires nothing but revulsion in even the purest souls."

No truer words had ever been spoken. "But if you knew Meallan was behind what happened to Raelina, why is he still walking around with a throat?"

Alisdair snorted. "Because I'm a fool. Two hundred years ago, I swore a binding oath to the alpha of the time that I would not cross their territory, or lay a finger on his wolves unless it was in self-defense."

"You what? Why would you agree to that?"

"Because he offered to do something even I couldn't do." He met my eyes. "Ana, the wolves protect us—everyone—from the Taken. Haven't you ever wondered why they lurk outside in the shadows instead of swarming our townships and villages?"

My jaw worked. "I guess I never truly thought about it but... yes. They're so savage. It didn't make sense that they attacked travelers on the road, but stay out of the villages." I fixed on him. "The whole time the wolves were the reason?"

He tipped his head. "They've never been able to live side by side with us. Their instincts wouldn't allow it. They wanted their own territory—autonomous of Lumenfell and our laws. So we came to an accord. In exchange for keeping my people safe, Domhan wanted the same. For them to be safe from me.

"I agreed because he was a good man. He still wore clothes and ate at a table. He wanted his own piece of Lumenfell, not all of it. His terms were equal and fair, and my people were safe. There wasn't a reason to refuse." He scoffed. "I didn't imagine we'd be where we are now. I didn't know I'd just sworn the oath that would leave Raelina unavenged.

"When that truth humbled me, I'm the one who became mad and obsessed with revenge. I plotted to ruin the only person left that I could"—his stroking finger traced my lips—"and it brought me you."

"Why now?" I whispered. "Why tell me all of this now?"

"Because you've asked so little of me while I've asked everything of you," he said, surprising me. No matter how many times he did, it still shocked me when Alisdair gave me the sincere truth. "All you've wanted was to know the true me. Well, this is it, Ana. This tale—my past—it's all there is, and all I'll ever be."

"That's not true." I cupped his face in turn. "You are so much more than what she's done to you. Every other king in Elva built their throne on the weapons of oppression she handed them. You're the only one..." I gazed at him with true clarity. "You're the one who won't rest until you've given back what she stole, and rebuilt what she ruined.

"Constance lost everything and it turned her into a power-hungry, narcissistic kakka who spread misery everywhere she went. You lost everything... and it only made you kind."

"Kind?" He arched a brow, laughing derisively. "You've called me everything but since you arrived. Don't puff me up with empty flattery, woman. I'm not yet so pathetic that I need your lies."

Sighing, I rolled my eyes. "I'm not lying. You are kind. You're also an ass," I added, giving him a look. "But a kind one."

"You believe this because?"

"Foalan—another child of your enemy who you gave a second chance." My grin was wide and knowing. "Treasa—you're the king of Lumenfell, but you trek out in the snow to see her to spare her the inconvenience. Bradach—you've kept a promise to your mother all this time, even though the man could fray the patience of Meya herself. Aydan," I said, for I had finally learned the little fox boy's name. "He had nothing and no one, and you gave him a home again.

"And me. You claimed the bitter, spoiled princess of the man who destroyed your happiness, and instead of taking your revenge out of my backside, you've treated me as an equal and your queen." I kissed his wrinkled brow. "I've always said the measure of a man is how he treats the people under him. With all you've done for your people, and the more you've done for the ones who let you down, I'd say that makes you the best man I know."

"Hmm. Well, you were raised in a sheltered bubble. You don't know very many men."

"But I've known a lot of jackasses," I snapped, "and you rise above them all. Why must you make everything difficult? It's a compliment. You take them with a thank-you."

"Why should I do that when I knew this would happen? You saw what became of the fox boy, heard my tale, and now I've softened in your eyes like a ripe peach baking in the sun. It's unacceptable."

My jaw hung open. "It's unacceptable that I should see a softer, kinder side of my husband?"

"I shall rid you of the belief that I'm either"—his claws sprung forth for the first time in weeks, and tore my dress to ribbons—"tonight. I had that cane brought up for you, little bird. You won't be singing of my softness when you're limping through the castle tomorrow morning."

Heat exploded in my lower belly, fed by the weeks-long wait it had no interest in. "Well," I said lightly, "if that's what you must do."

Alisdair was on me before I finished the sentence.

Chapter Fourteen

Alisdair healed quickly in the coming weeks, and with news of his recovery spreading through Wind and Wild, the wolf attacks on our people and the villages ceased.

"But I've yet to find my brother," Foalan said, his forehead stuck to the floor. "My failure is unacceptable, my lord. I insist I be flogged, then replaced. Your army deserves a better man than I."

Alisdair, Foalan, Eadaoin, Aeris, and I were out in the gardens. Aeris fluttered around Alisdair—giving him ale, adjusting the hanging orb-lights, fluffing his throne cushions. She agreed with me that he shouldn't be out of bed until the healers declared him out of the woods. But nothing, not even being outnumbered, stopped Alisdair from doing exactly what he wished to do.

I checked him over, then returned to my task. The little patch I scratched out for myself was just beginning to sprout. Eadaoin put on a polite face, and pretended to be interested while I gushed at her—explaining all the hows and whys of what I was doing.

I kept my other ear on Foalan and Alisdair's conversation.

"I will not flog or replace you for failing to locate your brother. Meallan knows Wind and Wild's dark and forgotten corners better than anyone. He hoards a thousand bolt holes, and he's an expert at covering his tracks. I never expected him to be easy to find. But—" A hard, vicious edge crept into his voice. "I will flog, replace, and behead you if you tell me once more that you haven't found the traitor who attacked and baited my queen."

My conversation with Eadaoin ceased abruptly. I half rose, ready and willing to dive in front of Foalan. I was beginning to understand Alisdair and when he was or wasn't being sincere.

And right then he'd never sounded more serious.

"On that topic," Foalan began, drawing me closer. "I will not disappoint you. The traitor has been found."

"Who is it?" Alisdair, Aeris, Eadaoin, and I asked at once.

"You're unlikely to know her, my lady," Foalan replied, lifting his head high enough to meet my eyes. "She's a kitchen maid. Her name is Eavan."

"Where is she?" Alisdair broke in. "Bring her here. Now. I will execute her myself."

"Hold on a moment." I moved between him and Foalan. "Why would she do this? Was Meallan threatening or blackmailing her? Was she helping him because she wanted the curse to remain unbroken?"

"The only thing that matters less than these questions are their response," Alisdair said. "She dies."

I gave him a look. "I would still like to hear the response, husband, so if you please...?"

He flapped a hand. "Very well."

"Foalan?"

"My lady, she did follow his orders in aid of his cause, but after speaking with her..." Sighing, he rose to his feet. "After speaking with her, I knew immediately something wasn't right. She was ranting and raving about how much she loves Meallan, that she would do anything for him, and they're going to be together forever.

"Absolute nonsense because I know enough about my brother to know he'd never mate with a chimp faeriken. I don't need to be a healer to know she's under the influence of a love spell."

I felt Alisdair's silence like a weight against my back.

"Is there any way to cure her of its effects?" I asked.

Foalan nodded. "It takes time, and she'll be a danger to you until then, but the healers can return her addled mind to its proper state."

"Then, we treat her, but we do so far from the castle. She cannot return until she's well." I faced Alisdair. "Do you agree?"

Face shadowed, a sharp bob of the chin was his only agreement.

Damn fucking Meallan and his love spells. His pack may have sworn an oath warning them off attacking Alisdair directly, but they were wreaking more than enough havoc on his life through the loophole.

"We're leaving," Alisdair barked in my direction. "Now."

He grabbed his cane and entered the castle, leaving me to trail behind. I followed—catching up to him easily.

These days, Alisdair was more and more open to talking to me and having real, honest conversations. But not in front of an audience.

"I'm sorry," I whispered. "I wish I could hunt down that bastard and kill him for you myself."

"It's not for you to apologize to me. It was you he tried to have killed not once but four times."

"Let's both agree we hate that furry little shit and want him dead."

"Agreed," he growled.

I squeezed his hand. He squeezed back, leading me around the wrong corner, going the opposite direction of our bedchamber.

"I have something for you."

"Ooh, a present?" I half joked.

"You may call it that if you like."

I was even more intrigued. I pelted him with questions as we turned down hallways, and found ourselves in the east wing.

The hard line of my shoulders went taut, remembering the night he found me in the east tower, and flayed my heart alive, shouting that I would never mean more to him than a good fuck.

Don't think about that. Things are different between you and Alisdair now. He's different. He asked me to stay with him.

But he hasn't told you he loves you, whispered another, quieter voice.

I pushed both out of my head, along with my memories of that horrible night. If Alisdair was willing to forgive me poisoning him and throwing me off a cliff. I could forgive him for losing his temper when he found me trespassing in the one room he asked me not to enter.

We turned one final corner, and came face-to-face with glass-paned double doors.

"What's this?"

"Another hidden part of the castle," he replied. "Or at least it was hidden until it was ready for you."

Alisdair pushed open the doors, and the gift of speech was stolen off my tongue.

My mind flashed back to that first night wandering the halls with Eadaoin. I peeked out of a blurry, frost-covered window and saw what looked like a conservatory. I forgot all about it when Alisdair chased me away from the tower.

Warm, misty spray washed over me—delighting my skin as it did the thirsty plants. Lettuce, peas, tomatoes, peppers, spinach, carrots, and herbs. Strawberries, blueberries, melons, cucumbers, and figs. I named all the plants and fruits I recognized, then jumped up and down, clapping to see even more that I didn't.

The greenhouse was incredible. So big, my gleeful cries echoed against the cavernous ceiling. I walked the rows of the plant stands, stretching my arms out wide, and just barely brushing their leaves from fingertips to fingertips.

"Alisdair, what is this? It's amazing!"

"I told you everyone in Lumenfell must be self-sufficient." He plucked a ripe, juicy strawberry and tossed it to me. I took a bite and moaned. "Castle Riagin is no different. This is the greenhouse that feeds our table. I thought you might like it to be your greenhouse—"

"Yes." I knew culture dictated that I hemmed, hawed, and demurred before accepting a large gift. We were supposed to go back and forth with me saying that I *couldn't possibly accept.* "Fuck that. I want it. I want it so much, Alisdair, it's perfect. It's the best gift anyone has ever given me!"

I ran to him, arms out—then abruptly remembered I couldn't go around throwing myself on men who were only days out of their sickbed.

Chuckling, Alisdair came the rest of the way, tugged me off my feet, and buried me in his arms. I melted against him—bursting with so much love for him I couldn't breathe for wanting to shower him in it.

I hadn't told him I loved him since that night I held him dying in the snow. It wasn't possible he heard me, and with each day that passed with me not saying it again, the words hung heavier around my heart.

Alisdair asked me to stay, but I didn't know what that meant for us. For me. As much as I wanted to go home to my family, it was Emiana, not me, who would walk through their door. It was also Emiana who would walk right out and return to Lumenfell.

I knew this because over the last few weeks during the times she'd taken me over, she was nothing but pleased that *I* fixed things with Alisdair, and now *she* would get her war. If anyone could've wanted to be high empress of Elva more than Constance, it was Princess fucking Emiana of Lyrica.

She wanted to stay here so that Alisdair, and his spies, and his army could give her everything she desired. I wished to stay because Alisdair was everything I desired. But only time, and not very much time at that, would tell who would get their wish.

All I knew was that the war plans were already in motion. And Alisdair still hadn't told me he loved me, and he didn't know my true name.

I slid out of his arms, dropping back down on the floor. "I love my gift," I said, forcing my mind away from my thoughts. "But I will need help if I'm to feed an entire castle."

He chuckled. "You will have it. This area is your domain. Request all the help you need."

Smiling, I curled my arm through his, resting my head on his shoulder. "Will you show me around? Tell me what some of these plants are?"

Alisdair did just that—giving me the tour and introducing me to the foods they nurtured to thrive in their cold, barren home.

"And in here"—we passed through a small door into another enclosed section of the greenhouse—"is where we grow the tropical flowers. You needn't continue scratching away at the ground outside. Grow your flowers here."

I poked his side. "I quite like what my scratching away has produced, but yes, I can do so much more in here." I tossed my head, mind blown. "We have to introduce Lumenfell's greenhouse system to all of Elva. Especially the magics used to keep plants growing in the wrong climate happy. This would feed so many struggling families."

"These systems and magics used to come natural for us," he replied. "Before we built cities and kingdoms in envy of humans, we lived simple lives in the forest where we grew and traded what we needed, instead of hoarding what we don't. We've lost much in our pursuit of power and wealth. I can't say if we'll ever truly get it back."

We passed by a collection of brilliant red roses, and I instantly flashed to that horrid, life-sucking thing in the tower.

"What is it?" Alisdair asked, feeling me stiffen against him. "Something not to your liking?"

"What—? No," I cried. "Everything's perfect, it's just... Alisdair, are things truly different between us now? If I ask you something, will you tell me the truth?"

He frowned down at me. "I have always told you the truth."

"You told me you were born with a full set of teeth."

"One is allowed to flex the truth when blowjobs are involved."

"That is not a rule anywhere," I replied with a giggle, then I sobered. "Seriously, Alisdair. It's about that rose you have locked away in the tower. What is it? Why is it so...?" I shuddered, not able to go on. "Will you tell me?"

Lifting his head, he nodded. "I will. Honestly, I'm surprised you waited this long to ask me. I've been expecting this question for a while, and— What did you say it looked like to you?"

Looked like to me?

"It's a rose. A thorny rose encased in glass."

"A thorny rose," he repeated, gaze drifting off. "Beautiful but dangerous. Like you. Of course that's what you see."

"I don't understand."

"It's not a rose, Ana, but it's not wrong that you see one. A soul looks like different things to different people."

I stopped dead. "A soul?"

"Constance's soul," he said, walking on ahead of me. "The one I ripped out of her chest and locked away in a cold, dark tower—forever imprisoned. Forever suffering."

I stared after him, eyes wide.

"Did you know a soul could suffer?" Alisdair sounded almost conversational. "People value the body and the mind, but the body is just a vessel, and the mind is unreliable. It changes so often, it breaks so easily.

"All we are is our soul, and when ripped from its protection, it never recovers. It never stops screaming." He laughed. "Or did you believe that was the wind howling?"

A chill raced up my spine, standing my hairs on end. "Alisdair..."

"Constance and I faced each other on a burning field, but she was prepared for fire. She laughed as her weapons shielded her from the flames—taunting her victory and my failure. She laughed while walking headlong into my trap.

"I tore her filthy, rotting soul—bloated and fed by the souls of innocents—out of her carcass, and on that burning field I built my kingdom. Over the centuries, all have wondered how I wield such limitless power, but I have no power. No more than any other faeman. Like them all, I must drain magic from another source."

"The rose." It wasn't a question.

He laughed louder, his malice washing over the flowers as he moved further away from me. "My final victory. Wind and Wild is everything she despises, and it was her magic that made it happen. I created her hell on earth, and forever this prison ensnares her while voiceless, sightless, and helpless, she screams.

"So, what say you, my queen?" Alisdair passed over the threshold, leaving me behind. "Do you still think me soft and kind?"

It was my fault. It was me who stupidly thought Alisdair telling me the truth was a good thing.

***

"I was a horse breeder in my previous life."

Alisdair walked side by side with me through the square, his hand firm and tickling against the small of my back. He nodded to people we passed, but his attention was on me. Despite all the time he spent teaching me archery and how to rule a kingdom, it was only now that I felt what it truly meant to have his time and attention.

And the result was I was wishing harder for my litter than ever. I refused it to keep Emiana at bay, but I regretted that decision as I leaned heavily on Alisdair—sore in places I didn't know I could be sore. I swore he was determined to make up for all the nights he couldn't chase me down and have his way with me.

But even so, our nights together weren't like they were before. I didn't need to tempt him with favors to get him to open up, and he didn't have to maintain tight control of himself every minute of every day. The result was for the first time since we stood at the altar, he was my husband, and I was his wife.

"I've always had a more natural affinity with horses than I did other animals."

Alisdair looked exceptionally handsome that morning, and that was saying something. His scars were all but gone. Only faint, fading lines marred his stomach and chest, but those would be gone soon enough.

He bound his hair back, pulling it taut around his horns. Horns that were smaller than I'd ever seen. After weeks of being forced to rest and not using magic, he was strong enough to take in more than ever. His horns were smaller, his claws were blunt, his fangs couldn't be seen behind his full lips.

All of that was well and good, but it wasn't what kept my eyes drawing up to bask in him.

Alisdair looked calmer and more relaxed than I'd ever seen him. Since we'd met, he'd been that hungry, stalking wolf—prowling unfamiliar streets warning off anyone who dare make themselves his prey.

Since telling the truth of his history with Raelina, Constance, and his daughters, the burden weighing down his own soul eased just that little bit, allowing it to come up for air in a sea of pain, hatred, and rage.

Seeing him like this, I could imagine the young, handsome horse breeder who ignited mad obsession in Constance, and such pure love in Raelina that her heart led her back to him, even after lost memories stole him away.

"Were you able to mind-ride with them?" I asked when he caught me staring at him.

"I was," he confessed. "The only animal that I could, but I wasn't complaining. The joy and freedom that a wild stallion feels as it gallops through the plains..." He shook his head. "There's nothing quite like it."

"Amazing." We strolled around the fountain—having nowhere to go, and not rushing to get there. "We don't see those gifts much these days. Do you think Meya really is punishing us? For leaving the forests? For betraying her daughters?"

"I believe we have come too far from what she expected of us, but we are punishing ourselves. Meya didn't make us do the things we've done, and isn't preventing us from stopping. We are steering our ship toward the rocks all on our own."

I hummed, turning that over in my mind. It was easy to forget Alisdair was wise, amid his harshness and jackassery, but when I thought about it, he rarely said a thing I disagreed with. He was even correct that he would one day corrupt me.

"Do you know how to ride?"

I shook my head. "I had a lesson when I was five years of age. The horse threw me and I never got on another again." That was Emiana's story, not mine. I knew how to ride, or... I think I do?

"Are you still afraid?" Alisdair gestured at Riordan's stables. "Or would you like to learn?"

"You'll teach me?"

Smirking, he backed away—lightly kissing my fingertips as they slipped out of reach. "I intend to teach you a great many things."

He crossed to the stables, leaving me a smoldering pile of lace and satin.

Eadaoin whistled, falling in at my side. "My lady, don't take this the wrong way, but I deeply regret that I was never chosen to be one of my lord's companions. The man exudes sex, and he's exuding it all over you."

"Ew," I cried, giggling. "That phrasing did not conjure a sexy image."

We cracked up.

"But truly." She bumped my shoulder. "I am happy to see this change. You both look so happy. Not that you didn't look happy before," she mused, cocking her head to the side. "It was obvious to everyone watching how much you two enjoyed riling each other up. Bet it made the sex de*licious*. Be honest, how hard did he fuck you the night you told the whole court he had a hairy mole on his cock and bursts into tears when he completes?"

"Oh, Meya," I groaned. "I think you and I could stand to be less honest with each other."

She laughed that growly, tsking laugh. "You never did tell me. How did you do it in the end? How'd you get him to fall in love with you?"

"I haven't." My reply was instant. "I mean, he hasn't said that he does. Assuming his feelings didn't work out well for either one of us, so I refuse to repeat the mistake." I lifted my chin, nose high. "If and when Alisdair has something to tell me, he will," Emiana said. "I won't be the lovesick fool—nipping at his heels and making sappy declarations that are never returned."

"Oh, my lady." She slipped her hand into mine. "I'm sorry."

Emiana's consciousness faded as the sympathy left Eadaoin's lips, giving me an opportunity to clarify her harshness and say that I didn't mean it that way.

The opportunity passed without a word from me. If it was possible for Alisdair Shadowsoul to be mostly right, it was also possible that Emiana wasn't always wrong.

The last time Alisdair broke my heart, we nearly killed him. It wouldn't be amiss for me to keep my heart in my chest this time around, instead of giving it to him to crush in his clawed fist.

"Are you ready?" Alisdair called, drawing my head back up.

Eadaoin winked. "Don't get into too much trouble out there— Actually, what am I saying? If you don't come back limping even worse than you are right now, don't come back at all."

"I was being generous when I called you a wicked minx!"

She took off, laughing. Eadaoin didn't need to stick by my side when Alisdair was around. No one did. He proved he was all the army I needed.

I entered the stables and went directly to the sweet brown mare who listened while I hogged her stall and bawled my troubles. Alisdair bent to help me up.

I halted. "Wait, I'm not sure about this."

"What's wrong? You said you wanted to learn to ride."

"I do, but maybe it's not a good idea to have another great big animal bouncing between my legs, after the first one left me so sore, I can barely walk."

He hummed. "Well then, you'll never learn to ride, because this great, big animal will fuck the sense out of you tonight, and every night that you're mine." Alisdair smiled wide, holding out his laced fingers. "After you."

Sniffing, I placed my foot on his palms. "Your mouth is as filthy as you are handsome."

"That as may be, but after you got on your knees and did what you did to my cock this morning, we can safely say your mouth is filthier."

I told him something filthy he could do with a horse, which set him off laughing. "You will not distract me with that naughty mouth for a second time today." He pointed. "On the horse."

"You're commanding me now?"

"You're delaying because you're scared, but you don't have to be." His smile almost knocked me on my back. "I'm with you."

My heart pounded so loud in my ear, it drowned out Emiana's memories and her fear of being thrown. *When you indulge her, it only makes it easier for her to climb a toehold into your mind. You must do what Emiana wouldn't do. And she wouldn't get on this horse.*

Mind made up, I got on the horse.

Ten minutes later, my sweet, gentle companion was doing her best to tip me face-first into the snow.

"This was my worst idea! I want to get off!"

"Take a breath." Alisdair's grip was steady on my waist, leaving me clinging to the reins of the excitable animal. "You're doing well."

"She's going to throw me!"

"Only because you're making her nervous."

"How am I the problem!"

Orna tossed her head and reared, her forehooves kicking the air.

My scream echoed through the forest. The only thing louder were his guffaws.

"This isn't funny!"

Alisdair leaned over me, gently patting and murmuring to the horse until she settled down. "She needs to feel your calm, little bird. Take a breath, sit up straight, don't pull too hard on the reins, and I will handle the rest."

"Okay, okay," I breathed, willing stillness into my jittery limbs. It was a strange sensation navigating someone else's terror. I held on to the fact that I still knew it wasn't mine. The days were coming when I wouldn't. "Breathe, sit up straight, don't pull hard on the reins."

I repeated that over and over to myself as Orna resumed a steady trot.

If not for our mode of transport, I would have enjoyed our quiet trip through the forest. A light dusting of snow rained from above like a confectioner's treat. Orblights hung along the path, casting a gentle glow on the winged rabbits and other critters who came out to see the guests trotting through their home.

It was morning, so the blazing sun and azure sky dominated the horizons. All behind a black curtain of clouds and ice. Even so, I didn't miss it. There was something serene and private about this little pocket of Elva, where everyone came together against the cold and dark. Every day there were parties in the square, and every night families huddled together with cocoa before the fire.

They loved each other harder because eventually the one they loved would be gone in mind, if not by death. They took nothing for granted—not the light, not the warmth, not food, and not freedom. It could all go away one day, so let's love it harder while it deigns to stay.

A stiff wind blasted me, ripping straight through my layers.

Alisdair instinctively drew me closer, shielding me with his warmth.

Oh yes, I missed the sun less and less every day.

I was so caught up thinking of the ways Lumenfell and Lyrica differed, that I didn't notice Alisdair's hand under my skirt until—

"Oh!"

Two fingers slipped past my folds as mischievous as the thumb pressing firm against my clit. "Shh," he crooned. "I told you. I'll take care of the rest."

"Is th-this"—I jostled on the saddle and came down hard on his fingers, rolling my eyes up in my head—"a part of the lesson?"

"Vital part." Alisdair nipped my ear, making me bite my lip. "I did say it was all about being relaxed."

"I see now why you were s-so popular." He flicked my little nub and I snapped forward, body bending in half as lightning demolished my defenses. "Women must've come from far and wide for your lessons— Ah!"

He chuckled. "You are the only woman to receive my private instruction." Alisdair slipped in a third finger and I nearly pitched off the horse. "But you'll find me a suitable teacher."

Suitable was not the word. Every bump and jostle impaled me on his fingers and struck that spot dead-on. If the goal was to calm me down, it didn't work. I was a moaning, shuddering mess who long ago gave up any pretense of guiding the horse and bent back, draping my arms over his shoulders, and holding on for dear life as I bucked and bounced on his hand.

A glowing, furry mass shot out of the trees in front of us, zipping across the path.

Orna neighed and reared, tossing us shouting off her back. We tumbled to the snow in a mass of limbs, satin, and shattered orgasms as she took off into the dark.

Alisdair and I flailed around righting ourselves. Hooking me around the waist, he finally sat us both up, getting our knees under ourselves. We took one look at each other, and burst out laughing.

I was laughing so hard I could barely speak. "Far be it for me to—to critique your teaching skills, but I think we're supposed to be on the horse when she gallops off."

Alisdair fell back over, clutching his stomach.

I hopped on top of him—straddling his waist. "I hope you don't think this means you've gotten out of that orgasm you owe me."

"I am not a stupid man." He grinned wolfishly. "So why would I have such a stupid thought?"

Alisdair waved his hand, and simmering white fabric appeared out of the air—spinning and floating all around us.

I shrieked in delight as the fabric formed, crafting a beautiful castle-shaped tent around us. Beneath my feet, the powdery snow both firmed and softened, becoming a fluffy, bouncy mattress.

I was allowed another second to admire the glittering, starry flecks woven through the silk before it all spun. We tore each other's clothes off in a frenzy, both whispering filthy promises to each other that burned my ears even as they left my lips.

Alisdair kissed me hard—scrambling my mind like the plate of eggs I devoured that morning. I gasped as he broke away, coming up for air but wishing he kept me drowning. Drowning in him.

Down he went, dropping soft, nipping kisses over my chin, along my neck, and between the valley of my breasts. Goose bumps popped in his wake as if my very skin was reaching out to him for more.

I moaned as his mouth closed around my nipple, sucking the soft nub into a hard, little pebble eager and desperate for more. He pounced on the other one and worshipped it in kind, making my core melt under his blisteringly hot ministrations.

Somehow, I got my hands between us and flipped him over, guiding him onto his back. I sat on his face like I'd been longing to do for weeks, and then I fell forward across his chest—gripping his rock-hard ridge. "I trust you know where I'm going with this."

"I do. You weren't content with one day of celebration, so now you bargain for a second."

I wiggled my pussy above his lips, giggling. "You did teach me to only bargain with what you desire."

Alisdair reared up and captured my lower lips—all talking over.

"Oh, Meya," I cried when his fingers immediately joined the party, rapid-fire plunging in and out of my hole while he sucked on my apex.

My back nearly bent in half as my head threw back—knees quivering beside his ears. Bolts of electricity shot through my veins, tightening me around him. I dropped and swallowed him to the hilt, letting him feel the vibrations of my moans and what he did to me.

For a while, our tent was filled with nothing but moans, grunts, cries, and the glorious music of flesh slapping flesh.

Alisdair stretched my hole past its limits milking the poor innocent for my cum. I fisted the snow mattress, barely holding myself up as I pumped him hard and fast.

"Yes, Alisdair, there— Right there! Gods, yes!"

He gave me no warning. Hot, sticky ropes of seed exploded on my face, shocking my razor-thin tether of control into snapping.

I came hard—jerking and flopping on his stomach as each resounding shock wave rocked my body hard, hard, and *harder.* It was an eternity before I collapsed on top of him, grinning like a lunatic. "Wow," I breathed, chest heaving. "I swear those get better every time."

"Let's test that theory."

"Uh-uh," I sang, wriggling away when he tried to flip me over. "I have you right where I want you, husband, and it's right where you're going to stay until I say otherwise."

"You are sexy when you think you're in charge."

"Oh, but I am." I winked at him over my shoulder. "I've told you, I have many ways of putting a man on his back."

A furious growl split his lips. There was something wrong with me that I found that deeply arousing.

"Now, now, don't be like that," I purred, gripping his knees. "You'll find that there's nothing I can do in this position that you won't like."

I didn't give him a chance to rebut. I rose up, slowly twisting and wining my hips, pushing out my ass, then slowly coming back down—grinding on his member. Taking my time, I teased, danced, and kissed his ridge with my pussy, sending it shooting back up and eager for more.

"Still think I'm a bad dancer, husband?"

He panted hard, his growls raising the temperature within my body. "You are the best dancer in all of Elva in this and every other century. You make all other dancers weep for their failure," he growled, "for they will never surpass you."

Now that's more like it. Fuck you, Honora.

"You've watched my mouth do it more times than there are numbers." I swirled my juicy hole on his tip. "Want to watch my pussy swallow that big, fat cock, lover?"

Alisdair didn't waste time with words. Snarling, he grasped my hips—pulling me slowly, but firmly down on his middle. Despite the inevitable way this was going to end, I was determined to take my time—drive him as crazy as he drove me.

I rose up all the way to the tip, enjoying his low hiss deep inside a newly awakened naughty part of me. Just as slowly, I impaled myself on him—groaning as my eyes fluttered. The man filled me to bursting, and then some. Alisdair said it was his looks that had all the men and women swooning in his younger days, but I knew for a fact fae weren't so married to clothes back in the old days. They were swooning certainly, but they weren't looking at his face when they did so.

Alisdair's warm, firm grip was the anchor pulling me back when I drew away. Caught in our eternal push-pull, I rode his lap much more happily than I rode a horse.

"Faster!"

Biting my lip, I rolled my hips—making him choke. "I could go faster," I mused, "but you'd have to do something for me first."

"Very well, if that's what you were waiting for, you should've said so sooner."

"What are— Oh!"

My brows bounced up to my hairline as a wet finger pushed past my puckered entrance. I opened my mouth to tell him that was not what I was going to say, when his other hand came around and rubbed my clit so vigorously, the explosion of pleasure popped me off his cock.

"Okay, that's better than what I was going to say."

"Faster," he ordered.

I knew when to give in to the will of a god. Nails digging in his knees, I bounced up and down on his lap—driving his length and his fingers deeper and deeper inside of me with each thrust.

Our heat filled the tent and burst out, banishing the cold from Wind and Wild—from the world. My moans were screams. I couldn't stop myself. I couldn't slow down.

Alisdair and I were like one—meeting thrust for thrust. Groan for groan. Scream for every relentless strike of my inner bull's-eye.

Every muscle in my body went rigid, tightening harder than my lower belly. I screeched myself hoarse as I came—body seizing and clamping my walls down, strangling his length till it burst.

We collapsed back in a sweaty, sated pile.

"Fucking hell, woman." It brought me immense pleasure that Alisdair was so out of breath. "You make it easy for a man to forgive you anything. I've already forgotten about that pesky little cliff you threw me off of."

My smile tightened around the edges. "Have you? Well, that's good. Since you only keep me around for my mouth and pussy, I'd hate for either to disappoint." I shoved up, but I was still too weak and shaky from my orgasm. My storm-out ended instantly when I flopped stomach down on the mattress—steaming.

I felt Alisdair's eyes on the back of my head. He was no doubt pondering what went wrong again that I was having another tantrum.

He's such a fool. I swear, it wasn't his heart that he ripped out. It was his brain!

"Ana."

"What!" I snapped.

Alisdair flipped me over. I squawked as he pinned my hands over my head, and pressed our foreheads together.

"You are aware, little bird, that I am hopelessly, madly, irrevocably, irrationally in love with you?"

I stilled.

"I would love you, my short-tempered, violent biter, even if you had no mouth and no pussy? Although, I would never wish you had no mouth, because it is your constant challenge of me, pushing me to grow and be a better man than I was the day before—that makes my heart beat mad for you—in or out of my chest."

I stopped breathing, my own heart shooting into my throat. I couldn't speak. I couldn't swallow. I couldn't process a word coming out of his mouth! Did he mean it? Was this truly happening?

"You knew this, yes?"

My jaw worked as my tongue strained to remember how to form sounds. "If... If I didn't," I croaked, "I do now."

"Good." He kissed me hard. "Because I wouldn't want there to be any confusion on that topic."

I ducked my head, hiding my smile in his neck. "No confusion here. We understand each other perfectly."

For a long while, we just held each other—safe and secure in our own little world. Lazily, I traced the runes on his arm—fingers skating over the cooling sweat on his body.

He loves me. I can't believe he loves me.

The thought brought a wide, goofy grin to my face every time. I'd been wishing for this for so long. At first I thought getting him to love me was impossible. And then I thought it was a miraculous feat that not even Meya could achieve. But here we were—two cursed people in love.

Cursed. Of course, the curse, I thought, a sliver of urgency sneaking through the fog.

I was cursed and Alisdair just brought me closer to freedom. Now all he needed to do was say so to my *true self* and make it so by declaring my true name.

But... what is my true name? I frowned, searching the depths of my mind. *I think it starts with a D— Oh, no, an O. O-r-a... Or is it O-e-a—?*

"What is it?" Alisdair smoothed down my frown lines. "What's upset my queen?"

My smile returned. "Not a thing. How can I be upset on such a perfect morning?" I chewed my lip. "Actually, I was just thinking. If you truly love me, I was hoping you'd do something for me."

He shrugged. "If you insist." His hand traveled between my cheeks.

"Behave yourself, beast," I cried, swatting his arm.

Alisdair laughed unrepentantly.

"What I was going to say was that I want us to get married again. Properly this time."

"Huh," he voiced, cocking his head. "You mean a marriage ceremony that doesn't end with me getting stabbed through the chest, or you fleeing into the night? That would be quite an accomplishment for us."

I giggled. "I think we can manage it, don't you?"

"We'll find out in a week's time." He kissed my fingertips. "At the ball celebrating our marriage."

Squealing happily, I tackled Alisdair and kissed him soundly. In typical fashion, he flipped me back over and had his way with me—making me very glad I had a pussy and a mouth.

All too soon, Alisdair and I headed back to the village with me enjoying the journey much more on foot. He listened to me chatter about wedding plans, stopping only once to pick a starflower and tuck it behind my ear without a word—just a smile. I swear I fell deeper in love with him on the spot.

Walking into town, my stream of chatter was interrupted a few times by a strange sight. Every villager we passed was stopped in the middle of their day—standing frozen in the square, on the side of the road, outside their homes, or beside the fountain.

They weren't moving. They weren't talking. They were just staring at something Alisdair and I couldn't see.

Cautiously we passed through and stepped onto the castle bridge. Eadaoin stood in front of the entrance, staring straight up.

"Eadaoin? Eadaoin," I called. "Are you okay? What's going on?"

"The ice..." she whispered.

"The ice? What about it?"

She pointed up, her finger shaking. At that moment, the icicle shed a tear, dripping its gift on her fingertip.

"It's melting."

Chapter Fifteen

"I said red roses, not coral, not scarlet, not carmine, not cerise, and not cherry. Red!" The offending roses were promptly thrown out the window. "Now!"

"Yes, ma'am," the servant cried, taking off running.

Another problem dared enter the room. The man carrying in the ice sculpture pulled up short when a swirling thundercloud of stress bore down on him.

"No, no, no. This is an elegant affair. Think swans, peacocks, and butterflies. Not dragons!" She sliced the rearing ice creature's head off without blinking. "Take it away!"

Eadaoin made a harsh noise in her throat. "You'd think she was the one getting married."

All I could do was nod in agreement, watching Aeris flit about the ballroom—making everything perfection, and tearing to shreds anything that wasn't.

Everyone was excited when we announced we were getting married for the third time, but no one was as excited as Aeris. She immediately took over the wedding planning—finding little need for my input. I simply sat back and left her to it.

It was safer that way.

"Take note, Bradach." I winked at him. "This is your future."

His smile shone upon Aeris. He didn't mind that at all.

The three of us walked the length of the ballroom, watching the wedding prep come together, but staying out of Aeris's way.

"I never imagined anyone could love my lord so much, they'd marry him three times." Bradach eyed me. "Are you certain you weren't also struck by that love spell? Or is this more of your stunted sickness?"

"Quite certain, and no," I returned, voice flat. "I love him. I want to marry him for real. A true ceremony where neither of us is being tricked, blackmailed, or plotting to kill the other." I eyed him right back. "Bradach, can I ask you something?"

"Yes?"

"Why do you call Alisdair 'my lord' instead of 'my brother'? Actually, why didn't you tell me from the beginning that he was your brother?"

The ever-present, affable smile evaporated, shocking me so much that I came to a halt. Bradach didn't.

"I lost the right to call him my brother a long time ago. When he needed his brother, I was... lost," Bradach replied. "I will live with that shame for the rest of my days." Then, he was gone. Bradach walked out the side door and didn't come back.

Eadaoin whistled. "Complicated history there, and that's the most I've ever heard him speak about it."

"That was?"

She nodded. "For all Bradach's joking, flirting, teasing, and tumbling—he's the most closed-off man I've ever met. Even more so than Lord Lumenfell."

Now that was a real shock.

"No one knows a thing about his life before Wind and Wild. The man is a vault of secrets."

I fiddled with my bracelet, chewing my lip. Should I try to talk to Bradach? Tell him that Alisdair told me the truth about his history with Constance, and all that led him to where he is today? Would that make Bradach feel more comfortable doing the same?

"Where are the utensils?" Aeris squawked. "We will have a neat, civilized wedding feast tonight, or none of you will eat!"

Sighing, I let it go. That wasn't my place. Alisdair opened up to the woman he loved and trusted. When Bradach was ready, he would do the same.

"I can't believe the ball is tonight." Eadaoin jumped up and down, clapping and squealing. "We've never had a ball here, Lady Ana. *Never.* I'm so excited to wear a beautiful, flowing gown and spend all night dancing with Keefe.

"You really have brought hope back to these lands again."

I followed her gaze out the window. The snow had been melting all week. That morning, I put on my shawl and had my coat sent back to the wardrobe. It was too hot for it.

I didn't know what to think seeing the melting snow. There'd been celebrations in the village every day and every night—rejoicing the coming end of the beast curse, and my alnihaya. But how had we lifted the beast curse? Assuming it was even something Alisdair and I did.

I still didn't know how the curse came to be, or where his heart was. Due to the silence that ensnared every cursed tongue, that was no surprise, but it did make me wonder. Did Alisdair do what Meallan claimed? Did he rescue his heart from its hiding place, and begin the process of destroying it, so that he could love me fully? Was that his choice—to reign as a strong, all-powerful beast, or love as a regular man?

And he chose me.

The doors opened and I turned—the smile already on my lips. I didn't have to see to know it was my Alisdair.

He walked inside wearing loose linen breeches, and a shirt unbuttoned to the waist. My heart picked up speed soaking him in. He was all mine. No matter how many times I told myself that, pinching myself barely made me believe it.

"It's coming together nicely." He came over and dropped a kiss on my forehead. "*Aeris*. I'm certain I have you to thank," he told the servant.

I sniffed. "Only because she's been barking and screeching over me all morning. I did not ask or approve of any of this, Alisdair. Send it away!"

"I quite like it," he mused, voice calm and relaxed. "Elegant, but understated. It pleases me, and it makes me want to carry you into an empty room and spend all night pleasing you." The corner of his mouth curled up and it did funny things to my insides. "Still want me to have it taken down?"

"Well, I... It's of no surprise to me that you have horrible taste just like that bird woman, but she did get one thing right. As long as everyone eats like civilized fae tonight, I guess it can stay," Emiana said grudgingly.

"Are you ready?" He flicked over my shoulder. "Eadaoin is supposed to whisk you away for a day of pampering."

Emiana disappeared, throwing me back at the reins. Relief flooded me. That was only a short episode, and thankfully Alisdair defused her before she could destroy the wedding of my dreams—again.

She'd been inserting herself all week—overriding my decisions, pissing off my helpers, degrading my friends, and all around making everyone wish I cracked my jaw falling down the stairs that day. I finally had to write a list of everything I wanted, hand it to Aeris, and tell her to ignore me if I told her to do anything in contradiction.

I had to make those kinds of strange declarations more and more, because Emiana was taking me over more and more. The only way to stop it was for Alisdair to declare his love to Cliona? Etain? Bedelia?

Fuck's sake! What is my name!

"Lady Ana, let's go." Eadaoin tugged me away. Alisdair and I barely had time to kiss goodbye before our lips were pulled apart. "First, you'll have a long, hot soaking bath in the finest bath oils in all of Elva. Then, we'll do your hair and nails. And finally, your dress will grace your body. Ah!" she cried, making me jump. "You're going to swoon when you see it. It's the most gorgeous thing in creation. I swear I wept."

Eadaoin whisked me away. As excited as she was for me to enjoy a day of pampering, she almost shed out all her fur when I insisted that she join me.

I offered the invitation to Aeris too, but she gave me an exasperated look, said she had too much to do to be lying around in a bath all day, and if I was late for the ceremony, she'd come and fish me out of my oversized, oily soup pot herself.

Sometimes I wondered which of us was the queen of Wind and Wild.

Despite her rejection, Eadaoin and I had a great time soaking, not only because halfway through the bath Bradach returned—his normal, affable self—and joined us, taking the place of his lover.

I had long since given up on keeping this man away from my bathroom. Especially since he was smart enough to bring glasses of spiced mulled wine, so my usual order to get out faded at the sight of them.

Bradach jumped in—splashing us both. "Ahh, lady and my lady, forgive me for my abrupt exit earlier, I had to put the finishing touches on your wedding gift."

My brows shot up. "Wedding gift? I get gifts?"

"Of course." Eadaoin bumped my shoulder. "Just like you got tributes when the people accepted you as queen. Your wedding tributes will be even better."

"Wait, no," I said, rising up. "The people of Wind and Wild already have so little. I felt guilty enough when they gave me the food off their tables. Please, spread the word that I don't need wedding tributes."

"Of course, Lady Ana," Bradach said, bowing as deep as the water allowed him. "We will be doing no such thing."

I nodded until the rest of the sentence penetrated. "What, why?"

"It'd be a terrible insult," Eadaoin hissed. "These are our customs. The tributes are the people's way of saying they accept you and your marriage—well, third marriage to our lord. Rejecting their tributes says you piss on their acceptance."

I sighed. "Okay, okay. I wouldn't want to offend anyone, but dare I ask, what is your gift to me, Bradach?"

"It is a manual on different sex positions and acts," he dropped. "You have to perform your wifely duties tonight, and you still blush at a man's naked body. Figured it wouldn't hurt to brush you up on your sexual education. If nothing else, the illustrations I drew in that book will banish the remains of that wide-eyed innocence right out of you. You're welcome."

"Hmm. How about I save us both a lot of time, and piss on that right now!"

Eadaoin and Bradach burst out laughing. I shook my head at the both of them. It didn't surprise me Bradach would give me such a gift. What surprised me is that Eadaoin didn't think of it herself. The kingdom of Wind and Wild was truly nothing like the borrowed memories of the Crystal Palace.

Wind and Wild was as harsh, brutal, cold, and unforgiving as its name, and still Alisdair was able to create a small community of happy, hardworking people—all of them as different as the day is long—but all of them working, living, and loving together while they patiently wait for the snow to melt.

"Do you think it's really happening?" I broke in, cutting off their teasing of me. "The curse is lifting?"

Bradach's grin faded. "I don't know." His jaw worked, but nothing came out. "We still can't talk about it, so as excited as everyone is, they haven't gotten their wish yet."

That was true. The curse was still abound on the furry faces, beaked noses, and tails trailing out of passing pants. *Curse lifting* and *curse lifted* were not the same things.

"Is it everyone's wish?" I asked. "Could there be others like Meallan and his wolf tribe who would want the curse to stay?"

"No."

"Absolutely not."

Eadaoin and Bradach weren't slow with their denials.

"We believe the formerly bound women will still keep their magic after the change disappears," Bradach said, "so there's no reason for anyone not to want this. Only Meallan thinks he needs to be a wolf to be a king."

I frowned.

"What's wrong, my lady?" Eadaoin asked. "Are you worried someone will try to kill you? We've doubled your security, and I promise, I will never leave your side."

"No, no, no, that's not it. It's just... something doesn't make sense." Once I finally voiced it, the uncertainty settled in my bones. "About the beast curse, about the melting snow, about all of it.

"Bradach, I know you don't like to talk about this, but you were there before Wind and Wild. Before everything. Do you know the origin of the beast curse?"

He peered at me through hooded eyes. "You know I cannot say, my lady."

"Can you also *not* say how to break it?"

"I cannot."

"But you do know how." I put my hand under his chin, drawing it up without touching him. We stared into each other's eyes. "Don't you?"

He didn't speak, and he didn't have to. I knew the answer.

Yes.

"There's more to all of this, isn't there? More to the curse, more to Wind and Wild, more to—" *That rose in the tower.*

"I cannot say, but I don't need to. The ice melting is a good thing," he said. "It's what we've been waiting for. Soon, we'll be free."

"That's good, but—"

My attendants walked in, loaded down with baskets holding face paints and all the tools made to transform the famed beauty of the east into a creature even lovelier.

"Are you ready, my lady?"

"Ready," Emiana said, rising from the water. "I will allow you to attend me, but will endure nothing pink, red, or orange. You, bring me spiced cider, and you, send the bird man away." I glared at the smirking beast. "Or I'll have him flogged if he comes near me with another bucket!"

Bradach rose up. Winking at me, he bowed before leaving—taking all six feet of dripping wet, naked, and gorgeous with. *It's a shame he can't mask those disgusting feathers and wings like his brother can. Shamer still that he's so insolent. And more's a shame on top that I couldn't bed him without his brother's marking revealing the affair.*

I hummed, slipping into the robe they held out and claiming my seat before the vanity. *There must be a way to rid myself of that mark, and these blasted marriage runes. Affairs aside, I can't stay faithful to the beast king. As surprisingly great a lover he is, one day I will need daughters to continue my line—claiming the throne of the true high empress. I cannot have his filthy blood sullying them.*

Sighing, I closed my eyes as they spread the tightening and shadow-reducing cream. I could confess to myself that I would rather go the route of removing the mark and finding a secret lover. Alisdair Shadowsoul was proving to be a kindred spirit and powerful ally. Everything that mattered had been stripped from me, and then he came along, promising to give it back and then some.

I did not want to kill him, so for his sake, he'd better free me from the marking scent, so I won't have to.

Emiana faded from my mind, but she didn't leave behind shock or horror. Honestly, it was a relief to finally know her true intentions. She was happy to go along with the wedding and all that came with it, because Alisdair was prepared to hand her the highest power in the land.

Of course she didn't love him, and of course she was willing to kill him. This was the same woman who wanted her father and all of his allies dead.

The only good news to come from that horrible train of thought was that she wouldn't try to harm Alisdair until *after* she was crowned high empress, and *after* she decided she was ready to have kids. I had until then to remember my fucking name.

"Ladies," I spoke up, ending their chatter. "Would you mind telling me all the female names you know?"

"Names? I'm not sure I understand," Carlin replied.

"Never too early to start thinking baby names." I patted my stomach. "I'd love some ideas, if you wouldn't mind helping me." *Because maybe you'll say the one that triggers my memory.*

That set them off jumping up and down, squealing.

"Oh my Meya, yes! We'd love to help," Carlin gushed. "What about Brona? That's my mother's name."

"Oooh, so pretty," I murmured, but felt nothing. No tingle of recognition.

"Evaleen?"

"Kiara?"

"Finella," Eadaoin threw in.

They pelted me with names from all sides. Mine would come up eventually. I was sure of it. Meya knocked sense into my stubborn head, so I'd finally wake up and see the man she had meant for me all along. No one was going to take him from me.

Alisdair loved to speak of the little bird who belonged to him, and that was fine. Because every night I lay next to the beast who belonged to me.

"—life or death! I must speak with her now!"

"Let him through," I heard Bradach bark from the other side of the door.

Riordan, the vegetable-seller burst in and slipped on the wet floor—crashing flat on his back.

I blinked at him, robes high. "What on earth is going on? Are you okay?"

"I'm fine!" He shoved up, huffing and puffing. "I'm sorry, my lady, I... I ran all the way here."

"I assume it wasn't to wish me well on my big day?"

"No, it's—it's terrible, my lady. Terrible, terrible news!" He surged at me and a blur shot into my path.

Riordan bounced off Eadaoin, nearly winding up on his back again. "That's close enough."

"Riordan, just calm down, and tell me what's going on," I said, rising up.

Riordan sought me over Eadaoin's shoulder, face stricken. "My lady, it's Aya Olene. She and Meliora have been arrested for treason. Some of the treasures I gave them had the Wind and Wild crest on them. They're saying it's proof of payment for espionage!

"Queen Ana, they're to be executed tomorrow at daybreak!"

I clapped my hands over my mouth. "That's horrible. You have to tell Treasa at once. She'll know what to do."

"What? My lady, I... I don't understand."

"Treasa," I cried. "I can't say too much, but she'll know how to help." He didn't move.

"Well, go on!" I flapped a hand. "Hurry. They don't have much time, and if Treasa knows them, they're vital to the kingdom."

"But, it's Aya Olene," he repeated, giving me a strange look. "Olene, Meliora, Gisela, Jaclan, and Savia. You've done so much for them. More than anyone ever has. Aren't you going to do something? Don't you care?"

"Of course I care, but what can I do? I have no idea who these people are." I returned to the vanity. "Treasa will. She'll think of something, so hurry. Find her."

"But, I—"

"You heard your queen." Eadaoin grabbed his shoulder and dragged him out. "Go downstairs, find the steward, and she'll help you find Treasa."

"But, my lady!"

Eadaoin tossed him out on his ear.

I shook my head, holding my hand up for my nails to be painted. "Those poor people. Hope they'll be okay."

"You can't worry about such horrible things right now, Lady Ana." Eadaoin beamed at me. "This is your big day. Nothing but smiles. I order it."

I laughed, bringing my smile right back. "You're right. This is my perfect day. All that matters is me and Alisdair."

***

"Are you ready, Queen Ana?"

I stood before the ballroom doors, listening to the hearts beating. The one in my chest, and the one in my ear.

I didn't know why I'd been hearing a disembodied heart. There were many chances for me to ask Alisdair about it, but it wasn't as though he could tell me because of the curse. Lumenfell brought me as many mysteries as it did joy. But one mystery had been solved that day. Did Alisdair love me? Yes. Did he want eternity with me? Yes. And did his heart, in or out of his chest, beat for me?

I smiled listening to the slow, steady thrum. *Yes.*

"I'm ready."

The guards swept the doors open, transporting me to paradise.

Starflowers drifted down from the ceiling, falling like snowflakes on the guests before disappearing just as magically. There were no chairs. Faeriken of all types and animals stood, crouched, and flew around the room—calling their love and congratulations. Not the silent, solemn affair of two great kingdoms watching a mistake, but the happy, joyous occasion of watching two people in love.

Tiny orblights strung together and wove around the rafters, chairs, and walls—twinkling like starlight. All at once, I was transported to that first night Alisdair ravaged me in the snow. I think even then I knew... that we were meant to end up here.

A sea of rose petals cradled my feet, guiding me down the path that led to my love, my Alisdair.

He was perfect, but of course he was. His long, curling hair hung loose and free. His ceremonial robes were similar to the ones he wore the day we married in Lyrica, but he looked nothing like he did on that day. Because on this one, he was smiling. No smirk or wicked grin. But a beaming, heart-breakingly beautiful smile that stopped my breath.

And his stopped in turn, when he saw me.

Eadaoin could've gushed the praises of my dress for an hour, and still wouldn't have come close to how gorgeous it was.

The yellow, gossamer gown clung to every part of me, softer than a whisper and lovelier than a sunrise. A tight, beaded bodice glittered with onyx jewels, as stark and striking as the yellow-and-black spotted wings rising from my back.

I didn't know for certain whose idea it was to turn me into a butterfly, but I wept to see myself in the mirror. Just like Eadaoin said I would.

It wasn't that it was beautiful, or unique, or expensive. It wasn't that the pattern of the delicate wings continued down my skirt, making it so I looked like I could take flight that very moment.

No, I cried because this dress was *me*. Emiana hated yellow, and she thought butterflies were no more than nasty bugs. It's the true me who loved and would've chosen such a magnificent gown for her wedding day, if such a day had ever been possible for her in more than her daydreams.

As I walked, all the well-wishes and congratulations faded, their eyes widening to behold me. All except for one.

Aydan, the little fox boy, made faces at me as I walked past, mimicking the funny ones I made to him the many times we played. Laughing, I screwed up my face right back, sending him running away cackling.

I was giggling when I stepped up to the altar, and took his hand. Alisdair pulled me up and drew me close, snapping me to his chest. Swooping down, he captured my lips—exploding suns and stars behind my eyes as our tongues tangled, caught in their unending battle dance.

Breaking away, I laughed. "I'm pretty sure the kiss is supposed to come at the end, husband."

"Rules only apply to those too weak to break them." He kissed me bold and free—grinning against my lips. "That's never been me, or you."

Foalan, our officiant, cleared his throat—forcing me to step back, though I didn't let go of his hands. "Let us begin. One and all, we are gathered here in these hallowed halls to witness the joining of Lord Alisdair Lumenfell, and his queen..." Foalan looked to Alisdair, who nodded.

"His queen," Foalan continued, "Shoua Callidora of Lyrica."

My smile froze.

"*Callidora...*"

"*Callidora, where are you, faywen?*"

"*Calli, come play!*"

"*Callidora, ha! Terrible name for such an ugly girl.*"

"Meya, we ask your blessings for this union." Foalan brushed an oil-covered thumb across my spinning, drowning head, then did the same to Alisdair. "Lord Lumenfell, it is time," he began. "Make your vows before the All Mother."

"Wait..." I choked. "I—"

"Do you, Lord Lumenfell, vow to care for, honor, and obey Shoua Callidora?"

"I do."

"Wha— What's going on?" My voice was a thin rasp.

"*CALLIDORA!*"

"I don't understand!"

"Do you, Lord Lumenfell, vow to give your title, your love, and your life to Shoua Callidora?"

"I vow to give you everything, Callidora, because I love you."

My mind broke.

I clutched my head, screaming as two decades of a lifetime flooded my head. Little Calli playing peek-a-boo with Mama. Callidora and Meli singing while they hung the washing. Riordan knocking on Calli's door, inviting her out to play kickball with him and his friends. Calli tickling Jaclan's and Gisela's feet under the covers, so their shrieking giggles covered the shouting fight Mama and Kirwan were having in the same room.

Callidora saying goodbye to her faywens outside her home, promising she'd come back.

No, not she. Me. It's me!

One after the other, the memories crammed into my skull—splitting it apart. Darkness bled into my vision, dragging me to a peaceful, painless realm of unconsciousness as all the while...

I screamed.

****

"—dora? Are you alright?"

"Everyone, out! There won't be a wedding here today."

Those words drilled into my skull, peeling my eyes open. A blurred shape came into view.

"Wake up." Alisdair leaned over me, holding me in his arms. He brushed the hair from my forehead. "You don't have much time."

"What's... going—?"

"It's Aya Olene. She and Meliora have been arrested for treason. They're to be executed tomorrow at daybreak!"

I bolted upright. "Mama!"

"Good," Alisdair said, "you already know what's going on. Callidora, you don't have much time."

"Calli," I blurted. It all came back to me. Every single second and every memory of my life, including the long months I spent losing it. "No one calls me Callidora. It's old-fashioned and embarrassing. It never suited me. It means—"

"Beauty." Alisdair grinned that grin, making my heart stop. "A name never suited anyone on this earth more."

Even with everything going on, he could still make me blush. "But you can't say that," I cried, pushing him back. I looked around at the wedding that would never be as the last guests left through the main doors. "You don't know what I truly look like. You don't know so many things!"

"Don't be ridiculous, woman. Of course, I know what you look like. Why do you think I got so angry when I found you snooping in the tower? You were about to tear the covers off the portraits of you. The *real* you."

"What? How? Why!"

"Come on." He helped me to my feet. "There's a lot to say, and not much time to say it. Follow me. Don't waste time with questions."

"But I—"

Alisdair grasped my hand and took off. I hoisted up my skirts, fighting to keep up.

"I've known you weren't the princess since you plunged a sword in my chest," he announced, dropping my jaw. "I told you so in the carriage ride that first day. Every report on Emiana said she was a meek, wilting flower whenever her father's disappointed gaze turned her way. But then suddenly, a tough, crass, violent, warrior of a woman was standing before me, promising to be the nightmare you became."

"Hey!"

He chuckled. "I know of few things that can cause such a drastic personality change. A body-switching spell was top of the list."

We bolted through the castle, going where I had no idea. I had to get to my mother, my sister, my family!

"But if you knew the whole time," I huffed. "Why did you marry me? Why didn't you let me go?"

"It's not that simple. That fool girl didn't have a fucking clue what she was doing when she decided a curse would solve all of her problems," he growled. "If that's what they did, they'd have another name." We raced around a corner. "I'm amazed she even completed the curse without outright killing you both."

"She practiced," I recalled. "She tested it out on servants first, and killed them all."

He cursed. "That doesn't surprise me. It only sickens me that she kept going, and didn't take it for the warning it was." Alisdair shook his head. "But it was what it was. When I realized what curse took hold of you, I confess, my first thought was to toast my good fortune. You were the heir to Lyrica in anyone's eyes. You were the key to my victory over Lyrica, and Salman's head on a pike."

That truth didn't sting. Alisdair had told me as much when he made me his mate.

"That being the case, I had to protect you," he said. "By making sure you couldn't leave."

"How did that protect me? I could've ended this horror so much sooner." My heart twisted. "We could've been together in a true and honest way much sooner. Why did you do this?"

"We're here." Alisdair skidded to a stop before a door I didn't recognize. Kicking it in, he tugged me over the threshold into a weapon room.

Weapons of all types, sizes, and lethality covered every inch of wall—from manmade to magic. An entire case to my right was filled with coudarian crystals.

"You'll need this," he said, taking down a bow and arrow.

"Alisdair?"

"I wish I had more time to teach you close combat. The bow seemed the right choice at the time, but now you need a weapon you can both handle and hide." Alisdair crossed to a display loaded with daggers. "Oh well, we'll have to make do."

"Alisdair!" I shot to his side. "Why didn't you free me sooner!"

He spun on me. "How was I to do that before we were in love with each other? I told you, it's a curse, Calli. It leaves no one with any good choices."

The hot ball of rage and betrayal burning in my chest shrunk, allowing me to breathe again. Of course, he couldn't free me before he loved me. The imposter they shoved at him was a stranger in every way, and love took its own time. He was bound by the limits of the curse as much as I.

"All right, but why wouldn't you let me leave?" I asked his back.

Alisdair was a whirlwind sweeping through the room, gathering every weapon I might need. "Because I knew what you would do. You'd go looking for Emiana to force her to break the curse, and that couldn't happen." A fist-size coudarian crystal thudded on the small table between us. "Crossing paths with yourself would've snapped your mind in half. No one could reconcile the contradiction of your mind being in your body, but your body isn't your body, because your body is looking back at you."

My mind spun simply trying to follow that sentence.

"I've lived a long life, my queen. Of the few I've witnessed who survived the spell, they spent the rest of their days in an asylum, because one or the other tracked the body thief down—and it was the last thing they ever did."

Alisdair went to the door and stuck his head out. "Foalan! With me, now!"

"But that still doesn't explain why you didn't simply tell me all of this? Or how you knew I was Calli?"

"Everything I told you about yourself would've faded along with everything else when Emiana claimed you." He finally stopped rushing about and came to me, grasping my shoulders. "And most importantly, I had to be careful with you. I've never known a soul to successfully break this curse with their mind, body, and soul still intact. Me continually telling you you're Calli while your mind is shouting that you're Emiana could've caused more harm than good."

As angry as I wanted to be with him... what he said made sense. Curses didn't play fair. Their sole purpose was to cause misery and pain, and they didn't want to be lifted, or they wouldn't silence our tongues when we tried.

"But you knew I was Calli," I whispered, cupping his cheek. "Not any of a twenty million women, but Callidora. How?"

"It was rather easy to figure out when you looted my coffers and gave the spoils to that Riordan boy to give to your family."

My brows popped, face heating. "You knew that I—?"

"Was stealing from me? Yes. Pretty much immediately." He grinned lopsidedly. "A natural thief, you are not."

Of all things, why did this embarrass me most of all?

"I ordered him to tell me who my jewels were going to, and then I had my spies track down Olene, Meliora, Jaclan, Gisela, and Savia." He stroked my cheek, catching a stray tear. "I wasn't surprised they were a family. I was even less surprised that they were missing their oldest daughter, Callidora, who walked into the Crystal Palace one day, and never came back."

"Oh, Alisdair." I fell against his chest, hugging him tight. "What am I going to do? Riordan said their execution is tomorrow. It takes a fortnight to get to Lyrica. I'll never make it!"

"I will get you there on time, Calli, I promise."

"Me?" I dropped my head back, gazing up at him. "Aren't you coming with me?"

"I'm sorry." He truly sounded it. "I can't leave Lumenfell right now. Meallan is still out there—waiting."

"Right, of course," I sighed. "How could I forget about that bastard? I've been so happy the last few days, I almost convinced myself all was right in our world."

"And I almost convinced myself Meya would bless us, but some fates she won't change," he said softly. "This wedding will end with you fleeing into the night, and me left with a hole in my chest."

Tears flooded my lids, spilling fast and free down my cheek. "My love, I'm sorry. I never wanted—"

The door burst open. Foalan rushed in with Aeris on his heels. She held a pair of boots and a pretty, but comfortable shift dress.

"Get her dressed," Foalan told Aeris. "I'll get her ready."

I was pulled away from Alisdair as they descended on me—stripping off my beautiful wedding gown, tugging the dress overhead, pulling on my boots, then strapping the myriad of weapons to every free spot on my person. I didn't know what I'd be walking into in Lyrica, but they seemed to believe I'd have to fight my way out.

The second they were done, Aeris and Foalan pulled me right back out the door.

"There's something you need to know," Alisdair called after me. "The night I found you in the tower, I thought I was speaking to Emiana. When I saw her about to endanger the woman I love by revealing that portrait, I snapped.

"I said horrible things to you, but every word was for her." His smile—so beautiful. So sad. "I never could've loved that spoiled brat. It's you, Calli. It was always meant to be you."

"I love you too," I gasped, straining to keep pace. "I—"

A blast of cold air smacked me, turning my head around.

Bradach waited in the flower garden, standing next to my litter. He wasn't alone. Seven other raven men and women stood by his side.

I realized immediately what they intended.

This is all happening so fast, I thought as Aeris lifted me onto the litter. *But of course, it has to. I have to save Mama and Meli!*

I twisted around, reaching for Alisdair. "What do I do? How do I save them? No one's going to listen to me. No one ever listened to a Gutter girl from the Galley."

"More the fool them." He kissed my fingertips. "But you're not a girl from the Galley, my love. You're the queen of Wind and Wild."

The bearers took their place, Bradach leading in front, and lifted the handles. They took off, jolting me flat on my back.

I twisted around as we took to the skies, shouting down at my Alisdair. "I love you! I'll come back. I promise you!"

Alisdair waved, and walls shot up from the sides—enclosing me in against the cold.

"I promise, my beast, my king, my husband," I whispered. "I'll come back for you."

***

Bradach and the raven faeriken flew all night—not stopping to eat, rest, or make waste.

I prayed to Meya as the snow, clouds, and darkness vanished in the distance, and the sun returned.

Heat beat down on the litter, as blazing as the beaming sunlight penetrating the slats and dazzling my eyes. How was this the world I grew up in? I felt like a stranger embarking on a new land.

"The Crystal Palace," Bradach bellowed, shouting over the thunderous hum of faeman-sized wings beating the air. "It's there!"

I wanted to see but Alisdair didn't make a window. All that mattered was that he could see it. We were close.

"Mama. Meli, I'm coming."

Despite what Bradach said, we flew for ages more. The light coming through the slats grew duskier and dimmer. Reds, golds, and purples danced before my eyes when I peeked out—Meya's final parting gift before day left us, and her moon and stars reigned.

"How much longer!"

"Almost there!"

I popped off my butt, thrown against the wood as Bradach and his brethren put on a burst of speed.

"What is that?"

"There!"

"Faeriken! It's faeriken!"

"They're attacking!"

Never did I think I'd be happy to hear those words. "Bradach," I called. "I can't see anything!"

Suddenly, the entire front wall of the litter blew off. I screamed, throwing myself back as the rush of wind and light blasted my sensitive eyes. Blinking rapidly, the Crystal Palace came into sharp view—as did all of Lyrica.

Little specks moved this way and that way on the streets, scurrying about their day. From high above, the stark difference between the royal residences and the Galley was impossible to miss. Trash rolled through broken cobblestone streets, falling off the piles stacked behind ramshackle huts, and homes that were old and falling apart from the day they were built.

We left behind my old home, flying straight over the marketplace and the shouting people below. Fruit and day-old vegetables took to the skies, pelting my litter and its bearers.

I gritted my teeth. "So much for the arranged marriage bringing peace and tolerance to the kingdoms."

Bradach and the others didn't let them slow them down. They went straight to the palace gates and carried me over, igniting fires under the feet of the palace guards.

"Back, beasts!" Soldiers flooded the courtyard, their swords aloft. Coudarian crystals embedded right on the hilts. "Leave this place or—"

A blast of wind blew them off their feet—sending them and their weapons scattering. Bradach, the others, and my litter touched down as they clambered up—filthy curses and violent promises pouring from their lips.

"That was your second mistake, beast," hissed a tall, freckled soldier. He spat blood on the pavement. "Coming here was your first.

"Atta—!"

I jumped out. "Stand down! Everyone, stand down now! Weapons on the ground!"

"Excuse me?" Derisive laughter filled the courtyard. "Who do you think you are, bitch?"

I raised my head, glaring into his eyes. He jerked back so fast his feet tangled, and the stupid fool fell on his ass again. "Queen Emiana, Royal Highness of Wind and Wild, and former princess of Lyrica. That's who the fuck I think I am."

"P-Princess? How—?"

"Silence!"

The boy about swallowed his tongue.

"I am a witness for Olene Waterrose and her daughter, Meliora. You're to take me to them," I barked. "The execution will not go ahead!"

"But, I can't—"

Bradach flashed—moving so fast, he was on the soldier before his fallen feather touched the ground. "Is there cotton in your ears, boy?" he growled. Bradach's dagger pressed to his quivering throat. "My queen has given you an order. The execution is canceled!"

"But, I can't help you," he cried, eyes bulging. "It's too late. The sentence has been carried out. The execution is over.

"The traitors are dead."

Chapter Sixteen

"The traitors are dead."

One of my raven guards gasped, clapping her hand over her mouth. "Oh, no. My lady, we were too late. I'm so sorry."

"No." Expression hard, I advanced on the captured soldier. His companions raised, lowered, raised, then lowered their swords as I stalked past—not knowing what to do against the woman that was once their sovereign. "They're not dead. Stop wasting time and take me to them now."

Bradach tightened on his throat. "Are you certain?" he asked me.

"Yes. Salman holds his executions after daybreak so that the temple priestesses can attend. It delights him to lord over his victims that their slaughter is divined and sanctioned by Meya. We still have time, but not much, *so take me to them now!*"

Emiana living in my head for months was worth something in the end. Faced with her knowledge and her face, the soldier gave in—ordering for the doors to be opened and the queen invited inside.

I chased him through the halls, and then he chased after me. Emiana's memories were fading from my mind like water through my fingertips, but the place where Salman forced a small child to watch men and women be beheaded... that memory would stay long after she was gone.

Something caught my eye.

Emiana's hair draped over my shoulders, the gorgeous flaming crown known by all in the kingdom. So striking and uniform, except for the ebony tips dipped in ink.

"Oh, no," I breathed. "Bradach!"

He raced to my side, and quickly noticed what I did. "I was afraid of this." He craned his head around farther than an unchanged faeman's could go. Our followers were too far behind us to hear. "The body-switching curse works in reverse when it's broken. First, you lose your body, then your mind. Now, you've regained your mind and next will come your body.

"You have to do this quickly," he forced through clenched teeth. "You said it yourself. The only voice they'll hear in that room is that of a queen."

I urged my feet on without a huff or puff. I wasn't winded in the slightest, even though I was running faster than Emiana's limit. My true body was returning, and it wouldn't wait.

"If I fail, get my mother and sister out of here." I whipped around a corner, blowing past a servant who screamed and dropped her bucket. "I don't care if you have to leave me behind. Get them to safety."

A thousand emotions warred on his chiseled face. "If I do so, it's an act of war. I'd be proving they're spies of Lumenfell who violated Lyrica's sovereignty, and then we violated it again by preventing them from executing two traitors to the kingdom."

"So be it. If it's a war Salman wants, it's one he'll get soon enough. But promise me you'll save them, Bradach. They will not die today!"

I burst through the doors.

"—the reading of the charges. Olene Waterrose, you are hereby sentenced to death and—"

"Stop!"

The same officiant who married me and Alisdair dropped his book, whirling around.

My stomach heaved at the sight before me.

The room chosen to be the final stop of Salman's enemies was a bright, plain, circular space. A ceiling-high window faced the west, soaking in the final rays of the setting sun. Standing beneath the window were the officiant and two temple priestesses. Across the room, Salman, his advisors, and Kirwan Dawnbreaker observed my mother and his daughter chained to the middle of the floor—hatred rimming his red eyes.

Meliora didn't cry. Head held high, she was resplendent in her new, expensive gown as she held on to my mother's hand—her lips moving in silent prayer as red, bubbling blisters traveled up her wrist.

Rage welled in my chest, choking me. They bound an innocent girl of only sixteen years of age with iron chains.

My mother knelt beside her, her wrists burning horribly, but I doubted she noticed. Mama doubled over, clutching her stomach and dry-heaving. Even now, the wasting sickness wouldn't give her peace.

Two soldiers stood above them both, holding the swords that would separate their heads from their shoulders.

Salman shot forward. "What is the meaning of—? Emiana?" He looked at me dumbfounded like he didn't recognize his child. "What on earth are you doing here!"

I lifted my chin. "I was about to ask the same question. This farce is over. You!" I snapped my fingers at the officiant. "Release them. Now."

"Do not move," Kirwan barked at him. "You have no authority here, *former* princess. You renounced all ties to Lyrica when you married, so it is you who will cease this farce, walk out of this room, and return to where you came from. This execution is lawful and will proceed."

I didn't so much as glance in his direction. "You will shut your fucking mouth in my presence."

Kirwan choked. "Excuse—! How dare—!"

Salman's expression hardened. "You've gotten big for your crown, girl. Why doesn't it surprise me an ignorant beast has no control over his women? We are not so lax in my palace, as you well know. You will leave my castle now, or—"

"I have every right to be here," I pushed on, ignoring both fools. "The charge is that they are spies for Wind and Wild. I am the queen of Wind and Wild and know every spy under employ of my kingdom. These two are not among them," I said, tone even. "So I repeat, release them, and after you've done so, thank me for saving you from carrying out an *unlawful* execution against your own citizens."

Meli flicked from me to Salman, wide-eyed. Her lips still moved in prayer, but this time I knew what she was saying. *Please, let them believe her.*

Another of Salman's advisors stepped forward. I couldn't access Emiana's memory of his name. "Forgive me, my lady, but your word is not evidence, while the payment confiscated from their home is. We have proof they were paid for services to the faeriken. While you have no reason to be honest about who does or doesn't spy for your kingdom." His brow arched. "If anything, your rushing to their rescue proves they're valuable to you, and a traitor to us."

My eyes narrowed on him, then flicked down. Before my gaze, my nails shrunk—returning to the short, blunt, gardener's length they were before. *Hurry!*

"That's a lot of words to call me a liar," I replied, folding my hands behind my back. "Here I was believing I'd be entering a civil conversation with my allies, not the insult-slinging match of enemies. And this is after my husband was kind enough not to declare the treaty broken after the events of our wedding day."

"Events caused by you!" Salman bellowed.

"Regardless, he remains committed to keeping the treaty, while you all appear committed to falsely accusing us of espionage and violating your sovereignty. Both acts that declare the treaty null and void.

"If it is your assertion that you have irrefutable proof that these women are my spies, then you have proven your case against Wind and Wild too," I stated. "We have violated the treaty, the ceasefire is at an end, and the war continues." I turned my back on them, marching for the door. "I will send word to prepare our forces to march on Lyrica. Good day."

"What!"

"Hold on a moment!"

"Stop," said one clear voice, halting my hand on the knob. "The voice of Meya will speak in this place and be heard."

I spun and dropped to my knees, thudding to the floor as quickly as Bradach, Salman, Kirwan, the advisors, the officiant, and the executioners.

Everyone bowed before the voice of Meya, and the representatives chosen to deliver it. Everyone—even a king.

Through my lashes, I watched as the temple priestesses stepped forward. They weren't chosen for their beauty, but they were all the same. A fact that couldn't be concealed by their heavy, white face paint, voluminous white robes, or their shaved heads—as bald as the moon.

"Meya weeps for the ravages of war, and the death and destruction it has caused to her creations." She swept over our bowed heads. "If there must be war, the passion and ferocity for which it is waged will be equal to the passion and ferocity in preventing it."

Stepping back, her sister and fellow priestess continued without pause. "Queen Emiana of Wind and Wild, and Lord Kirwan Dawnbreaker will present their evidence against these women, and then it will be Meya who decides their sentence. Her word is law. Her judgement is absolute. So mote it be."

"So mote it be," we echoed. "In Meya's name."

Bradach nodded to me out of the corner of my eye. This was my one and only chance, and—

My toes jammed against the front of my slippers, outgrowing a princess's dainty feet.

—I was running out of time.

Kirwan rose up. "I will happily repeat my evidence at the behest of Meya. The facts are these—only months ago, Aya Olene and her children lived in poverty in the Galley. Her eldest daughter, Callidora, owed a significant debt to House Dawnbreaker that she agreed to repay by signing up for the noble service of becoming a war wife.

"I myself escorted her to Crystal Palace so that she may begin her duties by servicing the faeriken in attendance of the royal wedding," he said. "The coward immediately fled and abandoned her responsibilities and her family.

"Or did she?" Kirwan brushed his thumb over the crystal on his lapel. A familiar silver chalice appeared in his right hand. "This is one of the items confiscated from Aya Olene's home. As you can see, the crest of Wind and Wild and its beast king is on the bottom."

I hadn't noticed that when I shoved all those treasures in a sack for my family. Alisdair was right. I was a terrible thief.

"What I now believe to be true is that Callidora bedded one of the faeriken and convinced him over pillow talk to whisk her away to Wind and Wild, where she'd be a go-between for her family and Shadowsoul. They spy on our kingdom in exchange for wealth and riches. That's the only explanation for the millions' worth of jewels, gold, and treasure discovered upon search of their home."

Anger laced his tone, but it wasn't for the loss of his war wife or child. I'd come to know this monster too well over the last sixteen years to mistake his true feelings. Kirwan was angry... at my mother.

I suspected the minute those jewels arrived, she quit working as a war wife, and dumped Kirwan in the trash where he belonged. He could no longer delude himself into thinking they were in love, when the door kept slamming in his face.

Finding the crest on the treasures gave him his ultimate wish—ensuring that if my mother didn't belong to him, she belonged to no one.

Meliora swung to me, face stricken.

I had no idea how Kirwan got her included in the charges. I assumed he did so just to cause my mother the ultimate amount of pain before the end. She would've known whatever trumped-up bullshit he spun to get a young woman executed, but I couldn't ask her.

By law—Salman's law—the accused weren't allowed to speak in this room, and naturally, the entire trial from start to finish always took place in this very room. Meaning, she couldn't speak one word in her defense while these uncaring monsters spouted lies and determined her fate.

Salman truly was a vile man.

"Thank you, Lord Dawnbreaker." The priestess inclined her bare head. "Now, Queen Emiana, what have you to say for these women?"

"I have only the truth, O Holy One, for I dare not speak anything else into Meya's ears," I replied. "There is another explanation for this money, and I shall tell it to you. I sent these treasures to Aya Olene because Callidora wouldn't accept it for herself. She wanted my thanks to go to her family, precisely because she cares only for them and her responsibilities."

"Your thanks?" Salman questioned.

"Precisely so, Father. You see, the night before my wedding, I was targeted by an assassin who wanted nothing more than to stop the signing of the treaty, and keep Lyrica under the grip of war. It was Callidora who saved my life."

Salman stiffened, eyes sharpening. "An assassin?" he barked. "How? Who!"

"The how was frightfully simple," I replied. "Poison slipped into my evening meal. You can imagine my surprise when a peasant girl burst into my chambers, screaming at me not to eat a morsel. I almost sent for the guards to have her flogged, but then she told me of the awful plot she overheard... while in the home of House Dawnbreaker."

Kirwan's head snapped up. "Excuse me? What did you say!?"

I sniffed. "Again my would-be assassin addresses me. You truly have no shame."

"Would-be assass— That's preposterous!"

"Silence," Salman ordered.

"But, my king—"

"Silence!" Salman shoved out in front of him, bearing down on me. "Explain this. Immediately."

"It is what I've said," I replied, lifting my nose in the air. "Callidora overheard a plot to kill me, and fulfilled her rightful duty—saving my life. It was me who asked her to come to Wind and Wild with me, not some love-addled faeriken. I did this to protect her in case Dawnbreaker figured out who foiled his plot, and attempted to kill her next."

"These are lies!" Kirwan roared.

The advisor who spoke up before separated from the pack. "I beg King Salman, Meya, and the priestesses for pardon, but I must say, I find the accusations against Advisor Kirwan highly unlikely. He has served my king faithfully for hundreds of years."

"Because we've been at war for hundreds of years," I sliced in. "Callidora and I have had many discussions in the months I've been away. House Dawnbreaker has been the exclusive military miner and seller of coudarian crystals since the war began. He's profited tens of millions, but with the treaty in place and the war over, that money goes away.

"Isn't that correct, Father?"

Salman turned on his advisor. A million emotions warred on his face, but one was clear as day—suspicion. "Yes, my child. You are correct."

Kirwan advanced on his king, and the soldiers reacted. Swinging their swords away from my family, they leveled them on his chest.

Halting, Kirwan raised his hands, away from his weapons and crystals. "King Salman, none of this is true. These lies are fabricated by—by—by that worthless brat, Callidora." Kirwan half-bowed to me, suddenly capable of deference and respect. "I do not blame you, my lady, for being taken in. Callidora is a troubled child and an accomplished liar. She'd have said anything to indebt you to herself, and beg a carriage ride out of Lyrica."

I scoffed. "What am I? A fool? Of course I checked her story before believing a word of it. While the poisoned food is gone and can no longer be used as evidence, there is more proof of sabotage. Proof that was witnessed before the entire court, and before you, Father."

"What is this proof?" Salman demanded. "Tell me, child."

My gaze swept the room, expression solemn. "My out-of-control, crazed behavior the day of the wedding. You are my beloved father," I demurred. "You know me. You know I never would've behaved that way unless something horrible was done to me."

Shocked hisses filled the room. Salman placed his body between me and Kirwan, as if he actually cared a whit about me.

"It's true," Salman barked. "I said myself that my Emiana wasn't herself that day. She never would've behaved that way unless her mind was addled by a spell. A spell intended to destroy the marriage before it began, and nullify the treaty." His lips peeled back from his teeth. "You."

"No! Someone may have spelled her, but it was not me!"

I shook my head. "You stand under the judgement of Meya, and still you lie. Very well," I said. "Since it has come to this, I will provide my final proof. Callidora told me much in our time together, including that Kirwan bragged about slaughtering the village of Lutin, because it was discovered their homes sat on a wealth of crystals. Proof of his insatiable greed."

I left out that Salman sanctioned that atrocity. That wasn't something Emiana was supposed to know, nor was it something Salman would ever admit.

"But there's more. He also—" I hitched a breath, sorrow drawing the corner of my lips down. "Father, I'm sorry to tell you this. But it was Kirwan who hunted your other sons down, and slaughtered them."

Kirwan's eyes bugged. "What?!"

"It was all part of his plan to leave you without an heir so that you'd be forced to make the same decision my grandparents did—give your throne to someone not of the bloodline. As your *trusted* advisor and supposed *friend*, he knew he would be at the top of your list."

"Lies, lies, all of it, lies," Kirwan bellowed.

"How can it be a lie?" I snapped, stepping out from behind a shaking Salman. "Not even I knew I had half-siblings before Callidora told me what she overheard that fateful day. My father protected the information because he wanted to protect them, but he told you, didn't he?" I spun to Salman, hoping against hope my desperate gamble was correct. "Didn't you, Father?"

Face a mask of shadows, Salman looked at Kirwan... and nodded. "It is so," he rasped. "I trusted you with the knowledge and location of my only sons, and you killed them."

"I would never!" Kirwan ran at him and was roughly thrown back.

Not a single word of defense came from behind him. His fellow advisors had distanced themselves as far back as the wall would let them. They looked at him with nothing but betrayal.

"I deny this slander utterly and without reservation," Kirwan roared, spittle flying. "Not a word she has spoken here today is truth!"

"Very well," I shouted over him, my voice rising partly due to him, and partly due to the screaming pain of my crushed feet. "If you deny my truth, I ask that you hear my logic."

"Speak, child," Salman said. "You will be heard in this place."

"Then I say this, my final witness." I moved toward my mother and sister, and Kirwan. "Kirwan claims my gift for saving my life was actually payment for espionage. To assume Aya Olene would have information valuable enough for my husband to listen to, you must assume these poor women from the Gutter had an equally valuable source.

"Who else would that source be but their war husband and father, Kirwan Dawnbreaker?"

"No," Kirwan cried. "That's not— You're twisting everything!"

"Am I? Or am I merely being logical? These two could know nothing of worth unless they heard it from *you*." I smiled mirthlessly. "Which would make you the spy, would it not? You're the leak. *You* are the one sharing information that wasn't meant to go further than your king's ears."

The advisors exchanged looks, murmuring amongst themselves. The expressions as they beheld Kirwan made him lurch back a step.

"But, no," I said, voice heavy. "You're not a spy for Wind and Wild, because *they* are not spies for Wind and Wild. They had no opportunity to pass information from you to my husband since we married, because I will bet anything Aya Olene has refused you every single day since she received my gifted treasures.

"So, speaking only logically, how could I have been paying her to spy, if she's refused to have anything to do with the only person worth spying on since she received said payment?"

An oppressive atmosphere smothered the room, but it wasn't a silent one.

"She's right."

"The princess speaks only sense."

"The real traitor is here, and it's not these poor women!"

"She's a liar!" Kirwan bellowed. "None of this is true, you must believe me!"

Facing the priestesses, I bowed. "Thank you for allowing me to speak as an ally to Lyrica and to peace. I give all that I've said to the judgement of Meya, for she is wisdom and truth. She will make the right decision here today."

"She will, and she has," said the priestess. "Meya declares these women innocent—"

"No!"

"—release them at once."

"NO!"

I stood, rising up beside Kirwan. "I told you," I whispered. "Everything you do to my mother, I'll do to you—tenfold."

Kirwan stilled. Flicking down, he latched immediately on my darkening ends. The ebony had climbed high enough to be unmistakable. "You…"

I brushed past, flashing a smirk that was just for him. "Have fun in the Burning Plains, bitch."

He shook, face turning an alarming shade of purple. "You!"

Kirwan lunged at me, slamming into my back. We crashed to the floor in a shower of punches, roars, and screams.

"Imposter! It's her. She's Callidora!"

"Help me!" I shrieked, covering my face. "He's gone mad! Help!"

"Get off of her!"

Half a dozen coudarian crystals were whipped out, but none were so quick as Bradach. He grabbed Kirwan under the arms, wrenched him off, and threw him at the stone wall. His bones collided, snapping on impact, then dropped the wretch groaning and broken on the floor.

"Arrest him," Salman shrieked, showering spittle. "Execute him!"

"Can you stand?" Bradach whispered, dropping next to me. "You must leave."

I lifted my face and he blinked, jaw slackening. There was something on Emiana's face that shouldn't be.

"We must go now!"

I didn't need to be told again. Shoving up, I bowed my way out of the room—keeping my head lowered. Escaping out into the hall, the peasant queen and the bird man ran. Ran as fast as their feet and wings allowed them.

Bradach shot me a smile. "You never cease to impress me, keva. All of Elva has met their match in you."

I winked. "You should see what I can do to a man with a brick and a few berries."

Our laughter rang through the hall.

***

I rocked her in my arms, listening to her giggle, babble, and coo.

"I can't believe I ever forgot you, sweet girl."

Savia shrieked, equally outraged by the insult.

The front door swung open, beckoning in a wild-haired, panting Meliora. She landed on me sitting on the couch holding Savia—the real me. The last traces of Emiana faded by the time I stumbled barefoot to my family's new home.

"Calli!" Racing past the twins, she threw her arms around me, hugging me as tight as our baby sister allowed. "I can't believe it's you. It's really you." She snapped back. "But where have you been? We've been worried sick! We thought you were killed by the faeriken until Riordan brought all those jewels, and we figured they had to be from you. But how could that be possible? You—"

"Meli," I cried, cutting in. "Slow down. I will tell you everything, I promise, just as soon as Mama comes. I want to tell you together."

Her face fell.

"What? What is it?" I bolted upright. "Oh no, did they not let her go!"

"No, no, that's not it. She was released with an apology, just like me, but..." Meliora's lips trembled. "She only walked as far as the hallway before she collapsed. I needed help to carry her back home, so..."

"Collapsed?" I got to my feet. "Why would she collapse? What's wrong?"

"You know what's wrong," she snapped. "The wasting sickness. It's only gotten worse since you've been gone."

I put a hand on Meli's shoulder, stopping her saying anymore when the twins' round, curious faces turned to us. I gave them a bright, carefree smile like I always used to do, and they smiled back.

When Bradach and I left the castle, I turned left immediately, making for Gutter Galley. He pulled me up short, reminding me my family would've moved after coming into wealth.

It took little asking around for us to find out where. It seemed the poor family from the Gutter who suddenly became wealthy and bought a home in the noble district was the talk of the town for weeks.

I knocked on the door and Jaclan threw it open. I barely got out a greeting before he tackled me, throwing himself into my arms. Gisela wasn't far behind him.

After talking to the twins, it was clear they had no idea their mother and sister were sentenced to be executed that day, and just as well. It haunted me the whole flight to Lyrica thinking of the terror they were going through, believing everyone they loved would leave them and never come back.

On the contrary, they were their happy little selves, giving me the grand tour of our new home, and even showing me my new room.

Even though Mama had the coin to buy the biggest mansion in the district, she didn't. She bought the home Papa left for her. The one that was always meant to be ours.

It had sweeping, vaulted ceilings; three floors of extra bedrooms, dining rooms, servant quarters we'd never need; a grand dining room with a mile-long table, and huge, four-poster beds in every room, *perfect for jumping* as Jaclan assured me.

"Children, have you had dinner yet?" I asked. "Why don't you go into the dining room, and I'll be along soon with your supper."

"That's okay, Haeowen," Gisela said, pulling Jaclan up on his feet. "Peri makes supper for us now." She lit on my wrist. "Oooh, I like your charm, Haeowen. It's so pretty."

"Thank you, sweet one. I'll get you one just like it." I watched them go, chuckling. "I've been replaced by Peri. Glad to know they didn't miss me too much."

The look Meliora gave me could've peeled paint. "They missed you, Calli. They cried every night for three weeks. They were inconsolable. We thought you were dead while the whole time, you were hiding out in Wind and Wild. How could you?"

"That's not what happened. Just let me explain—"

The guards chose that time to walk in, carrying my mother on a litter. My explanation was on hold while we got her settled in her room, placed baby Savia next to her, and covered them both with soft, downy sheets.

The baby fell asleep almost instantly. My mother stared at me like she'd never seen me before.

"Explain," she croaked, lips paper dry. "Did you truly overhear Kirwan plotting an assassination? Have you been sheltering in Wind and Wild all this time?"

I perched on the side of her bed with Meli sitting on the other side. She wasn't going anywhere until she heard my story, so I told them everything.

From the night Kaelan kidnapped me out of my bed and forced me to switch bodies with the princess of Lyrica, to getting word that they were about to be executed and flying across the Wastelands on the back of raven men.

"Speaking of, I asked Bradach and the others to hang back and give us some privacy, but they're going to need a place to shower and sleep. They haven't taken a break in over a day."

"Well, of course they must stay here," Mama cried. "Sounds to me Meli and I wouldn't be here without them. And you left them out in the cold, Calli, shame on you." Even lying in her sickbed, Mama scolded with the best of them. "You go send for them right this minute."

"Yes, ma'am."

"Calli, wait for me." Meliora jumped out and followed, trailing me out of our home and into the night.

"What is it?" I finally spoke up. "Say what's on your mind."

"I'd rather know what's on your mind. After your faeriken have rested and eaten, what do you plan to do?"

I frowned. "What do you mean? I'm going back home to Alisdair."

"Home," she repeated. "You used to call Lyrica home."

"And I still do." We skirted a couple walking down the sidewalk. "But Lumenfell is my home too. It's also where my husband is. Now that I know you both are safe, I have to return."

"Love has made you blind, Calli."

"What? Why would you say that?"

She gave me a hard look. "Mama is not safe. She's dying, Haeowen. She hasn't kept a single thing down for weeks. We can afford the best healers coin can buy now, and they're all saying the same thing. She doesn't have much time left."

I flinched like she punched me in the gut. "That's not— That can't be—"

"It's true. You saw her yourself. You know it's true."

My lips flattened into a thin line. Of course I saw that my mother was thinner than a skeleton with the cracked lips and thin, sluggish skin of a parched soul lost in the Wastelands.

"What will you do, Calli? These are the last days we'll get to spend with our mother before she... before..." Meliora blinked rapidly, eyes bright. My little sister—never wanting anyone to see her cry. "Are you really going to fly away and leave us to face this alone? Again?"

I balled my fists, mouth clenched tight. I was furious, but not at Meli or Mama. I was angry at the evil, sick system that stole my mother's magic in the first place. I was angry at the power-hungry, bitter witch who gave them the means to do it. She came here to destroy our way of life, and we played right into her hands. As a result, my innocent, loving mother was slowly wasting away.

"I'm not going to leave you alone, Meli. I made a promise to you, all of you, that I never would. I'll stay," I said softly. "I'll see Mama through this, and then we'll all go back to Lumenfell together.

"You'll be safe and happy there, and"—I took her hand—"we'll be together again. As a family."

Meli shook me off. "There's no family without Mama."

I didn't know what to say, because I couldn't disagree.

We walked the rest of the way in silence—both of us lost in our own sorrow.

Eventually, we arrived at the inn where I sent them to eat and relax. Egan's Inn and Tavern was owned by a nice man who never had a raised voice or bad word for anyone. I figured even if faeriken weren't welcomed with open arms, they at least wouldn't be harassed or chased out by Egan.

"—warned you! You are to leave by order of the king."

"And I've told you." Bradach faced the palace guard down, wings rising and casting long shadows over them both. "We're not going anywhere without our queen."

The small, cozy tavern was completely cleared out of everyone barring the raven faeriken, Bradach, and the fifteen guards sent to meet them.

Egan stood behind the bar top, eyes darting between them and looking like he wished both groups were anywhere but in his peaceful pub.

"What's going on here?" I demanded.

The leader of the guard turned and frowned at me. "This is of no concern of yours, shoua. Leave this place, for your own safety."

I winced. Of course, I was back to being the peasant, not the princess.

"We've been ordered to evacuate," Bradach told me flat out. "The terms of the treaty forbid faeriken from *invading* Lyrica, and King Salman means to hold us to those terms to a pedantic degree. He's granting us pardon for bringing the queen here for an emergency, but now that it's resolved, we must leave. What say you?"

"Excuse me?" the guard scoffed. "Why are you asking her? You were given your orders. Leave!"

Bradach didn't even glance at him. "Well?"

I peered at Meliora out of the corner of my eyes, heart squeezing. I wanted to be home with Alisdair, but there was never any choice. These were my last days with my mother, I wouldn't forgive myself if I wasn't here with her—and my family—to the end.

"The queen has sent me with a message," I replied carefully. "Rest, and then go on without her. She has to stay for now, but she'll return home as soon as she can. She promises."

"I understand." Bradach tipped his chin to me. "I will pass on her promise."

My lips parted. "And tell him that—"

"Let's go, Calli." Meliora tugged me away. "Mama's waiting."

"I know," Bradach said, his smile following me out the door. "I'll tell him."

****

I stroked Savia's hair as she cooed and babbled at our sleeping mother, smiling even as sadness choked me.

We'd been keeping them together, only taking Savia away to change, feed, or calm her. Our youngest sister wouldn't get nearly as many years with our mother as she deserved. The least we could do was let them spend this time together... before the end.

"Faywen?"

I started, blinking at Mama's open, watching eyes.

"What's wrong?"

Sighing, I set down her cooling bowl of broth and stretched out next to them. "Do you have to ask?"

Mama drew Savia closer, tucking her under her chin. "We knew this was coming, Calli."

"Yes, but..." Tears beat at the back of my eyes. "You should've had more time. If you did, then I could've—" I bit hard on my lip.

"Could've what, darling?"

"Could've saved you," I burst out. "With more time, I could've saved you! It's not right, Mama. It's not fair."

"Oh, Calli." Of all things, she smiled at me. "My precious girl, so full of fire."

"Don't do that. Don't treat me like a silly little child lost in her day-dreams. I could've saved you, Mama. I had a plan! But now I'm here and you're here, and I'm not that fiery, precious girl. I'm that useless, power-less girl again who's watching life step on the people I love, and not doing anything about it."

"Because it's not your job to do anything about it!"

Savia and I jerked, gaping at her. Mama never yelled at us. She never yelled at *me*.

"Mama?"

"Oh, Calli," she sighed, squeezing her eyes shut, looking like even that much sapped her starving body of energy. "I don't blame you, fay-wen. I put the weight of this family on your shoulders before you could walk. All those times I was called to the battlefield, you were left alone to care for Meli, and then again to care for Jaclan and Gisela.

"And then when I was finally allowed to stay home with my children, the wasting sickness took hold. Your whole life, I've either been absent, or sick and dying. It all fell down to you to be to the little ones what I was supposed to be—their mother."

I frowned. "But, none of that was your fault."

"It wasn't yours either. You should've had a real childhood, faywen. You should've been a big sister, not a borrowed mother."

My frown deepened. "Why are you saying these things? I did what I had to do because you're my family, they're my siblings, and I love you all. I'd do everything all over again even if *couldas* and *shouldas* could change a thing in this life. And why are you torturing yourself with these thoughts now? There's no sense worrying about what we can't change."

She smiled with her eyes closed. "Exactly."

"But…" The rest of my sentence died on my lips, chased away by my own words. "Very clever, Olene," I deadpanned. "Well done."

She laughed and I was sucked in, giggling along with her. "Seems your old mama still has some wisdom to impart."

"You're not old," I protested. "You're a young, beautiful woman in your prime. You still can't walk in a straight line for the men throwing themselves at your feet."

Mama's laugh was thin and raspy like rubbing paper. "I knew there was a reason you were my favorite."

I rolled my eyes, though I couldn't help chuckling. It'd been so long since we just sat around, laughing and joking. I was always focused on keeping everything together, while Mama struggled just to get out of bed in the morning.

"Jokes aside," Mama said, eyes still closed. "I need to tell you that I'm sorry, Calli. Your father and I never wanted any of this for you. You don't know the shame it brings me to know that the first time in your life you've felt true joy, power, freedom, and love… was when you were far away from me."

My smile melted away. "How can you say that? That's not true."

"No, no, my darling, I don't say that to make you feel bad." She found my hand across the sheets. "I'm happy you found those things. They're everything I wanted for you. Seeing your face when you talked about your king, it reminded me of the love I had with your father.

"You're finally happy, my sweet girl, so listen to me and listen well." Sternness crept into her voice. "Do not let it go. Do not let *him* go. Don't stay in this place and be small, when you could be there and be great."

"Oh, I see." I pushed up. "You overheard me and Meliora last night."

"She doesn't want to go with you to a land of ice, dark, and beasts," she said knowingly. "And you don't want to stay."

I chewed my lip, slumping against the headboard. It was true. Meliora held her tongue that first night, but in the seven days since I returned, she'd made her feelings about moving to Lumenfell loud and clear.

It didn't matter that we'd live in a palace where I'd be queen, and she'd soon be free of the binding. All Meliora heard was that she, the twins, and Savia would be put away in a separate, hidden part of the castle because the inhabitants couldn't control their urges. That is until she turned into a beast like the rest of them.

She wanted no part in the life I carved out for myself in Lumenfell. Even though I knew a big part of her resistance came from rejecting another change after a massive one ruined all of our lives. While I struggled to convince her the move was best for her, that quiet part of me had been asking for days, was I uprooting my family for their happiness, or mine?

"I'm not their mother," I whispered. "You are. So you tell me what to do, Mama? Isn't it better to be free in the dark than chained in the light?"

"A profound question, but even so, there is only one right answer. Freedom is all, Calli. There's nothing else that matters more than you five being able to love and live on your own terms, and you *cannot* do that in Lyrica.

"But if you must ask again, then I say to look to nature. Meya gave freedom to bugs and bunnies. She blessed the birds with wings. She bestowed fangs and fight on the prowling lioness. Why on earth, my precious girl, would you believe you deserve anything less?"

My lips trembled, shaking the teardrop balancing on the tip of my mouth. "So, you forgive me, then? For wanting to take the children away from all of this? Even though they may not thank me for it."

"You don't need my forgiveness, faywen. You don't even need my permission. As borrowed mothers go, you've proven yourself the best of them. I learned to trust your judgement a long time ago."

I roughly rubbed my stinging eyes, willing the gushing flood pushing against them to retreat.

"Mama, I... Thank you." I tossed my head. "But no more tears, and no more speaking with such finality. I won't have to make any decision Meli will curse me for, because the target will remain on your back," I said, earning a soft chuckle. "All that matters now is you focusing on getting well and hanging on long enough so I can save you."

She hummed. "So, tell me more about this Alisdair."

"Ah!" Savia shrieked, reminding us she was a part of this conversation too.

I didn't remark on either of their subject changes. The wasting sickness and what waited at the end of it has hung over my mother for years. I understood her wanting to speak of something else—if only for a little while.

"There's not much more to tell. He's strong, powerful, handsome, funny, and the biggest jackass in Elva."

She snorted—a weak, sudden sound that was over as soon as it started. "Jackass was an addition I wasn't expecting."

"I may love him, but that part is undeniable." I smiled despite myself. "Even though he drives me crazy, he's the only one that could make me... run slower."

"You should never slow down for anyone," she replied, not knowing the reference. When I told her about my time in Lumenfell, I left out the terms of our marriage runes, and that Alisdair would chase me down every night and fuck me until I saw the stars.

A mother didn't need to know everything.

"But despite his hard and prickly exterior, it's his soul, Mama. The real and true him is... so..." I trailed off, muscles winding tight.

"His soul," I whispered, eyes widening. "Charm."

"Calli?"

"Oh my Meya." I gaped unseeingly at the bedsheets. "So, that's it. That's how you break the curse."

"Calli, darling?"

I shook myself, coming to. "Sorry, Mama. I was just saying that despite how much of a raging jackass he can be, he's my soulmate." A small smile danced on my lips. "I know that more than ever now."

She hummed. "I admit I understand the appeal. I loved my fair share of jackasses."

"Wait, what? Asses? As in more than one? But I thought you said Papa was your true love."

"He was my one true love and mate, but it took me hundreds of years to see that. All the while your father was patient, caring, supportive, and yes, a bit of a jackass too." I sensed her rolling her eyes behind her lids.

"He loved telling me that I could deny it all I wanted, but one day we'd end up together. Want to know what the bastard said after I told him I loved him for the first time? *I told you so.*" She snorted. "With the biggest smirk on his face too. I almost followed the confession with a punch to his throat."

I giggled.

"Even though he could infuriate me like nothing else, what I wouldn't give to go back and tell him I loved him sooner. It's the biggest regret of my life that I wasted hundreds of years not feeling as blissfully happy and loved as he made me.

"Don't make my mistake," she whispered. "Don't spend a single day being less happy than you could be. Meya gave blessings to the bugs and birds. She has even more wonder and adventure in store for you."

"Oh, Mama..." I fell on her other side, clutching her tight and blubbing against her shoulder.

It was a while before my tears stopped, but that was okay. They weren't all sad tears. Some were hopeful for the promise of happiness to come with the man who made me want to punch him in the throat and kiss him until I couldn't breathe—all in the same measure.

Taking a deep breath, I let it out slow—hugging her tighter. "You know, I was actually thinking of you and Papa when I was trying to get Alisdair to fall in love with me. Will you tell me more stories about him? What was it, in the end, that changed everything for you two?"

She didn't reply.

"Mama? Are you asleep?" I peeked over her shoulder, and froze. "Mama? Are you okay? Mama?"

I shook her gently, then harder. She flopped in my grasp—eyes closed shut.

"Mama!"

Jerking in surprise, Savia started bawling.

I grabbed my baby sister and scrambled off the bed. Feet tangling, I fell hard on my butt and kept going, crawling back until I hit the wall. Clamping my hand over my mouth, I screamed—nails piercing my cheek smothering my cries.

I thought I knew pain. I suffered unbearable agony trying to force the magic through the bindings around my soul—shredding myself from the inside. What I wouldn't give if it only hurt that much.

Tucked in that corner alone with my crying sister, my smothered wails leaked through my tear-soaked fingers. I cried and cried until there was nothing left in me, then evermore I cried.

"Calli?" *Knock-knock.* "Is everything okay? Does Savia need a bottle?"

I sucked in hard, shuddering breaths—roughly wiping my face.

"Calli, open up. I've got Mama's medicine."

By the time I got to my feet and crossed to the side table, my tears were gone.

I blew out the candles, plunging the room in darkness, and opened the door. Meli tried to come in and pulled up short when I held out Savia, keeping my red, puffy face cloaked in the shadows.

"She is hungry," I croaked. "Would you mind feeding her? I'll give Mama her medicine."

"Oh, but—" She tried to peer around the baby. "I was hoping to spend some time with Mama. Gisela and Jaclan are doing their lessons now, so I can spend the rest of the day with her until I start supper."

I squeezed my eyes shut as a wave of sorrow drowned me. "How about a trade? You feed Savia now, and I'll cook supper, so you have more time sitting with her."

"Hmm. Okay," Meliora said—so light. So unaware. "That's a fair trade. Come here, baby." She took our fussy sister and held her close, dropping a kiss on her crown. "Be back soon, Mama."

Only when she descended the stairs did I shut the door, resting my forehead upon it. Of course I couldn't hide the tragedy that just cratered the soul of our family. I simply... wanted her to be as happy as she was for a little while longer.

My feet carried me away, bringing me to her side. Carefully, lovingly, I rested her on her back, crossed her arms, and tucked her in tight. "I love you, Mama," I whispered. "I already miss you more than there are stars in the sky.

"I promise, I'll take care of them. It won't be right away. It won't even be soon, but one day you'll look down from the Meadows, and you'll see us all as you were—blissfully happy and loved." She swam in my vision. "Good—"

"Ahh!"

I jolted upright. "What was—?"

"Get off me! Let me go!"

I took off, bursting out of the room and racing down the stairs. "Meli? Meli!"

He stood in the entrance—so still and silent, I almost didn't register him as a threat until I saw the coudarian crystal sharpened into a blade... pressed to her throat.

I skidded to a halt. Grabbing the banister saved my feet flying out from under me and dropping me on the steps.

"Okay," I said slowly. Calmly. "Let's all just stop and take a breath. You don't want to hurt her."

His lips peeled back from his teeth, snarl bleeding through.

"Put down the crystal."

"You don't give the orders anymore," Kirwan hissed. "Not without a stolen princess's face. How did you do it? Huh!?" He clamped harder on a struggling Meli, making her cry out. "Was it a trick from the beginning? All of it a plot to bring about my downfall!"

"Don't be absurd, you narcissistic kakka!" I shouted back just as loud. "Not everything is about you— Actually, nothing I do is for or about you! I saved my mother and sister, and should your downfall have come about as a result..." I shrugged, my smirk nasty. "That was just a happy accident."

"Lies. Whenever that disgusting, siren's mouth opens, nothing but lies and destruction falls out." Kirwan's eyes were bright with rage. "It's the greatest regret of my life that I didn't run you through with my sword the first time I laid eyes on you."

I barely heard a word the bastard said. My attention was fixed on Meliora and the weapon at her throat. A pinprick of blood smeared on her neck where it cut her.

"*Where are the children?*" I mouthed to her.

"*Safe.*"

"*Can you break free? Stomp his foot, then—*"

"What are you two doing!" Kirwan hauled her screaming out of the entrance, ducking into the side hall.

"Hey," I cried, chasing after them. "What do you want! Why can't you leave us alone?"

Kirwan stumbled against the wall, fighting to hang on to his struggling captive. He wrenched her head to the side so she couldn't communicate with me anymore. "What do I want?! You destroyed everything," he roared. "The king stripped me of my land, home, and title. He seized my vault. He sentenced me to execution for treason! I have nothing because of you!"

I couldn't have glared at him with less sympathy if I tried. "And what, Kirwan? Threatening your own daughter will get all of that back? Come now, you're smarter than this. You somehow managed to get away from the palace guards. Stop wasting time, let her go, and make your escape from Lyrica."

He smiled, and the shiver it sent up my spine stood my neck hairs on end.

"I'm not going anywhere, bitch, because I'm not threatening my daughter. I'm threatening your sister." His grin widened. "Here's how things stand, I didn't get away from the palace guards, they were murdered. *Slaughtered.* Undoubtedly your doing."

My doing? What was this madman talking about!

"They left the bodies next to my cell, so I took the keys and escaped. But not to save myself. I tried to stop them! Save my people, but it was too late for anyone else. Your dogs have overrun the palace and the streets, but that's fine," he hissed, talking mostly to himself. "I can make it right. I'll be Lyrica's savior, her leader, and—thanks to you giving me such a brilliant idea—her king."

I goggled at him. "What are you ranting about? You're insane!"

"Silence! For once in your life, keep your worthless mouth closed!"

"Ahh!" Meliora screamed as the crystal cut deeper. Blood flowed freely down her neck.

Balled fists shaking, I bit hard on my lip—falling silent.

Kirwan laughed. "Finally. So this is what it takes to keep your tongue in your head? Just like I knew it would." He sobered quickly. "Now listen up. You're going to get every jewel, every chalice, every bit of your stolen loot, put them in sacks, and bring them to me. I'll need coin to recruit the soldiers needed to take back Lyrica.

"And I'll need you."

My forehead crumpled but I didn't speak, gazing at Meli. *His mind has snapped. How do I get my sister away from him?*

"When the time comes, you'll recant every one of your lies and accusations. Admitting that you impersonated the princess and recruited faeriken mercenaries to help sell your lies. No doubt using your pussy to addle them under your sway."

It was entirely certain he didn't need to add that last comment. But leave it to Kirwan to be vile to the end.

"Go," he ordered. "Get the coin, and get your sister."

I stilled. "Excuse me?"

"Not the infant, I've no patience for those. Get the curly-haired blonde brat. Now," he bellowed when I didn't move.

"No."

He arched a brow. "You either take one sister with you, or I slit this one's neck right here on the carpet."

I breathed hard, hands clutching the other behind my back. "You don't have to do this," I rushed, mind spinning. "I'll get the jewels and go with you quietly. Just leave my faywens alone."

"Go with me quietly? Don't make me laugh," he gritted. "Nothing and no one keeps you in line, except these brats. Last chance, get the girl, or I'll kill—"

I slipped the dagger from my shift and threw—aiming right for his vile mouth.

Eyes rounding, Kirwan reacted on instinct. Hand flying off Meli's throat, he threw out the crystal and shouted a runic word.

The dagger collided with an invisible barrier, bouncing off and skittering across the floor.

"Meli, run!"

Throwing her head back, she smashed her skull in his face. Blood spurted from his ruined nose, freeing her from his grip as his hands flew up.

"Monster," she shrieked, stomping his foot.

Bones crunched in my ear.

"Go," I cried, grabbing and pulling her away. "Take the children and get out of—"

"Argh!" Pure, magical force slammed into us, blasting us into the hallway.

We dented the wood crashing into the wall. Pain surged through every limb and screamed out every pore. We crumpled on the floor—my head ringing.

"You just never... learn, girl."

Through the haze, Kirwan limped over—waving his hand. Before my eyes, he healed his foot and nose with the crystal.

He towered over us whole... and angry.

"I said I'd kill the girl if you disobeyed." A sword appeared in his hand, its hair-thin edge dancing the light off its tip. "I'm a man of my word."

"Wait!"

"Stop!"

The blade sliced the air, falling on Meli's neck.

Kirwan blasted off his feet.

Spinning through the air, the faeman never reached the ground. He propelled up and slammed against the ceiling.

How? I shoved up and crawled to Meliora. Holding her close, I whipped around—searching for whoever was doing this. Was it the twins? The only two of three people in this home who still had magic?

"Gisela? Jaclan?" I called. "It's okay, faywens, you don't have to do this! Haeowen will take care of him, I'll—"

A figure stepped into the hall, shadows cloaking all but her legs and bare feet, but that was all I needed to see to stop my heart.

"Mama?" I rasped. "You're— You're—" *alive?* stuck in my throat.

Unseen hands seized me and Meli, and lifted us into the air. I swallowed a shriek of surprise as we flew over her head, and wound up behind her—protected by her.

"Mama, how are you doing this!" Meli cried.

Our mother didn't answer. She had one focus and one focus only. Dropping her fist, Kirwan slammed to the floor, his head bouncing off the wood.

"O... lene, wait—"

"Agh!" She twisted and he moved with her, flying into the opposite wall.

"Olene!" Blood wept from a dozen cuts and wounds on his horrible, hideous face. "Wait, stop, please! I didn't want it to come to this!"

Mama picked up his sword.

"None of this was my fault!"

One of the crystals on his lapel glowed. Mama snapped her fist back and they tore out of his many hiding places, bouncing across the floor—one of them hitting my slackened jaw.

"It wasn't me," he bellowed. "It was *her*! That demon child!"

I didn't have to ask to know he was speaking about me.

"She's the reason we could never be happy. I love you! I've always loved you, but she destroyed everything!" Kirwan strained and thrashed, his limbs pinned to the wall.

Mama halted before him, her back facing us. "I can promise you two things here today, Kirwan. I never loved you. You are the most despicable of men. Lower than a worm. Filthier than the scum-sucking bottom feeders found crawling through shit. I've hated you from the moment we met, and every day I prayed to Meya for your death. How could any woman love you?" she hissed. "You don't even love yourself. The only thing you've ever done right in your life is Meliora."

The delusional fool had the audacity to gape at her in slack-jawed surprise. "Olene, what are you saying? This isn't you. This is *her*! Ruining everything. Coming between us!"

"And my second promise," Mama continued on, raising her sword. "You will never hurt my children again."

I grabbed Meliora, covering her face with my body.

"Olene, don't—"

Mama's sword struck true—severing his head from his shoulders. It thudded on the ground, the bug-eyed look of surprise still on his face.

I held Meliora close, not letting her look. No matter how much she despised the man, she was only sixteen. I wouldn't have her watch her mother kill her father.

"Mama?" I croaked. "Are you okay?"

She didn't respond for throwing out her hands. Snapping them together, Kirwan's head flew off the ground and pinned back to the wall. "Eldur!"

The body burst into flames, smacking us over the head with heat. Greedily they consumed him, reducing the great and fearsome Kirwan Dawnbreaker to nothing but ash. She swept it out the door and slammed it shut with a cold efficiency that reminded me of something I often forgot. My mother went to war right alongside my father. She was never a wilting flower... and she never feared a monster.

"Mama?" I said softly. "Are... you okay?"

"Of course I'm okay, faywen, but I need you to check on the children."

"But—"

"Now."

Her tone brokered no argument. I loosened my grip on Meli standing up. My sister broke from me and ran to our mother, burying her face in her chest as she sobbed.

I left them be, knowing Meli was with the exact person she needed at that moment.

I continued on through the hall, calling for Jaclan and Gisela, but inside, my head was a wreck. Putting aside that my sister's father threatened her life, so he could steal our coin and kidnap me and my little sister, the mind-shattering shock was watching my mother perform magic.

How? I thought she was gone, but obviously she just fell into a frighteningly deep sleep. Or did she, somehow, pass away, but then Meya allowed her to return to us—save us—with her true and natural state returned?

"Jaclan—?"

"Yes?" Jaclan poked his head out of his room—whole, healthy, and curious. "Is Mama awake? Can I show her my drawing now?"

Slowly, I stuck my head inside. Gisela and Savia were inside too. Savia napped in her cot while Gisela sat at the small table Jaclan vacated, drawing her own picture for Mama.

"Haeowen?"

"Oh, yes," I said, pulling out of my thoughts. "Mama's in the front room. Go and show her your—"

Screams pierced the air, invading through the cracked window. "Faywens, take Savia and go to Mama now!" I ran to the glass and peered into the street.

I choked on a cry. "Alisdair?"

My love wasn't in the street, but faeriken were. I watched bug-eyed as the source of the scream raced through the alley, shrieking her head off as a pack of rhino faeriken charged her. I wrenched back just as they closed in on their target.

"What the fuck is going on!" *The faeriken were invading? Why would Alisdair do this? We had a plan. As far as I knew, no secret female assassins have slaughtered Salman in his bed, so why would he attack now?*

"Calli? Calli!" Meliora called. "What do we do?"

I took off, racing out of the room and making for the back entrance. "Stay inside!" I burst outside and shrieked, hugging my arms to my chest.

Cold! Oh fucking Meya, it was cold! A blast of freezing wind struck me, chattering my teeth.

The pack of rhinos had moved on, but they weren't the only ones. A monkey faeriken scaled the walls of the home across the street and jumped on the roof. He had to. Two leopard faeriken were on his tail—snarling and snapping at their lost prey from below.

Cries and howls drew my attention, making me run around our building to the alley. Three cat faeriken ripped off their clothes and pounced on each other. There was a cock in an ass, and another in a mouth before they hit the cobblestones.

Their noise startled a bird faeriken into taking flight.

I followed their path up, my eyes turning to the skies as the dark, heavy clouds rolled in—blotting out the horizon. The sun. The light. The warmth.

The world.

"Alisdair didn't launch the invasion," I whispered, lips numb from more than the cold. "And these—these people—" Slowly, I backed toward my door.

"Argh!" A group of fifteen, maybe twenty women charged down the street with a familiar face leading the pack.

"Mykel Starsinger," Shadi screeched. Her hawk eyes bulged in sync with her ruffled feathers. "This will teach you that no means no. Eldur!"

The mansion windows three doors down blew out—the very glass fleeing before the flames.

I bolted inside, slamming and locking the door. "They're not from Lumenfell," I cried. "The faeriken are Lyricans! They've been changed! The curse—"

"We know," said a calm, clear voice. "You did say that in Lumenfell, their ordeal frees them from the binding..."

Stiffly, achingly, I turned, and met my mother's now small, beady eyes and thick, furry face.

"I was skeptical," Mama continued, "but I confess, it feels a fair trade."

***

The three of us sat at the dining table.

The twins were there too, but Jaclan and Gisela were busy poking Mama's face and scurrying off giggling. She looked at them fondly, while she devoured an entire chicken.

"At least, they're not afraid of you," Meliora remarked in a small voice.

"Mama's fuzzy," Gisela shrieked in agreement.

"Are you afraid?" I asked Meliora.

She paused, then shook her head. "I think it would be wrong to be afraid. I mean, the—saved you, didn't it? It cured you of the wasting sickness."

"Almost immediately," Mama said around her gnawed chicken leg. "All I remember is being somewhere dark and warm, and then just like that, I was awake, the nausea was gone, my magic was thrumming under my skin, and I was hungry. *Starved.* Like I hadn't eaten in months."

"But now you're a...?" Meliora blinked at her. "What are you?"

"I'm not sure."

"Me either," I echoed.

"A koala." Gisela blew in, poked Mama, and scurried off again.

"How do you know?" I called after her.

"I just do."

Mama shrugged. "A koala. I've heard of those. They can only be found in Rajadom. I never thought my inner animal would be a creature I've never seen before."

"Why are you so calm about this?" Meliora burst out. "You're— All of Lyrica is—! Fae-beasts are running through the streets! It's the middle of the day, and it's pitch black outside! Why aren't you yelling, scream-ing, raging, something!"

Humming, Mama tipped her head, actually considering the ques-tion. "I think maybe koalas are calm creatures—"

"They are," Gisela assured, not slowing her whirlwind race with Ja-clan for a second.

"—because I feel panic, stress, and fear, but they're all very quiet voic-es in my head," she finished. "The only emotion screaming loudly is re-lief that my faywens are safe." Mama stroked Meli's cheek. "And love, my treasure. Always love."

Meliora calmed a bit. "What about me?" She looked at me. "Why haven't I changed? Or you? Or the twins? Or Savia?"

"The curse changes people in its own time." I hesitated, not wanting to say the rest. "And it already has you."

"What? What are you talking about?"

"Meli, haven't you noticed that you can't say cursed?"

She stared at me, brows wrinkled, then understanding dawned as quickly as her paling face. "Oh."

I reached for her hand. "The good news is that you'll get your magic back. That's exactly what we wanted."

Two heads swung to me. "We?"

"Well, yeah," I said, drawing back slightly. "The beast curse is the only thing known to break the bindings. I had to save you, Mama. And undo what was done to you, Meli. Done to every woman in Elva. Animals get to live free." I looked to my mother. "Why should we accept less?"

Mama sighed. "Your intentions were good, Calli, and I am very thankful that I'm alive, and you're all finally safe from Kirwan, but, my love, I very much doubt what's going on outside is what you planned."

I winced. Rising up, I went to the window and drew the curtains back. Somehow, the chaos outside had gotten even worse.

Smoke rose from multiple locations, telling of the numerous fires that fed them. Of those that weren't fucking passionately in the streets, the rest of the faeriken were fighting, clawing, snapping, and snarling at each other.

I winced when two fox faeriken bodily threw themselves through our neighbor's window, then came racing out loaded down with their looted treasures.

"Why are they avoiding our home?" Meliora asked. I hadn't noticed her come up behind me. "None of the mob or looters are even looking this way."

"Calli's father." Mama crossed to the larder and claimed the cheese and sausage. "It's why he left us this house, and why I would have no other. Protection runes were carved into every brick and cinder," she said. "I'm feeding them my magic to keep them strong, so I can't go with you, Calli."

"Go with me? Go with me where?"

"Outside," she replied, calm as could be. She immediately set about reducing her meal to ground-up bits in her newly awakened stomach.

"Mama, why on earth would I go out there?"

"Because it appears that koalas also have excellent hearing," she replied. "There's someone in the square right now—shouting, carrying on, and whipping up a mob to invade Wind and Wild."

"What!"

"She's saying that..." She tipped her head. "This is all the doing of Alisdair Shadowsoul, and if they want to save themselves and Elva, they must march on his castle and kill him now."

The world dropped out from under me. "But they can't! They don't—"

"Wait." My mother held up a hand. "There's more. She's saying—shouting—that killing him will be no difficult feat. All they need is a little purple flower? Is that right?" Mama screwed up her face. "Wait, yes. She definitely said flower. All right, all they need is a flower, and..."

"No, please—"

"...she has dozens of them."

"Dozens?" I cried. "How is that possible!"

My mother shook her head. "I can't say, but she is whipping the mob into a frenzy. I can't hear her anymore over the shouting and hollering for Shadowsoul's blood."

"But they can't do this." I rose on tiptoe, straining to see the square. "They have it wrong. We *all* have it wrong! Killing Alisdair won't break the curse. They're about to make everything worse, and take away the man I love with one horrible mistake!"

"Unless you stop them," Mama said firmly.

"Yes, yes," I breathed, running to the door, then back to the window, then to the door again. My mind spun in faster circles than I did. "How do I get there? I sent Bradach away. It takes two weeks to get to Lumenfell by carriage."

"Same for them too," Meliora reminded. "It's not like the mob can get to him tomorrow."

"The ones that fly can. The ones that have mastered speed and transportation magic can even faster than the rest."

She winced. "Oh, right— But, wait," she cried. "Mama has her magic back. Can't she put a transportation spell on you?"

I spun on my mother, expression hopeful, until her shaking head obliterated my smile. "Transportation spells are dangerous. A single mispronounced word, or badly written rune, and you appear a mile above your destination and fall to your death."

"What about a speed spell?" I asked.

"Those burn out quickly, my love. After fifty miles, someone would need to feed it more magic, and you can't. I'd just be stranding you fifty miles away."

"We have to think of something!"

"Why not go with the mod, Haeowen?"

Our conversation halted. Mama, Meli, and I turned to Gisela.

"What was that, sweetling?"

"The mod," she repeated. "Mama said all the angry people are going to the Wild place. If that's where you want to go, go with them." The little eight-year-old shrugged. "Just say you're angry too and they'll help you."

I opened my mouth, but nothing came out.

"Meya, take it, Gisela," Meliora cried. "Are you, like, a genius?"

Gisela burst into giggles. Grabbing her twin's hand, she tugged him out the door to play.

I blinked at the spot she was standing in. "We've been jokingly calling her a prodigy. I think it's time we stop joking."

Even Mama nodded, surprise shattering her koala calm. "She does have a point though. They must know they need numbers to take on Alisdair Shadowsoul. They won't have them if most of the mob is taking the slow path," she said. "They're likely figuring out a way to get everyone there. You need to be there when they do."

"Okay, okay, okay." I bounced on the balls of my toes, liking the plan more and more. "This makes sense. It's not ideal to get there at the same time as they do, but it'd be infinitely worse to get there two weeks *after*. And I know Lumenfell better than anyone in Lyrica. I know I can get to Alisdair first and warn him. Save him."

I halted mid-turn. "But wait— What about you, guys? Mama, how long can you give magic to the protection runes? At some point you have to sleep. And, Meli," I cried. "The curse has already taken you. I can't leave you to face the change alone. And—"

"Calli, stop." Mama rose up and grasped my shoulders. "My love, hear me and hear me well, you're officially relieved of the position of borrowed mother. I will take care of everything," she said gently, kissing my forehead. "So you go. Go and save your one true love and mate. You both have waited long enough."

"I..." My eyes filled. "I will. Thank you, Mama. I love you. All of you. I'll be back as soon as I can."

"We love you too, now go."

I didn't waste another minute.

Racing upstairs, I rescued all the weapons Alisdair gave me on the way out, slung the bow and quiver on my back, and then I ran back downstairs to the kitchen to get some more. Only when I positively clinked and jingled did I kiss Savia and the twins goodbye, then head out the door.

The streets were no better than they were before, but I kept low and out of the way of the chaos, racing to the square with one thought in mind—saving Alisdair.

I'm coming, my love. You've waited hundreds of years for someone to finally see the truth. Just wait a little longer.

The newly born faeriken ignored me. They were all too busy fucking, fighting, or unleashing pent-up rage on their enemies. Most of the people out on the street were women, and most of the bellowing victims they were chasing with rage in their eyes were men.

I rounded a corner, turning down an alley that was a shortcut to the square, and I saw the bloodied, clawed-up mass that used to be Mykel Starsinger. I didn't know if Shadi caught up to him, or if the other women he forced himself on did. Either way... he wouldn't be forcing himself on anyone else in the Burning Plains.

I backed away and went down another alley.

Up ahead the statue of King Salman loomed high over the darkened horizon, lit up by the fires burning in the square. He loomed, but not as high as he should—thanks to the stone head I skirted tripping out of the alley.

Someone knocked the thing clean off his inaccurately broad shoulders, and then they vented on the rest of him, blowing chunks of stone off his legs, arms, and abdomen. As angry as those gathered here were at Alisdair, it seemed a few of them knew who the true enemy was. Part of me wondered if any of them got their hands on the real thing.

But I couldn't ask... because the square was empty.

"No!" I whipped around, eyes huge in disbelief. "Already? How have they found a way to Lumenfell already!"

"Did you say Lumenfell?"

I jumped, backing away. A figure had appeared before me—a woman, I assumed, from her light, musical voice. But assume was all I could do. Something was wrong, I couldn't quite... look at her.

My gaze traveled in her direction, then flicked away, flicking on Salman's head or piles of tattered, bloodied clothes that would come with a horrible explanation. The most I could make out were the leather tips of her boots, and a flash of auburn hair. But truthfully, her hair color could've been a trick of the firelight.

"That's an impressive concealment spell," I stated, blunt as ever. "Those are supposed to be rendered useless when the caster draws attention to themselves. Hmm, just like in reality, I suppose."

She laughed. "One's magic is only as limited as the books they read and runes they know. Thankfully, I have never been limited."

I tried to study her as much as the corner of my eye would let me. "There were people here. They were planning to go to Wind and Wild. Where are they?"

"Wind and Wild of course."

I tensed, chest tightening around my thumping heart. *No! Alisdair!*

"But you didn't say Wind and Wild." She circled me, forcing my eyes to spin wildly in my head until I squeezed them shut. "You said Lumenfell. You've been there before."

It wasn't a question.

"Yes, I've been, and I'm trying to get back. Were you here when they left?" I asked. "Can you tell me how they did it?"

"I was here when they left, and I'm how they did it."

Alarms chimed in my head, clenching my teeth. Mama was very clear when she said the person whipping the mob into a frenzy was a *she*.

"The better question is who are you?" her voice whispered into my ear, making my skin crawl. "There is no rage or revenge in your soul, so what business do you have in Lumenfell? And don't lie. I do so hate being lied to."

"Why would I lie? I will happily say to your face, or next to it, that I need to get to Lumenfell to stop a mob of feral idiots who are about to make a huge mistake. Alisdair isn't a monster, he only looks like one, and the reason he does is because of a curse no one truly understood... until now," I said, voice shaking. "I know how to save him, Wind and Wild, and all of us from the beast curse, and that's exactly what the fuck I'm going to do!

"So get me there, right now, or I'll beat your ass, and trust me," I barked, "I don't need magic or sight to do it!"

Silence reigned in the square, broken only by shouts, screams, and booms in the distance.

The mysterious stranger hummed. "Well, when you put it like that, who am I to deny you?"

"Wait, what—"

"Good luck."

A swirling pool of silver and blue opened up beneath my feet, reflecting my blown brows and gaping mouth.

She laughed. "You'll need it."

"You—!"

I fell. Scream clogging in my throat, the ground pulled out from beneath me, ripping me away from the square, Lyrica, and that chilling *she*.

Tumbling through the air, I landed face-first into a bed of powdery cold. I shoved up, gasping—and immediately choked on the burning air.

"Smoke?" I staggered to my feet. "How..."

I ordered that woman to send me to Lumenfell, and sadly, that's exactly what she did. I stood at the mouth of the path of Bevin, gazing out at the beautiful, peaceful town of Lumenfell as it was consumed by flames.

Heavy clouds of acrid smoke blanketed the shadowed town, hazing the air and stinging my eyes. Everywhere I looked, there was fighting. Villagers fighting the attackers destroying their home. Soldiers battling the intruders in air and on land. All of it was horrifying, but none of it struck as much fear in my heart as the flowers.

Dozens— No, hundreds of purple flowers floating through the air, burning in the snow, littered on the street, or clutched in the hands of the mob.

"How?" I breathed. "How did they get all of—?"

A feather-faced man dragged a cat woman screaming out of her home. Howling, he raised his hand high—knife tip glinting in the firelight.

My arrow soared free, sinking in his throat.

Dropping the knife, he clutched his neck and collapsed—dead.

"Thank you," she sobbed. "Thank you so much."

"Of course." I accepted the thanks, saying nothing of the fact that I missed. I was aiming for his knife arm. "Get out of town," I ordered. "Get to safety."

Nodding hard, she ducked back inside her home, then came running back out with two furry-faced children under her arms and another hanging on her back. I covered her until they disappeared into the trees, and then I returned the arrow to my back.

Alisdair was a great teacher, but I wasn't a good enough shot to risk it again. The next time, I could hit the wrong person.

Not that I know who the right people are!

I winced, sweeping through the blinding flames and attacking smoke. All I saw were faeriken fighting faeriken. How was I supposed to know who the victims were?

And weren't they all victims? They're all trapped under an unforgiving curse and desperate to get out. They don't know another way but to fight who they wrongly believed is the enemy.

"Stop!" I screamed. "Stop this, please! You have it all wrong. This won't break the curse, but I can! I can put everything back to—"

"Argh!" Out of the corner of my eye, a gorilla man picked up a burning barrel, and readied to throw it on a familiar figure.

I burst into a sprint, tackling him around the waist just as he let go. "No!"

We tumbled head over feet on the snow and cobblestones, painfully crunching a different part of my body with each strike. The barrel soared through the air, crashing on Riordan.

"I hope he was your lover, whore!" The gorilla man guffawed. "Enjoy watching him burn!"

Roaring, I seized my dagger and smashed the butt into his skull—bouncing his head off the stone.

He flopped flat on the ground, not laughing anymore.

"Riordan? Riordan, no!" I dropped to my knees, sobs wracking my chest.

He was my friend. In the end, the truest friend I ever had. He saved my family not once, not twice, but three times. And his reward was to die under a burning pile of compost.

"Oh, Riordan, I'm so s-sorry. I was supposed to save you. I was supposed to save all of—"

"Calli?"

I choked, blinking through the haze as the smoldering mound of fruit peels moved.

"Calli, is that you?" The trash blew off him. Riordan rose up, clutching a crystal in his hand. "What are you doing here? Wait— Did you come with them?" he barked, shouting at me for the first time in our life. "I can't believe you, Calli! Someone tells you faeriken are monsters and you just believe them? You used to be someone who judged based on action, not reputation! Fucking shame on you—"

"Riordan, can you save the scolding on prejudice for after I save my husband and everyone here from the beast curse, and no, I'm not going to do it by hurting anyone." I got to my feet, swiping away my tears. "This curse was born of hate. More hate was never the answer."

"You're going to what?" All of the angry bluster whooshed out of him. "And who is your husband?"

"Alisdair, obviously."

He blinked at me. "I've missed something very important, haven't I?"

"Yes, and it can all be summed up with this—body-switching spell."

Understanding dawned even as his eyes bugged. "So the whole time... it was you."

"Yes, but we don't have time to get into the details," I shouted over the melee. "There are flowers everywhere! If the mob gets to Alisdair, they'll be able to hurt him. Kill him! We can't let that happen. You have to help me get to him first."

"What can I do?"

I pointed at his crystal. "You can use magic. I can't. Just help me get to the castle, and I'll take it from there." I made to run, then stopped. "Wait, is your wife safe?"

"She's visiting her family in the Yararill Caves, and thank Meya for that."

"Then let's make sure you get back to her. We'll stick together, yes? Have each other's backs?"

He snorted. "I learned a long time ago that the safest place is by your side, Volka. Let's go save Lumenfell."

No more talk was needed. We took off for the trees, trying to avoid the crush as much as possible. Skirting around the outer edge of the village, Castle Riagin loomed over the horizon—swaying through the stinging, teary haze of smoke.

Flying figures surrounded it—pummeling the windows, walls, and doors with fire spells. But just as many flying figures faced them with weapons of magic and bronze—the proud uniform of the Lumenfell Army on their backs.

"Hold out a little longer," I whispered. "I'm coming."

"Riordan, what happened?" I called to him. He ran from my left side to my right and back to my left, keeping an eye out for anything that might come from the light, or the dark. "It's taken centuries for the curse to bleed over the borders of Quatassa and Sarabai, but now it rips across two thousand miles and transforms half the people in Lyrica within a week? I asked Treasa to trigger the spread, but I didn't expect this!"

"I don't know who Treasa is, but I do know what happened on the day the temperature in Lumenfell dropped a life-crushing fifty degrees, and the sky grew so dark, not even the orblights could brighten our days."

"What?" I asked, keeping my dagger out in front of me as I ran. "What happened?"

"The kingdom received word that Queen Emiana, ruler of Wind and Wild, had died."

I tripped. Stumbling over a tree root, I pitched forward—knife flying out of my hand. Dazed, the pain took longer to reach me, because his words had first.

"Dead?! Alisdair thinks I'm dead? Why?"

"I don't know, Calli, it's just what we were told. All of Lumenfell has been in mourning for days, and then today, the sky just opened up and..." He gazed out at his burning home. "They attacked."

"Oh no," I cried. "We need to get to Alisdair now!"

I raced off leaving Riordan to follow.

"Get him!"

"Kill them!"

"Shadowsoul did this to us!"

We burst out of the trees beside a burning home. Broken glass crunched under our boots, the shattered remains of the greenhouses I so admired. Was it really me who walked side by side with Alisdair, beaming so wide my face hurt while he led me through the greenhouse that was to be mine? It was hard to remember being so happy while everyone and everything I came to know and love... burned.

"He turned us into beasts! He's robbed us of the sun and stars, forcing us to root around in the muck and dark like pigs while he sits on a throne of gold!"

"That's not true," I burst out, charging around the cover of building. "You have everything all wrong! Alisdair didn't curse you! He didn't curse anyone! He's the one who—"

I rushed into the street, and locked eyes with Meallan.

He stood before the raging, torch-carrying mob wearing clothes. Not just any clothes, but light, breezy, colorful breeches and a silk shirt—the style of Lyricans. In that second, I knew.

"You," I hissed, lips peeling back from my teeth.

Meallan looked at me, then flicked away—turning his back on me completely. He didn't have a clue who I was.

"Today we fight back!" he hollered, sending the mob into a frenzy. Behind them, a wall of wolves clashed with the Lumenfell soldiers, ever obedient to their alpha. "We take back Lyrica! We take back Elva! We free our home from the scourge of Alisdair Shadowsoul!"

"Yeah!"

"Take the flowers, everyone!" Meallan presented the delicate, purple flower crushed in his grip. "Rub it over your fists and weapons. Weave it into your magic. It will protect us, and kill him!"

"Yeah!"

"No!" I screamed against the wind—a lone voice in a raging sea.

"Attack!" Meallan shouted.

They charged the drawbridge, the most unnatural sight with beautiful flowers in their hands, and hate etched into their faces.

"Don't do this!" I ran out in front of them and was roughly hauled back.

Riordan snapped me to his chest, throwing us both out of the way of the stampede.

"Riordan, the mark!"

"Was on Emiana's body, not yours," he finished, helping me up.

I slapped my forehead. "Of course, you're right. That means he can't scent that I'm right here. Fuck's sake, he thinks I'm dead and—"

The mob threw everything they had, magical and physical at the castle doors. Palace guards dropped down or charged around the structure to meet them, but the wolves were coming from everywhere. Pouring out of the forest, overwhelming the town, leaping on fleeing villagers and tearing out their throats. They were Meallan's army.

"That stupid, bitch-ass pup is using more trickery and manipulation to steal Alisdair's throne, and his li-fe!" I spun to meet two wolves who broke off from the pack, bounding straight for us. I earthed two vials from my pocket. Lobbing them overhead, they flew true—smashing on the wolves' faces.

They yelped, skidding to hard stops. Shrieking and whimpering, they frantically batted at their faces trying to get the stuff off.

Dropping on all fours, they turned tail and ran as fast as their hands and legs could carry them.

"What was that!" Riordan goggled at me, the crystal he'd been about to use hovering in the air. "How did you do that!"

"You can do it too." I shoved three vials in his hands. "Now, move!"

I sprinted for the drawbridge, then veered sharply left—jumping off the edge to the frozen lake below.

"Artisa!"

Magic washed over me—warm like the rush of dipping your toe in a hot, steaming bath. I lifted into the air, flying over the angry mob. "That's it, Riordan! Higher!"

Yes, finally! Once Riordan sets me down in the outer gardens, I'll find Alisdair and set everything right. I know this castle better than anyone. All of its secrets and hidden corners. All I have to do is—

"Die, stunted scum!"

A hard force slammed into me, vaulting me out of the sky.

"Calli, no!"

I plummeted to the ground. My head collided with hard, unforgiving, frozen earth.

Darkness claimed me.

***

"What were their names?"

Alisdair leaned against the glass, tearing apart a pilfered apple, and watching me tend to its brothers and sisters.

"Caitriona, Ashling, and Nora." A soft smile withered away the sharp edges of his features. A smile I only saw when he spoke of his children. "All so different, but in many ways, the same."

I packed in the muddy dirt, loving the feel of living earth squishing through my fingertips. "What were your days like? Were they like this? Did you watch your girls do all the work with the horses while you kicked back munching on apples?"

Alisdair chuckled. "I'll have you know I did all the work. My faywens told grand tales every morning of all the help they'd be to me, and then Nora would spend all her time petting, grooming, and riding her favorite horse. Ashling, my dreamer, chased butterflies through the field, and Caitriona... well, she would sing." He shook his head, laughing softly. "Like you, she had a beautiful voice."

I blushed like the silly mare I was.

"Her crooning could calm the wildest stallions. Looking back, those are the days I miss the most. Not the carefree days of my youth, or causing trouble with Bradach, or galloping across the plains with the herds.

"I miss the common days where nothing really happened, because it didn't have to. I didn't need any more love or adventure than being with Raelina and my girls."

I ducked my head, not wanting him to see me cry.

"That'll be what I miss most about you."

"What?" I frowned, raising my chin. "What do you mean?"

"When immortality takes me away from you like it has everyone I've loved, I won't miss the days you bit me, rolled in manure, or announced to the court I have a hairy growth on my cock that's bigger than my cock itself."

I snorted, bursting into giggles.

"I'll miss this," he said, smiling that smile. "Listening to you sing while you play in the dirt."

I both laughed and rolled my eyes. "You won't miss me, my love. We didn't start together, but we'll end together. That I promise you."

"...promise..." I rasped. "Alisdair..."

I peeled my eyes open, vision spinning.

Pain assaulted me—roaring through my head and ripping out a groan. Every part of me from my head to the bottom of my feet ached. I lost my boots in the fall. Whipping winds beat and froze my bare feet. How long was I gone from this world? Strolling in a land of daydreams while the world fell apart around me?

Somehow I pushed up to my knees, clutching my head. In the distance, I heard clanging swords and the rage of battle.

"I'm... not too late." I tried to stand and pitched to the side, my aching head spinning the world upside down. "Alisdair... I'm coming."

Flipping over, I screamed.

Riordan draped over the snowbank, blood staining his perch red. Long, vicious gashes raked lengthways on his chest—not the slash of a wolf, but the mangling of a falcon. Riordan tried to protect me from the flying faeriken who knocked me out of the sky. Her, or one of her comrades.

To the end, my friend saved me.

"Oh, Riordan, I'm sorry." I threw myself on him, my heart cracking in half. "You're a new husband. You have a baby on the way. Now you'll never get to see your child's face, all because of me. Ahhh!" I screamed, frustration strangling me. "Why was I so stupid? Why didn't I realize how to break the curse sooner!"

"Cal... li..."

I shot up, gaping at his fluttering eyes.

"...help..."

I sprung into action. Ripping the hem of my dress, I bound his chest with the strips, grasped his arm, and heaved him onto my back.

The weight of him bent me in half. Gritting my teeth, I took a step, then another, then another. "It's... going to be okay. I'll get you help, my friend." The gaping hole where the palace doors used to be beckoned me forward. "I promise."

I stumbled over the threshold and clamped hard on my lip, holding back a cry.

Talulla beheld me with unseeing eyes. My little, quiet taste-tester, who was saved the same night as I when I refused the poisoned meal and decided to eat with the rest of the court. Turned out I only saved her for a few more weeks, only for her to meet her end with a sword driven through her chest—pinning her to the wall.

Tears soaked my face as I forced myself on, refusing to look in the faces of the guards resting still and quiet at my feet. "Healer! Healer Soul-stitcher!" I called. "Someone! Anyone, help!"

Creeping around the corner, Riordan and I fell down the stairs to-gether—following the roar and misery of fighting. If the healers were go-ing to be anywhere, it'd be in the middle of the battle.

"You're not dying today, Riordan!"

He groaned.

"That's right. Keep talking." I clung tight to the banister, straining to keep us upright. One slip and we'd tumble to our deaths—for good this time. "Tell me about the baby. Have you thought of names yet?"

"...ric..." he wheezed.

"Gilric? Oh, yes, Gilric. After your father. That's a great name for a boy." I injected my dry, raspy voice with all the enthusiasm I could muster. "A strong, warrior's name. What about for a girl?"

"C-C-C-... Cal...li."

The corner of my mouth tugged into a trembling smile. "Really?"

He grunted. "Fuck no, keva... it'll be... Keelin."

I let out a short, sharp bark of laughter, igniting shaking chuckles in Riordan.

Good. If he's laughing, he's alive.

I climbed off the final step. The sound of breaking glass muffled under—

"ARGGHH!"

"Alisdair?" I lurched into the throne room, and there he was.

Aeris, Eadaoin, Bradach, Foalan, and the big, hairy, hulking beast that was the love of my life held a shrinking line against the fray.

My friends were bleeding, sweating, and gasping—all of them fighting to beat back the mob, and destroy the flowers they so eagerly wielded against Alisdair. But some were slipping through.

Alisdair bled from dozens of cuts. He was huge, but not as big as he could be. He was terrifying, but his fangs weren't as sharp. His claws not as long. He was weakening, and somewhere in the chaos, Meallan was waiting for the right moment to finish him off.

"Agh!" The Lyricans surged, slamming into Foalan's hastily erected barrier.

Both sides were pushed back with Aeris and Eadaoin tripping over the dais.

"Help," I shouted, addressing the jumping, screeching stragglers bringing the rear of the mob.

No one bothered to turn around.

"He's dying! We need help!" I swiped at someone's arm, and they swiped back—nearly knocking me off my feet. "We're Lyricans," I burst out. "We followed you to aid the noble cause of saving Elva, and now one of our own is dying!"

Two, three, half a dozen scrunched, glaring faces turned our way.

"Help me save him," I demanded, "or you're no better than the dead-inside animals you're trying not to become!"

It took a beat, but two of the faces stopped glaring. They moved in our direction.

"Calli? Riordan?" Suddenly strong hands lifted him off my back.

I blinked at her. "Shadi?"

"Oh, Meya, look at him," Shadi hissed, feathers ruffling. "Of course I'll help. I used to be good at healing spells," she said, carrying him outside the door and away from the fighting. "I'll do what I can for him, while *you*"—her face hardened—"help them kill that beast."

I just nodded.

Only when I saw her begin the healing spell, did I turn away, and ram my shoulder against the wall of bodies. "Down with Shadowsoul! Down with the faeriken!"

I shouted my nonsense, shoving through the crowd, and they parted way. Seeing a *normal* fae, hearing my chant—they let their sister-in-arms by, and chanted with me.

"Down with the faeriken! Down with Shadowsoul!"

I made it to the front, my soul coming alive to finally be near him. "Alisdair!"

Foalan's barrier collapsed. No less than seven magical blasts sped through the air, hitting Bradach all at once. He plummeted to the floor, and Foalan reacted on instinct. Spinning, his hands shot toward his falling friend—the crystals sewn on his sleeves glowing.

The stampede surged up the dais, slamming into Foalan's back and trampling him. Bradach crashed onto my throne, tipping it over on top of him.

He didn't get up.

"No!" Aeris and I screamed.

The mob descended on Alisdair—kicking, punching, tearing, stabbing, and attacking with their stolen purple flowers.

My love disappeared under the mass of bodies.

"Stop it! You don't know what you're doing! This isn't how to break the curse!"

"She's right," someone shouted. "This won't break the curse."

"Yes!" Hope soared as I fought harder, shoving through the crush and flying limbs. "Leave him be and I'll—"

"We need his worthless rotting heart to save Elva!" shouted that voice. "I bet the beast will be more open to sharing its location when he's short a few fingers!" A sword lofted high over the bobbing heads, and fell in a swift arc.

"Arrggh!" Alisdair roared, shredding my heart.

Boom!

The floor heaved, exploding us off our feet. The entire mob blew off Alisdair, taking me with them. I whipped through the air, screaming as the cold, hard stone rose up to meet me.

"Gotcha!" Hands seized me under the arms, yanking me up just in time. "Don't worry, my lady. I've got it from here."

Bright, iridescent wings fluttered on Aeris's back, so beautiful and radiant, I couldn't look at them for too long without being dazzled like the sun.

The curse hadn't given her wings yet, so of course, the resourceful, unstoppable Aeris made her own.

She dropped me down beside Alisdair. He slumped against his throne—broken and bleeding. Gaping wounds covered his mangled, twisted beast form.

I fell on him, taking his face in my hands. "Alisdair? My love, can you hear me?"

"What are you doing, girl!"

I twisted around. Groaning and bruised, Alisdair's would-be assassins staggered to their feet.

"Kill him before he rises! The blade is right there!"

"No!" shouted another voice. "We must torture him. Get him to tell us where the heart is, then we kill him."

"The heart is here! It must be. This pit is a trove of stolen and looted treasure," argued someone else. "After he's dead, we'll search until we find it. But we kill him now!"

I listened with half an ear. "Alisdair, please, wake up." I patted his grizzled cheeks. "I finally figured it out, love. I know how to save you, but you have to wake up. Look at me, please!"

He stirred.

"Alisdair!"

A single, swollen eye peeled open. His red, bottomless orb swept my face... and he smiled. "Calli," he rasped. "Thank you."

"What? Why are you thanking me?"

"I wanted your face... to be the last thing I see."

My chest squeezed. "It won't be the last, and it won't be today."

"Calli, look out!"

A blur roared out of the corner of my eye. The brutal thud of bodies colliding forced me upright—standing between Alisdair and whoever dared to think they were going to take him from me.

Eadaoin tumbled head over heels with him. Landing hard on his back, Meallan got his feet between their bodies and propelled her off—throwing her clear into the heart of the mob.

"Stay back," Meallan growled. He raised his one clawed hand, ever lethal even without its twin. "There is no discussion. There is no argument. I know exactly where Shadowsoul has hidden his heart. He needn't be alive for one more second, so tonight, I finish this."

"Yeah!" they sounded off. "Huzzah! Huzzah!"

The furry, scaled, clawed, winged, and beady-eyed Lyrican fae-beasts were a living mass—surging forward and back as one. I sensed their eagerness to storm upon the dais and finish Alisdair off, but they halted before their leader, trusting him to finish this like they trusted him to get them this far.

Fishing out one of my vials, I threw it at Meallan. It shattered at his feet, splashing on his foot and pant leg.

He arched a brow. "What is wrong with you? Get out of the way, girl!"

"No." Breathing hard, I took my stance. The dagger Alisdair gifted me clutched in one hand, and a vial in another. "You're not touching him, Meallan. You can whip up as many mobs and spell-addle as many kitchen maids as you like, but you'll never win. You'll never be king.

"To the end of your days, you'll always be the cowardly little pup who was too shit-down-his-legs scared to face Alisdair when he's not on his back."

His eyes flashed, lips peeling back in a snarl. "Who are you?"

"You know who the fuck I am, bitch." I threw another vial, ripping out a furious growl when it broke on his chest. "I'm the queen of Wind and Wild."

If I expected a gasp, or shout, or any reaction whatsoever... I didn't get it.

"Enough of this," he drawled. "Move aside."

He flicked his wrist and I went flying, crashing into Aeris. I flailed—just managing to untangle myself and sit up as Meallan conjured a bronze blade ringed with purple flowers, and plunged it in Alisdair's gut.

"No! Stop it!" Frantically I emptied my pockets, flinging vial after vial at him—bellowing my throat ragged. "Get away from him!"

One of the vials shattered over his eye, slicing his brow apart. He jerked, driving the sword deeper. "Fuck it to Meya, someone kill that bitch already!"

Half the cheering, celebrating mob came to life and surged toward me.

They tripped over themselves coming to an abrupt standstill.

Pure, unadulterated fear filled my heart, and theirs. Turning away from me, they faced the throne room entrance... and screamed.

"My lady!" Aeris seized and hauled me back, getting me out of the way as half the Lyricans trampled, stomped, and shoved each other running for the village entrance. Over their heads, five—seven—thirteen—twenty Taken stalked into the room.

"Wait— No!" Meallan cried. He sniffed himself and his eyes bugged. "NO!"

"That's right," I sang, smirking more wickedly than my husband ever could. "Linseed, rosehip, and suet, wolf bitch. Just for you. You really shouldn't have given me that tip." I laughed in his bulging, stricken eyes. "Or you should've been as smart as your other wolf friends, and run when you saw me coming." I threw another vial at him, making Meallan roar to blow my eardrums out. "At least I won't have to tell you twice."

He ran.

Streaking past me, Meallan shot out of the village entrance, leading a snarling, charging horde of Taken like a dangled apple before a horse.

His howls faded in the distance.

"Should I go after him?" Aeris gritted. "Make sure they kill him."

A groan sounded to my right.

"Someone else needs you more."

"Bradach," she cried, abandoning her queen, her duty, and her games—and racing to his side. But Aeris wasn't nearly as fast as me.

I fell next to Alisdair, and grabbed my dagger. "Alisdair? Alisdair, can you hear me? Don't you give up on me!" His eyes fluttered at my shout, but I could feel it. He didn't have much time. "Alisdair, come on, please. Don't you want to know how I figured it out?" I cried desperately, tears clogging my throat. "It was something Gisela said when she saw my bracelet. She called it a charm, but it's not. It's a jewel. A black stone. My sister had no reason to reduce a glittering, expensive jewel to a little trinket... unless it looked like something different to her."

I brought my hilt down, smashing it on the jewel. Alisdair grunted.

"That's right, love," I said, seizing on any semblance of conversation. I had to keep him talking.

I had to give him reason to hold on.

"I almost figured it out that night when Meallan tried to kill us in the woods. He said he had to stop you destroying the cursed heart, so that you could love me back." *Bang! Bang! Bang!* "If he said that's how you break the curse, then that's exactly how you *don't* fucking do it.

"He's under the beast curse. He can't speak about it, and he definitely can't speak about how to end it, so where did he get that from? Where did we all get that from? For centuries, this lie has spread through the kingdoms—fed by guesses that became rumor that became truth."

"Cal...li..."

"I'm here, Alisdair. I'm here, and I finally understand." I sensed them approach. Felt the weight of dozens of curious eyes, but no one rushed us or attacked.

They were listening.

"That day, when you faced Constance on a burning battlefield, you didn't create the beast curse," I gritted, lips twisting. "She did.

"Her very soul is a curse. An evil, horrid thing that sucks the light, and the warmth, and the joy, and the faemanity from everyone and all. That terrible, rotten thing that puts everyone around it through the same pain it goes through. Constance turned herself into the worst kind of beast to have love and power, so what do we who fall under its influence become?"

"Beasts," someone whispered.

Bang! Bang! Bang! "You didn't know that would happen when you ripped her soul out of her chest. But when you realized, you did the only thing you could, and ripped out your own."

"What?" Aeris cried, helping Bradach to his feet. "What are you saying?"

"I'm saying Alisdair never ripped out his heart. His heart never had anything to do with this, because it's been here the whole time." I paused only briefly, resting my hand on his scar. "It's there, but it's not beating. The body is just a vessel." *Bang! Bang!* "For the soul."

"Wait, wait," someone cried. It sounded like Shadi. "I don't get this. It doesn't make any sense."

"It does make sense. Constance was a soul eater, and her soul never stopped. The final stage of the beast curse isn't turning into an animal. It's losing your soul. Alisdair ripped out his and protected it, so that he could never reach that stage," I said. "Over the centuries, the beast curse has ravaged and maimed him beyond recognition, but he retained his mind. He protected his true self. And he never stopped waiting for the sun to return."

"But how... do you know all of this?" Foalan swayed on his feet.

"I know because Alisdair told me."

Scoff. "Make sense, girl!" another voice put in. "You just said if he told you, then it's not truth, because he can't speak of his affliction."

"What he did to Constance isn't the affliction," I snapped. "It's what she did to him that is. You can exploit the rules of a curse if you're clever, like telling a princess the names of your family, so you hold on to them just long enough."

Whispers broke out behind me. They didn't understand that last comment, and they didn't need to.

"Alisdair could tell me about a horrible woman and the misery she spread everywhere she went. But he couldn't tell me that misery took his soul, and turned him into a beast. Even so, he gave me the final piece of the puzzle, hoping my slow wits would put it together. Argh!" I belted, hitting the stone harder. "How the curse came to be, and how to break it."

"Do you know how to break it!" a voice shouted.

"Of course, I do."

Alisdair's lips moved. I couldn't hear him over the clamoring, but I thought he whispered, *I love you.*

"Well, it'd be more honest to say your soul gave me the final pieces. Hanging off my wrist, it beat that deceptive heartbeat in my ear when I thought fondly of you, pondered you, lusted after you, and loved you." I laughed softly. "All the while, it was banging the truth into my head.

"If hatred ripped out your soul and turned you into a beast"—I cracked the jewel in half—"then only love could give it back. And I do, Alisdair." Gathering the broken black diamond, I blew on it—sending all of my love with it.

"I love you too."

Glowing, golden wispy tendrils rose from the jewel that wasn't a jewel—enveloping his fur-matted limbs, curved fangs, black snout, and long, fuzzy ears.

His eyes snapped open.

"Alisdair? Alisdair!"

He shot into the air, toppling the throne and hovering above it. The glow swirled around him—faster and faster. Glowing brighter and brighter.

I reached for him, then clapped my hands over my eyes—crying out. *Too bright!*

Alisdair burned as bright as the sun itself. He was the sun itself.

Warm and protecting. Harsh and steadfast. The same sun that nourished the flowers in the meadow, scorched the desert soil. He was maddening like long, summer days that beat on your neck while you wished for clouds and rain. He was brilliant like those same summer days—spent laughing and splashing in the river with your siblings.

Like the sun, his soul was always there, always protecting me, always guiding me, always loving me. Even if some days, the clouds came between us. Alisdair never left me.

"Little bird." He kissed me, trapping my gasp.

And he never would.

Hot, fiery, and passionate—our tongues tangled, battled, and curled around the other, no part of us ever wanting to let go. I moaned, throwing my arms around him. Alisdair, Alisdair, Alisdair! He was finally mine.

We broke apart, grinning into each other's eyes. Our real eyes.

The real him.

"No horns," I whispered. "No claws. No fangs. I did it."

My love was whole and handsome. He once told me I would've fainted if I saw him as he was, and Meya, take me, I swayed on my feet—stunned not by the beauty of his perfectly sculpted face, but the way his true and genuine smile transformed it.

"I can't believe I really saved you."

His gaze traveled over my head. "Not just me."

Foalan touched his handsome face—again and again. No matter how many times he did, the fur and snout didn't come back.

Bradach spun in circles searching for the wings on his back. *Gone.*

"Eadaoin?" A tall, muscled soldier broke through the pack of joyous, tearful people, and stopped in front of a young woman with smooth skin, a pert nose, and full lips. "Wow," he breathed. "You are... hideous without fur."

"What! Keefe!"

Bursting into guffaws, he swept her up, spinning her off her feet. "I jest, my love. You're the most beautiful creature I've ever seen. And you always were.

"Marry me."

Eadaoin hid her face in his chest. That didn't stop me seeing her beaming smile. "Maybe," she purred. "If a better offer doesn't come along."

"It worked." I shrieked in delight, jumping up and down. "And—Wait!" I spun on Shadi. "Do you still have your magic?"

Twinkling, colored sparks burst out of her hand. "I would say so."

"What about Riordan? Where is he?"

"Don't worry. True healers came halfway through and took over. They heard someone screaming for help," she said. "He's going to be okay."

"Of course he is." I threw myself in Alisdair's arms. "Because nothing can go wrong on such a perfect day. Make it more perfect by telling me everyone, everywhere, is truly free of the beast curse?"

"They are, Calli. All of Elva." He nipped the tip of my nose—naughty to the last. "I've taken so much of her power within me, I gave more power to the beast curse infecting me. I fed it. I helped it spread. But of course, if I was the cause, I was also the solution. Freeing me from the curse freed everyone."

Happy as I was, I shuddered. "But what about the rose?" I whispered. "Shouldn't we get rid of it now? It's still a soul-sucking leech. It's not safe to keep around, even if it's locked in a tower."

"I've wanted to every single day," he returned, keeping his voice low. "But I couldn't until the binding spell was reversed for every woman in Elva. Until everything she destroyed was put right. I needed her power for such a massive undertaking, and well..." He gazed around. "It's almost done."

"Almost?"

He captured my chin between two fingers. "Are you unbound?"

I shook my head. "Come to think of it, I don't know if it freed Meli yet."

"Then the work isn't done. The good thing is now we know how to trigger the beast curse, and how to end it. You," he whispered, stroking my cheek. "As long as your love protects my soul, the snow will always melt. The darkness will forever lift."

"Alisdair," I whispered, eyes swimming.

"If any woman out there is still bound, she need only come to us to be freed. We can control the curse now. We can—"

"Make it so no woman in Elva is ever bound again," I finished. "And if they are, we can give them their life back." I sighed, eyes drifting to the ceiling. "I just wish we didn't have to keep that thing around to do it."

"Constance has done nothing but spread evil and hate since she set foot on our land. Now she'll finally do good for the people of Elva." He smirked. "Which is what the deluded, would-be tyrant wanted, so what a fitting way for her to spend eternity."

I laughed. "Sounds good to me." I rose on tiptoe, eager for more of his lips on mine.

"Well done, well done." A voice turned our puckered mouths toward the door. "You did even better than I knew you would, my lady."

I stared at the woman, having no idea who she was, until six small baby cots floated through the air after her.

"Treasa?" I blurted.

She spun on her heels. "That's me. I don't normally acknowledge the part I played, but I have to say, I cried when the curse saved your mother. Life has pulled you all apart so many times, it tore my heart out that Meya should take her from you again."

"Umm..." I blinked at her. "I don't understand."

"I do," Alisdair growled. He was no longer a beast, but the threat was no less ferocious. "She did this."

"Did this?" I repeated. "Did what?"

"I planted items marked with the Wind and Wild crest in your mother's home, knowing that monstrous man would—well, do something monstrous."

My jaw dropped. "You did what?!"

"I did as ordered, my queen. As your humble servant, I—" One of the babies started fussing. "Oh, hold on." Treasa floated their cot around, and picked the little one up—bouncing her in her arms. "Hmm. Where was I— Oh, yes! I got your mother and sister sentenced to execution because I had to give you a real reason to leave Lumenfell and Alisdair's side," she dropped—calm as could be.

"I noticed that after Raelina died, the curse worsened. It ripped through the land quicker than ever, and bled over the borders of Quatassa and Sarabai. Which is of course why I had to convince my lord that you died too."

My eyes bugged wider with every word. "Treasa!"

"Yes, yes, I was surprised too by how quickly his despair spread like plague," she mused. "You are his one true mate, my lady. Never doubt that."

My mind twisted into knots putting the scale of her manipulation together. "You! It was you in the square! You sent the mob here?"

"Nope, that was my daughter. Firstborn," she explained. "She was born six hundred years ago, and has lived with her father outside of Lumenfell, and the curse. My first husband also hid and protected her, so she'd never be forcibly bound. Fortunate for she grew into a prodigy. She claimed the gift I gave her, and then surpassed me. Truly, she is a wonder.

"Anyway," she breezed, still sounding like we were having a fun conversation about Elvan beaches. "I told her she had to keep sending people until she was sure she sent you. Thankfully, you caught on quickly."

"And the flowers?" Alisdair barked. "How did you get so many of them!"

"Those flowers can pop up farther than you know when you perform great magics, my lord. Whenever you missed one, or more, I helped myself." She shrugged. "Never knew when it may come in handy, and this time it did." She beamed. "Lit a fire under our lady and she—voila!—broke the curse! Huzzah, huzzah! What a great day for Elva."

Every soul in the room gaped at her in disbelief.

"Treasa," I said slowly. "I don't think I like you very much."

She laughed heartily. "I did ask you if you were willing to accept the consequences of spreading the curse faster. I do regret the lives that were lost today," she said, losing her smile. "I never wanted that, nor do I take it lightly, but freedom is everything. There is no life without it. So, thank you, Queen Callidora Cursebreaker, High Lady of Wind and Wild. You saved us all. Long may you reign."

"I—"

"Queen Callidora Cursebreaker." Foalan dropped to his knees. "I pledge my fealty to you. Long may you reign."

"Foalan, you don't have to—"

"Queen Callidora Cursebreaker, I pledge my fealty to you. Long may you reign," Bradach grunted out. "I won't kneel, if you don't mind, keva. Can't inflate that ego too much."

Bradach never ceased to send my eyes rolling.

"Queen Callidora Cursebreaker."

"Queen Callidora Cursebreaker."

All over the room, everyone dropped to their knees, and pledged their respect and loyalty to *me*. The poor girl from the Gutter. The stolen princess. The queen of nothing.

The cursebreaker.

Amidst it all, Treasa ducked out of the village entrance—floating her babies behind her. She sent me one last wink as she disappeared.

"Um... I..." My jaw stuck forming words as I turned back. "Call me Calli?"

Alisdair laughed. "How could they call you anything else, my beauty?" He planted a searing kiss on my lips, scrambling my mind. "My little bird, my nightmare, my queen. My wife."

"Till the end, my love. Forever and always."

"Aww, now isn't this a pretty portrait."

I froze. *That voice. I know that voice...*

A figure crossed the threshold. "But you're kneeling before the wrong person. I am your queen," Emiana announced, smiling upon us all. "It is me who will have your undying fealty for forever and a day, as your high empress."

"Meya, take it!" Alisdair shouted, shoving me behind him. "What are you doing!"

His shock was real and necessary. It wasn't the surprise of the long-lost princess. It was what she held in her hands.

Emiana clutched the glass case to her chest, and within it, the glowing, dark rose.

"Put that down! Get away from it!" Alisdair bellowed.

"Hmm, I think not, husband." Emiana's smile was nasty. "Why would I do that when this tangled ball of ivy is going to give me everything I want—"

"Stop prattling and find me," someone snapped. "Find me!"

I frowned. Peering around Alisdair, I searched for the owner of the voice.

"I want to thank you, little whore." Emiana fixed on me. "You were only supposed to be a little distraction that gave me time to search for the soul in peace, as well as saving me from the bed of a beast, but then you did so much more!" She laughed—delighted with her fucking self.

"You broke the bindings and destabilized every town, village, and city from Quatassa to Sarabai. It's total upheaval, and what they all need now, is for their true queen to rise to her throne. I will bring order." Her smile tinged around the edges. "On my father's bones, I will rise higher than a son of his ever could."

"—me," someone shouted. "Find me now!"

Who is that? Where is that coming from?

"Aww." Emiana mockingly pouted. "You look confused, little whore. Need me to explain it all? In simple words you can understand?"

Alisdair growled, launching off the dais at her. I shot in his path, holding him back. "Don't," I hissed. "Something isn't right. She's goading us for a reason."

"Oooh, well, aren't you the clever one." Emiana was losing her sweet tone fast. "So clever, you tricked yourself into thinking you earned everything I handed you! Wealth, riches, power, magic, and the handsome king falling at your feet. All of this belongs to me! Their fealty belongs to me. Get off my throne, whore! You won't be told twice!"

"I won't need to be told twice, but I'll tell you once, nothing here belongs to you," I said lightly. "You're not very subtle, Emiana. And even if you were, it was all right here." I tapped my temple. "In your head. You spoke about running away with your true love, and living a simple, quiet life in a cottage in Rajadom. But those thoughts were never in your mind. *Kaelan* was never in your cesspool of a mind. He was so insignificant, he never came up at all.

"Not like your hatred for your father, or your obsession with taking back the power he ripped away from your mother, and then from you. I had a feeling we'd be seeing you sooner rather than later, but this!" My calm broke gesturing at Constance's mangled soul. Just its nearness sucked the warmth from the room "That's the desperation of a madwoman!

"So let us end this right now." I yanked up my sleeve, revealing my runes. "You are no queen, Emiana."

Her eyes flashed.

"Find me! Find me!"

"The runes that bound us in marriage were inked on our souls, not our bodies. I am Alisdair's true mate and the queen of Wind and Wild." My smile was just as wide. "And you are not welcome in my kingdom.

"Arrest her," I announced, "for theft and treason."

Foalan, Keefe, Bradach, and our soldiers sprung to action, narrowing on her.

"Carefully," Alisdair barked. "Don't break the glass—"

Holding my gaze, Emiana opened her hands, letting the case slip through her fingertips.

"Noo!"

Alisdair sliced the air. A fallen throne cushion shot across the room, slipping beneath the falling rose. It landed softly on its bed—glass intact.

Foalan and Keefe seized Emiana's arms, dragging her back and away... just as her kick connected.

The case flew off, shattering on the floor.

Boom!

The soul burst free, blowing us off our feet. We crashed into the walls—Emiana and her captors included. None were safe in its path.

Alisdair collapsed on top of me. Through his arms, I saw.

The rose petals ripped free of the stem and swirled around the room, summoning a whirlwind maelstrom of malice and magic. It was as if the whole of the howling, cursed forest was brought down on our heads.

"Calli, we have to run!"

Chilling, whipping winds tore at our clothes, hair, skin, and his shouts—trying to rip away and smother them.

"We have to run now!"

We both tried to stand and were blown back, pinned to the wall.

"What"—wind rushed down my throat, ballooning my cheeks—"is it doing!?"

"It's looking, Calli!" An emotion I'd never seen in his eyes before, terrified me to my core. "It's looking for her."

The swirling roses descended on Eadaoin, swallowing her and her screams. They flung her away, soaring across the room and dumping my friend still and unmoving on the floor.

Shadi tried to run but they were too quick for her. Lifting her into the air, they threw her away just as fast—bouncing her body off the stone.

"Stop!" I screamed. "Stop it!"

The petals were flying toward the entrance and the stairs, when they veered sharply off course, and came straight for me.

"No!" I thrashed against the wind—fighting to run. Fighting to move! "Stay away!"

The petals loomed over me, a dark, ominous cloud of screaming, tortured souls—that veered away again.

They slammed into Aeris's chest, tearing her from Bradach's arms. She screamed—kicking and flailing as the petals lifted her into the air... and poured into her gaping mouth.

"No." My voice lost to the wind. "Please..."

Aeris shrieked, her body jerking, twisting, and contorting as she changed. The woman I knew melted away before my eyes.

Hard, unsmiling mouth.

Dark eyes.

Severe cleft chin.

Sharp cheekbones casting their own shadow over gaunt cheeks.

Raven hair falling in wisps and tangles around her shoulders.

I'd seen her once before... in a painting locked in a tower.

"Constance."

Her head snapped around, those dark eyes latching on mine. "Callidora," she mocked. "Are we on a first-name basis? I don't remember bestowing you the honor."

My skin crawled. This was *not* Aeris. Not her face, not her voice, not her kind, stern smile.

Constance floated down to the dais, her foot touching the platform just as the wind died down.

Alisdair grabbed me and ran.

"Not so fast!"

Invisible hands seized and ripped us apart.

"Calli!"

"Alisdair!"

She threw us clear across the room, slamming us against opposite walls. I didn't have a chance to think before golden manacles surrounded our ankles, wrists, and throat. Alisdair and I weren't going anywhere.

Alisdair roared—the veins in his purpling face bulging.

Constance clicked her tongue, mock-pouting. "Ah, my poor love. Not so easy to fight me when you don't have my own magic to use against me!"

"You!" Bradach charged her, hate contorting his face. He truly hadn't known the woman he was falling for was the body? vessel? of Constance, and he didn't give a shit. Looking into his eyes, all he wanted was her dead.

Constance flicked her finger. "Ferramenta."

Bradach vanished in a cloud of dark smoke. Thudding to the ground, a golden candlestick dropped at her feet.

Roaring, Foalan unsheathed his blade—his crystal-studded hilt glowing. "Eld—!"

"Ferramenta."

The cloud snatched Foalan. A mantel clock fell on the pile of his empty clothes.

"Attack!"

My guards came at her from all sides, Eadaoin leading the charge. Magic burst from her palm—soaring straight at Constance's smirk.

"Ferramenta!" She clapped, her voice resounding through the throne room.

The feather duster that was my first friend in Lumenfell thudded next to her love, Keefe—the broom.

The cloud shook out its collection of furniture, utensils, plates, and cleaning implements—striking the entire room dumb.

"Hmm, that was always my favorite spell." Constance swept the room, grinning. "Anyone else?"

No one moved. No one breathed.

Except for Alisdair.

"Evil, rotted bitch!" He fought against his bindings. "I put you down once, Constance! I'll do so again! I swear it on the deepest depths of your black heart! Your victory will be short-lived."

Her smile twisted, teeth clenching. "You've become quite ill-mannered during our time apart, darling. A few *hundred* years in a dungeon ought to help you remember your manners."

"I'll remember them when I burn the flesh from your bones and piss on the ashes."

She snarled, that disgusting grin finally gone. "How dare you! You should be begging for my forgiveness! You betrayed me," she shrieked, madness in her eyes. "You turned me into a filthy servant, bowing and scraping after *that*!"

I didn't know what she was talking about, until she pointed at me.

"You dared to marry that worm. To make it your mate and promise it the throne that belongs to me!" Constance roared, red eyes popping out of her head. "You will atone, Alisdair, and you'll do it in silence!"

Her hand slashed the air, and Alisdair's jaw snapped shut.

"Hmh! Hmpf! Hmm fmnnm!" he shouted, but nothing got out. He couldn't open his mouth. He couldn't speak.

"What did you do to him?" I yanked on my manacles. "Undo it! Release us and undo it!"

She didn't so much as look in my direction.

"My throne."

Constance twisted around. "What?! Who spoke!"

"Me." Emiana stepped forward, chin held high—not a trace of fear on her face. "I think you'll find the throne is mine, Constance. That was our deal. I free you, and you free me. It's me who'll become the high empress of Elva. No one else."

A thousand emotions flit across Constance's face—all variations of rage and disgust. Then they washed away, leaving her expression blank. "You're right, of course. Forgive me. I'm sure you know how a lover can goad you into saying things you don't mean."

My soul burned hearing this madwoman call my husband her lover.

"You held up your end of the bargain, and I will hold up mine." She snapped her fingers. "The binding spell is lifted."

Emiana cried out, joy filling her as she lifted into the air—cradled by the magic that was always there, but just out of reach.

"But."

Emiana's joy vanished. She dropped hard on the floor. "But?" she snapped. "What but?"

"Well, surely you know it's not as simple as declaring yourself high empress," Constance breezed, shrugging. "As the worm told you, you didn't marry a king. It did."

I bristled at the way she spoke about me.

"You have no claim to the throne of Wind and Wild. You don't even have a claim to the throne of Lyrica. You are a princess in name only. Your father made sure of that."

"You said you could fix that," Emiana cried, rushing the dais. "You promised you could make me high empress!"

"If it was as easy as waving my hand, I'd have done it myself!" she shouted back. "I said I could give you a throne, I never said it would be easy!

"There will be war, girl. War, and death, and pain. Are you ready to accept the toll—?"

"Yes," Emiana sliced in. "This is my birthright. I will fight for it. No matter the cost."

"To everyone else," I exploded. "You will plunge the nations into war to force their submission to an empress that has no business breathing the same air as them! And I don't speak of you, Emiana." I glared at Constance. "I speak of her. Whatever lies she told you, she will not give you rule of Elva!"

Emiana's expression flickered.

"Once she's gained control of the kingdoms, she'll slaughter you and take—"

"Silence."

My jaw snapped shut. I shouted—yelling and cursing through lips that wouldn't open.

"As I was saying," Constance continued. "If you accept the cost, then we will begin here. Today."

"What must we do?" If I planted any doubt in Emiana's mind, she promptly ripped it out and tossed it away.

"There are ancient texts within these walls. They will aid us," Constance said, receiving Emiana's bobbing acceptance. "Also, hidden in the dungeons, is a siren."

"*Hhhmph!*"

"Alisdair had brilliant plans for the creature. An idea so good, I wish I thought of it myself," Constance said. "We will take it with us."

"Very well. What else?"

"There's a rat woman somewhere nearby, who has power not even I possess. She will serve us or die."

"Naturally. All are my subjects. They serve me loyally, or they burn in the Plains."

"And the witnesses," Constance said smoothly, "who have been listening to your treason and now know I am the power behind you. They must die."

Emiana held her gaze unflinchingly. "Kill them."

"*Hhhhm!*"

Constance snapped her fingers, and the world ripped away.

A jolt resounded through my chest, twisting my stomach. It was like falling from a sudden, unseen cliff. Blinking, I found us on the other side of the drawbridge, standing at the edge of the burned-out, smoking village. Us being me, Alisdair, Constance, Emiana, and a large, glass orb—filled with seawater, and the siren within it.

I couldn't even marvel at the sloshy, cold puddles everywhere I could see. The ice was melting—beaten down by the humid heat sweeping freely through the green, verdant trees—chasing the stars across the horizon.

I couldn't even move.

Alisdair reached for me, his eyes frantic. I couldn't respond as his wrist manacles snapped together, then plunged to the floor—dropping him to his knees.

Something living—something powerful—slipped inside of me. Racing through my pores, it surged through my body, filling me to bursting, latching on the chains around my soul, and taking hold.

"Pay attention, Alisdair," Constance called. "I want you to watch this.

"Nabud Kardan!"

The ground rumbled beneath us. I had no idea what she'd done, until the first tower came down.

"Hmmh!"

Castle Riagin imploded. The walls crumbled, the windows blew out, and the towers collapsed—tumbling down on the people inside.

"Hmm! Hmmhh pghh!" Alisdair threw himself side to side, near wrenching his arms from their sockets.

It was no use. Our home. Our people. Our friends.

Gone.

And I registered none of it.

Tipping my head to the sky, the moon peeked through the clouds, took hold of my bindings...

...and tore them free, shattering my chains—erasing the clamps around my magic.

I exploded.

My magic roared like a wildfire, burning all in its path. Incinerating my insides. Scorching my nerves. Decimating my bones. Wiping out my mind. Breaking the manacles.

Emiana nodded, folding her arms. "Unfortunate, but it had to be done. What about the books?"

"Those will be easy enough to fish from the wreckage. It is the rat woman who will be hard to track down. And her daughter," Constance added. "We will find and take them both."

"What about her?" Emiana's hateful gaze turned on me. "We don't need a Gutter rat. Why did you take her?"

"It was necessary. The worm only serves one more function now, but it is an important one," Constance said. Once again, she did not deign to look me in the eye. "Torturing her in front of Alisdair will bring him endless pain, and me endless pleasure." She turned. "I think I'll start... by..." Constance trailed off, eyes widening as they landed on me—rigid and shaking. "Meya, help me..." she breathed, daring to call upon our deity.

"What?" Emiana snapped. "What are you—? Oh, her hair. Revolting, isn't it? You don't know how it disgusted me to wear the skin of a moon-kissed whore, but thankfully, her affliction didn't pass to me."

Constance didn't seem to hear a word Emiana said. She backed away from me, eyes rolling in her head raking me up and down. "You're moon-kissed?!" she shrieked. "A worm like you? Bestowed such an honor? How? Ho—!"

Ripping open my jaw, my screams let loose.

I screamed. I screamed and screamed as overwhelming, unnatural power consumed its weak and fleshy wrappings—the poor, little woman ill-chosen to be its host. My little body couldn't contain it.

Nothing on this earth could.

"No! NO!"

Constance turned to run, her grin nowhere to be seen.

Moonlight burst from my skin. Surrounding Constance, it enveloped her and hardened—holding her still in her tracks with only a stray thought from my mind.

"You fool," Constance screamed at Emiana. "Why didn't you tell me she was moon-kissed?! Why didn't you—?"

"*Die.*"

The command erupted from my soul, spoken with a voice that was and wasn't mine. Pure, magnificent light wrapped around Constance's arms, legs, neck... and pulled.

She choked—eyes bulging and body uselessly flailing against unseen chains. Her limbs lengthened, spreading in all directions over the newly awakened land.

"N-noo!" she rasped. "M-Meya, please! I am... your rightful... chosen! I was b-born for this... world! It's mine! IT IS MINE—!"

She tore to shreds, showering me, Alisdair, and a screaming Emiana in blood and gore.

"Ahhh! What was that?" Emiana cried. "What did you do? What did—?"

I snapped to her, my whole body glowing—my whole body singing with pain and power. Lifting my hands to the air, moonlight collected on my palm like starlings hopping along the branches—safe and knowing they were exactly where they belonged.

"Don't you dare, you filthy Gutter whore!" Rage contorted Emiana's face into something hideous. "Stay away from me! Eldur! Eldur!"

Fireballs soared at me, crashed into an invisible barrier, and glanced away—burning the ground around me.

"I am the high empress of Elva! Eldur! Eldur!" She rushed me when magic failed. "You will bow before me! You will obey—"

I swung my hands down, bringing the blinding, impossible light down on her like a ton of bricks.

It crashed on her skull, cracking it open and snapping her neck with her final insult still on her lips.

She was dead before she hit the ground.

Kicking away the useless creature, I turned on my gaping husband.

"Now, what were you saying before we were interrupted, my love?" I snapped my fingers, and his chains fell away like wet wastepaper. Just as easily, the power fled my body—leaving me weak but whole. "Something about loving me and worshipping my body until the end of time and after?"

A slow, wonderful smile spread across his lips. Surging forward, he scooped me into his arms—kissing me breathless.

"Yes," he teased, nipping my nose. "Something like that."

Epilogue

"Well, you definitely lied about doing all the work while your girls sat back and played."

His chuckles washed over me before we entered the stables.

Alisdair looked up from his grooming of the stallion. His affinity with horses returned with the end of the curse, but this one in particular refused to break. Seeing that he let my husband close enough to brush him while he ate his oats was a surprise indeed.

On the other side of them, our twin daughters, Clara and Dearla, hauled hay bales out through the stable's side door.

Alisdair crossed to us and pressed a warm kiss to our baby and youngest child's forehead.

Rikdash screeched a greeting to his father, waving his tiny fists.

The next kiss was for me. "I wouldn't be so certain they're getting work done."

Curious, I handed the baby over to Alisdair, then followed Dearla outside. My brows shot up when she threw it directly at her sister, who then caught it with her magic and lifted it onto the top of their hay tower.

I planted my hands on my hips. "And what exactly is going on here, young ladies?"

The eight-year-olds jumped up and down clapping. They were adorable. Mirrors of each other, but also of their father, with their long, dark hair; sun-kissed skin; and twin mischievous smiles.

It was baby Rikdash who looked like me, sharing my hair, eyes, and plump cheeks.

"Mama, mama! We're making a castle just like yours and Papa's! Help us, Mama."

As if I was going to say no. Laughing, I ran back inside, magically lifted five more bales without breaking a sweat, and tossed them all out to my husband's shouted, "At least leave me one for the horses."

Teasing, tickling, and playing with my girls, together we built the second-finest castle in the land beneath the shadow of the first.

Castle Riagin.

Yes, on that fateful day fifty years ago, Constance returned and destroyed it.

And on that very same day, we rebuilt.

It turned out that when Constance turned the castle's inhabitants into inanimate objects, she inadvertently saved their lives. Of course she did, because you can do a lot of things to a candlestick, but you can't *kill* one. How can anyone kill something that isn't alive?

With the power of the Moon Mother humming in my blood, and Alisdair's guidance, we unearthed all of our friends from the rubble, and then cast the spell to turn them back.

With that done, together—we all of us—combined our strengths and our magic to return our home to its proper glory. And when that was done, we turned our attention to Elva.

I paused in the midst of securing the hay roof, my gaze spreading out over the verdant, rolling green hills of Lumenfell.

The road to peace and equality in Elva was not an easy one. Constance was right about that single thing—that there would be war, and death, and pain.

With the lifting of the curse, scores of women all across the land rose up and slaughtered their oppressors. Wives slaughtered their husbands. Queens beheaded their kings. Sisters stabbed their brothers. There was chaos, riots, murder, and destruction everywhere you looked, and everywhere you tried to hide.

The lifting of the beast curse freed their minds from the animal savagery, but the memory of the last several centuries, and the fight of the men to preserve them—didn't.

And that, it seemed, was why I was born. The moon-kissed child—knitted together in the womb by Mother Meya herself, to ensure her will would be done in Elva. And her will was that Constance, the binding curse, and all the evil it and she brought upon our land would finally be rid for good.

Yes, it was true. The whole time, the true meaning of my white-haired affliction was that it wasn't one. It was a blessing. A gift from Mother Meya herself—telling me and the world that whenever moonlight touched my skin, I had the ability to channel the power of the goddess.

And channel her power I did.

For decades, Alisdair and I swept across the lands, freeing every woman put under the binding spell, stamping out the lingering resistance, installing new—female rulers—in the kingdoms, and creating a new and central government to unite us all under one banner and one nation. A central government led by the new High Empress of Elva, Queen Callidora Cursebreaker.

Of course, quite a few people from the old regime didn't like the power shifts, the new law demanding the execution of anyone who casts the binding spell, the new central government, or its high empress. Those few tried more than once to assassinate me—first by attacking any time they saw an opportunity, and then after they wised up, they attacked during the day when I couldn't connect to Meya's power.

All such attempts were harshly and brutally put down. If not by my husband, Foalan, Bradach, Treasa, Treasa's daughter, or my many guards, then they were crushed underfoot by me.

Even without Mother Meya's power, I was a strong magic-wielder in my own right. It was the continued arrogance of those misogynistic fools that refused to let them understand that women were not, and never were, weak. Having your power stolen didn't mean you never had any in the first place.

That said, the war was long and seemingly endless—lasting nearly forty years. More than once, I thought of Alisdair's plan to unleash the siren's song on the lands, and let all the faemen just kill themselves.

But then, I would look at my friend and brother-in-arms, Riordan, and remember that love and acceptance can still grow in even the most hateful and toxic environments. I wouldn't be like our enemies—lumping us all into one, so they can hate us all without the need for pesky critical thinking.

No, I did not need the siren, but she did need to return to her home. So, with the power of Meya, I rescued her and her disappearing island, and hid them among the stars. She and her people were so thankful, they gave me a vial of something they called fairy dust.

They said if I ever needed their help, the dust would bring me, my daughters, and my daughters' daughters to them until the line of the Cursebreakers ended. Which was nice and all, but I didn't see what help we'd need from a band of pirates, orphans, and killer mermaids. For now, the vial sat safely in the castle vault.

"Calli? Calli?"

I turned around, catching Meliora's wave as she and Bradach climbed the hill—hand in hand. Behind them, Mama carried the picnic basket, while Jaclan and Gisela carried the blanket and the baby seat for Rikdash.

I looked for Savia, and found her at the bottom of the hill with Keefe and Eadaoin. The three of them had become firm friends in the time the married couple started training my sister in combat and military strategy.

She claimed she needed to be an expert in both if she was going to become the next High Empress of Elva.

"What do you say, girls?" I stepped back, admiring our handiwork. "Should we break for lunch, and then defend our castle from Uncle Jac-Dragon?"

"Yeah!"

"No," Jaclan blared. He spread out the blanket. "I'm not playing the dragon again. I use fake fireballs, but those little monsters use real ones. My nostril hairs are still burning!"

Giggling, the girls rushed and tackled him—setting him off hooting and hollering trying to peel them off.

A warm, steady hand curled around my side, drawing me in.

I smiled up at my husband, and received a searing kiss in return—and a chorus of gagging from our daughters.

"As complete and total was my misery before I met you, my beauty, that is how fantastically happy you've made me now." Eyes shining and full of love filled my heart to bursting. "Thank you, Calli, for running that much slower."

I laughed. Alisdair decided within the last few years that he caught me so easily the times I ran from him, because I wasn't really trying to get away.

"And of course, I wasn't," I whispered, holding him and our sweet baby in my arms. "Why would I run from you? You, Alisdair Lumenfell, are my happy ever after."

***

Keep In Touch

Join Ruby Vincent's mailing list for release dates, teasers, giveaways, and more: https://www.subscribepage.com/rubyvincentpage
Check out all of her books on her website: www.authorrubyvincent.com

ABOUT THE AUTHOR

Ruby Vincent is a lover of all things enemies to lovers. From fantasy romance to contemporary romance, she loves saucy heroines, bold alpha males, and weaving a tale where both get their happy ever after.

www.ingramcontent.com/pod-product-compliance
Lightning Source LLC
Chambersburg PA
CBHW021329310726
48971CB00001B/49